DIVINE
BLASPHEMY

DIVINE
BLASPHEMY

Those That Burnt Rome
Still Live Among Us...

A HISTORICAL NOVEL OF MYSTERY
& ESPIONAGE

EMILE LEON

Copyright Information

ISBN-10: 0994062109
ISBN-13: 978-0994062109

To my Mom, who taught me how to pray

To my Dad, who showed me how to play

To the friends who blessed me with their trust

And to those who preferred to betray

To Heidi, my wife, who chooses to believe

And to Hala, my daughter, who has yet to make her way

I dedicate this work of verities

Or fiction, as some may say

Contents

Glossary

Julia Agrippina: Mother of Emperor Nero, Sister of Emperor Caligula and wife of Emperor Claudius.

Ananias: Son of Nedebaios, according to the New Testament was a Jewish high priest who presided during the trial of Saint Paul. He was tried in Rome for violence but acquitted by emperor Claudius. *In this story, he is a power-seeking priest who agrees to conspire with Marih to gain personal favours.*

Antonius: *In this story, he is a high-ranking Roman military officer. Antonius runs the Damascus military training camp and is a close friend of Seneca, a father figure to Paulus and a mentor to Marih and Cornelius.*

Barnabas: One of the earliest Christian apostles in Jerusalem. A friend of Saint Paul. He was born in Cyprus. *In this story, an Aleph operative.*

Caesarea: a city built by the Jewish king Herod the Great in Judea, two decades BC. Currently on the Israeli coast of the Mediterranean.

Centurion: a Roman military officer that led a group of 100 soldiers (80 soldiers at certain times.

Cephas: also known as Simon Cephas or Saint Peter. A prominent figure of the twelve disciples of Jesus and an early Christian leader.

Claudia Achte: also known as Claudia Acte, mistress of the Emperor Nero of non-Roman birth. *In this story, daughter of Paulus of Tarsus, raised as an adopted sister of Elisa, and an Aleph operative.*

Cornelius: a centurion in the Roman army, mentioned in the New Testament as the first gentile turning Christian. *In this story, son of Silvius and husband of Elisa. Also a Roman intelligence officer.*

Damascus: One of the oldest continuously inhabited cities in the world. Today, Capital of Syria.

Elisa: *In this story, princess of the Phoenician royal house of Abdmelqart, Aleph operative, and Cornelius' wife.*

Imperial Intelligence Agency: *A fictional incarnation of a Roman Empire intelligence gathering organization.*
Ishtar: In this story, *wife of Marih, daughter of an Aleph Elite family.*

Joppa: an ancient Jewish city, today incorporated with the Israeli city of Tel Aviv, also known as Jaffa.

Marih: *In this story, prince of the Phoenician royal house of Abdmelqart, brother of Elisa, Aleph operative, Roman Centurion, and husband of Ishtar. Also a Roman intelligence officer.*

Melqart: the ancient God of the Phoenician city of Tyre. He was the God of king Hiram who was King David and King Solomon's friend. The Temple of Jerusalem was built to resemble the Phoenician Temple of Melqart.

Nero: Roman Emperor from 54 to 68 AD in whose era the famous great fire of Rome took place.

Paulus: also known as Saul or Saint Paul. Considered the most influential early Christian missionary. *In this story an operative for the Imperial Intelligence Agency.*

Phoenicia/Canaan: An ancient Semitic civilization based along the coastline of modern Lebanon with colonies across the Mediterranean coast and islands.

Praetorian Guard: a force of private bodyguards and a special force whose main role was to provide personal protection to the Roman Emperor and his close circle in Rome.

Praetorian Tribune: A high-ranking officer in the Praetorian Guard.

Seneca: also known as Seneca the Younger. A famous Roman philosopher, statesman and dramatist. He was one of Nero Caesar's teachers. *In this story, he is one of the founders and masterminds of the Imperial Intelligence Agency*

Silvius: *In this story, Cornelius' father, a Roman Tribune.*

Simaan Ben Aaron: *In this story, a wealthy Jewish merchant, political liaison between Rome and Judea, family friend of Cornelius and Silvius.*

Simon the Tanner: mentioned in the New Testament, lived in Joppa. *In this story, a double agent for both the Imperial Agency and the Aleph Lodge.*

Tarsus: An ancient city that exists today in modern day Turkey. Mentioned in the New Testament as the hometown of Saint Paul.

Tyre: an ancient Phoenician city in the south of modern day Lebanon. Among other things, Tyrians are credited for inventing the Royal purple dye, building the temple of Solomon, creating the alphabet and spreading its use across their Mediterranean colonies.

Yeshua the Nazarene: Jesus of Nazareth.

Historic Timeline

Years (AD)	Events
28	• Graduation of Cornelius and Marih • Seneca is 32 years old
29	• Jesus was baptized by John the Baptist
31	• Death of John the Baptist
32	• Jesus dies
33	• Achte is 8 years old
36	• Saint Stephan is martyred • Saint Paul (known as Saul) converts to Christianity • Cornelius the centurion converts to Christianity at the hands of Saint Peter
37	• Last year of the reign of Tiberius. Tiberius is murdered March 16 at age 78 by his 25-year-old nephew, Gaius, who becomes Caesar, known as Caligula • Birth of Nero Caesar • Start of the rule of King Herod Agrippa
38	• Paulus (Saint Paul) meets with Cephas (Saint Peter) for the first time
39	• Paulus goes to Damascus but ends up having to escape by being lowered in a basket over the city walls
41	• Claudius becomes emperor after assassinating Caligula • Achte is 16 years old
42	• Agrippa I, a friend of Claudius Caesar, is given control of parts of Judea in the absence of Roman military
43	• Paulus is sent to Tarsus and stays there for a year or two before Barnabas comes searching for him
44	• St Peter escapes the prison of Herod Agrippa • King Agrippa becomes sick and dies, and the Roman military returns to Judea
46	• Claudia Achte is 21 years old
47	• Rome celebrates the 800th anniversary of the foundation of the city

Years (AD)	Events
48	• Ananias becomes High Priest
49	• Seneca (age 53) is asked back to Rome by Claudius and Agrippina the younger to tutor Nero, then 12 years old • Claudius marries Agrippina • Claudius passes a law expelling all Jews from Rome
50	• Claudius adopts Nero as heir • Agrippina (Nero's mother) is 35 years old • The Council of Jerusalem takes place • Gamaliel – Paulus' old teacher dies
51	• Nero becomes an adult at the age of 14
52	• Ananias, the High Priest who tried Paul, is sent to Rome accused of violence but is acquitted
53	• Nero Caesar marries Octavia, the daughter of his stepfather, Claudius Caesar
54	• Nero becomes emperor • Jews are allowed to return to Rome
55	• Nero (age 18) takes Achte (age 30) as a mistress with the support of Seneca (age 59)
56	• Saint Paul is captured and imprisoned in Caesarea
58	• Ananias is resigned as High Priest
59	• Agrippina is murdered by Nero Caesar, her son
60	• St. Paul leaves Caesarea to Rome, and stops in Malta after his ship crashes
61	• St. Paul arrives in Rome
62	• Nero Caesar marries Poppaea
64	• The great fire of Rome takes place • Nero accuses the Christians and starts a campaign of persecution • Allegedly, St. Peter is crucified in Rome, upside down
65	• Seneca (69) is ordered to commit suicide by Nero, after being accused of taking part in the Gaius Piso conspiracy

Years (AD)	Events
66	• Start of Jewish revolt • Ananias is trapped by Jewish nationalists while hiding in an aqueduct on the palace grounds (of Herod the Great) and killed
67	• Nero dispatches Vespasian to resolve the Jewish riots
68	• June 9, Nero dies at the age of 31
69	• Year of the four emperors
70	• Titus, the son of Vespasian, ends the Jewish-Roman War

Acknowledgement

My deepest gratitude goes to my developmental editor, Molly Aine Moore. Your dedication to the project, coupled with your sensitive yet strong guidance, went above and beyond all expectations. It was such a pleasure spending those many hours discussing the finer points of Divine Blasphemy with you.

I also owe a special thank you to my friend Samuel Tharmaratnam for the generous support on design and formatting.

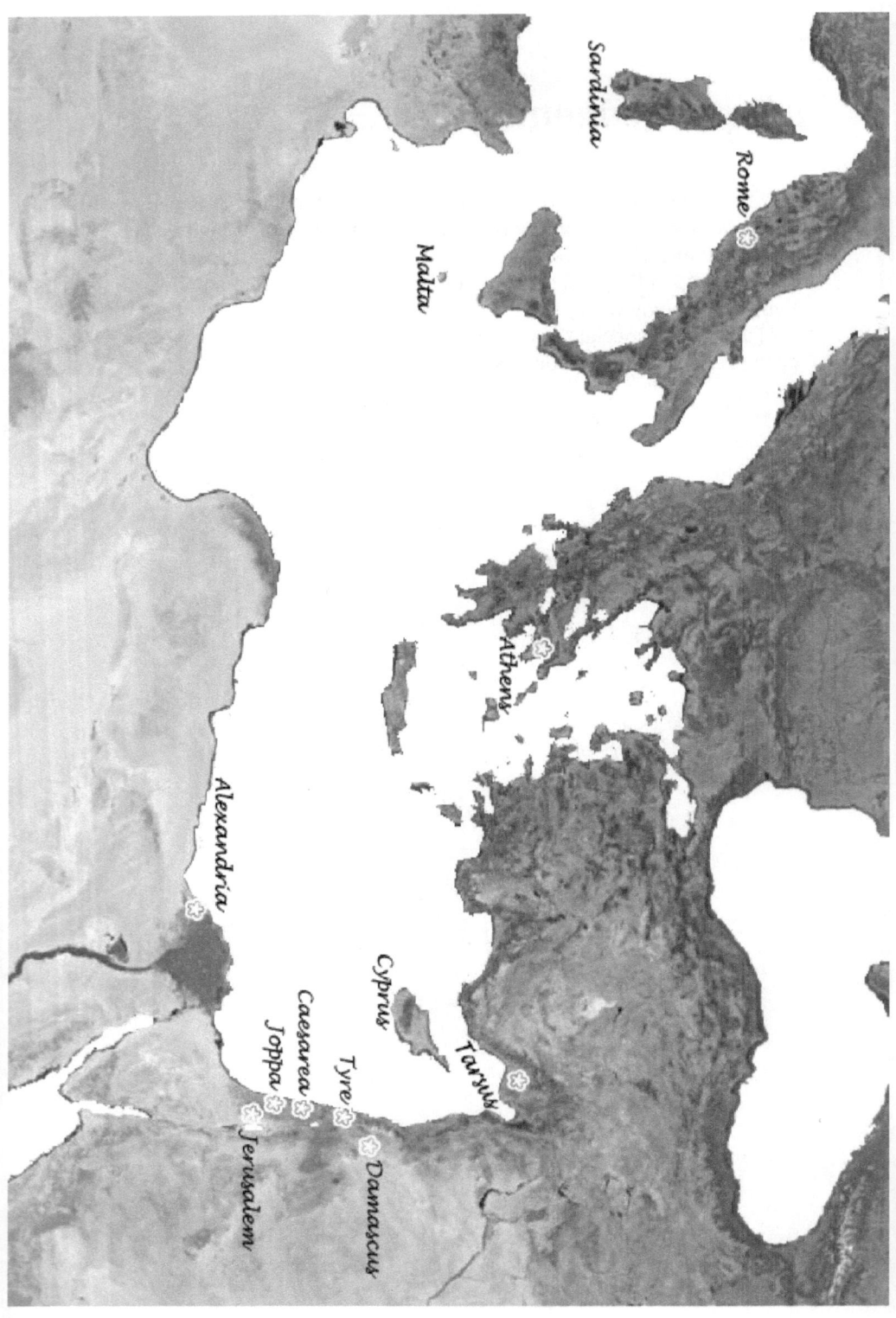

Preface

My uncle was a master historian and the best storyteller in the world. When I was eight years old, he began telling me a story I would never forget.

The premise that stories have as many versions as there are storytellers to tell them was as yet unknown to me. Truth be told, I wouldn't realize this fact until I was much older. I was amazed that one person could know so much – so amazed that I barely realized what mysteries he was working on me.

Uncle had been staying at my parents' for a year or so. My young mind only remembers him holding some fancy jobs at newspapers and radio stations. Every morning, he woke before first light to do his exercises. I remember getting up early myself to find him preparing his breakfast before heading out to work.

My father slept in. His job as a transportation manager required him to stay up late. My mother, a dutiful housewife, followed his schedule. As Christians in a Muslim-dominated culture, our household routines varied slightly from most of our neighbours'. For instance, we didn't have to be up early for a pre-dawn prayer. The house was quiet in the mornings for Uncle and me.

This brief daily encounter with my uncle started off on the wrong foot. Like most kids, I needed a crane to pull me out of bed on school days, but come summer I'd spring up before dawn, for no other good reason than not to miss a single moment of not having to go to school. My uncle didn't want me disturbing his quiet time – speaking broke his breathing rhythm – so I would grab a bunch of my comics and lock myself in the bathroom, flipping through my favourite pages over and over again.

The struggle began when he wanted to take his shower and a stubborn eight-year-old denied him access by claiming first right to the only bathroom in the apartment. The struggle escalated into a war after a couple of mornings of lost battles forced my un-showered and unhappy uncle to plead his case to my parents. Their swift interference set solid boundaries for my awkward desire for lavatory education at that most inconvenient time of the day. The new rules forbade me taking the magazines into the bathroom. Fortified by adolescent wisdom, I responded by abstaining from reading altogether. I'd show them! My journalist uncle had always praised my precocious reading talents, giving my parents cause to brag. I thought there'd be a stalemate of sorts, so Uncle's soft heart surprised me. He took my restrictions harder than I did. To make it up to his early-bird nephew, he offered to spend some twenty minutes with me every morning telling me a story while preparing and eating breakfast. I accepted on one condition: he had to make me a grilled cheese sandwich.

His story was nothing like I expected. There were no talking animals, no fantastical creatures, and no super-powered heroes. Yet his tale kept me enthralled from one morning to the next, week after week, all summer long.

It was such a unique story that I was sure none of my friends had heard anything like it. Lacking the oral history skills of my ancestors, I couldn't get my chums to let me even try to tell it – so I stopped trying. As summer drew to a close, Uncle and I moved on with our lives. He got his own place and I went back to school. I didn't even notice how quickly I forgot about it all.

Fifteen years later, when I was in medical school, my father called me with the sad news. Uncle had passed away after a lengthy struggle with that horrific memory-eating disease, Alzheimer's. He was much too young for such a fate. As I returned home that summer, my intentions were to locate some of my uncle's work, wherever it might be, and try to reconnect with him. I had long since reconciled with reading. Not at ease with showing my emotions, however, I needed some way to grieve the untimely departure of my childhood breakfast partner. Some of the papers I found surprised me: such a variety of topics, with the passions of some so lacking in others. I wasn't too keen on his political writings. They felt too journalistic, too matter-of-fact. These topics were nothing out of the ordinary, just routine compilations of then-current news with some analysis too polished to trigger much interest in a modern reader. It wasn't until around the end of my summer vacation that I came across a manuscript of a much different flavour.

Late one afternoon my father realized I was paying my uncle's writings more than casual attention. He spoke as if we were resuming an ongoing conversation, "You know, he used to call you his partner. He passed away too early. Big loss. Still so much potential."

I wasn't sure I knew where my father was going with his comments. I mean, up until then, I hadn't been able to get myself too excited reading through his papers. "I'm sure he was excellent at what he did," I said, trying to figure out where the conversation was headed. "You know, I don't know that much about journalism. Was that pretty much all he did?"

"The poor man couldn't get around to publishing any of his private works. He spent his life writing for a living. His other manuscripts were never finished," my father said. "If he had lived longer, I'm sure he would have been able to turn them into books. I have saved a few of his things. God bless his soul, he wasn't too organized and left things behind wherever he went."

"So what kind of things do you have?"

"Oh, a Masonic pin and a thick notebook where he jotted down some thoughts," my father replied.

It surprised me a little that he felt no duty to return these keepsakes to Uncle's wife and kids. But after all, they had known each other longer than anybody. "Are they handy?" I asked. "I'd like to see them, you could tell me about them."

Before long, my father returned from his room with the pin and notebook. I didn't intend to spend more than a few moments examining these two pieces out of my father's locked-closet collection of treasures, yet I found myself immediately grabbing the notebook and fanning the pages with my thumb, as if I were looking for a loose paper among them. I stopped at a random page. The few words I read stunned me. I flipped to another random page, then another... what my father called a collection of thoughts, maybe drafted for some potential project, was way more than that. It was a complete piece of work, in rough form, to be sure. I knew deep inside that no one had ever read or heard any of these thoughts... except for me, fifteen years ago.

As memories flooded back, this jewel of all my uncle's works hidden away among my father's possessions became very precious indeed. The words awakened something deep inside me, touching that emotionally skewed Middle Eastern boy, raised amidst what often felt like never-ending wartime, trying to escape through self-taught English by reading comic books in the bathroom. Suddenly it was all very important to another kid not so much older, struggling to become a medical doctor.

I don't know if I can do Uncle's thoughts justice. I don't know if I can even approach his mastery of storytelling. Forgive me, Uncle, for taking some liberties in telling your story with my inadequate skills.

One

Touched by Ceremony

In the time of Yeshua the Nazarene, a young Roman by the name of Cornelius was coming of age. The youngest child and only son of Silvius, a Roman tribune, he was already demonstrating the hard work and loyalty that would earn him honours within the ranks and make him an idol among his peers. Like his father, Cornelius was a patriot of the first degree. His occasional travels with his father, sometimes accompanying the emperor to Roman provinces, gave him some experience interacting with the not-always-so-grateful people of these conquered lands. Cornelius came to realize that the supremacy of the Roman legions was anchored in their thorough preparation for any sudden contingency.

Although he lacked the ideal stature of a warrior, Cornelius was braver than a cornered lion when standing his ground. His stunningly solid base of confidence supported his mountain-upright personality. Well educated, becoming his warrior class, he excelled in the sciences of war and politics. It was not uncommon to find him engaged in debates with his father's visitors on the strengths of political or military strategies. It soon became evident to all that Cornelius was not a conventional thinker and definitely would not become some ordinary Roman politician.

His father's influences were further enhanced by an unusual relationship: Cornelius drew additional inspiration from a wealthy and successful businessman of Jewish origin. Simaan Ben Aaron was not only his father's business partner in Judea, but also an important native liaison for many Roman politicians doing business in the province.

Apart from his business acumen, Ben Aaron was known for his generosity and charity. Giving back to the community was more of a Jewish concept than a Roman one. Having observed Cornelius from infancy, this family friend always held high hopes for his future. Still, despite the stubbornness only tolerated in favourite sons, Cornelius' great respect for Ben Aaron allowed him to at least listen to the older man's ceaseless advice. He wasn't so dense as to not realize the good counsel in the older man's push for him to join the military. Simply being born to the warrior class was no indication that any son would follow the father's example. In the Roman Empire, a career in politics had a relatively low ceiling; however, for accomplished military officers, the sky was the limit. Ben Aaron recognized the potential of Cornelius adding military experience to his mounting political talents. Perhaps he even saw evidence of a phenomenal sense of analysis beginning to surface in the youth, a rare potential to be reckoned with.

Bending to the friendly pressures of Simaan Ben Aaron and his own father, Cornelius finally decided to acquiesce to the military strategy. Together, they reasoned that upon returning to Rome after establishing himself in the field, he could start establishing his political position in a manner seldom seen at such a young age. Influenced by Simaan again, Cornelius decided his future would lie within Rome's eastern provinces, where military service would necessitate visits to Syria, Phoenicia, and the infamously unstable cities of Judea. Having always regarded Simaan as an uncle, he had a profound empathy for the faithful devotion of the Jewish people. He supported them publicly and refused to brand them as terrorists, a common stance among Romans. In Cornelius' mind, the troubles that took place in Judea were diplomatically workable. He disagreed that war was the only solution, and detested the idea of shedding the blood of the Jewish people in order to maintain peace. After all, how dangerous could these people be to mighty Rome? Their cities were flung far from the heart of the Empire and their interests were regional, bogged down as they were with internal matters of politics and a religion so alien to Rome.

Once decided upon, with his father's influence and support, Cornelius was able to arrange the first of his goals. He would leave for the training camp in Damascus where other military students from provinces scattered across the Empire were gathering for indoctrination as Roman warriors and citizens.

. . .

The first leg of his trip was by sea. Upon reaching Tyre, Cornelius left the ship to stay at the house of Marih, a young Phoenician also on his way to the camp in Damascus. A colleague of his father and representative of the Roman legions in Tyre had arranged for this prominent Phoenician family to billet young Cornelius.

Cornelius couldn't have been received by a more excellent host. The two young men immediately recognized a kinship, as if they had been at school together for many years. For generations, Marih's family had been Roman citizens, so it had long been the plan for him to join the military for reasons very similar to those of Cornelius. His was a Phoenician family of royal blood and political standing. Minor princes the both of them, Marih's older brother was already busy leading the family in the local political arena; being the younger son, Marih's would be the family's military face.

Despite his understood position in life, Marih didn't seem to care much for politics or what his family had planned for him. His positive attitude toward life was more in line with the pleasures he gratefully found along his path.

Cornelius thought that Tyre must have been just the right city for someone like Marih. It had a lively market that never slept and its citizens were accustomed to dealing with the casual passersby as travellers, merchants, or pilgrims. The Phoenicians had carefully crafted their legendary reputations by becoming powerful sea merchants for well over fifteen hundred years. Their generous hospitality was the natural result and had become an integral part of their customs, assuring their economic success above most others of their age.

. . .

A few days before Marih and Cornelius were to depart for training in Damascus, Marih used the pretence of taking his guest on a quick pilgrimage to the Temple of Melqart so that he might offer traditional prayers to the ancient god of the city before becoming a military man. The trip was shorter than Cornelius had expected. Still within the boundaries of the city and amidst crowds of people intent on other destinations, there was no evidence of a temple of any shape or size, at least not to his way of thinking.

Cornelius stood in confusion, waiting for his newfound best friend's explanation. "You didn't tell me it's an invisible temple," Cornelius said with light sarcasm.

"It's not invisible. Look around you. Don't you think it's weird to have a plot of ruins in the middle of a crowded city? This is where the original Temple of Melqart stood. Melqart is the god and the founder of Tyre; that's what his name means, king of the city. Our people, as you can see, have preserved these sacred ruins of his temple."

"I see," said Cornelius, unconvincingly. "You wanted to visit these holy ruins to ask your god's blessings?"

Marih responded with a patient grin. He turned toward the rubble and started walking awkwardly among the deserted aisles of building stones.

"Where are we going now? Can't you just stay here and pray? I don't think the priest is around anymore!" Cornelius grumbled without really expecting an answer.

Not realizing he was following so closely, Marih stopped short and turned around right in Cornelius' face. "This is it! Have a seat, my friend." Marih pushed down on Cornelius' shoulders, forcing him to sit on the very stone beneath his feet.

Cornelius obeyed, eyeing Marih, thinking that some strange worshipping practice was about to follow. To his disappointment, Marih sat next to him, seeming to enjoy his curiosity and confusion.

"Aren't you going to pray?" Cornelius asked.

"Not yet..."

"What are we waiting for?"

"My friend, my Latin tutor would say, '*Maxima enim, patientia virtus.*'"

"Maybe patience is the greatest virtue to those who have it."
Cornelius smiled. "I have it in short supply most of the time. Isn't
good communication a valuable virtue as well?"

Marih tilted his neck as if puzzled at this line of questioning.
"Uh... huh?"

"Communicate! Talk to me. Why, out of this whole field, are we
sitting right here, and what are we waiting for?"

"You are sitting right where the great priest of Melqart stood to
perform wedding ceremonies."

"Come on, you know what I mean. I don't mean this–"

Before Cornelius could finish his sentence, Marih was distracted
by figures approaching in the distance. Cornelius followed Marih's
gaze to see two girls holding hands, wandering purposefully towards
them.

"Are you expecting them?"

"The girl in the red shawl is my sister."

"Your sister? I thought I already met your sister."

"This one is Elisa. You haven't met her yet. She's been away
visiting for about a month now."

"And the girl in the blue is, what? Your third sister?" Cornelius
never seemed shy of a sarcastic tone.

"No, she's my bride."

Cornelius thumped Marih on the chest harder than he meant to.
"You son of a... your bride?"

"We're getting married today."

"Impossible! Where and when? I don't get it. Is this some kind
of a joke?" Cornelius' face ran a comical range of expressions as each
thought occurred to him.

Marih put Cornelius at ease as best he could, considering. He
summarized his plans for an official tie to the girl who owned his
heart before leaving for Damascus, and said that a formal wedding
celebration would be scheduled for later. When the girls had
approached to within a few steps of them, Marih introduced his new
friend.

. . .

Phoenician culture – like most other cultures – had elaborate
etiquette and protocols for betrothals and wedding ceremonies,

starting with family approvals of either proposed spouse. Free-spirited Marih had decided to avoid all the accompanying social noise so close to his departure into the military... at least temporarily. Absolutely unavoidable when it came to matrimony was to have a small, private ceremony binding the couple to each other, legal in the eyes of their god. Both parties would still live apart, awaiting the public ceremony validating the marriage in the eyes of the community. Public announcements of formal spousal relationships were a means of bringing witnesses together to sign the marriage contract and thereby avoid any religious sin or public shame. Should anyone object to the union, a judge's best rulings were based either on admission of the alleged crime or the sworn word of a witness to the contrary. Witnessing was the strongest way to close any agreement – especially in betrothal and matrimony – and to ensure its binding power.

. . .

The four sat in a circle as the couple explained to Cornelius how they had long planned for this event. Marih and Ishtar had been in love for years and they didn't want to wait any longer. Listening and nodding sympathetically, Cornelius couldn't take his eyes off Marih's sister Elisa.

She was an attractive girl by all accounts. In addition to her dark hair and olive skin, her large eyes spoke back to him even as her full lips remained silent. Cornelius had yet to learn that her composure sprang from her professional training as a choir leader at the temple. She was learned in royal etiquette and was educated beyond most of her peers. He was aware that she and Marih were of a house of royal blood, the pinnacle of the Phoenician elite. Had he been able to think beyond his fixed gaze, he would have noticed they were all speaking in Latin, instead of translating back and forth into Aramaic or Greek, as was customary in Phoenician middle classes.

Cornelius drifted back into reality as Marih began explaining why their gathering in these ancient ruins was still so holy to them. The original Temple of Melqart remained a holy place regardless of whether or not it still stood. Marih's people kept the knowledge of the original plot of the temple, metre by metre, so that they were able to picture walking in its hallways and chambers as if the walls were still standing. Cornelius thought to himself, this explains the awkward paths Marih and the girls had taken over the ruins to this exact resting spot.

. . .

Gathering his usual aplomb, Cornelius clapped a huge hand on Marih's shoulder in a friendly game of blame. "You're lucky these two ladies showed up! I'm thinking they are the only pleasant part of this odd pilgrimage of yours." Still not fully grasping the situation and not quite done with his playful sarcasm, he asked, "What now? Am I to wed you two?"

"That's the plan."

"I'm going to assume you're joking now... I know you are not that stupid."

Marih looked him straight in the eye. "Only a man can hold the ceremony. Otherwise, I would have asked my sister to do it."

"But how am I to know what to do?"

"There's not much to know. The ceremony only has a few conditions. The man officiating must first be standing in a corner facing the couple to be wed, at an angle, like this." Marih moved Cornelius and the girls around like he was setting a stage for a tableau.

"Next, you must state, '*Upon your acceptance, by the name of He who was at the first, the Majestic Builder and the Eternal First Teacher, the Architect of the Skies whose tools shaped the land, and by the holy name that was given to me and is remembered and glorified throughout the Earth by the first letter of the letters, I tie you one to the other by the Rope of Marriage and the Rays of Fertility.*'"

"Right. That's not too difficult. I can learn that if you give me another day!" Cornelius really had a problem with sarcasm sneaking into his voice; he didn't always mean it. He shook his head. "But I have a couple of questions."

"Like where this corner where you're to stand might be?"

"Now, aren't you quite the prophet?"

"In our religion, nearly everything is hidden in allegories or represented by symbols. Hence, you will be standing on one of the cornerstones of the temple, symbolic to the first cornerstone."

"And how exactly are we going to find this one stone?"

The girls giggled as Marih pointed between Cornelius' feet at the stone on which he stood.

"I like this symbolism thing. You can make things work for you simply by imagining whatever you want, huh? Alright, let's imagine that this stone is the cornerstone," Cornelius said.

"No imagination here, Cornelius. This stone really is the cornerstone we need. While it's true there's little left of the old temple, our priests still know where each stone should have stood. This exact stone has a long story. But, to be brief, perhaps you have heard the saying 'The stone that the builders rejected became the cornerstone?' It is with our faith that this story arose. This is that rejected stone, our cornerstone."

"You're beginning to make an impression on me, my friend. But here's another question for you, what about that part where I say I was given a holy name?"

"Not to worry. I have given all the small details proper consideration. For this condition, you must have been given a holy name since birth in order to conduct such a ceremony."

"Exactly my point. I don't have a holy name!" Cornelius thought he had finally found a loophole out of his strange predicament.

"It might not be holy to you as a Mithraist, but it is holy to us. Your name, believe it or not, links back to our god Melqart whose symbol is the horned head of an ox."

"I get it... my name means 'the one of horns,' which makes me the perfect fit for your symbolism-based rites. Incredible! This is all too much. I wonder why I never heard of any of this before now. Perhaps now I will be honoured as a very special person in Phoenicia... like a prophet or something?"

"Oh, you are special, indeed. You only have to compete with the king, the head priest, and... well, the rest of the population!" The friends found that two could play at the sarcasm game. Marih laughed. "Almost every Phoenician has a name based in religion. Our names are mostly composites, almost always with the name of God in them somehow."

"Alright, alright. I stopped paying attention when I heard you say I was special." Finally realizing his friend's dead seriousness, Cornelius succumbed. "I guess I have no way out now. Repeat to me what I need to say and I'll do my best to memorize it."

"Before we get there, there is one final condition that you should know."

Marih explained a delicate – and most essential – element of the ritual: the summoning of the essence of fertility so that the holy energy might be passed to the newly wed couple. The ritual required the man conducting the ceremony to be in a state of sexual arousal. More precisely, his condition must be visible to the couple and the witnesses; the more evident it was, the more content the newlyweds would be. Priests, of course, had mastered this technique to such a degree that some of them would faint (or pretend to) from ecstasy. The Adepts of Melqart had mastered the art of orgasm without ejaculation.

Cornelius was definitely not on board with this condition. Eyes wide, he stuttered his apologies: Although he wanted to help, he wasn't sure he could perform such an awkward act with the sincerity required. Marih assured him they were not expecting him to act like a professional priest in this matter, and that minimum requirements would suffice. Inquiring what these minimum requirements might be, Cornelius was informed by his sexually advanced friends that he only had to achieve an erection. Cornelius was in such a state of shock, he truly doubted such a condition could even be possible.

Marih attempted to distract Cornelius by repeating the marriage oath a few times, helping him memorize it properly. By the time Cornelius thought he was ready, the sun had almost set on the Mediterranean horizon, leaving a bright yellow line extending between the Earth's poles. Gradually blending with an evening sky, the night approaching from the east attempted to mimic the light of day with inadequate stars and a half moon.

Assuming confidence he did not feel, Cornelius stood on the cornerstone with Marih and Ishtar facing him, at the diagonal they had been placed in earlier, waiting to become husband and wife. Elisa looked on, standing three feet from Cornelius' left side. A few minutes passed as Cornelius tried different mental tricks to at least bring about an erection sufficient for this Phoenician ceremony. Not wishing to put additional stress on his friend, Marih maintained his silence; but his bride let a quiet sigh of impatience escape her lips.

Cornelius stood in deep concentration with eyes partially shut as Elisa took two steps closer, gently wedging Cornelius' left shoulder between her breasts. Her warm, female scent enveloped them both. She wrapped her right arm around his shoulders, resting her teasing fingertips just below his right ear. Those full lips he had fixed upon earlier tickled his left earlobe, wandering smoothly down the pulse throbbing in his neck. Her left hand played freely and lightly upon his chest and belly, ever-so-lightly tracing lower until she felt the unmistakable stirrings of Cornelius' readiness. With a satisfied grin and teasing breath, she slowly pulled back, latching her own aroused gaze upon his startled eyes. The groom's confident voice summoned Cornelius back to other matters at hand.

"Do you still remember the words of the ceremony?"

Cornelius smiled through his embarrassment and continued with the wedding of the couple.

Two

A Friendship Earned

The trip to Damascus proceeded uneventfully. With the training underway, Cornelius found the traditions of the eastern provinces appealing, especially when the actual training proved to be not very physically demanding. The Romans' complex system allowed enlisted men of privileged classes to choose from varying levels of difficulty among the different military roles. Cornelius chose to join a function responsible for strategic military planning and decisions. With his already well-developed analytical skills, it was only a matter of time before he staked his territory amongst his peers, distinguishing himself by his work ethics and advanced skills. Camp trainers used his work as examples for other students and repeatedly rewarded him for his continuous excellence.

One of Cornelius' teachers, Antonius, had given many loyal years of service to his emperors – there had been several already – as he advanced through the ranks. He quickly took Cornelius under his wing, not only because he was proud of his student's achievements, but because he knew and respected Cornelius' father. Antonius, like many of the Roman soldiers, was a Mithraist. For hundreds of years, Mithraism was firmly entrenched in the Persian Empire, but didn't find fertile ground to grow in the west because the Greek pantheon held sway as long as the Greeks controlled the Mediterranean. When the Roman Empire gained prominence, though, they exhibited a culture anchored in business principles rather than philosophical concepts. It was a practical system that approached other cultures with an open mind, or so it seemed. Theirs was a culture of domination by assimilation. This allowed Mithraism, one of the more advanced religious structures to a Roman's way of thinking, to flourish amidst the ranks.

Not to be slighted, the Roman soldiers stepped their Mithraist rituals up a notch. They established worship lodges everywhere they went, creating a method of initiation by protecting the integrity of the military organization as they assured against contamination by mixing with the common public. These security measures gave Roman Mithraism mythical stature by way of the time-honoured secret order.

Antonius introduced Cornelius into the Mithraist Lodge at Damascus, as per tradition, and tutored him through the increasingly difficult degrees until he became very well known to the members of the lodge. Many of the higher Roman military personnel recognized him as Antonius' favourite, being prepared for an honoured position in the Empire.

Months passed as Cornelius and his peers approached graduation. In preparation, the teachers split the trainees into groups and gave them different assignments as an integral part of their training. The assignments were chosen based on the assessments of the teachers as to who would be best suited to each position. Some were asked to complete a mission at a seaport, others were sent to the streets for tasks involving the public, and some were asked to offer tactical protection to travellers and pilgrims. Cornelius was matched up with two other recruits, and together they were given the responsibility for a strategic mission. By now it was no secret that he was being considered for a military intelligence position; one of the finest and most sought-after assignments, it was usually given to the instructor's prodigy.

Cornelius didn't even try to conceal his delight when Marih joined as the second member of his team. Despite the fact that he was not a Mithraist Lodge member, Marih came from a Phoenician royal family, and recruits like him were traditionally given access to top positions in certain provincial branches of the army. Even so, a recruit would not be trusted to such a position unless he had proved himself and earned such entitlement.

The third man to join their cadre was someone neither Marih nor Cornelius had met thus far in their training. He was introduced to them as Barnabas. Working undercover for the Empire's intelligence agency, Barnabas was not a trainee but rather an agent, a spy for the Romans in the Jewish community. Cornelius and Marih were informed of the peculiar status of Barnabas and of the secretive nature of his role. Their mission was to follow Barnabas to Jerusalem, in particular to the Temple, the holiest of holies for the Hebrew people. They were to keep a discreet distance from Barnabas, acting as if they were perfect strangers. Barnabas, in turn, was to surreptitiously guide them to the holy Jewish city. Once in Jerusalem, the two trainees had to use the best of their skills to enter the Hebrew temple, an entrance denied non-Jewish visitors. The two were to then return to Damascus without Barnabas, and bring with them proof of their successful entrance of the sacred temple.

To avoid discovery, they were to disguise themselves. At no time could they allude to the secret Roman intelligence agency or they would be denied any support, even by their own government. In other words, if they were discovered in their masquerade, they would be utterly on their own. Most importantly, they were not to expose Barnabas. Exposing Barnabas would not only be a loss to the agency, but would guarantee him a death sentence by the hands of any of the radical Jewish groups.

. . .

Trailing Barnabas didn't require much attention from Marih and Cornelius. As they were passing by a small Phoenician village, they noticed a monument of some horned deity that stood tall in the town square.

"Yell out my name," Cornelius said.

"What?"

"Just say my name out loud," Cornelius repeated in all seriousness to his confused friend.

"Cor-ne-li-us," Marih said quietly, still not sure what this was about.

"Louder."

"Is this some kind of a joke?"

"Do you see me laughing? I need the people in the town to hear my name. How often in my life will I be so honoured because I am called 'the one with horns'? Shouldn't these people know I carry the name of their god?"

Marih chuckled. "Your name won't help you much around here."

"Why not? Don't you see the horns on that monument? These must be of your people."

"Yes, they are Phoenicians, but in these little mountainous towns people won't understand the meaning of your foreign name." Marih flashed a smirk. "Here they call the horned deity the Aleph."

"Like the letter? The Aleph?" Cornelius' high tone clearly showed dissatisfaction at the loss of his presumed advantage.

"As in the FIRST letter, the Aleph. In fact, that's why our ancestors made it the first of the letters. No greater honour could be shown to our God than that His symbol should make up the first letter of our written language."

"Isn't Melqart your god?"

"Melqart and the Aleph are one and the same. The Aleph in our language means the ox, the nickname and symbol of Melqart."

"And both are horned... that makes sense, although I still think you should teach your people the name of their god in other languages."

Marih chuckled. Their minds wandered to private thoughts.

"Do you miss Ishtar?" Cornelius asked out of nowhere. The road was not short, and light conversations were their best ally.

Marih nodded.

. . .

Barnabas didn't take many breaks on the way to Jerusalem, covering the ground from Damascus in less than two days. As they approached the gates of Jerusalem, Marih and Cornelius were completely on their own. Marih suggested they waste no time accomplishing their mission, and they headed to lodgings north of the city for the night with plans to begin first thing in the morning. He wanted to get this over and done with so they might take time to return to Damascus through Tyre. Even in the midst of executing a dangerous mission, he missed his family, especially the newest member.

Suddenly, the two realized they really had no set plan for their dangerous mission. They had spent their travel time discussing everything but an actual plan. Setting about resolving their blunder, they agreed the flexible timeline for their mission needn't prevent them getting it done as quickly as possible.

For technically grown men of the age – Roman centurions in the making, no less – there was something very adolescent in their assault on the temple. To begin with, they had no idea what they would find inside it, let alone what they could snatch as proof they had been there. Cornelius thought they could pretend to be tourists and get into the temple or maybe bribe someone to let them in. That angle was not only weak, but very risky. With a native advantage, Marih was the first to come up with a potentially workable approach.

Marih tried to use his knowledge of the Jewish religious traditions to put together a potentially convincing story. According to his plan, Cornelius was to pretend to be the deaf and mute son of a wealthy Jewish family currently living in Rome. Marih would be his manservant, also a Jew, who spoke both Aramaic and Latin. The family had long searched for treatments for their son's ailment; they now resorted to Jerusalem's Holy Temple as their last hope for a miracle. They were sending their son, Josephus (Cornelius) with their trusted servant Nathaniel (Marih) to ask for the blessing of the Lord God at the Inner Temple, before the Holy of Holies. The proof for their mission, in Marih's plan, would be "holy water" blessed and then begged from the priests of the Inner Temple for Josephus' cure, with a generous donation for the poor as compensation. Marih's figuring was that it was not uncommon in Middle Eastern religions to have the priests perform prayers over certain kinds of food or drink in order to bless them. People everywhere believed that the blessing would somehow pass on to whoever drank or ate the blessed items.

Cornelius liked the idea and had no problem letting Marih do all the talking once inside Jerusalem's walls. After all, Marih was the one who spoke Aramaic, the local tongue. Maybe no one would notice his Phoenician inflections, perhaps a bit odd in a Roman Jew. They'd deal with that if it came up – no sense in worrying about such a small detail now.

The operation began with a long walk uphill toward the temple. Their Roman-style clothing fit their story of Jewish pilgrims from Rome. The streets became busier and busier the closer they got. Cornelius was relieved by the cover they found among the number of people who were either running a stall in the bazaars, tending to various errands, visiting, teaching, or involved in some other matters. They blended in perfectly.

. . .

Swept up in the street throngs approaching the temple, the two novice spies began to feel the heat of their situation. They climbed the stony stairs, continuing to blend in with the large crowds as if they belonged there. They reached a large square, right at the entrance to the temple, where people congregated in groups. Members of many and varied Jewish sects gathered separately at different sections of the square. It wasn't difficult to recognize their differences in the ways they dressed or even wore their hair, each according to their own sect.

Now unsure as to whom to approach or even where to go, it must have been obvious to some that they were lost or looking around for information. Two men walked up to them in a rather official manner and asked whether they were part of the ceremony about to take place at the temple. In Aramaic, Marih told the men their purpose for visiting, their hopes of receiving blessings for his deaf and mute master, Josephus. Cornelius didn't have to dig too deeply for his expression of confusion. He might as well be deaf as dumb, not understanding any of this conversation. The two Jewish men said they had to wait if they wanted to enter the temple, as it was reserved at that time for a ceremony. They suggested instead that Marih and his deaf master go down a certain series of steps to a small room at the lower level of the temple where they could inquire with the schedule-keeper as to when they might be able to enter the temple or even talk to the priests. With almost palpable relief, the two travellers offered their thanks with two silver shekels.

As they descended the designated steps, they noticed some

commotion at the landing just before the small room. Two crowds of young men with voices raised were standing behind what seemed to be a leader or rabbi of each group. Curious about the mounting tensions behind the two leaders, but careful not to speak, Cornelius gestured to Marih that he wanted some explanation as to what was going on.

Pretending to be seeing to his master's comfort, Marih sat Cornelius down on the ground within hearing distance of the loud crowd and proceeded to massage an imaginary cramp in Cornelius' calf. With his face turned away from any curious observers, Marih mumbled a translation of the debaters' Aramaic into Latin. Though it made little sense to him, Cornelius got the gist of the problem: basically different interpretations of Jewish Law. One leader was accusing his counterpart of being too strict on the physical (earthly) laws while completely ignoring the spiritual (heavenly) reasons behind them.

For his part, Marih was not surprised, as he was fairly familiar with the practices of the neighbouring Jewish culture. However, Cornelius was in the process of learning something totally new to him. This was something Uncle Simaan had never mentioned.

Still watching from a distance as the hubbub attracted more onlookers, Cornelius saw three people walk purposefully and with steady and straight steps up to the little room at the bottom of the stairs. He assumed this room was their original destination. He couldn't see their faces, but it was obvious they knew exactly where they were going. Otherwise unnoticed, they quietly disappeared inside the tiny room. Cornelius kept an eye on that door for few minutes, but he didn't see anyone leave. Driven partially by curiosity and partially by wanting to get on with their original plan, Cornelius signalled Marih to get up off the ground with him and walk with him to the room. Although the room wasn't far, it still took them a few minutes to get by the crowd now jamming the stairs.

When they arrived in that room, they were surprised to find only one person sitting at a high, square table placed against a wall, filling up half the space in the room. There was no evidence of the three men Cornelius had seen enter the room only moments before. Marih, assuming their original plan, proceeded to address the keeper of the temple's schedule, introducing himself and telling the story of the mute pilgrim Josephus who had come all the way from Rome seeking the blessing of the One True God.

Keeping a hospitable smile on his face as Marih spoke, the man's attention was on the growing crowd right in front of his room. He apologized to his visitors and ran out to talk to the debaters, asking them to move their discussion away from his door, thereby allowing access to those who sought to book time with the temple priests.

In an instant he was swallowed up by the mob, leaving the two men alone in the dimly lit room. Cornelius wasted no time. He began pounding on the rock walls around the room like a prisoner frantic for a way out.

"You are mute, possibly deaf, I get that, but you don't have to pretend you're blind, at least not with me!" Marih whispered loud enough for Cornelius to hear but not loud enough for his voice to carry out of the room.

"There must be an exit somewhere. I'm sure there's another way out of this place!"

"What? What makes you think so?"

"I saw three men purposefully walk into this room and they did not come out. Where did they go? They didn't just disappear. They had to go somewhere since it was not back out of that door." Cornelius hooked his thumb over his shoulder as he continued to search the room.

Puzzled with his friend's behaviour, Marih lowered himself onto a small stool by the large table, resting his forehead upon his folded arms. As if by instinct, he placed both arms under the table, under the edge furthest from the wall, and pulled up. Both legs of the table beneath him came up, bringing a layer of the wooden floor with them and creating a wide enough opening beneath to allow a grown man to descend a dark, steep stairway. A quick glance at the top of the table now revealed the hinges that attached it to the stony wall.

Surprised, as if observing a conjurer at close range, both men snapped their gaping mouths shut and, without further consideration, Cornelius ducked under the table and slipped down the stairway. He left Marih no choice but to follow him.

"What are we doing? Are we mad? Where does this go?" Marih,

more than Cornelius, realized the kind of danger they could find and made no pretence at hiding it.

"Aren't we supposed to get proof of entering the temple?" Cornelius reasoned. "This has to be a secret entrance. We may not get another chance." He whispered a confidence he barely felt, hoping to gain Marih's approval.

"A chance to die, perhaps? Do you think we'll just be welcomed with open arms when we get to wherever this passage leads? That the priests will just escort us into their secret vaults? We'd better think of a story fast... for when we get caught... for we *will* be caught!"

"Oh, calm down. I've never seen you so cautious. We are still in the Roman Empire, aren't we? The laws of Rome apply here too, you know. They will be on our side if we get caught. Nothing to worry about."

"What laws are these? You mean the ones Antonius told us to forget about if we get caught? Remember? They will disavow all knowledge of us should we be so unfortunate. We are right in the heart of the rebels' den. Within the walls of the temple a different set of rules are in play. Jerusalem is in turmoil, even on a good day. The priests will not care who we are or where we come from. They will throw us on the midden mound and burn us along with their house waste. I cannot believe I followed you in here, let alone jumped into the jaws of Hades!" Marih gasped, trying to catch his breath.

"What do you mean you followed me? You were the one who found the hidden entrance, remember?"

"I didn't say to jump, did I? I just wanted to..." Marih trailed off as another idea interrupted his ranting.

"You just wanted to what? You want a good adventure every bit as much as I do, snatching the proof out of the temple to bring back to Damascus. That's what we both want. So let's just focus and we-"

Before Cornelius was able to finish, Marih cut him off with a fairly louder voice, quickly checking himself back to a whisper. "I just wanted to prove something... something in our legends... to see if is true that the Temple of Solomon was built according to the design of the Temple of Melqart."

Cornelius narrowed his eyes, trying to grasp what Marih was talking about. Before he was able to speak, a loud noise above their heads froze their every movement, every breath. It was the schedule-keeper. Returning to his room from the fracas outside, he found his visitors gone. Shutting the room's small, wooden door, he checked under the table and immediately resumed his duties.

"Brethren, here's a torch to light your way. Sorry for running out on you like that. Those rabble-rousers are good cover for our purposes, but unpredictable. May your way be blessed." He lit the torch and handed it to a speechless Marih, then closed the trapdoor on them again as he returned to his business.

Cornelius didn't know whether to laugh or cry. Just seconds ago, he was trembling with fear of what they had stumbled into all the while thinking fast, out loud, for a courageous solution. Now, suddenly, he was awash in relief as a stranger handed them a torch and blessed them on their way. In stunned silence, the two looked into each other's torch-lit eyes. Cornelius found his tongue first. "You were saying?"

The two exploded into relief laughter, followed by choking coughs for a long couple of minutes as they regained their senses.

"That was very close," Marih said, gathering his wits and remembering what he was going to say. Feeling a bit unstable, he sat down on the narrow stairs for a moment, gesturing for Cornelius to do the same. "I was always told that the temple was built upon the original design of the Temple of Melqart. I was never sure which temple, always assuming that it could've been true with the original Temple of Solomon, the one that was destroyed by the Babylonians. Or perhaps Herod built the second temple also following the same design."

"Are you saying what I think you're saying?"

"I don't really know, but if my guess is correct, I might be able to get us out of here."

"So, with the Temple of Melqart, there was also a table in a room that opened into a dungeon, or wherever we're headed, like in here?"

"I never saw it because, as you know, the Temple of Melqart was destroyed long ago. But yes, this is what I was taught by our priests."

"And your priests told you about this dungeon and where it leads?"

"Theoretically," Marih said. "You see, we carefully study the sacred geometry in the ancient plans of the old temple as part of our religious beliefs."

"So where is this tunnel supposed to take us?"

"Several places, but only one of them along this underground path is important to us. This tunnel is supposed to branch out into different parts of the temple. The one we want goes to the east and exits behind the temple. We are told that... at least in our temple in Tyre... it exits into a House of the Trusted."

"A house of the trusted? Trusted what? Are we going to end up in some stranger's house? How safe is that?"

"The House of the Trusted is not an actual house of someone but rather a semi-public place where a group of people belonging to an inner organization gather regularly."

"So, we'll end up in a public place where we can simply disappear into the crowds again?"

"This is what I was taught, at least theoretically. Let's just hope this is all true." Marih slowly stood, with sturdier legs under him again.

"I'm afraid that when we get out of here we will regret not going all the way into the temple to steal something of value to bring back to Damascus as our proof," Cornelius complained.

"Oh, I can live with these regrets, my friend!"

Cornelius rose and prepared to follow Marih, the torch held in front of them as they began their descent.

"Trust me," Marih continued, "any regrets you can think of will be much easier to bear than the big alternatives... like getting caught!"

. . .

Marih took his first steps carefully into the depths of the dark tunnel, the torch not being particularly bright. He kept one ear on the footsteps of Cornelius, making sure he was following safely. The tunnel was completely built in stone. Its floor was paved with cobblestone and the walls met overhead in a rounded arch high enough at its apex for an average person to walk upright. They continued for a few minutes before they reached an intersection splitting off into three identical tunnels. Marih stopped for a quick breath, but quickly resumed his pace as he chose the path to the left. As they had entered the tunnels from the north and were walking south, Marih's left turn would be the one going east toward their intended House of the Trusted. However, in no more than a minute, Marih realized something was not right. The tunnel ended in a wide, cave-like chamber with no exits or doors. They felt their way around the dead-end room, as Cornelius had in the small room above, methodically pushing and kicking the stones to make sure they were not missing a hidden door.

They had almost given up when they heard dull voices approaching. They both held their breath, trying to identify where the voices were coming from. But the voices soon faded and disappeared. Now they knew there must be some way out of there into the other side, the side where the voices were.

Cornelius took the torch from Marih's hand and lifted it up in the air. He had noticed that the walls were not smooth like in the tunnel and the stones were not as well arranged on top of each other. Also, there seemed to be a bit of a stony ledge just above eye level.

As Marih followed Cornelius' eyes around the vaulted ceiling, Cornelius waved to him to come closer, to a section that had stones protruding, forming a nearly invisible, irregular rise of stairs. Marih climbed the first step, reaching for the stony ledge with one hand to keep his balance. The second step and he knew he was onto something. The ledge he was grasping proved to be the edge of a balcony-like wall, separating them from the real wall of the chamber. As they both climbed up the wall and over the ledge, they exchanged whispered words of astonishment as to how well concealed the inner wall was. Now they could see that the little space between the real wall and the outer balcony was not continuous around the room but rather formed half a circle along the wall of the rounded chamber.

Here they found a wooden door reinforced with metallic strips and heavy hinges, standing almost shut in the external wall of the chamber. They slowly pushed the door, moving it just enough to be able to peer through. Upon sneaking a peek inside, Marih slapped his forehead with his open palm and started mumbling something that Cornelius couldn't make out.

"I can't hear you," Cornelius whispered, nudging him.

But Marih, instead of raising his voice, turned around and this time put his open palm on Cornelius' mouth. The voices they heard before were approaching again. They quickly pulled the door to its almost-shut position and backed up into the darkness of the narrow balcony.

Cornelius, now being the one closer to the crack in the door, kept his cheek flat against the wall. As the approaching voices drew nearer, he could tell they belonged to two men entering from the hall beyond the door.

The two were speaking the local dialect that Cornelius didn't understand. Nevertheless, he didn't need to understand the language to realize that one of them was telling a very intense tale, keeping his listener enthralled.

The two men seemed to enter the room only to grab something and walk back out, as their voices turned away again. Something in the storyteller's voice was familiar to Cornelius. It made no sense to him that he should recognize any voices in this part of the world. Not only could he not recall knowing anybody here, but it was also unlikely he knew anyone who spoke the local language so fluently... well, except for Marih, who stood as mute as the stones about them, were it not for the shivering that kept reminding Cornelius of the seriousness of their situation.

Despite all that, Cornelius' curiosity got the better of him and, in a desperate attempt to catch a glimpse of the speaker, he bent forward, bringing his eyes into a position where he could look through the thin crack of the door standing slightly ajar. Marih's hand held his arm tight, forcing him back against the wall. But Cornelius had already caught the glimpse he needed. He may not have recognized the language, but the voice matched the face of someone he knew very well.

He couldn't wait for them to disappear down the hall so he could tell Marih what he saw – not because Marih would know this person, but because he thought he might be able to comfort Marih a little when he told him this person was an old and dear family friend, a well-trusted ally who wouldn't harm Cornelius or let anyone else do so, for that matter.

. . .

Simaan Ben Aaron was the last person Cornelius had expected to see there. By the time Cornelius turned toward his companion to divulge the startling news, Marih had already begun climbing over the balcony into the cave-like chamber, assuming Cornelius would follow. But first, with his nerves steeled a bit, Cornelius dashed through the door into the hallway, intending to steal something and thereby fulfill their mission. He cast about for a small item he could easily stow away in his clothing when he saw something on the side of a table, wrapped carefully in cloth after the fashion of protecting a precious object within. He grabbed it and dashed out. It was peculiarly light for the size of it, and he stopped briefly in the half-dark outside the door, hurriedly but carefully opening the wrap only to discover that it contained a piece of bread.

Disappointed with his failure at thievery, Cornelius stuffed the wrapped bread in his sleeve. He rushed to catch up to his friend, anxious to tell him the exciting news about Simaan. By now the panicking Marih had scampered down the uneven steps hidden against the walls and fled across the chamber, looking for another exit.

Really not expecting to find a solution to their desperate situation, Marih was relieved to discover another well-disguised exit on the other side; only this time there were no doors, rather a wide-open tunnel.

Careful to avoid discovery, Cornelius finally overtook his friend about ten metres into the tunnel and was able to slow him down with a gentle tug on his shoulder from behind.

"I knew that man! He is a family friend. You have no need to worry," Cornelius whispered.

By now the torch was guttering and the darkness threatened their retreat. Marih gaped at Cornelius, taking a short pause to think about what he was saying before he spun about and continued what he hoped would be a swift exit down the tunnel. Two more minutes of cautious marching into the gloom of the tunnel passed before they reached a massive wooden gate held shut by a large, metallic latch digging at least two inches into hard ground beneath the cobblestones. However, there were no locks on it. Marih reached down to the latch but didn't try to open it. He suddenly stopped and turned around to face Cornelius.

"Maybe we should wait a couple of hours first. What if I'm mistaken about this exit? In a couple of hours, it will be late enough into the night and the city will be asleep. What do you think?" Marih was clearly at a different level of fear compared to Cornelius.

"Whatever gives you comfort, my friend. I personally would have no problem going back to the temple. I was trying to explain to you that the man I saw there is Simaan Ben Aaron – he is like an uncle to me. I don't know why I didn't go to him then and there. If he learns I was there and didn't come forward, he will be very upset with me."

"Sure... right, about that family friend, Cornelius. I'm sure he would be upset, very upset to see you there. He might do to you what he did to the other man."

"Other man? What are you talking about?"

"Well, I'm not really sure, but I'm not willing to find out."

Cornelius grasped Marih's shoulders to calm him, interrupting again, "Cut to the chase, will you? I'm telling you, I know this man very well."

A knowing look passed over Marih's eyes. "That's right, you couldn't understand what he was saying! Your family *friend* there was telling the priest how he poisoned some big shot in Rome! They seemed to be plotting to bring some politicians or military leaders that sympathize with the Jews to power in Rome. I couldn't hear everything... their conversation had already started when they entered the room... but I didn't need to hear any more. I got cut of there fast!"

"Did he mention the name of the big shot person that was killed? I know most of these people. That cannot be true, you must have misunderstood." Cornelius had a patronizing half-smile.

"I didn't hear a name. But I heard well enough that he poisoned the man's wine and made it look like he drank bad wine instead." Shaking his head as if to clear it, Marih continued, "Anyways, how is he a family friend and who is he exactly, dare I ask?"

"He is the man that convinced me to come here for my military training. Thanks to his advice, I decided to join this class so I can further my position among the politicians in Rome. He has been my father's friend and business partner for as long as I can remember. He treats me like a son." Cornelius' voice was strong with conviction.

"Well, he might be *your* family friend but that surely won't spare my life if *I* get caught. Another thing, why would he be here if he lives in Rome?"

"Ben Aaron… he's a Jew. He's a very wealthy man and many Roman politicians rely on his financial advice and on his political relationships here in Judea. He might be here on a political mission. He is a very successful merchant, hence his wealth, and he has holdings all over the Empire. Jerusalem is only one of them. A man of his calibre is always sought after by leaders of commerce and nations, and it wouldn't surprise me if he is being hosted by the priests during his visit to Jerusalem."

"Glad to know you are on his good side." Marih couldn't hide his biting sarcasm fuelled by his mounting fear. "He is obviously capable of doing more than just supporting the politicians of Rome!"

"Oh, come on now! You have to trust me on this. One day I'll introduce you two and you'll get to know him better. This man is not capable of doing such harm."

"It's not that I don't want to believe you – I'm sure this will all make sense once we're out of here and out of danger."

Marih suddenly sat down, hard on the ground, as if his body had reached its limit of tension. He managed to support the bottom of the torch with his hand, like a soldier holding onto his flag in battle until his very last breath.

A couple of hours went by. The two friends talked quietly, their fears settling and their nerves calming. Their torch was definitely failing now, so Marih stood up and walked toward the door. He gently lifted the metallic latch. "It's flexible enough, indicating frequent use," Marih mused mostly to himself. The shocker was right behind the door. The doorway was completely blocked with building stones, as if this path was no longer in use and a wall had been built to close it off.

Marih and Cornelius laid their palms on the wall, trying to push each stone separately, hoping the wall might have crumbling mortar and they would find an exit somehow. Accepting their hopeless situation, Cornelius' thoughts returned to Simaan Ben Aaron.

"Uncle Simaan is our only hope. Let's go back to the temple."

"I will not go back there for any reason." Marih continued pushing on stones, thinking out loud, "It makes no sense."

"Not many things have been making sense down here."

"I mean the latch. The latch that locked this door is too loose. If this path was truly blocked, the latch would have been stiff. There isn't even any rust on it. Look at these hinges: well maintained and in perfect shape. These are not the hinges of an abandoned gate."

"What are you suggesting? Someone knows we were here and built a fresh wall to trap us?"

"Was it Ben Aaron who taught you all your superior skills of sarcasm?" Marih flared at Cornelius, all out of patience. "There must be a reasonable explanation." He started examining the door closely, swinging it open and closed a few times, back and forth.

Cornelius came closer to hold the failing torch for Marih, and as he did, he noticed two elongated holes in the wooden door extending about three inches horizontally and one inch vertically. He pointed them out to Marih.

Marih stared at the holes before he cried, "Of course! The door is just an illusion! What you see is not as it is. The real solution is just in front of you... you look but you don't see."

"What?"

"This door opens from left to right, and this is what we see and what we expect to see beyond, correct?"

"Uh huh."

"In reality, the door opens from right to left."

"But there are hinges on the other side of the door."

"That's because the real door is something you look at but don't see," Marih tried explaining again. He pointed at the stony wall to the right side that joined the gate at its hinges. The wall had many imperfections, cracks and holes in it, but when Marih opened the wooden door completely until it touched the wall, the two holes in the wooden door matched and overlapped with two corresponding holes in the wall. Marih took the metallic latch completely out of its socket and inserted it from the short-arm side into one of the holes in the door while it was open wide against the wall. He maneuvered it gently until it passed through with no resistance. Then he turned the latch so that the short arm became perpendicular to the ground. Met by minimal resistance, he turned the latch like a key, visualizing how it unlocked a simple mechanism on the other side of the wall. He then removed the latch and proceeded to repeat the process in the second hole.

Confident now, he proudly swung the wooden door shut, inserted the latch and turned it until it was hooked, then pulled slowly. Cornelius' eyes widened as a door-sized block of stone swung open toward them, away from the wall. Marih couldn't hide his glee. He jumped around like a puppy with a new bone.

Without thinking, Cornelius found himself hugging his friend and generously commending his near-mythical analytical skills. After they put the latch back on the wooden door and passed through the stony opening, they made sure to shut the door behind them and return the lock system back as they had found it.

They looked around to find themselves in a dark, narrow corridor which zigzagged four or five times, as if it was meant to block any light between the tunnel and the door. They cautiously advanced through the convoluted corridor.

At the last turn, Marih slowed, taking smaller steps as he flattened himself against the wall. The two realized they had found that proverbial light at the end of the tunnel. Straining to hear any voices and finding none, their tense nerves started to relax at the promise of safety. The chances of having to face someone so late at night were slight.

With the last light of their torch, Marih looked back into Cornelius' eyes for assurance. Getting a nod of confidence, he proceeded to inch past the last curve and into the light. Wasting no time, Cornelius strolled after Marih like a man with no worries. He walked right into Marih's back. Peering over Marih's shoulder for the cause of their abrupt stop, he realized they had ended up in a room with no less than fifty0 men seated along its four walls. Every single head was turned their way and every eye consumed them with interest. It was as if they had been expected.

One man was seated on a raised dais, in an obvious position of distinction. His clear voice broke the silence. At his command, one of the attendees stood with a sword raised before his eyes in salute and, with military steps, approached the strangers by circumnavigating the room in front of the seated members. Finally facing them, he spoke in a dialect foreign to Cornelius' ears, yet recognizable as part of a strict military ceremony. Marih understood and replied with a brief phrase. A short response came from the armed man, perhaps a sergeant-at-arms. Cornelius feared the worst as the man took a step back and raised his sword in an aggressive stance, pointing its tip at Marih's chest. Cornelius stepped forward, thinking he could perhaps attempt to negotiate their way out of this seemingly hostile situation, but Marih raised his left hand and placed it on Cornelius' chest, signalling that he was in control of the situation.

Not convinced, and at a disadvantage due to the language barrier, a confused Cornelius heeded his friend's gesture and stepped back. Trusting Marih was his best – and only – option. The exchange continued for several moments before the sergeant-at-arms lowered the sword in his right hand and extended an open left hand towards Marih. Cornelius jumped slightly at this unexpected gesture. But Marih extended his open left hand, taking the man's palm into his and performing a slight shake of both their arms before returning their hands to their sides in a military stance of mutual respect.

The sergeant-at-arms then addressed Cornelius in Latin, welcoming him among friends. After a nod of approval from the chair, their new comrade asked the two to follow him. They walked behind, along the side of the room, avoiding the centre. When they reached the end of the room, their escort made a sharp military pivot.

Staying along that end wall, they crossed to the centre, reaching a point where they were opposite the chairman of the meeting. At that spot, the sergeant-at-arms turned to face the chair and performed a ritual gesture. He then waited for the chair to nod in acceptance before continuing his walk towards the door. Marih followed in his steps and performed the same gesture, with clear comfort, as if he knew exactly what he was doing. Cornelius assumed he was expected to follow along; with no choice but to attempt to do the same, he turned to face the chair, attempting to mimic the gestures of the other two men. The chair gave him a nod with a slight smile, as quiet chuckles escaped some of the more seasoned attendees. No doubt his moves were clumsy, but Cornelius maintained his assumed decorum as he quickly walked behind his friend towards the exit.

At the door, the sergeant-at-arms knocked with what sounded like a ritual rhythm. Another patterned knock was heard on the other side of the door. The man knocked again and the heavy door swung open. They passed through silently, at which point their guide returned to the main hall and the doorman posted outside closed the door behind him. Everything appeared to Cornelius to be scripted and precisely rehearsed.

The doorman raised an index finger at arm's length, pointing the way. Following them to the external gate, he gave verbal directions to Marih in a friendlier manner and shook his hand with a smile.

Alone again, Marih and Cornelius climbed a long flight of steps to the narrow streets of a residential area. They were finally in open air, breathing the freshness of the Mediterranean night.

Three

No Questions Asked

Lost in thought, Marih and Cornelius silently followed the doorman's directions to the inn catering to Phoenicians, not far from the temple. Although exhausted from their long chain of ordeals, they were too keyed up to surrender to sleep. By the time the sky began to lighten with dawn, the two were ready to get going.

Stepping outside the door into a street already alive with the day's business, Cornelius needlessly asked, "Shall we head to Tyre now?"

Taking a deep breath of morning air, Marih smiled. "To Tyre!" His smile spread further across his face with their first few steps. "You know, I was afraid you still had plans for entering the temple to bring back our proof." He chuckled.

"Before we get too far, we just need to get something to eat. I've never been this hungry in my life."

"I know what you mean. We were so loaded up with... well, fear, I guess... just one thing after another. We haven't eaten since we arrived yesterday morning, and barely a few swallows of water besides." Marih raised his eyebrows. "You know, there is no treasure on earth that can convince me to repeat last night's experiences again," he said without reservations. "If this means we fail our assignment and are given another one, then so be it. I'm sure none of the other assignments could bring us even halfway as close to death as we came, more than once, last night. I'm just glad that we're still alive."

As Marih went on and on reliving moments he was only now beginning to remember, Cornelius dug into his sleeve as if reaching for a frustrating itch. Instead he pulled out the cloth-wrapped bread he had stolen from the table in the tunnels beneath the temple. He unwrapped it and broke off a piece of bread to hand to Marih. Marih's eyes popped and he choked on his words, hastily pouncing on Cornelius' hand with both of his, covering the cloth and the bread.

"Hey! What the...? I wasn't going to eat this alone. You'll get your share, you bread-wolf," Cornelius laughed.

Keeping his hands clasped over Cornelius' hand, Marih began to act as if he had suddenly lost his mind. A couple of hysterical chuckles escaped his otherwise sombre face while his feet alternated jumps and skips in a clownish show of madness.

Thinking such a reaction to the simple piece of food was an exaggerated joke about their hunger, Cornelius laughed even more. But Marih, in a break from his mad dance, opened the cloth and silently commanded with his gaze for Cornelius to look. Bringing his eyes down to the partially opened cloth, his smile disappeared as he looked back into Marih's eyes. Facing each other, backs half-bent over their hands between them, the mad dance claimed them both.

What Cornelius thought was only a plain white cloth wrapped around a piece of bread in the darkness of the night took on a whole new significance in the light of the day. The plane white side of the cloth was only a liner. The outer side was richly detailed embroidery upon the finest weaving found only in the most royal houses... or upon the holiest temple altars. The design consisted of a centered seven-armed candle holder, with two overlapping triangles below and one centered above it. The surrounding area was richly embroidered with decorative shapes of plants and animals in many-coloured threads, even threads of gold. This was no mere cloth wrapping some workman's simple lunch hastily left behind, but rather a ceremonial emblem of the temple, one worthy of holy rituals and ceremonies.

Their mad dance celebrated the happy accident of the proof of their mission. It was as if it had been placed in their hands by an unseen protector.

. . .

Fortified with assurance of their undeniable proof, and after a breakfast more substantial than holy bread, they rushed north to Tyre. Some local merchants directed them to a caravanserai where a porter leaving right away offered affordable transport services. He gave each a donkey and mounted one himself after loading the saddlebags with water and blankets for the road.

Once out of the busy city centre and into the quiet streets leading north, Cornelius and Marih held back a bit, leaving a good distance between them and their guide. Their conversation was no longer for the ears of their travelling companion.

Cornelius said in a low voice, "The more I remember of last night, I... what the hell were we thinking?"

"If you will recall, I was the one who asked that question first! Wasn't I? Scratch your head, my friend, you'll remember my regret at the first step I took with you under that table into that damned tunnel... the man in the room thrusting that torch in my hand like we belonged there!"

"Alright, alright, quit nagging and start talking. You owe me a whole lot of explanation. Where on... or under... the earth did that tunnel take us? Who were those people? You spoke their language, even knew their rituals. What did you say that made them let us go? They didn't just let us go, they showed us out with great hospitality!"

"I knew this was coming," Marih mumbled.

"Damn right!"

"Let me first ask you one question. Is there anything in this world, any favour, I could offer to avoid answering these questions?"

"Not even if you were the great Tiberius himself!"

"Well, I had to ask. No, really, I had to ask, and now that we have confirmed the matter, here's what I can tell you."

"I'm all ears."

"Last night, you had no idea you were the luckiest person who could ever find themselves in that situation, simply because I was with you. That huge room with all the men lining the walls was a secret Aleph Lodge. Anyone entering that lodge, unless he was an elite Phoenician, I assure you would have not have left it alive. They would've killed you and buried you right there under the lodge."

"They would do that? What kind of criminals are they?"

"Oh, save your righteous indignation! What makes you think you can have secretive Mithraist lodges but others cannot have, let alone protect, their own?" Marih sometimes ran short of patience with Cornelius' haughty Roman supremacy.

"I see!" Cornelius snapped back. "So you are jealous that you were not invited to the Mithraist Lodge in Damascus, aren't you? There was nothing I could do, my friend. They only allow important and intelligent Roman people, it's not my fault."

Marih repeated the last of what Cornelius said, only in a nasal voice, mocking him in a comic way that broke the rising tension. Correcting himself and lowering his voice again, he returned to his explanation. "Anyways, immediately recognizing our situation, I introduced myself as a member of a known Aleph Lodge in Tyre. We exchanged secret gestures and passwords verifying my claim, all according to mandatory procedures. Most fortunately for us, the master of the lodge recognized me and my lodge, having visited it before."

"So, you are a member of the lodge in Tyre?"

"Yes, but the lodge you must be thinking of is not the lodge that he knew me from. I also belong to a specialized, scientific lodge."

"Specialized in what?"

"In science, as I said." Marih kept the answer short.

"What kind of science?" Cornelius prodded.

"We're putting together a comprehensive map of the world. And that's it, there is nothing more I can say."

Cornelius had problems with barriers, obviously, for he rudely plumbed for details, "A map of the world? What do you mean? How many scientists are working on this? Are they famous people, people I would know?"

Marih stared back with a smile that affirmed his intent to answer no more questions. Instead, he asked, "Say, what's the password to your little Damascus Mithraist Lodge?"

"I get it, I get it. No more questions." Chastened, Cornelius stepped up his donkey's pace and the two rejoined their guide on the road to Tyre.

Four

Tyrian Tyranny

Because of their secret betrothal in the Temple of Melqart several months earlier, Ishtar couldn't move in with Marih's parents as tradition would normally dictate. She had to wait for the official public ceremony assuaging the honour and pride of both families as well as the community at large. Elisa, in on the secret, made sure her new sister-in-law did not feel disconnected. Far from the typical royal female of the time, Elisa didn't waste her time in idle leisure, practicing cultural refinements worthy of the marriage market. Elisa had other plans for her future. Or rather the wise leaders of her royal family had made sure their plans were hers. Since birth they had instilled in her a deep calling to fulfill a mission of utmost magnitude, one vital to the continuation of the Phoenician race.

The legendary powers of the Phoenicians were never truly based on iron swords and armour-piercing arrows. Instead, their dynasty was built through strategic decisions: well-calculated accommodations, flexible deceptions, unquestionable loyalties wherever changing circumstances warranted. Supported by vast sums of money, uncanny commercial prowess, and the new sciences emerging from Alexandria, the Phoenicians were biding their time as a world minority, subtly influencing political decisions as major empires came and went. Plots hatched in secret meetings of the Aleph elite were executed by wisely chosen loyalists, manipulating the Roman Empire, the Greeks before them, the Egyptians, Alexander, and many others. Elisa was the ultimate weapon, selected as many others had been selected over innumerable centuries for their intelligence, social skills, attitude, aptitude, and beauty. The final requirement was their royal blood, a guarantee of undying loyalty.

Elisa welcomed her single-minded dedication to her people's cause. Her mission was to make herself emotionally necessary to an influential Roman of rank – the higher the rank the better. Her status as second daughter in a royal house allowed more flexibility as to whether or not she needed to marry. As wife or priestess, her goal was to make certain that shared confidences with her Roman target were on the deepest level. Her mentors would then, periodically and throughout her life, assess Elisa's status, providing direction and help when needed.

. . .

Every three years, the Mother Lodge in Tyre met to launch the next generation of Aleph elite on their lifelong training for the missions that had been chosen for them. Among the representatives from lodges spread out all over the inhabited world were a large number of experts and high-ranking officials. They converged to introduce the latest home-grown crop of trainees to the network that would guide them surreptitiously throughout their lives. It was no mean feat to disguise the purpose of so many dignitaries arriving all at once. Luckily Tyre was the hub of a great many comings and goings in commerce, religion, and the military of many nations.

Shortly after Marih left Tyre for Damascus and his military school, Elisa was summoned to an exclusive meeting with the grand master of the Mother Lodge there in Tyre. She was one of no fewer than ten Phoenician royals of various ranks receiving their orders to embark on their missions, thereby applying the training received over their lifetimes. Also, these invited representatives reported to the Mother Lodge with updates and circumstances affecting their home provinces. This collective information allowed the Aleph elites to plan accordingly and conspire effectively in order to achieve their goals.

Elisa kept her humility knowing that every one of the ten was about to receive a life-changing audience, never questioning destiny in the service of their people. Up until now the dead seriousness of their official capacities had been merely academic.

Any who knew her would attest to her extraordinary confidence and stunning courage, yet Elisa found herself nervous to the point of irritation as the opening ceremonies approached. She tried to display an attitude of calm assurance, but her burning eyes and heaving chest betrayed her.

The ceremony began as the junior members were introduced to their senior peers from around the world. One by one they were asked to take a chair in the centre of the room where their skills, ambitions, and passions to serve were individually assessed. Assignments were presented and suggestions were made as to how best they could proceed in their life missions. Each felt a certain autonomy as they realized that the final decisions were in their own hands. Towards that end, the Mother Lodge provided ample discussions in an open forum where all those who had advice – which was never in short supply – could offer their opinions, defend their suggestions, and even attempt to influence the candidates, all in a most democratic fashion.

Two of these highly interactive visitors took a keen interest in Elisa, more so than in any of the other young candidates. One was the master of the Jerusalem Lodge and the other was the master of the lodge in the city of Tarsus. These two had collaborated on common projects for decades.

. . .

The Jerusalem Lodge had always been important to the Alephs, primarily due to its proximity to their Mother Lodge in Tyre. The Phoenicians endeavoured to maintain good relations with their Jewish neighbours, in order to prevent the political troubles continuously plaguing the area from spreading north towards their own people. The Phoenicians also wanted to preserve the business relationships with these most valued customers; Jewish merchants typically bought the largest portion of their supplies from their northern neighbour's markets.

As touchy as matters could be from time to time, the Alephs

had become adept at managing the situations beyond their borders, south or north. However, their chief concern for some time had been how best to manage the insidious power and greed of the Roman Empire, enforced by its massive, well-trained army and overly ambitious generals. One solution of particular interest to the Phoenicians was the city of Tarsus, situated as it was on the inner northern coast of the Mediterranean as the land route turned west from Tyre towards Rome. It was the largest non-Canaanite city that was neither Roman nor Greek. Tarsus claimed a history of relations with the Persian Empire before Alexander the Great attempted to impose himself upon the region. Neither Alexander nor any of his successors were able to alter the inhabitants' sense of belonging, cultural traditions, or religion. One of history's ironies would always be a conqueror's attempts to suppress religions and traditions, almost always driving said practices underground where they would thrive in the hands and hearts of those who held them sacred – until the conquerors were in their turn overpowered. Always simmering just below the surface are the heated passions of the people to bring their ethnic pride into the light.

This may well be why Tarsus retained a strong Mithraist tradition carried forth from the days of Persian relations. The fervour that had survived was barely matched by any other state, except maybe for the Armenians. One of Rome's tactics for assimilation of the conquered was to adapt the local gods into their pantheon. More than any others they had encountered, the ceremonies and traditions for Mithras were of great interest to the Romans. With certain modifications, the secretive ceremonies that came to define Roman Mithraism grew to be more important than the beliefs themselves.

The city of Tarsus accommodated the lifestyles of the Canaanites who lived in the city or frequented it. By treaty, all people of Tarsus carried the privilege of Roman citizenship. Not every occupied city-state or province enjoyed such rights and protections.

Besides the Canaanites honouring Mithras, other automatic Roman citizens of Tarsus were Canaanites of Jewish origin. This blend of allegiances in the north with ethnic origins to the south bred sympathizers in Tarsus who fed the Phoenicians certain vital intelligence with regards to Rome.

All these factors brought Jerusalem and Tarsus under the ever-watchful eyes of the Aleph elites. They achieved status historically enjoyed by major colonial cities like Carthage.

. . .

The two representatives from Jerusalem and Tarsus stepped forward to give their counsel to the Mother Lodge. They felt a need for the new generation of candidates to be not only Phoenicians of direct descent, but also incorporated with loyalists of mixed Phoenician/Roman origins. They told their brethren about the Roman troops placed in Judea with no other purpose than to smother the usual crop of rebellions that arose as regularly as the Hebrew Passover feast. Recent intelligence revealed the legions patrolling certain cities around the Sea of Galilee prone to unusually high-risk activities. In anticipation, the Romans were operating at all levels of their political and military influence, even with social developments, to keep the risks as low as possible across the region.

These two expert lodge masters had given these matters deep consideration and were ready to suggest actions. In order to manipulate various situations to their best advantage, the practice of incorporating solid insiders trusted to transmit essential information in a most confidential manner was key. They now proposed to Elisa and the body of the Mother Lodge a plan to produce a Phoenician child of Roman descent.

Amidst excited murmurs from the brethren, and a no less stunned expression on Elisa's face, the master of the Tarsus Lodge described a unique opportunity recently presented to him. For some time his social standing in Tarsus had earned him initiation into a Roman Mithraist Lodge there. At last his secret dual membership had awarded a most propitious opportunity.

The Romans had recruited and trained spies to plant in several troublesome Jewish communities in an effort to maintain their upper hand. One of these spies was working on an advanced plan and was reporting directly to Lucius Seneca.

All the body of the Mother Lodge knew of young Seneca. A highly educated and influential Roman officer, he was reported to be a philosopher, a statesman, and a dramatist. They also knew that the reins of Roman intelligence in the eastern Mediterranean were held tight in his grasp. Seneca's operatives were reported to be especially crafty. This particular spy's cover required he be an extremist Jew beyond reproach. To successfully fabricate the necessary background story, he had to present a clear and sinless past. A particular challenge to Seneca's plan was this candidate's three-year-old daughter. The carefully laid piety of his cover story would be overshadowed by a child, born from an unsanctioned relationship and whose mother had died in childbirth. His circumstances left him unable to care for the child on his own. His only desire was that his daughter be safe and well looked after. Seneca promised his spy that he would find the right caregiver for his daughter. Accordingly, Seneca brought this matter to his brethren at the Roman Mithraist Lodge in Tarsus, asking that a search be done for such a caregiver.

"Your royal blood will make you a very attractive candidate for such a child," the master said to Elisa. "This will also ensure that you develop a close relationship with Seneca, who has promised his man he will look after the child in person, as if she were his own daughter, and thereby ensure her well-being." The master of the Tarsus Lodge ended his sermon.

As the members took turns speaking in their democratic fashion, Elisa was building a list of questions in her mind. The discussion didn't contain many certainties, and by the end of the Tarsus representative's talk, Elisa was at the peak of her unease. A moment of silence passed before Elisa realized it was her turn to speak. She should say something to quell the audience's anticipation. With an unsteady voice, to say the least, she threw out her first question: "How can I..." Elisa hated the shiver in her voice and hoped that by speaking slowly she would hide it. "Um, make sure... that I will get the child?" Starting to gain some confidence, she continued, "I am assuming that there will be other candidates competing for her elsewhere in the Roman Empire!"

The representative of Tarsus had anticipated her question. "But they are not all located in Tyre. A condition is that this daughter be brought up in Tyre so the father has the opportunity to see her. If the child was in Rome, he might not see her for years at a time due to the nature of his work in Judea."

Elisa started again, "Won't they question why a young lady of royal Phoenician blood would adopt a Roman child?"

"Yes, they will." The representative of Tarsus' eyes opened wide and his cheeks pulled a light smile. "I said there was an opportunity, I didn't say it was guaranteed." He looked around the lodge, forwarding the question to the rest of the attendees, "Why would a young Phoenician lady of royal birth want to adopt a child instead of just having her own?" His theatrical gaze rested upon his Aleph brother from Jerusalem, acting as if they had not already rehearsed the reply.

The representative of Jerusalem spoke, "We received word that the Roman spy will be sent to a military camp in Damascus where he will stay for a period of time to receive more detailed Jewish religious training. The military camp is the same one that your brother Marih is staying at for his military training." He finished by looking back at his friend, passing the floor back to him.

The master from Tarsus took the stand. "If you were to go to Damascus to visit your brother, you will have an opportunity to see the spy and his daughter."

The grand master of the Mother Lodge of Tyre and the chair of the meeting took over, "Sister Elisa, as you can see, our brothers have thought this matter over very well and have worked very hard on gathering intelligence. What is the use of such information if we don't make the best use of it? You are a fine woman blessed with beauty and intellect, and with the blessings of Melqart you will be guided to perform your mission most effectively, of this we have no doubt. But remember that the best laid plans are never perfect and are not expected to be; plans are merely confidence builders helping us believe we know how to achieve our goals. The real plan, Sister Elisa, only appears clear and complete after its execution."

Elisa bowed her head in respect, signalling her agreement with the grand master's final advice. The following five minutes provided a ritualistic transition from Elisa's audience to the next candidate, allowing her to join the rest of the attendees around the sides of the hall. The calming traditions of the Mother Lodge helped her rest her nerves, and by the end of the ceremonies she had managed to regain her poise.

In the next few days, Elisa didn't stop thinking about her future and what her destiny as an Aleph operative would bring to her, until she was summoned to meet with the grand master and other Aleph elites to work out the actual details of her mission. The next step for her was to go to Damascus on an alleged visit to her brother Marih where she would meet with this Roman spy and his daughter.

. . .

One early evening as she was watching the sun prepare to take its daily dive in the sea, Elisa saw the long shadows of three men riding toward her parents' residence. She soon recognized her brother Marih and his now constant companion, Cornelius. She had just planned her trip to Damascus, and now here he was cancelling out her pretence for her visit. Was her brother returning to Tyre for good? Now how would she explain her important visit to Damascus? All these thoughts were overtaken by a wave of sisterly sentiments as she ran to her brother's welcome.

The two visitors had more awaiting them than Elisa's initial warm welcome. Marih's family was delighted by the surprise and his young wife clung to him like melted cheese on coarse bread. The convivial traditions kept the two travellers up way beyond their strength. Their adventures in Jerusalem had exhausted them and they were looking forward to some rest. By the time people started giving in to the night, Marih and Cornelius had explained to everybody that they were in Jerusalem on a mission and that they were planning on spending a day of rest in Tyre before they returned to their military camp in Damascus. The explanation brought comfort to Elisa's mind as she silently wondered if she could join them on their return.

Finally, Marih, Ishtar, Cornelius, and Elisa were the only people left in the visitors' hall. Marih's wife pulled him up out of his chair, hinting that the time had come for her to have him all to herself.

"Go to your rest, Marih, I'm sure you will get plenty of sleep tonight," Cornelius said with his usual sarcasm.

"That you will never know, will you?" Marih shot back.

Elisa walked her brother and his bride to the door and gave him a long hug. He whispered in her ear, "The master of the Jerusalem Lodge sends you his regards."

She shuddered in his arms. Attempting to hide her astonishment, she moved her embrace to her brother's other cheek and hugged him tightly again. She could feel his smile as he whispered again, "It's a long story. You have a story to tell me, too?"

Feeling Cornelius' gaze upon her every move, Elisa whispered three words, "Yes. Tomorrow morning?"

As she returned to him, Cornelius realized they were alone. He had never managed to forget the particulars marking his last encounter with her at the ruins of The Temple of Melqart. He was so obviously nervous, how could she not notice? Was it just that memory of an awkward Phoenician ceremony or was there more to it? He did find Elisa exceptionally attractive, but attractive women didn't usually make him this nervous. Could it be that he wasn't sure what to expect from her, or even from himself? The one thing he was sure of was that he didn't want to do anything to offend Marih. The easiest way out of his predicament would be to leave the room by calling it a night. He stood up, stretching his arms and pretending to suppress a yawn. "It's time I got some rest of my own."

Elisa realized his tenseness. "Of course, Cornelius. Your earlier quarters are being used tonight as we did not expect you. But we have a place with a comfortable bed and the quiet you need. Come with me."

They walked out into the front yard and followed a short path to the dormitory for visiting guests. Once inside, Cornelius found himself in a pleasant atrium with several wooden doors around him. She motioned towards one, opened it, and walked in. Cornelius followed with slow steps, pretending to be busy with his bag. Wondering what took him so long, Elisa walked back to the door and waved for him to enter.

"You should find this most comfortable. I will see you in the morning. Sleep as late as you like," she said as he walked through the narrow door, brushing lightly against her. She gave him a sisterly kiss on the cheek and turned around, in one fluid gesture pulling the door closed behind her as she stepped into the atrium.

Cornelius, still feeling the warmth of her lips on his face, now questioned whether he should feel relief at being left alone or stupidity at passing up an opportunity for another kiss. He was just happy to have his bag in his hands to fidget with as he got ready for bed.

No sooner was he sure he was safe from further anxiety, than Elisa suddenly opened the door, leaving an opening only wide enough for Cornelius to see her face. "Uh, Cornelius? What happened at the temple... during the betrothal... that was just ceremonial, a one-time thing. What happens in a ceremony stays in a ceremony. I thought you should know," she said with a soft voice to avoid waking up the guests in the other rooms. These words of intended comfort had the opposite effect on Cornelius, who stood there even more nervous than he had been before. Unable to find the right words, he stared blankly into the space between them and bobbed his head with what seemed more like a shiver with a lopsided smile.

She shut the door quietly and walked away.

. . .

By the time Cornelius awoke, almost mid-morning, Elisa and Marih had already found private time to brief one another. Elisa told her brother about the Aleph Grand Lodge meeting and about her new mission, which clarified to him how the master of the Jerusalem Lodge happened to know his sister. They decided to spend one more day in Tyre and depart for Damascus in the morning.

In what seemed to Cornelius to be a spontaneous, spur-of-the-moment behaviour, Elisa and Ishtar decided to join the men on their trip back to Damascus and help them celebrate their graduation.

Five

From the Horse's Mouth

On the way to Damascus, Cornelius shared with his company his happiness to have finished the course. He explained how Antonius, his supervisor and teacher, had hopes to officially enroll him in the Roman Intelligence Agency. Cornelius had been thinking about it for quite a while, though, and had decided to himself that he was not going to pursue any further involvement in the military, in any shape or form. He was just happy to have been initiated into the military and planned on carrying back to Rome his brief military record for his *curriculum vitae* and future political career. Cornelius knew Antonius was going to be disappointed with him, but he had to do what he had to do. His heart was in Rome and he had missed his family and friends very much, so much so that he was unable to imagine himself living somewhere in the peripheries of the Empire – which was where most intelligence officers would have to serve.

Ishtar was Cornelius' only attentive listener. Marih and Elisa pretended to be interested in the conversation, but were completely absorbed in thoughts of Elisa's mission from the Mother Lodge. Each of them was running different scenarios through their heads. Elisa didn't want to think too far into the future, and tried to keep her thoughts focused on the immediate objective of winning the child. The unknown made her mind play tricks on her nerves. It was difficult for Elisa and Marih to remain aloof around Cornelius and not mention the matter at all, but they managed to make it to

Damascus, their secret intact.

. . .

The graduation celebration would not be held for two more weeks after their arrival. In no particular hurry to report the success of their mission, they entertained their lovely companions seeing the sights of Damascus. Two days after their arrival, Antonius summoned Cornelius to his chamber.

"Oh, favourite son of Rome! He asks for you and forgets all about me," Marih teased his friend. "We were in this together, you know. The Phoenician deserves a promotion too, you know."

"You don't have to worry about me competing with you on a promotion. I'm going to tell Antonius today about my decision to return to Rome. But," Cornelius changed his tone playfully, "if you really want me to put in a good word for you to my fellow Roman Mithraist, I could deign to find you such favour."

"You have two more weeks of enjoying my company before you leave this part of the Empire for good. So do yourself a favour and make use of every minute you have," Marih said with a smile.

"I'll sure be missing your crazy traditions, especially that wedding ceremony of yours." Cornelius reached for the embroidered cloth they had stolen from the Jerusalem Temple to show Antonius the proof of their proud success and left.

On his way to Antonius' chamber, he played in his head how he would present the story of his adventures with Marih, some way to build up their achievement in a big way, before he broke the news to Antonius of his wish to return home.

Walking into Antonius' chamber, Cornelius lifted the cloth up in a fisted salute as if presenting his enemy's severed head by the hair. Making sure the embossed image was unmistakably visible, he looked about for his teacher. Antonius was sitting in one shaded corner chatting quietly with two other men. When he saw Cornelius, he excused himself from his conversation and stood to receive his visitor. A smile of encouragement and pride stretched on his face when he saw the cloth. The message was clear and impactful. His student was a success! He gave Cornelius a welcoming embrace, thumping him on the back a few times while guiding him to one of the seats at the table. The two men prepared to leave the room, but

Antonius said something to one of them quietly before saying to Cornelius, "You have a visitor from Rome." He asked his man to go bring the visitor.

"A visitor?" Of course! It could only be his father here to attend his son's graduation, knowing how proud he was and how much the graduation meant to the old warrior. After all, his boy would be coming back home with a certificate of manhood as testimony to his experience in the arts and science of war as only earned via the glorious Roman legion. Instead of answering right away, Antonius busied himself adjusting a Levantine-styled lamp on a raised, shapeless stone.

Antonius didn't let him wait too long. "You are now at an important crossroad of your life, Cornelius. Decisions that a man makes at such intersections direct the rest of his life. You need to ponder this deeply and then heed both your gut and your smarts."

"I do realize the importance of such decisions and I have been thinking about this for a while," Cornelius interrupted to introduce his wish to return to Rome, before Antonius could spoil the moment.

Antonius was visibly distracted, ignoring this statement just as he had the question before. He kept on talking as if he was racing his young student's thoughts to deliver some time-sensitive message. "You are a very intelligent man and we need leaders of your type for our agency. If you stay here and don't return to Rome I will personally see to it that you are offered the best options available in return for your patriotic service to this Empire by helping to manage this turbulent zone. However, if you decide to return to Rome – although that would be an unfortunate loss to me – I will support your decision, knowing full well you will continue to serve our Empire however you choose."

Antonius brought his thoughts to a close as he heard the expected steps approaching. Cornelius looked up, a twinkle in his eye, unable to hide his emotions as he anticipated his father's entrance. He fixed his posture quickly and touched his sword with his left hand, ensuring he looked his military best to impress his proud old man. When the faces became clear in the light of the lamp, Cornelius was ready to move forward and hug the precious Roman visitor. Instead, disappointment checked his joyous expectations.

The visitor was not Cornelius' father.

Gathering his wits, Cornelius quickly regained his composure and moved toward his visitor with open arms, gathering him up in a familial embrace. "Simaan! What a pleasant surprise. What are you doing here? You've come for my graduation?" Cornelius remembered the incident at the temple in Jerusalem and realized that Simaan must have been in the area on business and decided to drop by and attend his graduation. After all, Damascus had been his idea, and Simaan always treated him like a son.

"Your graduation is a matter of pride to all of us, my son." Simaan's sombre tone and posture gave Cornelius pause. He pulled back slightly to get a better look into Simaan's face, hoping he would only see signs of travel fatigue.

It wasn't fatigue. There was something darker in Simaan's already very dark eyes.

"I'm afraid I bring you sad news, Cornelius, my son," came Simaan's careful words. Cornelius' eyes bounced back and forth between Antonius and Simaan; he felt a sickness rising in his throat. "Your father has passed away."

Cornelius still had his hands on Simaan's arms, not yet having freed himself from the first embrace. "What? My father? When? When did this happen?" As strong a man as Cornelius had become, this news nearly brought him to his knees.

"I was in Rome when it happened. I came directly to you. You know how your father loved life and lived it well. He surely enjoyed good wine. Only this time it seems he had a few drinks from a bad wine pot. No others were harmed. A physician was sent for, to no avail. His passing was quick, yet good fortune would honour him one last time as he left this world surrounded by family and friends. Except for your absence, he was at peace. There are few better ways for a man to go."

As Simaan said his piece, Cornelius' senses clamped down, numbing him in the moment, as if everything was moving in slow motion. The words broke down into letters, each hitting his ears like the howl of a mother mourning her firstborn's dead body. Something else broke inside his mind. His fingers dropped off Simaan's arms as if he felt the filth of the skin of a despicable traitor. Simaan could sense the deathly cold rising; he stepped back to find unfathomable emptiness in his wide-open eyes, just before Cornelius turned his back to him.

He stood there in silence for a few long seconds. His right hand rested on the handle of his sword amidst a struggle between his heart and his mind. His arm tensed from the shoulder down while opposing muscles fought for control of that sword. How easy it would be to pull the sword and spin about, levelling it at Ben Aaron's neck! He fought it with every drop of his might. No, too quick, too rash. That would deprive him of watching him suffer through some as yet unplanned revenge. His mind jumped back the other way. He thought of burying his sword in Ben Aaron's chest and watching him die slowly. No, not that either. He began to savour the rage building in his gut and gloried in his mastery of it. In an honest gesture of remarkable self-control, he let the sword rest in its sheath. He looked over at Antonius and said, "I will take you up on your offer to stay here as your centurion. I no longer have reason to rush back to Rome."

Cornelius' quick mind made the connection between that overheard conversation beneath the temple in Jerusalem and the stupefying news of his father's death... death by poison, not an accidentally spoiled pot of wine. He felt like a man blind from birth suddenly gifted with sight – except what he saw were not imagined splendours but the bitterness of reality and deception.

Antonius was confused. He did not expect this response from Cornelius. He had been intently watching the exchange between the two men and couldn't be sure of what had happened. He did want him to stay and work with the agency, but there had never been any offer to become a centurion. Considering the circumstances, Antonius decided to leave clarification for another time.

Ben Aaron, on the other hand, had completely different expectations. He wanted Cornelius to return to Rome to fill his father's shoes. He spoke in his usual capacity as friend and advisor. "Rome is the right place for you now, Cornelius. You should return and manage your father's business and take his role in the society. You are a natural leader, my son, and we have always expected you to step up to such responsibilities – and now is the time. Your father's house needs you, Cornelius. Rome needs you."

It took extraordinary discipline to overcome the rock-melting hatred that was his emotions and stop it from erupting into action or pouring out in words. Still not looking in Ben Aaron's direction, Cornelius covered his face with one hand but spoke with conviction, "Rome will always be in my heart. I wish no other honour than offering myself – body and blood – to the glory of Caesar and the gods of Rome. These things I learned from my father, a soldier of splendid loyalty and unmatchable patriotism. No, I will stay here and serve Rome as a warrior, so long as I can breathe. Rome is not short of politicians."

Cornelius made his final decision quite clear, leaving Ben Aaron no room for negotiations. "Son, if that's your wish, you have my support," Ben Aaron said as he tried to hide his disappointment. "You seem to have made up your mind and obviously Antonius is taking good care of you. You will surely make a superb centurion. I am very proud of you and will make sure you see me at your new post when next I return to the east. I am heading back to Rome tomorrow morning. Allow me now to take your leave and go give this aged body of mine some rest."

Cornelius nodded but made no move toward him, not even to turn around and look at him. Simaan the family friend had entered this room; Ben Aaron his nemesis was leaving it.

. . .

After Ben Aaron left, Antonius searched for words of comfort and sympathy for the grieving Cornelius. His mind stumbled between empty platitudes and confusing thoughts about what had just happened. He kept coming back to the question of the centurion position and why his student had suddenly decided to stay instead of returning to Rome for his career in politics.

Cornelius could almost hear his analytical teacher's mind churning away, postponing his questions about what happened. His motivation to put his mentor at ease was over-ridden by his need to release the anger raging within his whole being.

"Ben... Aaron... killed... my... father," he said, slowly emphasizing each word, barely opening his lips as his teeth ground into each other.

"Simaan!?" yelled Antonius in disbelief. "Did you say Simaan? This Simaan? He... what?"

"Simaan Ben Aaron." Cornelius raised his red-rimmed eyes to meet Antonius' stunned gaze. "And you heard correctly."

"Where does this come from? He's a friend to your family, he came all the way from Rome to bring to you the–" Before Antonius finished breaking down his understanding of the situation, Cornelius interrupted.

"He did not come from Rome," Cornelius said with the confidence of a knowing man. "Marih and I saw him and heard him arrogantly pronouncing his achievement to a priest at the temple in Jerusalem, in the secrecy of their private chambers." Cornelius pulled out the piece of cloth from the temple in a tight fist, raising it to the narrow space between their faces. "Marih translated the words of the voice I know so well. Ben Aaron was in conversation with the high priest. Now I recognize it as the same story he told us about my father, except he told the priest that the wine was poisoned to make it look like he had bad wine. I am done with the treachery of politics in Rome. You wanted me to stay here. You got it."

"If you really believe this to be so, how did you keep your calm?"

"'It is at the peak of anger that one is tempted by the most destructive of decisions. It is at the peak of temptation that avoiding hasty destruction becomes a virtue. It is at the peak of all virtues to finally achieve destruction by wise planning and knowledgeable application.'" Cornelius repeated these verses, honouring the many times his father, in all his wisdom, had repeated them to him. His father was a known stoic and believer in the ability to control one's mind through discipline enhanced with knowledge. He had always instructed Cornelius to avoid knee-jerk reactions because they often result in the opposite outcome to what is desired. A well-planned, wisely executed, delayed reaction has the potential to completely overcome the instigating act and endure any rebuttals.

"Attributes of the true leader, Cornelius! Like father like son." Antonius lowered his eyes in silent honour to both men. In due time he continued, "But these attributes will serve no purpose if the son ends like his father. You have major decisions to make. So before you pledge to any commitments, I want you to meet somebody."

"Could there possibly be anybody I would want to see at this time?" Cornelius snapped.

"I guarantee you will want to meet Lucius Annaeus Seneca."

Six

A Persian, a Jew,
a Phoenican or an Arab?

Lucius Annaeus Seneca was born to a wealthy family in the city-state of Corduba on the Iberian Peninsula. He spent many years of his youth in the eastern provinces of Rome, exposed to Phoenician and Greek philosophies of stoicism and ascetic neo-Pythagoreanism. His education, brilliance, and familial descent made him an ideal candidate to become a consultant for recruitment into the Imperial Intelligence Agency.

The top-secret mission assigned to Seneca during the reign of Emperor Tiberius was to support efforts by the Empire to dismantle the strongly knit religious societies of Judea. Based on his guidance and advice, the Roman Empire had selected a team to serve Seneca's mission. In Damascus, his friend Antonius would frequently present the pick of his current recruits for Seneca's consideration.

. . .

Easily slipping into the role of father figure, Antonius truly believed Cornelius needed a few days of reflection before making any major life decisions. He waited three days after their meeting with Ben Aaron, then invited Cornelius to dine with him and Lucius

Seneca.

When Marih learned from Cornelius of the planned event, he wasted no time before carrying the news of what could well be a potential opportunity to his sister. Neither Elisa nor Marih had any idea of exactly who Lucius Seneca was, aside from what the brother of the Tarsus Lodge had revealed at the closed Aleph meeting a few weeks earlier. There was no reason to assume that some potential business was about to materialize between Cornelius and this Seneca. Marih's guess was that an invitation to one of Antonius' social events was intended as a device to help lift Cornelius out of his grief. The news of his father's death had landed with all the weight of an elephant on his friend's chest. Cornelius didn't even attempt to hide his sadness.

Marih and Elisa were completely in the dark about the details of Silvius' death. They had no idea Cornelius had connected the tale of murder and intrigue they had heard from Ben Aaron to the death – the murder – of his own father. Their interest in the dinner party was merely to cast a wider net of intelligence in order to increase their chances of their mission's success. Perhaps they could open a window of opportunity through Cornelius with Seneca, the suspected director of the agency.

In addition to his formidable military reputation, Antonius was a very hospitable host and a cordial conversationalist. Should his guest be but one of the general public, perhaps a merchant of no elitist skills or educations, Antonius would know just the right sort of conversation to make his guest feel at home, so much so one would think he was born and had lived all his life among the struggling middle social ranks. And should his guest be of the exalted rank of Lucius Seneca, Antonius could smoothly manage any dialogue in a fashion that allowed his guest to shine and feel the conversation was valued without creating an environment of comparison or competition.

Bringing together talents such as Lucius Seneca and Cornelius, Antonius anticipated a most stimulating evening. The potentially rhythmical blend of these highly intellectual and brave minds promised a unique evening with no fear of usually restrictive social limits. By way of launching the conversation, Antonius excitedly informed Lucius of Cornelius' plans to stay in Phoenicia and Judea.

"A correct choice is one that stems from one's nature." Seneca's tendency to speak in philosophical terms encouraged the younger man's response.

"What if one's nature has undergone radical change?" Cornelius challenged with a voice of confidence, intending to stimulate his host and the other guests with a lively debate.

Seneca astutely read in Cornelius' comment what lay hidden between the lines of their dialogue. He recognized the smoke concealing the blazing fire, all behind the outward calm of this well-controlled young man. He responded, "Natures are like solid mountains. They need earthquakes to shake them out of place."

Seneca directed his next comment to Antonius, "Yet, nothing is impossible. If we can conceive an idea, so might that idea come to pass. So it is when natures undergo change. All that remains to be seen is the magnitude of courage sufficient to bring it about."

"And this one lacks no courage, I can tell you," Antonius boasted with the pride of a father in a favourite son.

Antonius was happy with their initial conversation. Things were going just as he had hoped. No one could offer better advice and wisdom to Cornelius than Seneca; he knew that all along. He had known Seneca to enjoy analyzing personalities and to offer highly introspective opinions. He also knew that Cornelius was not one to shy away from philosophical conversations. Most importantly, he wanted Cornelius to be sure of his decision to stay in Damascus before he started executing any big plans he had for him.

"Cornelius, Lucius is the man who coined the saying, 'Difficulties strengthen the mind as labour does the body.'" Antonius tried to gently raise the perception of Seneca as a man of a heeded voice. Realizing that Cornelius was not completely oblivious to the fact that Seneca was someone of a high and well-respected rank in this part of the Empire, Antonius also assumed that Cornelius could have never guessed what exact role Seneca played – not only the secretive nature of his role but also because Seneca had been living away from the mainstream political society of Rome. Cornelius was already quite familiar with the latter.

The evening continued in delightfully entertaining debate, but dwindled away to just these three men sitting in close conversation. "This young man has a rare combination of skills seldom seen in one person of any age. He would be the right person for special operations, you know," Antonius said with a knowing look to Seneca.

"What skills could possibly differentiate me?" Cornelius asked with a self-deprecating tone while keeping an attentive ear in case Antonius actually had the answer.

"I think I understand what Antonius is trying to say," Seneca interrupted, beaming at Antonius. "I also tend to trust his judgment. If he thinks you're fit for a special kind of operation, I could only wish you'd concede to undertake such an operation."

Seneca and Antonius seemed to have already been discussing a matter in much more detail than the general conversation Cornelius had been having with them thus far. Still not sure if Seneca's comments were merely rhetorical or if he was actually extending an offer of employment of some kind, Cornelius took advantage of the liberal wine consumed amongst them and probed playfully, "Just like other humans, Antonius makes mistakes, you know. You might want to test my skill set first."

"Not Antonius, he doesn't err on this kind of assessment!" Seneca's reply was quick and confident.

With eyes almost begging for more clarity, Cornelius kept quiet, stretching his patience to admirable limits.

Seneca bent forward, bringing his thighs to the edge of the sofa like someone on the verge of reciting an interesting tale, "The skills we seek vary widely. In fact, it is not necessarily a specific personality trait we look for, but rather a combination of traits ensuring our people are capable of performing at the highest levels of reliability in positions where execution seldom tolerates mistakes."

"I am grateful for the flattering description of my skills, but I would only be pretending in my protest if I didn't ask you now to speak more plainly. Surely the time has come for games of rhetoric to be put aside." Cornelius had a strong feeling that both men were preparing him for the details he craved and he knew he had to offer them the opportunity.

Instead of answering him with more clarity, Seneca went rambling on about the need for a live example for him to truly discern certain people's traits and how these traits could be useful. Seneca was still talking when one of Antonius' guards walked in on them, apologizing and briefly informing Antonius there had been some sort of incident.

Antonius unguardedly spoke out loud in front of his trusted guests and asked the guard about the details of the incident.

The guard said one of their men had been caught trying to sell Antonius' favourite horse to a passerby. Antonius looked around at his guests, intrigued by the situation but embarrassed for having to handle such a matter in their presence.

"Come, my friend, don't let our presence deter you. I would love to watch you in action." Seneca begged Antonius to go ahead with his interrogation.

"Bring me the thief," Antonius commanded the soldier.

The guard presently returned with the thief already in chains, dragged by two more soldiers.

"What's your name?" Antonius roared.

"They call me Claudius, sir," the chained soldier replied in suitable fear.

"How dare you steal from my stable, never mind my favourite horse?" Antonius interrogated the soldier in a voice quite unlike the calm and hospitable one his guests had just been hearing.

"I assure you, sir, no one dares to extend a hand to your property with malicious intention," the soldier said, trying to speak in a formal manner, as if doing so could justify his conduct. "I was not stealing your horse. A stranger told me that your horse spoke to him in his dream and the horse asked him to come in person when he awoke and talk to him. He said the horse promised to reveal an important secret to him."

"Are you out of your mind? Did you really think you could come before me with such a pathetic account? The nerve!" His words carried just the right amount of intimidation.

"But the man was honest, sir," the soldier continued sincerely. "He gave me a detailed account of his dream and he was able to describe explicit details of your horse, details only your stablemen would know."

"You were caught receiving money from the stranger," Antonius sternly accused the profusely sweating soldier.

"Not at all, sir! The money I was caught with was my own. The man said that he needed money in order to seduce the soul of the talking horse, so that it would divulge the secret!"

"So he took my horse *and* your money? Tell me, were you born stupid or do you have to work at it?" In an effort to bring his temper under control, Antonius remembered the taunt from his nursemaid that always made him laugh. While he still didn't believe this soldier's story, he wanted to give the man the benefit of the doubt. "Describe this stranger to me. What is his name?"

"I'm sorry, sir, I realize now how incredibly stupid this sounds, but I don't know his name. He was so very convincing I forgot to ask," the soldier cried.

"What language did he speak? Was he Roman?"

"I... I don't know, sir. He spoke fluently in our tongue, but when he told me what the horse said to him in his dream, he spoke with a different tongue before translating it to me," the soldier said.

"What did he look like, then? In the names of all the gods, man, recover your wits! What was the colour of his skin? What was the colour of his hair?" Antonius looked to his guest, Seneca, for support.

"He is in between, sir. He could be dark but slightly light-skinned. His hair, too." The soldier knew his answers were not sitting well with his superiors.

"Was he a goddamned Persian? Was he a Jew? A Phoenician? An Arab? In what manner did he state his belief in his dream?" Antonius had run out of questions... and patience.

"Forgive me, sir, I would not dare to lie, the man could be any of those. He could fit as any. He sure has fooled me, I know that now, but he... he... you should have heard him speak, sir." The soldier barely finished his words before Antonius interrupted him.

"Are you saying that if I listened to this man he would convince me, too? Aren't you full of insults!" The pitch of Antonius' voice was mounting in continued frustration.

Seneca stepped closer to Antonius. "He did convince you once," he said with a lowered voice, looking down at his feet, arousing confused attention from the soldiers and Cornelius. Antonius' rage visibly drained away as he turned slowly to Seneca with squinting eyes, filled with no less confusion than the rest of those straining now to hear Seneca.

Before any further reactions were seen in the room, the soldier in chains started jumping about like a chicken, yelling, "This is the man! This is the man, sir! Sir... the man is here!" Then he turned to the stranger entering the room, begging, "Please tell them, tell them what you told me. Tell them the truth!"

All eyes turned as one to a man standing confidently in the doorway, with an impossible expression of a greeting smile on one side of his face and an attempt to look serious on the other.

"Paulus!" Antonius shrieked and jumped at the intruder, unclear to the audience if he was attacking or embracing. He was stopped midway by Seneca's hand clasping his arm at the elbow. Antonius immediately got the message. "Let the soldier go, he's forgiven." Antonius gestured to the soldiers that they were all dismissed at once. As the last confused soldier left, Antonius freed himself from Seneca's loosening grip and continued his way to this man, hugging him like a father finding a lost son.

"I should have known! A man that could fit any description and could convince a loyal soldier to hand over his money along with his master's talking horse!" Antonius exploded into loud laughter, quickly joined by Seneca and Paulus. Cornelius couldn't help but smile as the contagious environment maddeningly flipped. He kept searching for any clues to help him understand the situation.

"Cornelius, my son," Antonius called to him, sensing his distress. "This is Paulus, the cream of my career and the crown of my pride."

Starting to realize that Paulus must be a former apprentice to Antonius, Cornelius nodded his head in a gesture of understanding and extended his salutation to Paulus. "I am assuming that you two also know each other?" he asked, indicating Seneca.

Before either could answer, Antonius excitedly jumped in, waving one finger in the air, "Oh, they have met indeed, in circumstances like no other."

"Antonius!" Seneca's sharp retort reminded Antonius that now was not the right time to tell that story.

Antonius ignored Seneca's alarm and started talking while he prepared a seat amongst them and passed a drink to his flamboyantly late guest. "There is no better time or place to tell this story than tonight and in this chamber." Seneca acknowledged he'd met his match and acceded.

Antonius gazed at Seneca. "As you know, Lucius, I had planned all along to have Cornelius join us this evening so I could introduce the two of you. He clapped his huge palm on Seneca's shoulder and shook it. "I was right before... about Paulus, wasn't I? Trust me with this one, too."

Seneca settled back with an indulging smile and relinquished the floor to his elder comrade.

"Cornelius is, by far, the best in his class. His graduation is coming up in few days. He has had many trials and has handled himself admirably. None carry greater portent than the most recent turn of events." Antonius paused, letting that statement hang in the air. He resumed in measured tones, as if ticking off a mental list as he spoke, "Silvius, my dearest friend and his father, passed away very recently. This sad fact was unknown to him while was on his examination mission in Jerusalem. At one point during his escapade, he found himself hiding in an inner chamber of the temple." He watched their faces turn to surprise at the mere mention of Cornelius actually making it inside the Jewish temple. "Yes, indeed, hiding in an inner chamber in the tunnels of the lower level, he overheard a conversation between a Jewish priest and a Jewish man who turned out to be a citizen and resident of Rome. You see, Cornelius recognized the voice of the man as one belonging to a close friend of his family. He ventured to catch a glimpse of him, just to make sure. This man did not see him, did not even realize he was overheard. His field partner is a Phoenician recruit who translated the conversation for him. For Cornelius, that moment was nothing more than a strange coincidence. It meant nothing to them, so they completed their mission in what turned out to be a most unique... dare I say legendary? manner!"

Antonius winked at Cornelius and continued, "He visited me upon his return to Damascus and this very same family friend sought him out with the sad news of his father's passing. He was told the cause was an accidentally spoiled pot of wine." Antonius leaned forward with all seriousness. "I watched your face, my son;

you comported yourself most admirably." Sitting back, he returned to the cadence of his story, "As if struck by the gods, he immediately ascertained from that brief description that his father had actually been assassinated by this same Jewish man. In short, his father was poisoned!"

Paulus hammered his glass on the table in front of him. At the same moment Seneca sprung to his feet. Both stood there dumbfounded.

"In a display of self-control I have seldom seen in men twice his years, our Cornelius stifled a natural inclination to kill the man on the spot!" Turning again to Cornelius, he said, "You must have summoned all your father ever taught you about quick decisions producing poor results. The way you turned the moment around to your favour was marvelous!" Back to his guests, he concluded, "Cornelius took the news as his cue to announce that he had decided not to return to Rome where a guaranteed future in politics would otherwise await him. He has decided to stay here in Damascus and help us serve our great cause." Antonius paused for effect.

Lucius spoke first. "This explains the major change in your nature we bandied about so lightly before. I am sorry for your terrible news, Cornelius; such is life, but we never get used to it." He settled back into his seat, deep in thought.

Remaining quiet, Cornelius nodded, lifting one eyebrow in a sign of acquiescence to a bitter truth. He was beginning to truly like this man.

"Such is life. That's true," Antonius bounced in again. "This is Cornelius' story in a few inadequate words, but I'm sure that these are only the first few lines of an odyssey of distinction."

Antonius took a brave sip of joy from his glass, challenging the bitterness of life. When his head came down, a light and natural smile formed on his face as he watched Paulus approach Cornelius and give him a quick shoulder clasp of brotherly support.

Antonius turned his attention to Cornelius. "And now, *quid pro quo*, I give you the story of Paulus.

"A number of years ago when I was at the School of Tarsus, I sat as an honorary judge on a committee conducting a competition in applicable history. The top student was to win a sum of money and a proclamation of respect from the committee, a very prestigious honour sought by every advanced student.

"Our committee had met behind closed doors to compile a list of contestants for the competition when the door was flung open and a well-dressed, mature-looking young man – whom we assumed must be a teacher at the school – walked in on us. He had sharp, brave eyes. He stared directly into the eyes of each of the committee members and none of us could seem to return the gaze. Adding to his aura of mystical magnetism, he has a most singular black mole, centered in the middle of his chest, three fingers' width below his collarbone at the split of his cloak.

"His rock hard confidence and authoritative tone had us all on edge as he spoke. He proceeded to lecture us on the necessity of taking into consideration the ethnic and religious diversity of the Roman citizens of Tarsus, stressing that the minorities should not feel rejected. He was specifically emphatic about the need to enlist the participation of students from the Jewish community and, to that end, suggested we should aim a certain percentage of the questions at their peculiar history. The man's highly respectful attitude and professional reasoning was most convincing. Every one of the committee members felt commanded, but in a most agreeable way. He bowed and withdrew. We were all swayed by the validity of his argument. As I was the most experienced in the Judaic culture, the committee asked me to suggest questions suitable to the task. Of course I accepted the request."

Antonius raised his right fist, thumping it audibly on his own chest in mock Roman salute, "As a soldier, I never shy away from a challenge!"

This demonstration drew smiles of pride from his similarly patriotic audience. "Let me go back a few years to explain why I should be so chosen. You see, it was generally known among my colleagues that I had the honour to become acquainted with one of the most respected masters of the Jewish religion, a certain Rabbi Gamaliel. In a mutual effort to assure security and peace in the area, the rabbi and I developed a synergistic relationship whereby he helped resolve internal issues of any religious nature and I provided a physical presence whenever a situation seemed it might spin out of control. By showing respectful and sincere curiosity for his religion, he once invited me to spend a day at a teaching school outside the temple. Naturally, I accepted. As I said, this was some time ago. There happened at that time to be an unusually brilliant child among his students. Gamaliel assigned him to shadow me throughout the day and to mentor me on the basics of the religion. One day was nowhere near enough to teach me even one fraction of the ancient Hebrew religion. But I had certainly remembered enough anecdotes from that one brilliant boy to put several questions together a few years later."

"You mean your contest questions were actually some little kid's stories?" Emboldened by liquid camaraderie, Cornelius thought he'd tease his commanding officer.

Antonius threw back a withering look, shaming him for his inappropriate comment. With narrowing eyes came a promise there was more where that came from. Clearing his throat, he continued, "I submitted the questions and the committee approved them. They trusted me. However, they decided to use the questions only in the event of a tie between students at the end of the examination. And so, we went out to the anxious contestants and their audience... the crowd was so large we had gathered in a small amphitheatre."

"Each main contestant had a supportive team of four students from his class, selected for their various areas of expertise. As the contest progressed, two contestants were continuously tied for the lead with a third trailing by only three or four points. When we reached the final stage of the competition, it was obvious we would have to use my questions to decide the winner. Well, I'll tell you now, it didn't take long before we realized the questions that were supposed to break the tie had only complicated matters further. Instead of advancing one of the two leading contestants, the questions gave the advantage to the third contestant! He was lagging only slightly and proved to be the most knowledgeable about this topic. This dark horse, with the help of his team, improved his score to bring about a three-way tie."

"Then what? Did you have to create more questions on the spot?" Cornelius had no sooner spoken than he realized Seneca and Paulus already knew the answer.

Without missing a beat, Antonius shook his head. "I see by your expression you must be figuring this out as I go. No, we did not add any questions. There was only one thing left to do: announce them all winners!"

"So you split the prize money and the accolades among all three?" Cornelius wondered out loud.

"We thought we had!" Antonius turned a caricature of a serious face to Paulus. "As we were awarding the prizes, something didn't quite register. Little incidents, more than just coincidental, began to catch my attention." He rose and walked over to Paulus and, tucking his fingers behind the neck of his robes and pulling down gently, he exposed an unmistakably clear, raised, pea-sized black mole centered in the middle of his upper chest. "This young man was on one of the teams."

"Wait a second..." Cornelius needed to confirm what he thought he understood. "You mean that teacher who walked in on you during the committee meeting was on that third team?"

They all hoped Cornelius was intelligent enough to connect the dots, so lips remained silent a moment longer while he worked it through, thinking out loud, "So, Paulus was a support member of one of the teams, and he was also the pretend-teacher who convinced you to include questions about Judaism!"

"There you have it!" Antonius raised his hand to halt Cornelius' further thoughts. "So, I said nothing and allowed the prizes to be distributed to the main contestants. I tracked the students to where they had gathered to celebrate after the closing ceremonies. I was torn between catching the young whelp and sending him to a proper punishment and assuaging my curiosity as to who he was and what else there was to learn about him. Obviously, I chose the latter because what I soon learned made his pretence of being a teacher the most forgivable act of slyness he had committed that day."

Seneca interrupted with false acrimony, "Instead of delivering a proper punishment to Paulus, Antonius thought that he should bring him to me!"

"Oh please! What else did he do?" Cornelius was hooked.

"You see, this tricky deviant's subterfuge was unknown to his mates. He collected all the winners' money... contestant by contestant... by persuading contestant number one that he will deliberately undermine his own team with the condition that if that contestant won, he would give him an amount equal to one third of the total prize of the contest. Now that the prize was to be divided by three, one-third meant all the winnings of the first contestant. Paulus had slyly extracted the very same deal from ontestant number two. One would think he couldn't possibly know all three teams were going to tie. Surely he only assumed the multiple deals would at least guarantee him something, regardless of the winner. To hedge his bets, Paulus made one more wager with his own team leader, contestant number three, that he could convince the committee to include questions about Judaism, thus giving them an advantage over the other contestants. This bet was also equal to one third of the total prize. This way, if his contestant won, despite his attempt to undermine him as well, he would still stand to make a reasonable profit."

"Even though that tie thing was not expected, I must admit it was a possible solution to the equation!" Paulus tried to sound humble but his pride was overflowing and contagious as Seneca joined the conversation.

"Every mother will tell you to never encourage bad behaviour. So what does my dear Antonius do but send this walking problem in my direction!" Before Seneca finished, they had all exploded in laughter.

By now Cornelius began to understand what Seneca and Antonius meant about searching for people with specific personalities and characters. He wanted to know more about his predecessor, for it was not lost on him that he was being compared favourable to Paulus.

He wanted to know how Paulus was so learned about Judaic history. Perhaps Paulus was actually Jewish. Something in his subconscious couldn't rest with the idea. The matter with Ben Aaron had suddenly soured his mind to his previous generosity toward the Hebrew faith. He didn't even struggle with this new bigotry. He couldn't believe that Antonius and Seneca would put their trust in a person of Judaic descent when the core of their shared mission was to suppress troubles in the territory caused by the Jewish agitators.

"Am I correct in assuming that you, Paulus, are Jewish?" he said, trying to sound analytical rather than judgmental.

"Jewish by blood, Jewish by education, Jewish by practice," Paulus began but Seneca picked up his thread: "Roman by birth, Roman by upbringing, Roman by loyalty... Roman by choice!"

Seneca drained his wine glass and continued the story. "Paulus' father descends from a Hebrew family that immigrated to Tarsus generations before he was born. The family became dualists, which is occasionally practiced but not really sanctioned. They were Roman Mithraists who maintained a relationship with a branch of their family still in Judea, thereby practicing their Jewish customs at home. The two branches of the family maintained their ties thanks to a business arrangement that brought mutual benefits to them in their respective cities.

"The boy's conniving intelligence began to cause embarrassment to his family early on. At one point, his father decided to foster him with associates in Jerusalem, hoping that a life under stricter Roman military ruling - away from the Roman freedoms in Tarsus - and discipline among even more strictly religious Jews, might improve his behaviour and teach him some lessons. Part of his studies in Jerusalem was with other boys learning Hebrew from the rabbis and all the traditions that go along with such training."

"Just as with you, my boy, if you think the stories of Paulus can be told in one night, you are mistaken. This is not a bad thing, for either of you – just think of the many entertaining dinners to come!" Antonius promised Cornelius.

"To wrap things up for this evening," Seneca deftly concluded, "I'll tie the story up with a bow. You remember Antonius saying how he had once spent a day with the class of the Rabbi Gamaliel? Can you deduce who that precocious Jewish boy who played his mentor for a day in Hebrew school might have been?"

Seven

Challenge of the Apprentices

Elisa and Marih were intrigued by Cornelius' behaviour in the days after his meeting with Seneca and Antonius. They suspected he had been invited to join the Imperial Intelligence Agency, but Marih's attempts to probe his friend met with no success. Cornelius made no mention of Paulus to Marih, already assuming a level of trust put upon him to not share any information he'd been given. On the other hand, he had no cause to assume Marih was trying to extract information from him.

The week leading up to the graduation ceremony was one of intensive planning for Marih and his sister. They rehearsed various scenarios, role-played, and worked out different contingencies. A chance to achieve one of Elisa's objectives as assigned by the Mother Lodge could present itself at any moment. Their failure to recognize these rare opportunities could mean another long wait and more costly planning before another one opened up.

One major problem defied their planning: they didn't know what Seneca's man looked like or even how they were supposed to identify him. Should they succeed in approaching Seneca and earning his confidence, the odds were not good he would lead them to him. Well trained by their own intelligence mentors, they both knew there were different levels of trust among all the trustworthy Romans in Damascus for the graduation. Seneca would avoid publicizing the man's role with the additional crowds confusing matters. Just as Marih had not been asked to take part in a Mithraist Lodge, there were others like Marih at the graduation party: trusted enough to be Roman soldiers but not enough to reach the inner circles of confidence. This innate prejudice made it difficult for those not clearly born to Roman aristocracy to compete with the likes of Cornelius. Not to say it was impossible, they just had to work harder to earn the trust automatically placed in the Roman elite.

Marih and Elisa understood perfectly well. After all, it was no different with their Phoenician elite.

Their initial enthusiasm and confidence started to wane as the graduation date approached. They wondered if they had overestimated the potentials of this event. They also questioned their level of experience and blamed their excitement on being new operatives. Despite all, they had come too far to not carry on with their plans. If they failed, they would pass their lessons learned back to the Aleph brethren in hopes someone would in turn provide more information – perhaps a description of the man or possibly his name. For the time being, their best bet was to stick with Cornelius and use him to get closer to Seneca.

Eight

When in Doubt, Wing it

In the morning of the graduation celebrations, an official ceremony was conducted in the graduates' honour and the new soldiers were officially declared to be servants of the Empire. Marih and Cornelius were proudly clothed in their ceremonial uniforms: gleaming muscle cuirass over a snow-white tunic, a red-plumed helmet, a basic shield bearing the Damascus camp insignia, and an empty, tooled leather scabbard. Over the years to come they would earn shields and cuirasses of intricate workmanship, signifying their status in the mightiest fighting force the world had ever known. But for now, with banners and standards waving in the breeze, an aura of majesty prevailed. In the large field beyond, the clamour of playing children and the buzzing of the crowd grew louder as local families, visiting Roman families, and Roman supporters residing in Damascus and the countryside filled up the usually quiet and tightly controlled military zone.

Mingling with their brethren, the two friends went their own ways for a moment. Antonius seized the opportunity and signalled for Marih to walk with him casually until they were out of sight of the gathering and could hear each other speak.

"Son, you know how proud I am of every one of you. I don't

need to tell you that, but I also know it is good to hear these words privately so you surely know I wish you all the best. You, Marih, have a special position and a noble responsibility. Being a royal Tyrian, I was hoping you would understand if I asked you for a favour." Antonius got straight to the point, as was his way. "I realize that you might not have the intention to carry on with a military career or might decide to give up a potential position with the intelligence agency for the sake of other royal and family responsibilities, but for now I need you to help me with your friend Cornelius."

"Of course, anything I can do," Marih agreed, although he couldn't think what Antonius would possibly want of him. After all, Antonius was close enough to Cornelius if for no other reason than being Mithraist brethren.

Antonius welcomed Marih's cooperation, "We have a need for Cornelius to stay here in these provinces. We ask you to help make this happen. I suspect one of the challenges for him will be having friends and people he trusts around him. You already are a good friend to him. It would help him to know he can continue this good relationship with you and your family. Is this something for which you could give your support?" Antonius smiled, already anticipating Marih's answer.

"Gladly and with pleasure, Antonius! Cornelius and I have been like brothers since the start of our training. My family likes him and would love to consider him a son. A very easy and pleasant favour you're asking of me."

"I'm indebted to you, son. This greatly eases my mind. If you have any interest in pursuing further training or in assuming a certain role... if it's in my power to help you, do not spare me your request. Please, join my guests at my table tonight. Cornelius also will sit with us. Do you have any family here?" Antonius asked.

"In fact, my wife and my sister have come with us to Damascus by way of our return from Jerusalem through Tyre."

"They, too, should sit with us. That settles it! You are at my table tonight." Antonius shook a fatherly finger in Marih's face; he nodded his obedience with a smile.

The invitation brought mixed emotions to Marih. While nothing but gain could come from attracting such a favour from Antonius, perhaps his sister's plans to approach Seneca's man might be completely lost in the bargain. It was too late now to seek out Elisa and learn her plans. What else could he do?

. . .

The commencement ceremony was a lengthy process whereby every single graduate had to individually recite an oath of allegiance to the brotherhood of the military and the might of Rome all while at the point of a sword resting upon his left chest, a symbol of precaution and selectivity by the military. Upon swearing their oaths, each received a shining new *gladius* to fill their empty scabbards. Thinking themselves unique in the annals of military history, the ceremony was to a large degree inspired by Phoenician Mithraist rituals.

Throughout the ceremony, Marih kept thinking of his talk with Antonius. He and Elisa had to come up with an alternative plan, and time was not on their side. Immediately after the graduation rite he found his wife and sister and informed them of Antonius' invitation. He lowered his voice and told them of Antonius' interest in keeping Cornelius in Damascus and the favour the old soldier had secured from him to help make it so.

Clearly concerned, Marih thought out loud with the two women, "We should tell the Mother Lodge about our situation with Cornelius. If we fail to connect with Seneca's man... maybe a connection to Cornelius is a good alternative."

"Elisa won't have a problem with that, will you, dear sister? He's attractive and intelligent enough!" Ishtar goaded her with a playful, lopsided grin.

"Actually, we have to be very careful not to involve ourselves in anything we can't control. We also don't want to harm our relationship with Cornelius." Marih fixed his eyes on his sister with stern caution.

Elisa returned his glare as she parried Ishtar's sweet jabs. "There is no room for capricious dreams in my life! My passion lies with my loyal mission and none other, dear sister!" Her entire being attested to her loyalty to her mission. "He's just Marih's friend."

"Just so! Now what should we do about tonight? We can't get out of this!" Marih's urgency brought them all back to the main point.

"I don't think we have much of a choice," Elisa said, clearly disappointed; then her mercurial eyes suddenly sparkled. "Let's improvise..."

Nine

Close Enough
to Hear a Princess Breathe

Cornelius was looking forward to the graduation night feast. Since Antonius had invited him to sit at his table, he was eager to enjoy the company of Seneca once again. He had enjoyed every bit of that company last time. It hadn't yet occurred to him that these men might behave differently in an open-air event surrounded by ten times the number as had been in the privacy of Antonius' chamber.

His mind had been racing all day, continuously thinking about his future as it became clear to him that the centurion position would be his. What better cover for his involvement with the agency, and it was a duty he could do with eyes closed. Not to be too flippant, he had to admit at first it would bring him challenges that would keep his leisure time down and interest up.

Seneca's recent involvement with the intelligence agency – or, as the younger men liked to say, the agency – promised just that type of routine-breaking lifestyle. Being a centurion would probably become more of a hobby, while working with the agency would become his passion-filled career. He knew that he had Antonius' complete support with this matter and didn't expect too many challenges. Being as it was that he was filled with that almost attractive hubris of the very young and intelligent, it almost seemed too easy.

As the partygoers started gathering and drinks were generously employed, Cornelius was soon thrown off his cloud: Seneca had left Damascus the previous day. In disappointment, he sought out Marih from amongst the crowd. At least he would have the company of his loyal friend and they would make the best use of the night. In a night full of surprises, this one much more pleasant, he found that Marih and his beautiful little family were joining him at Antonius' table.

The first half of the night they hardly had any free time, as stranger after stranger dropped by the table to pay their respects to Antonius and congratulate him on his stellar class of graduates. With the second half of the evening prompted by many pots of wine, Cornelius and Marih started regaling their company with all the unforgettable, awkward moments of their camp experiences. Of course the top story was their mission to Jerusalem, which Marih commandeered to his advantage as servant to a mute Jewish Roman on pilgrimage for a miracle cure. With theatrical embellishments, they told of their fear as they crept through the underground tunnels until they stumbled upon a gathering of some certain secret society. They remembered the high points in tandem and laughed to entertain their company. Simaan Ben Aaron's talk with the rabbi was not part of their tale, nor the details of the Aleph Lodge.

As they ran out of stories, Marih and his young wife turned their intimate attentions towards each other, as most of the others around them began to pair off. An expected culmination for such Roman parties, these practices were embraced by the upper classes of the provinces of the Empire – be they Phoenicians, Jews, or other ethnicities – adapting them to suit their sensibilities. Even fatherly Antonius had his arm around the waist of an attractive young woman who was playfully making him drink from her cup.

Under the circumstances, Cornelius couldn't help but consider the attractive and very available Elisa sitting right next to him. Ever since that incident at the ruins of Melqart's Temple, her presence always gave him a feeling of pleasant unease. Another memory surfaced: Elisa giving him a brief kiss on his cheek after showing him the guest quarters at her parents' place. But he also remembered her specifically telling him that the temple incident was just a ceremonial thing. That was the hardest part for him to accept. It was very difficult to think of her as just a friend's sister after such an incident, ceremonial or not. These memories were made no easier by his growing admiration for her beauty and intelligence... and none of this was helped by the fact that they had both been drinking.

"It seems our companions have singled us out by their neglect," Cornelius said, gesturing towards Marih and Ishtar, and again towards Antonius and his attentive young partner.

"This is a great day for you, Cornelius, and there is no reason you should not enjoy every minute of it. Why, look around you, many beautiful women must be yearning to enjoy your company." Elisa's attempt to project a sense of sincere, friendly advice was not working on Cornelius.

"Many beautiful women, indeed! Everywhere, and especially right next to me." He was under the influence of more than wine.

"I meant you could enjoy the beauty of any woman of your choice," Elisa said, trying to remain in control.

"I knew what you meant," he replied and turned to face her.

Elisa looked to her brother and sister-in-law for help, but found them completely involved and paying absolutely no attention to her conversation with Cornelius. "You cannot mean that. I don't even compare to many of these beauties. Still, it is a good and entertaining deceit, please continue." She giggled in spite of herself.

"After all the wine I've had, please believe I have lost the capacity for deceit. I am honesty in its purest form." Cornelius was encouraged by her giggles.

"With all the wine you've had, I don't think I should trust your judgment." She placed her hand over his, resting them both on the table. "I'd wager I'd never hear such talk when you're sober."

"If that's the case, I'd rather be drunk for the rest of my life." Cornelius pulled his hand from under hers, only to wrap her small hand in both of his. "I assure you I've had these thoughts completely sober." The two looked into each other's eyes for long seconds. Many unspoken words were passed through that gaze.

Despite the alcoholic buzz, Elisa's mind quickly replayed images of her discussion with her brother earlier that day. She remembered her mission and Marih's warning about being careful not to do anything that might affect the relationship with Cornelius. She knew that the stakes were too high to risk, and her strong will surfaced. She sat up with an air of playful determination and said, "You know what I think I'll do? I will take my own advice and go find someone of my choice and celebrate my drunken brother's graduation!" She laughed as if she was only teasing, but she stood up, turned, and walked away – if not in a very straight line – into the crowd, leaving a trail of giggles behind her.

Cornelius blinked... and blinked again. What had just happened? She got up and walked away! In his romantic fog he thought maybe he had misread Elisa and allowed his imagination to run away with him. He was perplexed by her mixed signals, and a sliver of indignity jabbed at his mood. He, too, got up and walked away... in the opposite direction... leaving nothing much in his wake.

Antonius noticed the incident. Disengaging himself from his flirtatious companion's attentions, he caught up to the slightly meandering Cornelius and pulled him into a game he was about to play with a small group.

Elisa had two major disappointments to cope with, neither of which had anything to do with Cornelius. Not only had her plan for discovering Seneca's man flopped like a dead fish on cold marble, but Seneca didn't even show up! Now she was robbed of the introduction to the great man who had been a major key to her mission.

She had left Cornelius to fend for himself after coming so close in their flirtation. There was a mutual spark there and she had walked away from it. Mission. Mission. Always the mission.

Ten

'Mary!

Has No One Condemned You?'

Despite their pride in Marih's graduation, the Mother Lodge in Tyre was disappointed by their failure to contact Seneca or locate his man. Running out of ideas and excuses to remain in Damascus, the women readied themselves to return to Tyre.

"Cornelius and I are soon heading to our posts in Caesarea. We will go by Tyre. Maybe you can wait a few days and travel under our protection," Marih said.

"Are you leaving your wife behind in Tyre again?" Ishtar feigned the shunned bride.

"You are now wife of Roman Centurion Marih. You will have a hundred servants and their commander at your service in Caesarea, my lady," Marih flirted.

"There has to be something about you becoming a centurion that can benefit our lodge and cause," Elisa mumbled, deep in thought as was usual these days. "I cannot believe that you, a Phoenician royal, so easily received the rank of centurion."

"Antonius personally asked me to join with Cornelius and make his decision to stay in Judea a positive one. Remember, my role as a centurion is just a cover within the agency. Our main purpose is to infiltrate and weaken the Jews from inside. Either way we're in for good intelligence for the lodges."

"But still, for the Romans to accept a royal Phoenician into their ranks... it doesn't happen every day. Luck is on our side." Elisa was referring to the historic hatred between the two nations since the Punic wars when the Phoenicians of Carthage almost took over Rome. Over the decades, the Romans forgot what Hannibal did to them, yet retained an innate caution towards certain nations, especially the Phoenicians.

"Well, sister, their memory fades to our advantage. The Romans are beginning to sink under the weight of the constant pursuit of power and lavish luxuries. A nation such as ours – full of purpose and faith – will never lose its way."

"As long as there is one Phoenician standing, our national identity will survive. Our enemies are blind. They don't see how revenge smolders under the ashes and is quick to spark!" Ishtar surprised them all with a growl like a rabid dog after fresh flesh.

"We should have been on the road to Caesarea by now, but Antonius is holding us up. He wants to send some friends of his with us. There's always more safety walking under the protection of Roman soldiers."

. . .

Back at Antonius' chamber, a secret meeting of Cornelius' so-called friends was underway.

"She is to be well cared for. I want to make sure she is completely happy in every facet of her life. He cannot afford any distractions while he's in the field. It's too dangerous for him." Antonius adopted his fatherly tone laced with authority when speaking to Cornelius.

"Do not worry, I will make sure she and her new mother are well looked after. She is a fortunate child to have such a proper Roman lady to mother her." Cornelius bowed courteously to the woman with the child in her lap, quietly seated beside Antonius.

"Indeed. Our lady was hand-picked by Seneca out of many hopefuls within the intelligence community." Antonius smiled at the woman and caressed the head of the little girl.

"You will see to it that Paulus sees his daughter discreetly from time to time. You will be the agency's contact with him. Seneca will pass the directions to you, so from now on you are the main person from the agency to be in touch with Paulus." Antonius took a deep breath, checking his mental list to make sure nothing was left to chance. "We have spent too much time and energy planting Paulus in the Jewish community; there are major plans for him. Losing such a valuable operative would be a great setback for us."

"You have my word, Antonius, I will not lose track of Paulus," Cornelius confirmed, his new hatred for the Jews burning like an ember deep inside.

"In two days you head to Caesarea. Your soldiers are awaiting you. And so is your new house. Go now, inform your fellow centurion Marih to get ready. But remember, within the agency, we give our people only as much as they need to know."

"Rest assured, Claudia and her new mother will not be a topic of road-chat with Marih."

With that assurance, Antonius took another deep breath, this time content he had fulfilled his commitment to Seneca and guaranteed a safe transport of Paulus' daughter to her new home in Caesarea. There could be no better arrangement. Caesarea, the newly built Roman oasis in the heart of Judea, would provide Paulus with frequent opportunities to see his daughter discreetly and conveniently.

. . .

The custom in peripheral Roman provinces with their widely scattered city-states was to plan travels according to military convoys, especially on the internal roads, away from the busy coastal roads. Cornelius' party was no different. Close to two hundred people began the caravan, travelling to various destinations en route to the Jewish territories far to the south. Young and old, men and women, merchants, families, and tourists, all of different colours and loyalties, travelled the ancient trade route that connected Tyre to the interior. The caravan moved slowly as many were on foot. The centurions were on horseback, but the upper classes travelled in litters. Their next segment would take them along the well-secured coastal road from Tyre to Caesarea.

The call to start the return trip made Elisa uncomfortably

anxious. It was time to go home and devise alternative plans for her current mission, but first she had to relate the details of their miserable failures to the Mother Lodge.

Marih had managed some intelligence concerning Seneca's man. At least they knew his name and that the agency had located an adoptive mother for his child. But would they ever see this Paulus? He disappeared just like Seneca. And now they had to move away from Antonius, their last link to this project. Not an exciting ending for the story her ambitious mind had built.

Elisa and Ishtar sank into a quietness of their own, deep in thought for the whole first day on the road. They altered between their litters and walking, to break the monotony of travel. Marih, on the other hand, kept to his fellow soldiers' party, where clamorous laughter erupted every now and then, reminding the civilians they were in the company of a mighty military force.

When the sun retired, so did the convoy. Barely minutes after the women's tent was raised, the thudding of urgent steps rapidly approached them. Elisa's heart jumped into her throat when she peered through the tent flap. She could see a woman in the failing light, her face contorted with panic and clasping a little girl to her breast, heading straight for their tent. Elisa jumped back as another woman, covered from head to toe in black robes after the traditional Jewish fashion, grabbed her prey and pulled them right into their tent.

The woman in black spoke fluent Aramaic, "Don't worry, Princess Elisa, the little girl will be fine."

"What's happening here? What's wrong?" Elisa rushed to help, but had no idea what help was needed or who these women were. This stranger called her princess, a clue she might be an Aleph agent under cover.

"The child was fussing and drawing attention, so I gave her a sleeping elixir. Her mother thinks I'm trying to help, but she's frightened, so she ran. She doesn't understand our tongue," the woman in black explained as she took the child from her mother's tight grasp and placed her on the carpeted ground just inside the tent. She quickly stuck her head outside the tent, looking in all directions, perhaps for help... or witnesses.

"Why did you give her a sleeping eli-" Elisa's words stopped in her throat. The woman in black pulled a Roman *gladius* from beneath her gown and stabbed the sobbing adoptive mother with the short sword. At first, the blade didn't go all the way through; so the assassin steered right and left until she hit a softer spot and pushed deeper, forcing the woman to the ground outside the tent's door. Elisa gasped.

"Don't be afraid, my princess! I am your Aleph servant, Mariam. This little one is Paulus' daughter. She is now motherless. Your chance to adopt her has come." She pulled the sword out, stood up, and faced Elisa in the gathering darkness.

"What am I supposed to do?" Elisa said, at a loss.

"Run after me and yell out what I have done. I will escape into the valley, my way is prepared. Pretend you were trying to protect the mother and child from me when we invaded your tent." She didn't wait for Elisa's acknowledgment, only turned around and let her legs free, running with the wind. Elisa followed, screaming, until a slope in the camp hid them from the eyes of the caravan.

"Wait! You, Mariam…" Elisa whispered loudly.

Mariam, nothing but a shadow some ways ahead of her, turned, now walking backwards, answered, "My princess?"

"Of which colony are you?" Elisa asked.

"Of Magdala. Mariam of Magdala, my princess." With that, she turned and disappeared into the darkness.

Galloping horses came up quickly behind her. Elisa threw herself on the ground, face down, and pretended to be rising from a fall.

"Do not try to escape! Surrender!" a coarse voice from atop one of the horses shouted at her.

"Hold! All of you, hold I say!" Marih pulled up quickly with the rest of his men. "Elisa, my sister, is that you? What happened?"

"A woman in black killed another woman trying to escape her, right outside my tent! I went after the murderer, but I stumbled and fell and she outran me and disappeared in the darkness." She indicated the direction, but not the true line of escape. Marih reached down. She gave her left hand to him and jumped up behind him. "Back to my tent, the victim's daughter needs us!"

The horses quickly covered the distance back to the tent.

Holding tight, Elisa quickly whispered in Marih's ear, "The Mother Lodge sent a messenger, in the guise of an assassin. The adoptive mother is dead and Paulus' daughter was left at my tent."

The sudden news and burst of excitement left him short of breath. He turned his horse into the wind and breathed in the cooling night air.

The sight greeting them at the tent was sickening. A small crowd had gathered, alerted by Elisa's yelling. A woman lay motionless, her blood freely soaking into the ground. The limp child in Ishtar's arm began to squirm, tears and nose dripping with no free hands to wipe.

Elisa was first to jump off. She rushed to Ishtar, took the child, and ran into the tent. She placed the little thing on a pillow and wrapped a blanket tightly around her, like swaddling clothes, to calm her. She listened carefully to the commotion outside, soldiers trying to identify the dead body, a woman of rank. The chaos suddenly stopped. The quiet was almost as confusing as the noise. Unable to hear or predict what was going to happen next, the next few moments nearly choked her.

Her fears multiplied when Cornelius barged into her tent, pale as the body lying outside, lips quaking. "Where's the child? Is she alright?"

Elisa covered the girl with an outstretched arm, as if to prevent Cornelius from taking her. "She needs to rest. She is safe, she is quieting, sleeping again, but I can hear her heart beating fast."

"She has to wake up! You don't understand. She is in my protection." He paced towards the entrance of the tent where Marih now stood.

Marih had followed Cornelius into the tent. Sizing up the situation, he suggested, "We need a healer. We can take a couple of horses and rush on to Tyre. If we go light with few stops, we can be there by next sunset."

"I'm coming with you. I will not leave her." Elisa fuelled the passion of the moment.

She adeptly used Cornelius' weakness towards her to her advantage. She sensed agreement in his tone even as he protested, "But Elisa, this is my responsibility. I don't want to disturb you with this."

"Nonsense! This all happened at the door to my tent. The child has become my responsibility, too. From now on, she is my little sister!" Elisa flashed her persuasive eyes at Cornelius.

His dancing pupils exposed him. He was thinking fast. A decision had to be made, right there, right then... one of his first important decisions as a centurion and a Roman intelligence agent... he had no idea it had already become a cornerstone in the Aleph plot. "Alright, alright. Before we go much further, there is something I have to tell you about this child. We can talk when we're underway. Let's hurry."

Eleven

Talitha Kumi

By sunset of next day, Marih had successfully guided his wife, his sister, and Cornelius to the city of Tyre. They took turns carrying the little girl and had left a couple of exhausted horses behind. Although everyone was worn out, there was no time to waste. They summoned the head healer of Tyre, a high-ranked Phoenician by birth. Elisa knew he would be completely aware of their mission and of Mariam's secret mission. It was most likely he had given her the elixir for the child and held the antidote.

Once the girl was safely in the healer's care in a closed chamber, with strict instructions for privacy, the group finally had time to reflect on the situation. They had learned from Cornelius on the road that the girl they carried with them was a Roman businessman's daughter and that the man, a friend of Cornelius', was too busy with the family business to properly look after his wife and their child. Cornelius had promised to protect her and her mother. He explained that he felt responsible; he had failed to protect the mother and now he needed to find a solution to care for the child. The one person he told the truth about Paulus to, when the opportunity allowed, was Marih.

Unknown to him, his Aleph companions already had their story in place, and set about convincing him that Elisa was going to take the child in as a sister at her parents' royal household. If the child survived her current trauma, she would be treated like a princess in her recuperation. Besides, her father – this Paulus – would still be able to see her in Caesarea periodically as Elisa would bring her along whenever she came to visit Marih.

Their whole plan fell apart when the healer brought out horrible news. "The girl is dying. There is nothing more I can do for her. I do not understand, she should be responding."

"This can't be! There must be something! Is there another healer we can consult, no offense to you, but I cannot give up." Cornelius looked to Marih for support. This was his country, maybe he knew of other options.

The healer stroked his beard, flipping glances back and forth between Marih and Cornelius. "There is one thing to try."

Cornelius' eyes opened wide and froze in anticipation.

"We have a visitor, a follower of a healer from Nazareth." The healer waited for their reaction.

The silence dragged beyond Cornelius' patience. He raised both hands, pleading. "What does that mean? Who is this healer?"

"There is a Jewish sect that lives in the wilderness and devotes itself to prayer. Stories about their master healing the most difficult, even raising people from the dead, have flown all over Judea and Phoenicia," the healer explained.

Cornelius' frisson of excitement suddenly hit a wall of pure dread. He was not going to allow this girl near anyone Jewish. "I don't trust the Jews!" he firmly announced.

"This is a different group of Jews, my son. A new sect... they aren't even accepted by the other Jews. They openly announce they do not hate the Empire and call for peace." The healer raised an open palm towards Marih, seeking his support.

"Indeed, Cornelius. These people visit Phoenicia all the time and make no enemies," Marih confirmed, nodding in agreement.

"Then I must be at the girl's side at all times. Bring this healer."

At Cornelius' words, the old man waved for them to rest, take refreshment, and await his return.

Within the hour, four sets of eyes that had been fighting fatigue grew wide with joy at the site of the returning healer. Alongside him walked a somewhat disheveled young man dressed in a simply cut tunic of plain homespun, clearly from the common people. He said little, no more than a polite salutation, and stood quietly with his eyes lowered, waiting.

When summoned by the old Phoenician, he walked straight to the girl's side. From around his neck he pulled forth a small bag of cloth on a cord. He pulled out another piece of cloth, wrapped around a clump of mushy material, greenish gray and pungent. Still not saying a word, he moved his lips continuously as if quietly reciting a prayer. He spat into the mushy material and mixed it well, then placed chunks of it over the child's eyelids, in her armpits, and behind the ears. After what seemed like an eternity to Cornelius, the man spoke. "What is the girl's name?"

"Claudia," Cornelius eagerly answered.

The man kneeled by her side for few minutes, then raised his head and arms to the sky and commanded, "Claudia, Koumi!"

The loudness of his cry, completely unexpected from such a quiet man, drilled into the nerves of all there. They shivered in the breath of divinity of the moment.

The man rested his head, returning his gaze to the ground, then spoke, "Brothers and sisters fear not her death. For He who has taken her is capable of raising her."

Cornelius' knees weakened at the mention of death. He rushed to Claudia and placed his ear on her chest. He couldn't hear her heart beating. Had she truly died? Did this Jewish man kill her?

"My brother, you are a good man with good heart. You are full of faith and peace. Have some confidence. Trust in Him and she will be up and playing by tomorrow morning."

"You are to stay with us this night. If what you say is true, I will reward you generously." The threat behind those few words was clear: if Claudia didn't get better, this man's fate would fit his crime.

. . .

Hours of most needed rest knocked Cornelius out. A gentle touch to his cheek woke him up. Eyes opened but brain still half asleep, it took him few seconds to remember where he was. The realization that he had woken up to Elisa's touch tickled his spine, but the mission at hand came quickly to mind. Jumping up, he looked around in search of a sign.

"I have happy news for you," Elisa quickly comforted him. "Claudia is awake and playing."

"She is? She is? When did that happen? Where is she?"

"She's eating in the breakfast room. What a beautiful girl! I long for her to always be my sister princess."

Cornelius, still not believing his ears, asked, "Where is the man? The Jewish healer?"

"We let him leave. Since the girl was miraculously healed, we didn't want to keep him against his wishes."

"No, of course not, I just... I just wanted to, you know, this man brought her back to life. Only in tales of the gods do such things happen." Cornelius scrambled for words. "I wanted to reward him... I, I want to learn more about this knowledge he carries. Did he say anything before he left? Where can I find him?"

"Slow down, slow down. So many questions! Before he left, he only asked us to feed Claudia." Elisa smiled. "The followers of the healer from Nazareth don't live in one place. They don't own houses. But you will be able to find many of them in Caesarea and the surrounding towns. Caesarea can be seen from the hills outside Nazareth. Be patient."

Elisa in turn was patient for Cornelius' mind to relax and let things happen in their own time. He finally made peace with the situation. "Why don't you wash up and make yourself less scary," she said. "I'll wait for you."

Cornelius did as he was told. He didn't mind being bossed around by Elisa. "Very nice. Now, walk with me. Let's go see Claudia. Oh, and by the way, I have a nickname for her: Achte, 'little sister.' Do you mind?" she asked playfully.

Cornelius smiled at the reassuring words. Why would he mind? Claudia was being offered the best care anyone could ask for. A gentle and beautiful princess would raise her little sister princess in a royal household. Marih's family had been generous to him personally and continued to shower him with support. They made him feel like he was one of them, so once more he was happily embracing their gestures.

Twelve

Centurions in Action

Life at Caesarea proved quite agreeable to the new Roman centurion. There were no ancient ruins to distract from this idyllic little bit of Roman perfection set down in the rolling northern hills of Judea. Inhabitants of the city were predominantly Roman and friendly to the military. The locals, especially those holding various public positions, were little more than sycophantic toadies with selfish ambitions for material gain and power over their Jewish nationals. In other words: Roman puppets.

The situation didn't bother Cornelius; he enjoyed being courted by these brownnosers. He had three jobs here: his responsibilities as centurion, his duties to the agency, and his revenge towards Ben Aaron and his people. That all three goals should in some way serve one another was a bonus that made his life most interesting. Behind every one of his interactions with the locals, he made sure he had a sip from the cup of revenge over the people who spawned the killer of his father. Those little sips were never enough. The final revenge was brewing.

For the first three years of Cornelius' life in Caesarea, the agency never stopped plotting. They planted new spies; worked on growing the established ones, like Paulus; and gathered secret information about Jewish militants – their numbers, whereabouts, traditions, strengths, and weaknesses.

That said, it wasn't all one long chain of successes. The agency had one hurdle that defied their machinations. Seneca's analysis of collected intelligence lead him to realize that the only way the Empire could put an end to the turmoil that permeated the area was to infiltrate the various bodies of Jewish religious leaders and their headquarters. Politicians were easy to buy or control, but such was not the case with the Hebrew leaders. These men held real influence over the public. Not the conservatives, who needed a particular kind of management; no, it was the sects with their messiahs and baptizers and teachers that sprang up like swarms of locusts everywhere.

Some of these were peaceful ascetics who withdrew from the evils of the world as they saw them. Theirs was a spiritual war. The Romans had bigger fish to catch along the Sea of Galilee. Most of the other sects had a temporal philosophy, seeking their kingdoms in this world rather than the next. All it took for these sects to spur a militia into action was a questionably religious leader preaching feverish ideologies requiring his followers offer up their lives for the cause: the elimination of the infidel Romans from Judea.

The fly in the ointment was the rare sect that managed to blend the spiritual with aspects of the temporal. Hard to know whether to leave them be or snuff them out before they become bothersome, just to be on the safe side.

With Seneca's guidance, Cornelius' new job was to locate these packs of sometimes several hundred men gathered about each of these messiahs in their hard-to-reach hideouts and infiltrate their planned insurrections. That's all. *At last*, mused Cornelius, *a worthy challenge amidst all this easy living in Caesarea.*

Or so he thought. These bands of rebels with their religious trappings were very difficult to infiltrate, even for very seasoned and conniving moles like Paulus. Funnily enough, these tribes of zealots were not even friendly to each other. The agency should be able to plant moles among them, and then work to turn them against each other with self-destruction the logical outcome. Failure to accomplish so elegant a plan after a few years of trying did not sit well with Cornelius. Whatever humour the paradox held was wearing very thin.

In the fourth year of Cornelius' presence in Judea, the agency thought it finally had a sure thing. Seneca had received promising news from the governor of Jerusalem. Without the agency's meddling, the Jews had been troubled enough by one of these sects that they had captured its leader and surrendered him to this new Roman governor, Prefect Pontius Pilatus. They were so perturbed they even suggested his execution. Seneca sent immediate recommendations back to Pilatus to return the man to his people in the hopes that their own religious leaders and their followers would execute him. At last, a hot spot that could be manipulated into a Jewish/Jewish conflict. Exactly what Rome wanted: divide and conquer.

On a personal level, Cornelius was disappointed to see the teacher from Nazareth die. It had been this man's disciple who had saved Paulus' daughter, Claudia, from death. Resigning himself to that age-old excuse of orders being orders, Cornelius put aside his personal feelings. The bigger disappointment lay with the agency. Once again, pertinent intelligence was lacking in the agency's foolproof plan: the Hebrews had no law to put a man to death. But they could turn a blind eye should the Romans find a way to do it for them.

Failing to grasp this one simple concept of justice of the people the Romans attempted to grind into submission, when Pilatus sent this rebel back to Herod Antipas, he would in turn send him back to Pilatus. The crowds appealed to Pilatus to do their dirty work for them – to their way of thinking, a small price to avoid a rebellion.

Smack up against a wall, there was nothing to be done but acquiesce. The agency had run out of ideas. No simple punishment would do. There were several other undesirables ready to dispatch, so Pilatus simply added one more. When it was done, there was very little noise; the agency counted it a minor success despite the loss of the larger results hoped for.

. . .

Matters continued along familiar courses for several years after the death of the Nazarene. The sects of the Jewish messiahs rose and fell, all dependent upon the fickleness of the people towards their perceived saviours. Still, at all times the communities remained tightly shut. A breakthrough finally came from a most unexpected source. The almighty Roman intelligentsia was not immune to double agents; in fact, they were so cocksure they hadn't given the concept much thought at all. The idea was created and designed by the Aleph Mother Lodge and presented to the agency by their own agents above all suspicions. Marih had convinced Cornelius that together they had a solid plan.

Cornelius called for a meeting in Caesarea. Seneca arrived in person to hear what ideas his star agents had to propose.

Marih took the floor. "Remember the Nazarene that was crucified a few years back?" He knew they remembered him well. "I have information about one of his followers."

Seneca raised an eyebrow. "The Nazarenes are still a force to contend with? What, they have a new leader?"

"Well, this is not exactly about their leadership." Marih looked directly at Seneca. "They are still somewhat rudderless. As you know, the followers are growing in number just the same. I know one of them."

"This is not very impressive news. Did you bring me all the way from Rome just to tell me you know one of his followers? I could probably walk down a street and meet three of them in an hour." Seneca's attitude was not as much geared toward the responsibilities of the two centurions as it was to the success of the agency. These continual failures were affecting the confidence of all the operatives.

"We have a plan, sir," Cornelius said with confidence.

Marih continued, "Your man Paulus is currently the most advanced of our agents; still he has not earned the trust of any of their religious leaders. Perhaps this is because his roots are in Tarsus rather than the Jewish homeland." Marih looked to Cornelius, passing him the baton.

"There is a certain follower, one called Echeleel, in their tongue. He has been trying to bring new members – gentiles – into Judaism. The man is himself half Greek and has interested his Greek relatives. The Hebrew laws do not allow him to bring them to the temple and formally make them Jews, so he has been preaching and gathering support from sympathetic Hebrews among the Nazarenes to change these strict laws. He wants Judaism to be open to gentile converts."

Cornelius relied on Seneca's quick mind to gather where they were headed with their concept.

"I should never have doubted you." Seneca smiled. "This is surely a unique opportunity. If this man wins his battle, our agents will have much easier access to the inner circles. Just how much of an influence is this Echeleel? Has he enough people listening to him?"

Marih smiled, feeling more encouraged than before. "We have information that many of the Nazarene's followers agree with him. But he has not yet gained ears among the more conservative Jews among them. We were thinking that Paulus might lend him a hand in gathering more followers by starting a movement within the sect that would support him."

"Hold your horses. I am not risking everything we have achieved with Paulus thus far for this! Keep Paulus out of it. I do not want him involved. Don't think you can throw my best agents in your fires." Seneca was unmistakably adamant.

The sudden change in reception of their original plan threw Marih and Cornelius into a whirlpool of confusion. Without the help of the planted agents – Paulus chief among them – how were they going to support Echeleel?

"Oh, come on, you two." Seneca raised both hands, trying to get his men to think. "Does this Echeleel have another name?" Seneca referred to the common practice among Jews openly living in the Empire to employ a Greek translation of their names or a suitable Greek nickname.

"Yes... yes, Stephanos," Marih offered.

"There's your answer. This man will always be seen as Greek. He will never get anywhere. The temple priests saw to it that his teacher was neutralized, a real Jew the Nazarenes even claimed descended from their King David, and you think this half-blooded upstart could make them change their ancient laws?"

The two stood silent. Seneca had a strong point, but what other alternatives did the agency have at this juncture? None.

Seneca wasn't done with their idea; they should have learned by now how his philosophies came into play. "Let's support him without jeopardizing our agents. You, Cornelius, invite him here and talk to him about converting to the Hebrew faith. Tell him of your utmost respect for the crucified Nazarene and your belief in his ways, especially after one of your servants was miraculously healed by a disciple of his in the years before his death. Make sure he doesn't know the true identity of Claudia. Instead, keep to your miracle story about an unnamed servant." He paced back and forth a few times, deep in thought, while the other two stood quite still. "He must be made to believe he has your protection. Do not even hint at false security; he must gain courage in order to follow your plan. If he makes it, he will think he owes us. If he doesn't, he will be none the wiser and we will be in the clear. We don't need any more trouble from these people at this time." Seneca stared at them, awaiting acknowledgements.

"It's this kind of wisdom and advice that we sought from you, sir. Marih and I will plan and execute accordingly. You have our assurance."

Thirteen

Though He Die,

Yet Shall He Live

That very night, Marih spoke with Elisa. She had come to Caesarea with Claudia so Paulus could visit with his daughter.

"Seneca agreed to our plan of supporting Stephanos, the Nazarene follower. He's so protective of Paulus, he won't let him get involved... adamant about it." Marih's brows were heavy; he was practically fuming.

"I will inform the Mother Lodge. Another disappointment. We have come so close to Paulus and we still cannot use him to our benefit." They were a matching set of gloom and doom. "So. Are you going to keep him out of it?"

"I don't have a choice. Cornelius is his direct manager here in Judea and he will follow Seneca's orders to the letter."

Elisa brightened a bit. "Who said that Cornelius has to be the one to tell him anything? He is Paulus' manager, but I'm Paulus' family. I will see him tomorrow with Claudia."

"You're a sly one, dear sister. What do you have in mind?"

"Don't worry, I won't do anything risky. I will play the gardener and plant seeds for the future. I'll let him know..."

Marih followed her gaze to young Claudia Achte running in.

"Here comes my little princess." Elisa knelt with open arms, scooping her up and hugging her tight. "And what was Achte doing?"

"I was praying for our Lord Melqart."

"You're a wise young woman. How about some hugs for your big brother Marih?" Claudia pulled herself from one pair of arms and threw herself into another pair twice as strong.

"Do you remember we will see Paulus tomorrow morning?" Elisa tested her memory.

"Yes, and I will not mention anything about our religion or Lord Melqart to him."

"That's right," Elisa praised. "Your father Paulus is a good man but he is sadly misguided by the Romans. You will never hate him, Achte, because it is not his fault he doesn't know the True Light."

The little girl nodded with a guileless smile.

"The day will soon come when the Phoenicians prevail and we take our revenge for the Punic war." Elisa stood up and turned to her brother with fire behind her eyes, grinding her teeth to muffle her words and failing miserably. "This pseudo-Mithraist scum of an empire has been mocking our Lord with their pitiful ceremonies for years. They bastardized our ways when they celebrate the slaying of the bull, the very symbol of our Lord Melqart, the Aleph! But I swear, in the name of the Aleph, I will not depart this earth before seeing their false glory reduced to ashes."

"Patience, my sister, patience is our strongest weapon."

. . .

Paulus' relationship with Elisa was purely familial. He assumed her brother didn't involve her in agency secrets. Marih was beyond reproach and suspicion. Paulus' conversations with Elisa and his Claudia were of his family's textiles business and his expert knowledge that kept him travelling nearly all of the time. This was his actual cover story for everybody outside of the agency, including the Jewish community, so his stories came easily.

He also told Elisa that his family had not approved of his marriage to Claudia's mother and that's why he had to keep her a secret, only to lose her to a fever when the child was very young. Elisa's sympathy made him believe she believed it all.

They had met often enough that there was a certain level of comfort between them. It was this kind of relationship that allowed Elisa to implement her plot when Paulus arrived that morning to visit his child.

"You know, up in Tyre I've been hearing things that have made me very curious, and you're the only one I know who might know more about such things, with your travels and all," Elisa said, innocently interrupting Paulus' play with Claudia. "You go to Jerusalem all the time and have business friends there. Do you happen to know if it is true that the Jews have started allowing new members to join them?"

The question got Paulus' attention, but he didn't look up from their game on the floor. "That's an interesting question, why do you ask?"

"A Greek friend of mine asked me if it's true. She thought I would know because my family has dealings with all sorts of people, socially and in business, and I might understand the ways of the Jews." Elisa kept her eyes on the sewing she had in her lap, acting as if it wasn't a big deal and she was just asking as a favour for a friend. "She said one of her relatives, a leader in that Nazarene sect, you know the one? The one where their leader was crucified by the Romans? Well, his name is Stephanos, I think... and she says he is working on changing their rules or something like that."

"What else did your friend tell you?"

"That's it, really. I don't even know why she is so interested in joining them. Certainly would do nothing for her marriage prospects," Elisa continued in her indifferent attitude.

"Hmm. I don't believe I have ever heard of such a thing before this." Paulus dodged the topic, letting it drop. But like any good spy, he set the name and description of Stephanos in his mind. He would discover if someone was truly working on some way to get the temple to admit gentiles. This would be important news to take to his handler, Cornelius.

. . .

The next few weeks saw a great deal of activity concerning all movements around Stephanos. Cornelius and Paulus conducted independent investigations, each having him followed, neither one knowing of the other's actions or results. Paulus was shocked when he learned that this Stephanos had visited Cornelius' house. He quickly reminded himself that he was not the only spy at the agency and that Cornelius must have learned of Stephanos from another operative. Unable to clarify the situation with Cornelius – they met only periodically and under strict rules of secrecy – he decided to keep his eye on Stephanos.

Three weeks later in Jerusalem, he learned that the temple's high court, the Sanhedrin, had summoned Stephanos in order to try him for speaking out against the Law of Moses. Paulus made sure he would be in attendance for this particular court.

When Stephanos' day in court arrived, Paulus felt a black cloud hanging over the whole affair as he heard the arguments. Young Stephanos accused the high court of being party to the killing of many prophets sent by God and finally killed the King of Jews, The One, The Nazarene, and for this they deserved to lose their sacred privilege of being God's chosen people. He called for opening the Hebrew religion to new memberships from the gentiles, advocating that all converts may enter the temple and approach the Holy of Holies.

Paulus watched, fixated on the rage of the judges who reacted as one entity. The danger was palpable. Stunned at the blind courage of Stephanos, he hoped the young fool had prepared a plan of escape or arranged for some kind of protection. It did cross his mind that maybe Cornelius had given him some promise of protection. Why else would Stephanos speak so bravely, offering insult after insult directly at the Sanhedrin? If this was a ploy by the agency, then it surely was a brilliant one. The chances of getting out of there alive were slim to none, but should he succeed, it would open the door for many agency operatives – as gentiles – to convert to Judaism and serve their Empire from inside.

Wasted thoughts, Paulus realized as the judges passed the judgment of blasphemer and handed the condemned man over that he might be taken to a valley outside Jerusalem for his punishment. Paulus followed along with the crowd, as any pious Hebrew would, hoping against hope that something could still interrupt this fiasco. Upon reaching the valley, Stephanos was placed where many others before him had been stoned. Still confident that help must be on its way, Paulus didn't join the stoners. He would want to avoid any confrontation with the Roman soldiers coming to aid Stephanos. To further secure his own safety, he offered to wait on the clothes of the stoners and safe-keep them while they did their job.

Help never came. Four years ago that very court hid behind some law that would not allow them to put a man to death; now no one intervened as Stephanos became the first to be stoned into martyrdom.

Fourteen

Change is the Only Constant

When their duty was done, as the Jewish mob returned to pick up their clothes and belongings, Paulus made sure these men noticed him. Many praised the worthy young devotee for his loyal show of support while his brethren defended the Law of Moses. If they hadn't paid attention to him before now, he did not pass up this opportunity to meet them face to face by offering his own praise of their faithfulness and devotion.

In the following weeks, Paulus went about gradually building up his participation in the stoning, making a great show of his own devotion to the Holy Scriptures of Moses and his readiness to punish the deviates and infidels – like these misguided followers of the Nazarene – even unto death. He grasped every chance to gain favour wherever it would best suit him. His name was whispered about like a spark in dry stubble.

This did not sit at all well with Elisa and Marih. These dedicated Alephs had received clear directions from the Mother Lodge to influence Paulus to join the followers of the Nazarene, not work against them. Clearly, Elisa's plan had backfired. By telling Paulus about Stephanos, she actually led Paulus to pursue the more extreme Jewish position. True, she couldn't have known he would go off in the other direction, but the results amounted to nothing less than another failure. Before now, the Mother Lodge had always made sure backup plans would save her and her brother from any contingencies. But who was going to save them this time?

"We can't waste any more time. I must return to Tyre and inform the lodge that Paulus is further from joining the Nazarene's sect than ever before." Elisa dreaded her duty to take responsibility in person for their failure.

"Sister, hold on a moment. You know, this might not be so bad after all. There must be some use of Paulus gaining favour among the Jewish leaders. The Mother Lodge might have a way to benefit by this."

"Not according to the master plan. The lodge doesn't care about the Jews. They are but a speck in our plots against the Roman Empire. The lodge needs the Nazarene's sect to flourish because it is the only sect that has been hated by all Jewish groups and is the only one that has developed friends out in all the provinces, the ones they call the gentiles. Don't you see? This is the only one of the Jewish sects capable of invading the Roman Empire by their insidious call for peace and friendship among those external to the Hebrew faith. It's our chance to invade Rome, to introduce our own wolves in sheep's clothing. To put it another way, this is our chance to plant this monster of a Jewish egg into the nest that is Rome, and nurse it until it hatches and destroys our enemy from within."

"There must be someone else that we can plant there, someone other than Paulus. He's not the only Roman spy we can manipulate," Marih said in an attempt to soothe his sister. He admired her passionate devotion, but sometimes she frightened him.

"Speculations aren't enough. I must bring accurate solutions. I will be on my way to Tyre tomorrow morning." Elisa's sternness was non-negotiable.

. . .

The day after Elisa departed, Seneca came unannounced to Caesarea. He called an urgent meeting with Cornelius and Marih.

"Gentlemen, an opportunity has presented itself. Paulus is now closer than ever to the Jewish leaders. It seems to me the time has come for him to become a leader of people!" Seneca's words triggered their brains, but in very different ways.

"The agency has a plan?" Cornelius asked.

"There is no one in the agency closer to this project than the two of you. The agency has always set plans and passed them on to you. But to what end? Failure after failure. The fault does not lie with you. I see that now. I have come to change *modus operandi*. The plan this time will be set by the three of us, no others!" Seneca sat back, inviting them to speak.

"The Jewish leadership is not easy to infiltrate. Paulus has always been up against his status of outlander, raised in Tarsus, not being accepted by Jerusalem's leaders. They will not let him through." Cornelius was preparing Seneca for his suggestion. "The only way for him to lead from a position of strength is to establish a new one."

"Establish a new position," Seneca clarified.

"Correct. If we support him and provide him with weapons and protection, he can gather a number of people to the cause of persecuting the followers of the Nazarene, and start his own militia. In a couple of years it will grow enough to become a serious power to be reckoned with, even to the point of overturning their courts and religious leaders." Cornelius forced himself to contain his excitement while he waited for Seneca to mull this over.

Unbearable silence dragged well beyond Cornelius' comfort. His stomach knotted as Seneca deferred his opinion and asked Marih for his point of view.

Marih had been thinking of his discussion with his sister the night before. It was not in the best interests of the Aleph Lodge to have Paulus lead a militia. They wanted him leading the Nazarene's group.

"This might be doable," he said as his inner voice screamed *What the hell am I saying? This is the best I can think of? This is not serving the lodge. But I see no real weaknesses in Cornelius' plan. This is happening too fast.*

"I don't think so," Seneca responded, thinking out loud.

Marih held his breath.

"I can see two weaknesses in this plan. First, Paulus is not a violent, military kind of man. He is a thug, to be sure. He's a crook, a cheat, a master of deception, all of the above. His highest assets are not well-suited to the battlefield. No one knows him better than I."

"I absolutely see that," Marih immediately concurred. A kernel of an idea started forming in his mind. However, the insightful response he needed was not forthcoming, so he passed the ball back to Seneca, "You said two weaknesses?"

"The other one lies in the proven fact: military power is not the way to confront the Hebrew ideologies. You must know, the best way to counter a philosophy is through an equally convincing philosophy, one which carries the same ideological weight and supports equal manpower. Were it otherwise, the Empire would have eradicated their threat a long time ago. The Roman military force is undefeated when put against another viable military power. Weapons cannot fight ideas."

Marih made sure he looked deep in thought, interpreting the insight he had just received from Seneca. This time, however, he wanted the reigns of the conversation to stay in his grip. He spoke with conviction. "One Jewish movement offers us all we need... the followers of the Nazarene."

Cornelius looked at Marih with surprise. They had brought this idea to Seneca once before when they spoke to him about Stephanos. Seneca had clearly opposed it then. Why would Marih bring it up again?

"This group has continuously shown an indifferent behaviour towards the Empire. They are friendlier to the non-Jews and some of them are even open to accepting new members among those they call gentiles. This movement – for it isn't organized enough to be anything more – could be carefully nurtured as it spreads in the provinces, diluting the influence of the conservative Jews in Judea. We have already seen how many Jews since the destruction of their temple generations ago, in their diaspora afterward, have been influenced by Greek philosophies. This Nazarene concept can eventually permeate the Hebrew beliefs. If molded properly by us, we can turn them into friends of the Empire – thus achieving our ultimate goal of dissolving them from the inside out." Marih's heart raced, anticipating the impact these ideas might have on Seneca.

"And who better to understand the ways of the Levant than a

true man of the Levant, a royal Tyrian." Seneca smiled, walked up to Marih, and squeezed his shoulder with encouragement.

Marih sucked in a load of cool air. He could not believe Seneca's reaction to his thoughts.

"I suppose you deserve some explanation. I didn't mean to toy with you like this. Well, I did, I admit. I love a bit of theatre. After you two spoke to me about Stephanos, I carried the idea back to the agency as well as to my colleagues at the Mithraist Lodge, as many are one and the same. I was reminded that a man who underestimates a situation can all too easily pass up a once-in-a-lifetime opportunity." He smiled. "Many trustworthy men among the Mithraists saw great opportunity in these followers of the Nazarene.

"Don't get me wrong, I am still happy that Paulus was not involved with that Stephanos business. Look what happened to the man! However, if you two develop properly safe scenarios, I am willing to consider them."

"How much time do we have?" Cornelius asked.

"One week," Seneca pressed.

"If you agree, I think it prudent to include one more expert in our scheming, an expert who knows the field better than any one of us. Paulus!"

Marih thought fast. "Let's develop the plan, and then evaluate its validity with Paulus. Give us two weeks, can you?" Marih's real need for extra time was to consult with the Mother Lodge. At last, they had their breakthrough. Not a prospect to handle carelessly.

Seneca nodded a few times with wandering eyes, as if making mental calculations. "I'll see you in two weeks. Do not disappoint me."

Fifteen

A Miracle in the Making

Cornelius and Marih put their heads together and quickly developed a viable plan. Such a strategy, despite all its complications, had become a simple exercise for them. However, Cornelius felt the stakes were higher this time. Paulus was a risky sort.

Marih's opinion didn't differ much. The situation was grave. But he approached it from a different angle, so his motivations didn't concur with his fellow centurion's. Marih's priorities lay with the Aleph Lodge plan.

He needed to inform a local Aleph Lodge of the recent happenings and receive immediate directions. With no time to waste, Marih had to choose between the two Aleph Lodges closest to Caesarea, the one in Tyre or the one in Jerusalem. The latter would be the most reasonable as it fell within the same military jurisdiction as Caesarea. He could justify his trip as being work-related. Going to Tyre, on the other hand, would be more like a holiday and he'd be less likely to receive the needed support under the recently imposed pressures.

. . .

An urgent meeting was called the next evening at the Jerusalem Lodge. Marih had attended it several times before and since he used it as an escape route from the temple with oblivious Cornelius trailing along.

He informed his brethren of the recent Roman decisions and requested advice. The Brethren discussed plans for hours, taking into consideration the potential double involvement of Paulus and Cornelius with the Nazarenes. At last a viable plan was approved. Under the cover of night, Marih headed back to his barracks with his gut fluttering with thrills and fear.

Sleep wouldn't come that night. His mind was overexcited by the Aleph plot, one which went beyond his wildest expectations. Occasionally a tiny smile of pride would cross his face. He was tempted to wake his wife, asleep beside him. He just wanted to share his feelings with somebody. Patriotism peaking, he played in his mind scenarios of how one day, over the ashes of Rome, he would tell of the splendour of his Phoenician faith and the brilliance of its Aleph Lodges.

Racing the first rays of the Mediterranean sun to Cornelius' gates, Marih anxiously looked forward to preparing their planning table. Both men were accustomed to military routine; rising with the sun was as natural as breathing. Cornelius didn't let Marih wait long before welcoming him in.

"I haven't been able to think of one workable idea to justify the conversion of Paulus from his conservative-Jew side that hate Nazarenes to that of the knowledgeable Nazarene devotee." Cornelius didn't try to hide his frustration. "Besides, who'd believe him?"

"Let's start by asking, who's supposed to believe him," Marih said.

"Of course! The Nazarenes! We don't care what the Jews think of him. And if they pose any risk, we will protect him."

"Exactly. So we have to put ourselves in the shoes of the Nazarenes and think like them," Marih smoothly guided.

"That's exactly why I wish Paulus was here with us. He would know how these sects think."

"You're underestimating the dexterity of your Tyrian friend." Marih bowed with hand over heart, indicating himself. "Don't forget I grew up in this part of the world. I don't need to be planted like

Paulus."

Cornelius got the message. "Obviously, you have an idea."

"Was I that obvious?"

"My friend of many, many years, I can read you like a book! Please bless me with your wicked thoughts."

Marih took a huge bite of an apple; maybe talking around a mouthful would hide the shiver of excitement in his voice. "Remember when Claudia Achte was raised from the dead?"

"Uh huh."

"The Nazarene and his followers had done many of these so-called miracles. They had changed water to wine, used a few fish and loaves of bread to feed hundreds – some say thousands – of hungry followers, repaired the eyes of the blind and made them see." Marih paused for a reaction.

"Uh huh."

"Don't you see? These people believe in miracles as signs from their God; it sets them apart from the other struggling sects. They would see the conversion of Paulus to their side as a miracle."

"And... you expect me to perform that miracle?" Cornelius raised an eyebrow.

"Not exactly. But Yeshua will."

"Who?"

"Yeshua, their Nazarene leader."

"He's dead!"

"Exactly," Marih grinned.

. . .

Two days later and the two centurions were sitting at that planning table again, this time honoured with the presence of Paulus.

"Let me see if I rightly understand you two tactical geniuses... You want me to pretend that I go blind because Yeshua speaks to me from the heavens. He reprimands me and orders me to heed his word and go to the leader of his followers, some fellow named Cephas, who will pray for me. I will then pretend to be miraculously healed!"

Marih sensed sarcasm in Paulus' summary. Maybe he was not convinced by their plan? His eyes opened wide, hoping to assure him they were completely serious.

"Quite simply, yes." Cornelius was ready to face the truth.

Silence settled around the table.

"You know, this is why we wanted you here. We needed to see what you think, find the holes in our reasoning, refine the plan. This is in no way final, just an idea," Cornelius pushed in response to Paulus' blank expression.

Silence resumed, drilling through their nerves.

"So... do you think... you can do it?" Cornelius struggled with his impatience.

Marih felt his heart rise to his throat.

"I suppose... I mean, if I couldn't, who could, right?" Paulus sat back smugly. "It's brilliant!"

Sixteen

A Vision of Blindness

Their plan awaited the return of Seneca. Unlike his excited junior operatives, Seneca had justifiable concerns and insisted on modifying some of the details. He didn't like leaving Cephas' reaction up to chance. Seneca insisted every single part be worked out and completely under their control. In Seneca's version, Paulus was to create the event of Yeshua speaking to him in a deserted area, perhaps on the road to Damascus. Yes, Damascus would be perfect. This way no witnesses could confirm –neither could they deny – what had happened. Also, Cephas moved around too much, so instead of trying to find him to perform the all-important miracle, he should go to Anania in Damascus, an old man well respected among the Nazarenes and far away from the core group. If for some reason he should call their bluff, they could make him "disappear," thereby maintaining the secrecy of Paulus' identity. This contingency would not be so easily accomplished with Cephas in Judea.

Marih began to mentally check the Aleph plan, which had suggested Cephas be Cornelius' link to the Nazarenes, against Seneca's plan. But Seneca wasn't done yet, so Marih postponed his thoughts until the first phase was worked out. He was jumping to conclusions too early by planning for Cornelius before even knowing if Paulus' part in the scheme could materialize.

Planning the event down to the smallest detail, it was to be executed only upon Seneca's signal. Seneca would personally go to Damascus to prepare the agency and raise the level of readiness. Sometime in the next month would be an event completely diverting the Roman agency's focus from trying to infiltrate the conservative Jews in Jerusalem to infiltrating this pesky opposing sect, the Nazarenes.

. . .

Three weeks later, four dusty companions moved quietly along on tired horses: direction northeast, early afternoon, sun high in a clear sky. It had been a while since they last rode around the Sea of Galilee, so their travel talk was on how the surrounding wilderness had become so harshly dry, deprived of much of its former thriving vegetation. One of the travellers noticed a green horizon ahead, a promised change to their monotony. The travellers sighed, realizing they were not too far from Damascus and its famous gardens.

One of the four had wandered a bit ahead, when his horse gave a sudden, startled jolt. The horse reared up, hooves kicking in the air. His companions tried to see down the road for some explanation, a snake perhaps. Finding nothing, they exchanged puzzled looks.

Within seconds, the rider fell off the horse, hands covering his face. He rolled in the dust, yelling in pain or fear or both.

The spectators jumped off their horses but cautiously approached. They wished to help but couldn't ascertain the situation; perhaps they, too, were in peril.

"Saul, what's wrong, what happened?" one man asked.

Saul, as his Hebrew brethren knew him, lay flat on his face, arms and legs spread out on the ground. He turned his head, twisting his neck off the ground, trying to look at the sky. The yelling stopped.

"Who are you?" he gasped.

The companions looked around... who was Saul talking to?

"Yeshua? Yeshua the Nazarene?" Saul continued speaking to the sky. Tears streaked through the dust on his terrified face. He swiped at his eyes like a child, the dirt blurring his vision and smudging his cheeks. With eyes closed, he spoke again, "My Lord... my Lord..." His calls went unanswered.

He got to his knees and stood up slowly. His companions quickly ran to his aid.

"Did you hear?" the shaken Saul asked, trying to clear the caking mixture of sand and dust and dirt from his eyes and face.

"What? Hear what, Saul?"

"The Lord, Yeshua the Nazarene... he has revealed himself to me. His light blinded me. Didn't you see?"

"Saul, we didn't see anything but you falling off your horse or hear anyone speak but you!"

A shriek drove a shiver down his companions' spines. "I am blind! I cannot see! My Lord, my Lord! I have sinned!"

"Here's some water, Saul, flush your eyes," said one, offering his water skin.

"There isn't enough water in the Sea of Galilee to flush my sins from my eyes!" Saul cried. "Take me to Damascus. My eyes are shut. I beg you, brothers. The Lord Yeshua has revealed himself to me and blessed me with the Knowledge; He is the True Way; He is the Miraculous. From the darkness of my ignorance I have been persecuting the Light. I have always been blind. Yeshua the Lord has just given me true sight though I cannot see anything else about me.

"Take me to Damascus, I beg you!" Saul repeated this request to his companions over and over again.

Saul was the Hebrew name that Paulus used when among them or the Nazarenes. Any spy planted as a real Jew within the Jewish society surely had to carry a Hebrew name.

The agency had helped him carefully select his companions. They were junior Pharisees, easily influenced and, most importantly, weak-natured. They were not strong enough to oppose him, yet these devoted Pharisees could be trusted to carry the story back to Jerusalem and spread it among any of the temple visitors who would listen.

Once in Damascus, Paulus continued his pretence. The Jewish community did not appreciate his references to Yeshua the Nazarene, and many accused him of lying. And there were others who thought he was acting out to attract followers of the Nazarene in order to trap and persecute them, because his travel companions had already spread the word that they had been commissioned to go to Damascus for such a purpose.

Paulus could employ his crafty tongue to manipulate any audience, each according to their ways and his needs. Speaking with his "blind" eyes open, his face to the skies at all times, he was starting to get used to his new persona when a slight commotion was heard at the door to his room.

Three people of the community had come as Seneca had told him they would. Well known among the Damascus Jews was the older man, Anania. He was a Pharisee famous for his calls for peace among all Jews. When some of the Jews celebrated the beheading of a man called Yohana, who baptized people into a new sect and was connected with the early group soon called the Nazarenes, Anania opposed his own community and rejected the violent opposition against them. When Sufi followers of Yohana arrived in Damascus with his head, he gave them protection knowing they were harmless and helped them respectfully bury the head before returning to their wilderness, east of Jerusalem, in Arabia.

Paulus was prepared. He had heard of Anania over the original planning table and immediately recognized what was coming. However, not knowing the exact agreement between Seneca and Anania, he decided to focus on playing his role and just trust where Anania led.

"Leave us alone, folks, please, allow us a few minutes alone. I wish to examine him." Anania exerted his gentle authority and shooed the few people out of the room to wait in the courtyard outside the house.

"Saul, my son, what has happened to you?"

Anania began by taking a cup of wine left on the table, praying over it as if blessing the liquid within, and raised it above Paulus' head. Still looking up, he incanted, "My son Saul, may your sins be washed away by this blessed wine. May this cleansing be a baptism to open your eyes to the True Light." Lowering his gaze, he tilted the cup slightly until a few droplets lightly fell onto Paulus' eyes.

Anania's lowered gaze fixed hard on Paulus as he spoke the words and he read every muscle twitch. A normal reaction for a sighted man would be the anticipation of the drops, evidenced by an intuitive defense of trembling eyelids. Paulus' trembling eyelids gave him away. Anania didn't hide his observation.

"Aha! Lying in the name of God."

Paulus had seriously miscalculated the situation. Thinking fast, he exclaimed, "Oh my Lord Yeshua! You made me see through your devoted servant Anania! Thank you, Lord."

"Saul!" Anania roared. "Another pronouncement like that and I'll throw you out to let the community deal with you."

Paulus realized it was too late. How the agency miscalculated this one! How could Seneca send Anania to him when he was such a skeptic? "Alright, alright..." he switched his negotiating skills. Maybe he could at least save his covert identity. "Why are you here? You are a man of peace and I am a known persecutor. Why do you come here?" he asked Anania.

Anania blew a lungful of tight air, tugged on his long beard, and nodded a couple of times before speaking. "It's that man Barnabas. He came to me and asked me for help. He said you are at risk because some Nazarenes-in-hiding were after you. He said you would present yourself as blind and helpless and you would need help in your pretence in order to appear to be one of them. Some sort of miracle of conversation, I believe he said."

"So you knew I was faking and came to protect me from the Nazarenes?" Paulus had never been more alert and ready to negotiate his way out of a predicament. Seneca had not come himself, but sent Barnabas to set things up for him.

"Of course not. Are you crazy? You want me to play your friend's game by pretending I healed you? I only agreed with him so I could prevent whatever game you two are trying to play on the Nazarenes. Leave them alone. Damascus is not like Jerusalem. Here we all respect each other, even like each other. We don't want your politics here."

Anania was adamant, unmovable. He had Barnabas and the agency fooled. What a miscalculation on all fronts!

"So what do you want?" Paulus explored his opponent's needs, a negotiation technique that worked for him in the past, because it forced the opponent to give up information first.

"I want you and Barnabas out of Damascus. I never trusted that man anyways. One day he is casually talking with the Romans, the next he plays at being a Nazarene. He must think me a fool!"

"But where do we go now? In Jerusalem we are not welcomed because the story has already been spread about, that I have become a Nazarene. People will not believe me there. Those who commissioned us deny us, for to help us would scandalize them throughout the provinces." His second negotiation strategy was to assess his opponent's flexibility.

"How is that my problem? You come here, lie to us, and bring wickedness to Damascus. Then you ask for help?" Anania stepped back a few paces, turned sidewise, and took a deep breath.

Silence controlled the room. Paulus recognized signs of consideration and awaited his opponent's next offer.

"Alright, but my conditions are firm: this will be the last time you or your friend Barnabas ever set foot in Damascus."

"Agreed!"

"I will take you out, south. The Nabatean Arabs are always looking for slaves to trade. They will take you."

Paulus tongue dried in his mouth, eyes rounded, and his wits seemed about to abort their mission.

Anania kept a straight face for what seemed to be ages. Unable to read Anania, Paulus' veins popped out blue on his forehead.

A subtle smirk on Anania's face felt like soothing ice on a burning wound. Anania was just pulling his leg.

"Give it a rest, you moron. Are you truly the smartest they have?"

It finally dawned on Paulus that maybe the agency knew what it was doing after all. Anania was just killing time before inviting the people back in.

"A certain ascetic Jewish community lives down south in Arabia, removed from all your politics. They follow the way of Yohana the Baptizer. When we're done with this ridiculous theatre of yours, I will take you there." Anania now spoke seriously but with clear disgust in his voice.

"Deal!" Paulus jumped at the offer.

Anania opened the door. People walked in to find Paulus with clear eyes looking straight at them. His smile was mixed with tears and his facial expressions danced between laughter and fear. He proclaimed, "The Lord has cleared my eyes at the hands of his good servant Anania. I can see! Glorious is the Lord!"

Anania turned towards Paulus in repugnance. He shook his head, deeply regretting his part in playing along with this impostor.

Paulus, on the other hand, showed sincere happiness knowing that the plan was actually proceeding as expected. He should have known that Seneca deserved more trust. In all the years he worked with him, he had never let anyone down. He had allowed his nerves to take over, his excitement visibly real to those gathered about him. Oh! how reliable Seneca was, a true genius. But what had he done to ensure Anania's participation? Clearly no fool, Anania had him going for a while there. Whatever it was, Paulus was profoundly appreciative. If Seneca were there, Paulus would have covered his feet with kisses.

. . .

The crowds slowly dispersed, perplexed by Anania's role in this singular revelation. They respected him too much to doubt him, but there was no way they could believe what they saw. Confusion set in and they had no idea what to expect next.

Anania and Paulus left the house and headed to the inn where Barnabas had established himself. There Paulus learned of the agency's threat to Anania: "If you want to see your son again, you had better help Saul regain his vision." Anania's son lived and studied in Alexandria, and he had no way to confirm the seriousness of the agency's threat as delivered by Barnabas. No man would risk his son's safety, even unconfirmed, so Anania chose to cooperate.

Upon learning of how the situation had played out and Anania's masterful manipulation of Paulus by forcing the outcome, Barnabas found the story very entertaining. Even so, their deal with Anania was far from accomplished.

With no chance to say goodbye to Seneca or Cornelius, Paulus headed south with Barnabas and Anania to the Jewish community in the wilderness of Arabia. Their promise to Anania hinged on their safe delivery to these people in the wilderness; from there he would be free to return to find his son safe. Anania rested for a day before his return trip to Damascus under the protection of an agency operative.

In Arabia, these two spies *cum* Nazarenes had to temporarily succumb to a very different lifestyle, one bereft of the luxuries of large cities and the lavishness due citizens of the great Roman Empire. Theirs would be the life of the ascetic Jewish gnostics.

"How long must we stay here?" Paulus hoped Barnabas had good news on this front.

"Until Seneca sends for us."

"How will he ever find us?"

"This hiding place was his idea from the start."

"Huh," Paulus grunted. "And what if Anania told the community about us? What's the point of hiding, why don't we just go to Rome rather than live in this... desert?"

"Anania would not tell..."

"How can you be sure? Once his son is safe..." Paulus paused, sensing more to the story.

Barnabas didn't say a word.

"He's not going to make it back to Damascus, is he?"

Long-term projects like Barnabas and Paulus represented were far too precious to the agency. The deal they cut with Anania was not binding to such conspirers as these. He was but an unsuspecting pawn; they never had any intention of leaving witnesses behind. The disappearance of a wise man with a small party returning to Damascus and a couple of months in Arabia for their valuable agents seemed the safest choice all around. Unknown to them, these two spies were worth a few years' wait if that meant survival of their project.

Barnabas was better prepared. He explained to the volatile Paulus, "The way of the people here is very similar to the way of the Nazarenes. As we await Seneca's signal, we can learn much about them that will be useful to us in years to come."

Seventeen

A Neighbour
in Need is a Friend Indeed

After hearing about the success of Paulus' conversion and the noise it created in Damascus, Marih readied himself for another trip to Jerusalem. This time he had the other plan in mind, the conversion of Cornelius to the Nazarenes' belief.

The Jerusalem Lodge was well prepared for him. This time, members of the Mother Lodge in Tyre had been invited to participate in the much-anticipated discussion.

At the entrance stood two pillars in memory of the pillars of the temple ruins in Tyre. In the centre of the room stood a replica of the altar that had once honoured the great God Melqart. It was a careful recreation, passed down through centuries by oral tradition, and the focus of every Aleph Lodge.

In traditional ceremonial costume, the members all wore stone engraver aprons over long tunics. The body-length aprons were made of specially loomed thick fabric of the highest quality, meant to protect the stoneworker's body from the flying shrapnel of engraving.

After ceremonial prayers, members raised the wooden emblems

that hung around their necks up into the air with their left hands. The brethren chanted in a monotone the hymn calling their God to arise from the dead, as they believed he always did, and eradicate their enemies, reducing their glory to ashes.

This sacred emblem they carried was the Aleph: the first letter of their alphabet, representing the head of a bull ox, the mark of the God Melqart. Once the chanting concluded, the members placed the emblems on tables in front of them. The tables had the builder's square, two long arms of a right angle, engraved onto the tops so the angle pointed away from them. The Aleph emblems were placed so that the horns of the pictogram lay against the arms of the square. The master then announced the lodge to be open on the square.

The proceeding discussion was not any easier or shorter than their previous meeting. Theories and scenarios were offered and analyzed. The judging brethren seemed inclined to one particular scenario. Successful practicality was their trademark, and this scenario seemed to ensure it.

Marih offered vital intelligence regarding the agency's movements. Seneca had refused to include Cephas the Nazarene in the conversion of Paulus, so this movement must be reconsidered. Cephas was described again to the brethren as having been the closest of the disciples to Yeshua the Nazarene. However, after the death of Yeshua, Cephas' cowardly and timid personality placed him in a secondary role behind that of Yeshua's brother. He had been in hiding most of the time, and many of his hiding places were homes of Phoenician labourers.

These Phoenicians had often opened their doors for the Nazarenes – partially because they didn't much care for Jewish politics, but mostly because of the recommendation by the Aleph Lodges to do so. It was an unspoken rule among the Jews to avoid stirring up trouble with their northern neighbours and their colonies. While they considered them sinners beyond their aid to the Nazarenes and cursed their ways in closed circles, they found in the Phoenicians a major ally in commerce. Money was the ultimate mediator. Ironically, the homes of these useful sinners became safe havens for the persecuted Nazarenes.

The Aleph operatives had identified the man Cephas as a guest at a Phoenician tanner's house in Joppa. The tanner's name was Simon. After the death of Yeshua, rumours among the people told of this Cephas repeatedly escaping persecution by denying he ever knew Yeshua let alone being one of Yeshua's immediate followers.

However, as many of the Nazarenes did the same, they found comfort in what Cephas did. It was their way of accepting their own cowardice and explaining their actions. If Cephas himself, number one in Yeshua's eyes, had escaped trouble in this way, wouldn't they be excused by doing the same? By their reasoning, their Lord had meant for things to happen as they happened. This little difference of opinion, however, was becoming a matter of division amongst the Nazarenes.

Marih felt his new mission had certain unresolved complications. While he had received confirmation from the lodge that Cephas would surrender to their threats and would therefore submit to Cornelius' wishes to join the Nazarenes even though he was a gentile, convincing Seneca of all this posed a challenge. The lodge assured him all this would come to pass, but how was he to convince Seneca without blowing his cover? Seneca had earlier refused the inclusion of Cephas as a point in Paulus' plot because the Roman Intelligence Agency couldn't guarantee him. They simply had never had him under their surveillance and didn't have enough intelligence on him. Why would Seneca include him now?

Unresolved challenges of this type had become routine to Marih, which isn't to say he ever became comfortable dealing with such ambiguity; he had long ago accepted this life chosen for him by the Aleph Lodge and the great Melqart.

. . .

Ten days had passed since the meeting with the Jerusalem Lodge and Marih had been puzzling out how to broach the topic, when Cornelius brought it up right out of the blue.

"Seneca has informed me that he will be with us very soon to discuss my infiltration of the Nazarenes."

"I look forward to another success for the agency," Marih said, filling their cups to refresh themselves.

"A success for the agency is fine. But this will be a personal success for me, another milestone towards settling my score. With each one I come closer to watching Simaan Ben Aaron – that scum of a murderer – suffer alongside his people for what he did."

Marih still didn't know that the man Simaan Ben Aaron had claimed he had murdered was Cornelius' father. The time had come for Cornelius to tell his best friend about the secret of his father's death.

Eighteen

Brothers No Matter

Emperor Tiberius was dead. The ground-shaking news made its way around the Empire in no time. Gossip travels fast; bad news travels fastest of all. Uncertainty preoccupied the military leaders of all ranks as they feared losing not only their status but their heads.

A halt was put on all plans. Military institutions, including the agency, cautiously awaited their orders. Within two weeks of the emperor's death a new emperor claimed the throne. Despite acts of generosity towards the servants of the Empire and its institutions, Emperor Gaius had cunningly managed to impose several unnoticed changes. One of these changes proved disastrous to the agency.

Gaius summoned a number of high-ranking intelligence officers from throughout the provinces and retired them, one way or another. While some of his peers' retirements were mortally permanent, Seneca's orders placed him under forced house arrest in Rome. He stood by helplessly while his major responsibilities in Judea, along with the officers and projects that relied on his direction, were all put in the hands of unqualified, inexperienced favourites of the new emperor.

Such news was cause for celebration for the Alephs. But what brought joy to Marih wreaked catastrophe on Cornelius. Losing his mentor and idol was bad enough, but now years of careful work within the agency were at risk without Seneca's guidance. What did this effete band of politicians know of intelligence work? What if they changed the focus... or worse, killed their ongoing projects altogether?

The Aleph brethren immediately employed their underground network to support their Roman allies and various puppets, helping them fill the gaps of power created by the new rule of Emperor Gaius. Such politics didn't much bother the Phoenician people. They backed Romans who would come to their aid once they achieved positions of power; and, if they didn't, their sourness would turn them hostile to the emperor's administration. Either way had its benefits, developing allies on both sides of the equation.

As Cornelius and Marih were already centurions, it made sense to the Aleph Lodge for them to continue their work with the agency. Whether they knew it or not, the brethren would protect their roles. Instructions were distributed to all lodges to continue to support all arrangements for agency projects.

. . .

"Orders are finally in. I am to maintain my office here in Caesarea," Cornelius said with guarded relief. He knew Marih would have received his orders at the same time. He was hoping he wouldn't lose his closest friend in this upheaval. Marih was a major pillar in his support system. Life in Caesarea would be less tolerable without this brother-in-arms. Marih was his Aramaic brain, his sincere advisor, his accomplice in revenge, and one thing more... he was Elisa's brother.

"Orders came in for me, too," Marih frowned.

Cornelius' mood changed, unsure whether he could take any more bad news. There had been enough already.

"And I'm not going anywhere!" Marih bellowed happily, grabbing his old friend in a bear hug.

"You bastard!" Cornelius beat Marih's back with closed fists, sincere relief washing over them both.

"Brothers no matter!" Marih proclaimed.

"Brothers no matter!" Cornelius agreed.

. . .

Seneca was the Imperial Intelligence Agency's biggest asset. Restricting him by house arrest was Gaius' biggest mistake. With the great philosopher's absence, the Aleph plans met few obstacles. It didn't take much for Marih to convince Cornelius they had to carry on with their plans regardless of any changes in the agency's position. He reasoned: the current situation was time-sensitive; waiting for the new agency's administrators to figure out what was going on was intolerable; failing to keep the projects on track could be disastrous considering what they had already planned and achieved.

Cornelius readily agreed to Marih's clever plan: using Cephas the Nazarene as his link to the sect was a perfect cover on several levels. Marih wondered what Cornelius would say if he knew implementation of his scheme was already underway.

"What have you heard about this Cephas that makes you think he'll comply?" Cornelius asked after he'd thought for a moment.

"Our operatives tell us he always seems to be in hiding. We hear that when his teacher was still alive he had a position of honour; he's a big man, but gentle. But something changed him. Now he hides like a frightened animal. If we can corner him, he'll be too scared to oppose a Roman centurion's wish to join the group. But you've got to convince him you are sincere, and you can shore up your sincerity by making him think he has gained some kind of immunity or protection by befriending a centurion. Such confidence will give him the courage to defend his actions in front of the other Nazarenes. They surely will not be so gullible. This will also give him the confidence to come out of the shadows, raise his voice, and assume the role originally entrusted to him by his teacher, Yeshua." Marih's passion was contagious.

"I can do this! I will see he has the safety he needs through carefully selected soldiers. Caesarea will always be open for him and his friends," Cornelius added.

"And so will be Tyre. I can ensure Cephas' followers the comfort they need all along the chain of Phoenician cities north of Judea. You already know my people will offer any support they can to Rome, and with pleasure."

"That settles it! We shall waste no more time. I will send my

men to him tomorrow, instructing them to be polite and invite him...
escort him here. You should be here, too, don't you think? You speak
his tongue," Cornelius suggested.

"Yes, but don't have them bring him here. Let them just inform
him that you want to see him because you are interested in his ways
and want to learn them," Marih further explained. "If the gossip goes
out that he was forced – in any manner – to your house, it will put
the other followers on guard."

"But, what if he gets scared and escapes?"

"He will not. Don't worry, he'll be too afraid to run away."

"But just... let's just say for argument's sake... what if he did?"
Cornelius was still not convinced.

"He is currently staying with a man who is one of my agents.
This agent will advise him to come to you, and if he doesn't listen,
my man will tell us where to find him. Then and only then will we
bring him in by force."

Cornelius beamed, "I believe in your powers of persuasion. You
so astutely brought me from under the temple in Jerusalem, you can
surely bring me into Cephas' circle of trust!"

"Thanks for reminding me... I always meant to tell you that
things work out very well when you're mute."

"Aw, shut up!"

. . .

In the city of Joppa, by the seashore, was the humble shack of
Simon the Tanner. The tanner's profession was among the lowest
of the low in any Jewish community. Their religious purity laws
held tanning of hides an unclean activity. The pungent chemicals
and the dreadful smells accompanying the process of drying animal
skins wasn't the worst of it; it was all the blood and gore of the dead
animals before the hides were even ready to tan. Hebrew laws were
strict about cleanliness, especially where blood is concerned, and
certain parts of animals... even certain animals... were to be avoided.

Simon the Tanner served a purpose in the community, but
begrudgingly so. In commerce, his profession was a necessary evil.
Where else would they get the leather for their simplest needs, such
as their sandals? Still, his house and workshop were far removed
from the rest of the dwellings in Joppa, providing a safe place for

Cephas. Cephas had no such qualms about uncleanliness.

Cephas and the few Nazarenes who knew where he hid were constantly thinking of solutions for their unsustainable living situations and the constant threat forcing their immediate escape to safety. Simon the Tanner's advice to them was to make friends with the Romans.

"I don't understand why it should be such a worry. The Romans have the power to protect you," Simon spoke to Cephas and his friends upon returning from their morning fishing trip. They tied the boat a couple of hundred yards away, far enough from the tanner's house to be respectable, then would walk the shore pretending to clean their tools and untangle their nets. When they passed a huge line of hanging animal skins, hidden from view, they snuck up to the house.

"Simon, you know our laws. We are not allowed to mix with the gentiles," Cephas replied, trying to hide his annoyance. This wasn't the first time that Simon had pushed like that.

"You are mixing with *me*! For Ashtart's sake! You are living with me and you take your meals with me!"

"That's different, Simon," Cephas smiled. "You're one of us now. Besides, you are saving our lives by allowing us to stay here, so this is an emergency, requiring special consideration."

"Well, use the same reasoning for your more serious emergency. Consider working with the Romans." Simon took some dried pieces of salt pork from a jar on a shelf behind the table they sat around. "Listen, you break or stretch your rules all the time. You have allowed yourself to live with me and eat my food. Your teacher allowed you to do things on the seventh day. And here you are hiding like chickens because you are afraid what the people will say or do if you mix with the Romans. Tell me how this makes sense?"

The Nazarenes had no words.

"My friends, you know you are welcome to stay here as long as you want. I think of you as nothing less than brothers. A thousand years ago, our King Hiram and your King David and his son Solomon sealed this pact of brotherhood. I do not understand how it became so dishonoured, but I will honour it... even if it leads to my death." Simon searched his companions' eyes for agreement while trying to catch any hint of weakness. "All I'm saying is that you should try and give that Roman centurion a chance. He has sent many of his servants to Joppa searching for you and he means no harm. To the contrary, he heard of your teacher's ability to cure the ill; he wants your blessing."

"Yeshua performed many miracles for the gentiles. They were against the laws and look how he is honoured for it now," one of Cephas friends spoke up.

There it was. The words were accompanied by a scent of weakness, revealing itself to Simon's sensitive nose. His smelly profession didn't ruin Simon's senses, it heightened them. It was time. "An opportunity doesn't present itself twice, my brothers. Truth be told, I fear if you do not entertain the curiosity of this Roman centurion, you may lose any benefit of his protection, maybe even turning him against you."

"What? Why? We are no threat to him!" Cephas objected.

"No. And what did Yeshua ever do against Rome?"

The Nazarenes were speechless again. Simon knew he hit a sensitive nerve. *Seekers are so malleable*, he thought to himself, but he proceeded carefully, "Eventually, everyone against you will wheedle their ways into his mind and convince him you are liars. He will turn him against you, if for no other reason than to shut them up."

The men had all this time been chewing on the dried pork Simon had offered them. The sea hadn't been kind to them lately. Maybe the fish would be more abundant in the evening, and maybe they wouldn't. They were hungry in so many ways.

His companions picked up Simon's arguments: "Cephas, Yeshua trusted you. He called you Cephas, our rock. When you judged it was permissible to eat from the Phoenician's table, we did. If you judge that we can extend brotherhood to this gentile – a Roman centurion, no less – we will."

All eyes turned to this sensible Nazarene. No one could find an objection. Simon forced a smile from betraying his face. Was it working? Could it be so easy? Were they convinced?

"But what will our brothers in Jerusalem think about this?" Cephas hesitated, his fears surfacing, as they usually did.

"The brothers will honour your words. You are full of the Spirit; they believe Spirit speaks through you."

"I will pray on this. I will pray to our Lord for insight," Cephas finally seemed to agree.

"Perhaps you should do so now, my friend..." Simon gently nudged, "I believe the centurions' men are still searching and might come by any day, any moment. We should be ready."

Simon stood to leave the Nazarenes to do whatever it was they needed by way of fortifying themselves in their decision. He walked out to a partially skinned ox hide with a satisfied smile, getting on with his life.

Two days later, as the sun approached the middle of the sky, Cephas was lying flat on the roof of Simon's house, trying to catch a glimpse of his friends' boat upon the sea. He was careful to avoid standing on the roof in the daytime; someone might see him and identify him. In the corner of his eye, a motion on the deserted road leading to the tanner's house caught his attention. He looked carefully. His stomach knotted as he recognized a Roman soldier and what might be two servants. They were coming his way, with a purpose.

. . .

When Simon's messenger confirmed Cephas was ready, their careful planning was immediately put to use. Marih dressed as a Roman private, a trusted messenger of a centurion. With two servants to accompany him, they rode off to Joppa. One of the servants was Simon's messenger making the return trip. He knew Joppa very well and was able to guide them swiftly over the night. They arrived at the messenger's house in the early morning hours, refreshing and resting themselves for their mission.

Leaving their horses behind, the three had walked off the main road and took a side road that led to a lonely house with several outbuildings by the shore. The vile stench hit their nostrils while still on the main road, intensifying as they marched down the deserted path to the tanner's house.

The door to the house was open on a crack. Marih pushed it all the way and called for the man of the house in Latin with a Greco-Roman accent. Hearing no answer, they backed up to look around the property. One of the servants scurried behind the house, which gave on to the open beach. Marih recognized the voice returning with the servant. It was Simon. Hiding their smiles of recognition, they pretended to not know each other. Marih suspected Cephas was somewhere nearby, watching.

"Greetings from Centurion Cornelius of Caesarea, we come in peace," Marih addressed Simon formally. He looked around in search of something, and then back at Simon. "What is this stench?"

"I apologize, sir. An unavoidable result of my occupation. I am a tanner. That smell comes from the animal skins I hung this morning." Simon affected his reply in broken Latin.

Clearly unable to ignore the odour, Marih spoke with authority, "I wouldn't remain here a minute longer were it not for my orders." He turned his face and coughed, then continued, "My master sends me in search of a man known as Cephas. He is one of the Nazarenes, they say a leader among them."

Simon played his part and stood silently, as if thinking.

Enjoying the theatre, Marih continued with his lines. He had rehearsed them in his mind several times on his way to Joppa. "My master seeks him in peace, he need not fear. My master has heard great things about his congregation and he would like to learn more from Cephas, first hand."

"Sir, please be sure I fully intend to fulfill your master's wishes. However, Cephas does not seem to be here at the moment," Simon said, perhaps a little too loudly. With his back to the house, his finger pointed up, indicating the roof of the house.

"No disrespect to you, but I will have to confirm your claim. You see, we have been looking everywhere for a very long time and we must follow our orders." Marih also made sure his voice carried to Cephas hiding on the roof. "You! Go check the outbuildings. You! Go to the roof," he ordered his servants.

"Is there a well around here?" Marih asked Simon.

"No sir, we are too close to the shore to have a well. There is no place for him…" Simon hadn't finished his sentence when Cephas' voice was heard from the roof.

"I beg you, do not interrupt my prayers. I will be with you shortly!" Cephas' voice wasn't very prayerful.

No doubt Cephas was scrambling for excuses for being found on the roof, his fearfulness betraying his voice. Marih shot a quick smile to Simon, forcing himself to regain his play-acting sombreness. "Leave him to his prayers. Come down. Remember, we need him alive!" Marih surely enjoyed those last words. He knew they would fall heavy on Cephas' weak heart, an unspoken reminder that his death was not out of the question.

. . .

As Cephas lay on the roof watching the three men approaching, a million thoughts raced through his mind. He and his brothers had talked about this moment with Simon, they had anticipated it. They knew this was coming and they agreed to go through with it. So why could he not get his legs to move? Ideas of the Jewish community accusing him of mixing with the gentiles swarmed his head. Maybe he should think more about it. Maybe it was a bad idea altogether. Now that he was actually listening to the conversation of this Roman soldier with Simon, he found no comfort at all. Breathing became more difficult. Lying flat on his chest under the full sun, his heart hammered into the roof of the house. Cephas could hear his own heart pounding... could they?

"You! Go to the roof."

Hearing the Roman soldier's order convinced Cephas he was about to meet his doom. Any ability to think quickly vanished and Cephas regressed to the emotions of a child, caught by a parent in some prohibited act. He yelled – almost cried – the first thing that came to mind, "I beg you, leave me to my prayers!"

The one emotion that never failed him was his sense of fear. It now told him perhaps he had been too harsh, so he immediately softened his plea, "I will be with you shortly."

That is it. There is no escape. Cephas' knees struggled to carry him down from the roof. But why was he so scared? Again, he tried to talk himself into some courage. Hadn't he and his Nazarene brothers already agreed to open their sect to the Roman centurion? Surely, these were the wishes of the Holy Spirit. Yes, that's it. After all, Cephas tried and tried, yet some power kept resisting his refusals. Something kept pushing that centurion into his life. It all begins with the centurion's most unusual interest in the Nazarene way – unlike any Roman behaviour they had ever seen – and it ends with Cephas and the brothers in dire need for protection in order for their sect to survive, let alone thrive. Now three men have come asking for him at the best hiding place he had ever had. How did they find him? It could only be the workings of the Holy Spirit. Yes, the brothers would surely understand this reasoning.

"Blessed be your master who sends you here." Cephas' words began in a shaky voice, weaker than he wanted to let on. He cleared his throat in an attempt to recover some semblance of dignity. "If he seeks the Way, it's because the Spirit has enlightened him, guiding you here." Cephas didn't know whether the Romans' silence was a sign of respect and agreement or merely the calm before the storm. All eyes were burning straight through him as he nervously stroked his beard and announced, "Tomorrow I shall come to Caesarea."

"We will accompany you there today, if you wish." Although polite as he could be, Marih knew any words from a Roman soldier would drive a lump of fear into Cephas' throat.

"Ehhhm, I... you're..." Cephas' dry lips stuck to his teeth and his tongue struggled to let an arid gulp down his throat. "I need to talk to my brothers, ehmm, must have their blessings. It's our way, you know." Glad to have found the words, he now worried if they were convincing. He couldn't go alone to that centurion, like Daniel walking into the lion's den. He was scared enough just thinking about it in Joppa, how could he make it to Caesarea without the support of the brothers? They were his pillars, his confidence. Besides, who was to say this centurion wasn't going to deliver him to their enemies, the conservative Jewish persecutors. No scenario was a good scenario in Cephas' mind. He just wasn't going to Caesarea alone, and that was that.

"As you wish. We will stay in Joppa tonight and travel with you in the morning. Our master will be very happy to see you."

Marih's words fell like cool water on Cephas' burning brow. The fact that he was so flexible was a fine sign. Maybe things weren't so bad after all. This centurion who caused such fear in him could possibly be the source of relief he and the brothers had needed for so long. Perhaps by befriending him they really could find a protector; after all, they might regains some of their freedom and cease this life of hiding from their own shadows. The mysteries of Holy Spirit were not theirs to know.

"I look forward to meeting him. Have a peaceful night." Cephas saluted the visitors.

. . .

The evening came on quickly. After the Romans left, Cephas' nerves exploded into non-stop talking. Simon sat there patiently listening to Cephas' flights of ideas, jumping from one conclusion to another and one plan to the next. Tangents, although meaningful to Cephas, defied what Simon knew of logic. But he kept nodding until his friend finally exhausted himself.

"It is clear to me you are doing the right thing," Simon finally got few words in. "Your prayers on the roof, so quickly answered, are proof enough that the Holy Spirit is guiding you and will give you comfort." Simon recognized his main job that night was to keep Cephas from having second thoughts.

"That's the honest truth, the Spirit is my guide."

His peace was short-lived, for before long Simon had to listen to it all over again, only this time with certain embellishments as Cephas revealed every detail to his two Nazarene brothers.

"...and the Lord answered my prayer by causing me to fall on my face in a trance. In the vision, I saw a huge sheet come down from the skies carrying all kind of animals. Then a faceless voice told me to kill and eat whatever I liked."

Simon listened with fascination. A sheet with animals? Cephas had said nothing about that earlier. He was surely refining his story as he went to persuade his brothers of their course. What a wimp. Simon controlled his urge to smile; he thought, *There will be time to enjoy these stories in depth when I tell them again at the Aleph Lodge.* Cephas' story couldn't be a more perfect fit for their plans. And the more creative tales became, with the visions and all, the less Cephas would be able to pull back.

Cephas passionately continued, "I thought how could I eat of forbidden creatures, impure? But the Voice spoke to me twice more. Every time I thought I shouldn't eat these impure things, the Voice taught me to call nothing impure that God has made clean."

Simon watched the faces of the brothers, how their trust grew as he spoke to them. Why didn't they question him? Simon had a million questions by now, but he marvelled in silence.

"So I knew without questions the Spirit's message to us is to accept the gentiles among us. Who are we to call them impure if the Spirit teaches us otherwise?" Cephas concluded.

"So, Cephas, you are saying it is safe to go to the centurion's palace? Or maybe the Spirit wants us to accept him, but not necessarily go to Caesarea... or maybe the vision was really about food and not the gentiles?"

Finally, one brave question! By now Simon knew there was no return, so he sat back and enjoyed Cephas' imagination at work.

"The true truth is, just before I woke up the Spirit told me three men are coming to take me to Caesarea and I should not be afraid. I should go with them. And so, in the name of the Spirit, I ask you, my dearest brothers, to accompany me tomorrow on this holy mission."

Formidable closing, Simon thought. Amazing how some people have skills you would never suspect. Such a man – so well known for denying any knowledge of his teacher while he went to his execution, only to escape and leave his teacher's mother and women followers alone when they most needed him – one such as he can still find people to not only follow him but hang on his every word as if he were some kind of hero. Absolutely amazing.

Nineteen

Awkward

The fastest intelligence tool ever known proved itself once again: gossip beat Marih's official confirmation to Tyre. Paulus' conversion was accomplished. The Mother Lodge was ecstatic. Their plans were moving ahead with success upon success, challenges greatly reduced thanks to persistence and tactful execution.

But the celebration was short-lived. With the death of Emperor Tiberius and the rise of the new Emperor Gaius, all the Imperial Intelligence Agency's projects slowed to a crawl. What help could Paulus bring to the Aleph's machinations if he was not an active agent? The Aleph brethren's focus turned towards maintaining any and all projects that enhanced their cause in any way. Every lodge everywhere was pressed to coordinate and keep up to speed.

The Mother Lodge was still optimistic about Elisa's plan for bringing up young Claudia. Some missions, especially the long-range ones that involved the rearing of a child, must brook no interruptions. They could wait on Paulus and Seneca; their experience assured them this interruption with the agency was just another cycle, one eventually coming around to their favour. Of course, if either was permanently removed from the political or military picture, Claudia would become practically useless to them. Claudia's purpose was as a tool of influence over Seneca *and* Paulus. Elisa must maintain her role until further notice.

There were many times when the Alephs' needs overlapped with the agency's. Never going completely out of service, the agency suffered under the mismanagement of Gaius Caligula's minions. The Alephs decided to take things out of the control of the new leaders of the Imperial Intelligence Agency and put them in Cornelius' hands or, more practically, their own. The Mother Lodge decided not to sit idly by and watch Paulus and Barnabas' projects fall apart after investing years of shadowing them and refining their paths. Cornelius should take a more active role and should help in reviving these projects. After all, he was the direct agent and manager of Paulus. Cornelius, who had a personal vengeance against the Jews, would probably be a responsive target.

The Aleph brethren didn't make this decision easily. In fact, they were severely split along both sides of the argument. For many, these new ideas were too unrealistic, even for an organization steeped in long-range planning. They thought the lodges were becoming arrogant, taking too many things for granted. They did not believe they could lift Cornelius to such a powerful role. There were simply too many variables in such an ambitious plan. Even if Cornelius' sails tacked to their winds, who could say he would succeed at taking control of Paulus and Barnabas, independent of the agency's more public face? If uncovered, the Romans would take all this as treason.

As good as these arguments were against proceeding, the hesitant decision was still made to proceed. Marih was informed of the new directions and his orders changed accordingly.

Elisa's mission expanded. The Phoenician princess would now speak as their voice in Cornelius' ear. Despite Marih's strong ties with Cornelius, multiple fronts would be safer, more effective. Elisa accepted with her usual passion for her cause and more... a hidden desire. No matter how much she tried to convince herself otherwise, the idea of being close to Cornelius always brought an exceptional thrill.

. . .

Proceeding with their orders under the guise of their normal lives, Elisa brought Claudia for a visit to big brother Marih in

Caesarea. They needed to coordinate their individual instructions.

"Have they lost their minds?" Marih didn't hide his disappointment.

"I know... it is too ambitious. But an extreme disease calls for an extreme remedy," his sister said.

"What if we end up losing both, Paulus and Cornelius? Have they thought of that?"

"Brother, they know the risk is there. The lodges pondered all the angles for a great deal of time. It is done now, we are past the deciding. We only have to make it work."

"I guarantee that Cornelius will refuse. For him to act upon his own orders is tantamount to treason. He wouldn't do it. Ask me about him, no one knows him better!"

"Where are Paulus and Barnabas now?" she asked.

"What?"

"Where are the agency spies?"

"In Arabia."

"That's all I need for now. Give me two days and wish me luck."

"Elisa, whatever you have in mind, it needs to wait. Tomorrow I will be in Joppa to meet Cephas, the Nazarene. We need to bring him to Caesarea so Cornelius can be converted, or pretend to be..."

"I know, I know, brother. You focus on your task."

Marih was silent.

"And pass my regards along to the tanner," Elisa added.

Marih smiled as he pulled little Achte into a hug.

. . .

The morning brought a surprise visitor to Cornelius. He had not expected Elisa to come to Caesarea as it wasn't an appointed time for Paulus to see his daughter. They both knew he was still in Arabia. Emotions overflowing at the sight of her in the visitors' room, he wasn't about to question her reasons. "Forgive me, but have we met before, my lady?" he joked.

"In an occasional awkward moment, my lord," she played along.

"I have grown to like awkward."

"I'm afraid I've grown to be it," she half-whispered.

He grinned. "In my limited experience, I find when such matters are an accepted part of a culture, they stop being awkward and become the norm."

She gazed into his eyes with what? A hint of lasciviousness? The intensity of such a thought stopped his mind mid-thought. What had he been saying?

Elisa broke the silence. "Please, don't let my unexpected visit interrupt your day... be free to tend to your tasks."

"Oh, not at all, not at all. Would you breakfast with me?"

"I am a bit hungry, thank you for asking."

"Where is little Claudia? Isn't she as hungry as the princess?" Cornelius asked.

"She's at Marih's place. I didn't want to wake her up early. Besides, Ishtar dotes on her... practicing for their own."

"So, it's an all adults breakfast then?"

"Oh no, I'll still eat with you!"

He laughed and ordered their meal be brought to the small morning garden, lush with bright colours in the early sun.

The breakfast was serene. Unlike any time Cornelius had spent with Elisa before, it verged on romantic yet without an agenda. They simply were themselves, easy in the moment. Being himself, however, his uncontrolled thoughts strolled in and out of daydreams. He wondered if Elisa was feeling the same way. Or perhaps she found in his company the comfort of a brother? Talk about awkward... nothing was more awkward than his feelings towards her. He pushed back an overwhelming yearning to take her in his arms and explore every speck of her tanned little Tyrian body, with his fingers and palms and lips. *Get hold of yourself, man!* he chided his own mind. It was probably too late now anyway. He had already become the trusted family member, maybe too much like a brother to go back. Being with her like this was certainly enjoyable, gratifying, but incomplete. Yes, indeed... talk about awkward.

"You know, it wasn't a necessary part of the culture," she said as she left the table and reclined on a cushion in the dappled sunlight, leaving room for Cornelius to sit close by.

"I'm... uh... what do you mean? What wasn't part of the culture?"

"This awkwardness."

What the...? Is she reading my mind? How could she know I'm thinking awkwardness? He crossed to the proffered place on the cushion, clearly puzzled.

"You said that if the awkwardness was part of a culture, it stops being awkward and becomes part of the norm," she explained.

"Oh, yes, yes," he chuckled. "You lost me for a moment there, I'd already forgotten that conversation."

"So, you see, it was not a must-do part of the culture."

Now what? Why am I having so much trouble following her conversation this morning? Is it just me? She kept looking at him with those piercing eyes, waiting for his reaction, as if she wanted him to say something. "Ah," was the best he could do.

She smiled. "Marih's wedding, you silly man. Remember? That part of the ceremony... it wasn't really... *necessary.*"

"What do you mean?" he remained afraid of misinterpreting.

"It was an optional part. It wasn't a must. Of course it would bring good luck, but it wasn't... *necessary.*"

"So you just thought you would follow along in order to bring your brother good luck?" he carefully asked.

"No, not exactly..."

Cornelius' heartbeats sucked the air out of his lungs. *Is she saying what I think she is saying?*

"I did not do it for the ceremony alone," she said in a much more serious tone.

Bodies now inches apart, he quivered inside, like a bull before charging. Time must have stopped then started again, because neither could recall the exact moment they fell into each other's arms. But it didn't matter. All that mattered was that awkwardness finally making sense.

. . .

The sun had climbed very high in the sky before Cornelius spoke with some concern. "What will Marih think of this? Of us?"

"Let's not tell him."

"Not tell him?"

"It's too complicated."

"But he's my dear friend. Why would he object?"

"It's not about you, Cornelius. It is about my family and me. Remember, I am a princess to my parents and, by tradition, a princess only weds someone of royal blood."

"There must be a way..." he tried to interrupt.

"Well, unless you become the next Caesar, this must remain our little secret." She left no room for him to bargain.

Cornelius sat up and apart from her, their afterglow dissipating way too quickly. "I think I just missed my chance. The next Caesar has been chosen already. Gaius has robbed me of my future... my projects and my chance to be with you." His words didn't sound as playful as they were meant to.

"What do you mean he took your projects?" She pretended not to know.

"Our new Caesar suffers from paranoia, and rightly so. It seems to be a condition inherent with the title, especially with some of the military leaders. You have heard, no doubt, he has retired many of them in one way or another. These actions have put many of our projects to pause. For example, and I'm sure you know by now that Paulus works closely with me, so, his work might end up being cancelled. He might be able to spend more time with his daughter after all." Disappointment shadowed his voice.

"Oh!"

He wasn't sure of her reaction.

"You know... I have grown so attached to Claudia. I have never considered things would not continue as they are. Does this mean you, too, may have to return to Rome?"

He looked into her genuinely worried eyes. Why had she deprived him of this feeling for so long, this unfathomable affection where his soul felt at home? He had shut off so many emotions after learning of his father's death. Rage and hatred and duty had dominated for too long.

"Maybe you need to," she continued, slowly, as if thinking out loud. "You have already achieved such high ranks for your age. Nobody would blame you if you decided to return to Rome. It is not like you have failed anybody. Your family will be proud of you. Your father would be proud of you, more so than he already was." Elisa tactfully spoke of his father, her soft hand stroking his arm as she bent to kiss his chest, burying her eyes beneath his chin. The centurion quietly held her head with one hand and with the other wiped away the powerful tears that escaped his will.

No, if he returned to Rome, he would have failed, terribly. And yes, he would have failed somebody - his father. The Jews had to pay for what they did to his father. That was the reason he hadn't returned to Rome after graduation. In the years since, he had lost touch with what remained of his family and friends in Rome for no other reason than this. His decision to stay in Judea had surely changed what he had always thought his future would be: he was not married and had no children; he was not a politician arguing law in Rome; he would never hear his father's words of pride after a successful task; and he didn't even have a mother's loving gaze to nourish his waning confidence. Where did time go, dragging his life along with it? Here he was, living in Caesarea among strangers who either wanted him and his Empire dead or were pandering to him for personal gain. Was he feeling sorry for himself or was it the unresolved guilt over his father's murder in these confusing tears? Or was it merely release from Elisa's touch? His breath caught in his throat.

"I am sorry, Cornelius. Is it something I said?"

He smiled. "I haven't felt this comfortable since long before my father's passing. I am happy to be here now with you."

She kissed his lower lip then pulled back a bit, wiping his cheek with her thumb.

"I cannot return to Rome, Elisa. If I do, I will have failed myself. Even if the military retires me, I will stay."

Her heart danced within her ribs. This was the dedication she wanted to inspire in him. His revenge was surely his first weakness. She was obviously a close second. Well and good!

"Is there no chance to recover your projects? Couldn't you take things into your own hands, independent of the agency?" she asked, sounding innocent.

"That would be treason to Caesar!"

She thoughtfully continued, staying calm, "Surely the real treason would be to Rome. Such careless retirement of patriotic military leaders...risking the security of the Empire by discarding projects carefully nurtured for so many years...forgive me, Cornelius, but I fail to see who is best served, Rome or Caesar. I have tried, but I have never seen how they are one and the same."

He didn't answer.

She cautiously ventured further, touching his face with admiration, "A man like you should fear no one. You have all the support of the people around you, you know." She paused, as if to think then said, "Cornelius! What if you were to recover Paulus from Arabia. Why not bring him to Tyre?" Her words managed a gentle conviction.

Impressed by her knowledge... and softened by his emotions... he could think of no reason to hide secrets from her if Marih had already entrusted her with such information. After all, this wasn't official Roman business anymore. Though tempted by her reason, he held onto a little good sense by resisting a quick decision. "I'm not sure it's the best way..."

She feigned a gentle sigh. "Otherwise, I suppose I will have to go live in Arabia so Paulus can be close to his daughter. I cannot take her completely away from him."

"You? Go to Arabia?"

"Or to Rome, should they retire Paulus to Rome."

"No... I am staying here, and I want you to stay with me. Let me talk to Marih about Paulus."

"Then we stay... and I am yours. It won't be easy. We will have to be discreet and I must stay in Tyre with my parents for now, for Claudia's sake." She traced his jawline with her fingertips and smiled.

Everything about her became more attractive with this settled between them. Could he be any more in love?

Twenty

Rising Star Falls Again

Two days after Cornelius and Elisa assured one another they would stay in Judea, Marih arrived from Joppa with the promised Cephas. A festive welcome, well-rehearsed, brought all of Cornelius' house-staff, along with Marih's, to the gate. Despite such an impressive gathering, Elisa remained apart, just another one of the guests, quietly fading in the mix.

"Please stand, I beg you." Cephas came quickly to Cornelius and helped him up. "I am only a man." Seeing Cornelius kneel brought immediate relief to Cephas. The centurion was already on his side. All the worry, all the paranoia, and the sleepless nights faded away with the dust left behind on the road. He must learn to stop worrying so much. If the beginning of this adventure was to start like this, surely the mission would be easier than he imagined, and possibly a pleasant one.

The entire crowd, family and friends were there. How did they learn about the Nazarene's message? *And why me?* Cephas wondered. One would have thought they would send after someone from the congregation in Jerusalem. Of course, the brothers in the congregation would probably not want to mix with the gentiles, which is something to point out to Cornelius and his family. Little can gain people's trust as easily as a gesture or a favour.

"You know, to be as we are now here together is forbidden among observant Jews. To mix with peoples of other races by visiting their homes or breaking bread is anathema to them. But God has made it clear to me that I must not call anyone unclean, no matter who they are or what they have done," Cephas said with an odd mix of humility and pride. "That's why I come to you with ease." He walked with Cornelius, hand in hand, to the visitors' chamber.

"I am honoured to have you in my house. I thank you for coming such a long distance, a most tiring trip," Cornelius welcomed.

"It is one of our ways, to serve whenever asked. But let us speak plainly, my brother; exactly why have you sent for me?"

"What a pleasure to have such honesty between us so early in our friendship!" Cornelius saw that Cephas was seated comfortably and that his servants would tend to his comfort after his journey. He began, "It was about this time of day... oh, many days ago... I was alone in my house when I suddenly saw a man in shining robes, a shimmer in front of me. He said, 'Cornelius, your prayers have been heard and your charitable deeds have not gone unnoticed by God. You must send to Joppa and fetch Cephas, the head of the Nazarenes.' And so I did."

The head of the Nazarenes? Cephas raised his shoulders and puffed his chest like a peacock. He was the head of the Nazarenes? Well, if the Spirit says so... maybe this whole time the Spirit had been protecting him, planning his path. If only the brothers in Jerusalem would hear of this, those people who had been calling him coward, when it seemed everything had been the Spirit's plan all along. It wasn't his fault. Surely he needed to be protected after Yeshua's death so that he could lead the congregation when the time was right.

"You are most kind to visit us," Cornelius interrupted Cephas' thoughts. "Here we all are, to be assembled before you at your leisure after your long journey, to hear everything the Lord has told you so that we may follow him, too."

"Now I truly understand... God has no favourites... anyone of any race or nationality... anyone who loves Him and does what is right in His eyes is acceptable to Him." Cephas looked around at his gathering flock, fishing for some sign of recognition that he was getting through to them. Several smiles were encouragement enough.

"You no doubt already know what happened all over Judea, how Yeshua the Nazarene went about doing good and curing the sick and aiding any who had fallen under the power of the devil." He was warming to this! How rewarding to find ears that can hear... at last! No hecklers, no doubters, no one interrupting. They were as receptive as empty pots. He went on preaching and teaching, "They killed Yeshua by hanging him on their tree of shame, and even now my brothers and I remain under their constant."

"Dear brother," Cornelius spoke, "You are to be afraid of them no more. My men and I will protect you from all threats. I want you to feel that my house is your house and, in fact, I would like to invite you and your friends to stay over for a week to teach us your way."

With covert pride barely masked by his overpowering enthusiasm, Cephas spoke to his Jewish company, "Could anyone refuse the water of baptism to these people, now that they have been visited by the Holy Spirit?" He then asked for water to be brought to the room; he prayed over it, asking blessings, and baptized the crowd, one by one, in an exhilarating ceremony.

. . .

A little more than a week later, as Cephas and his friends were departing, Cornelius sent along two of his Roman soldiers to guard them. He ordered the soldiers to act as private guards and remain vigilant at all times so that Cephas would have full protection when in the city of Jerusalem.

Soon after they left, Cornelius and Marih met to speak about Paulus and Barnabas. Not surprisingly, Marih instantly agreed to Cornelius' plan to recover them from Arabia and bring them to Caesarea, so they could secretly spend some time there when Cephas returned from Jerusalem. Marih was impressed by his sister's cunning, following through with her promises beyond his expectations. He knew it had to be her influence behind Cornelius, but why hadn't she told him about it when they met? Maybe she wasn't sure of the results; it was in her nature to under-promise and over-deliver.

The two centurions wasted no time. They sent a messenger to Arabia and summoned Barnabas and Paulus to Caesarea.

The exiled spies were ecstatic to be summoned back to Caesarea. Life in Arabia was not nearly as luxurious as the simplest of Roman amenities. However, as soon as they arrived at Caesarea, it became obvious to Marih and Cornelius that having these two particular spies in the same place at the same time was a risky plan. If one of them was exposed, the other would soon fall with him, and the resulting losses would be too great a blow to the agency. After much deliberation and debate – including masterfully veiled attempts by Marih to sway the planning in favour of the Aleph elites' needs – Barnabas was kept at a safe house in Caesarea while Paulus was sent into similar protection on the peripheries of Tyre. Elisa had already returned to Tyre with Claudia, so sending Paulus nearby was a simple task.

Cephas was invited periodically to teach Barnabas, who was presented as a Jewish admirer of the Nazarenes, followed by a slow introduction to the congregation in Jerusalem. Accepted without suspicions, Barnabas was soon put to work on minor missions aimed at spreading the word of the Nazarenes and attracting as many Jews as possible. The congregation welcomed their Hebrew brethren, hoping to heal the rift; Barnabas' angle was to further widen it. The congregation wondered at his devotion to this risky undertaking, unaware of the covert protection by the Romans.

The situation was not so easy with Paulus. His reputation of extremism against the Nazarenes was still a raw nerve with them. In a more cautious approach, Cephas was sent to Tyre many times to communicate to him the teachings of Yeshua and the way of the Nazarenes. For all their professing of forgiveness of sins, his infamous acts hung about him like a shroud, and Cephas asserted Paulus was better off not visiting the narrow-minded congregation in Jerusalem.

. . .

After a couple of years of frustrations, the centurions spurred an alternate plan to better showcase the exquisite talents and skills of Paulus. In light of the growing political influence and financial power of the Jewish communities in Phoenicia, Asia Minor, and

Europa, they decided to direct Paulus' focus into these geographic areas. Weakening of the Jewish communities outside Judea was essential to limit the support they funneled back into the temple, for the wealth of Jerusalem relied heavily on the aid steadily streaming in from those living abroad. In Rome itself they influenced the decisions of Roman politicians who covertly sought the backing of large minorities of Jewish citizens of Rome and Greece.

The first attempt at launching Paulus back into action backfired, and with dire results. They thought the best place for him to start would be Damascus. After all, in Damascus the people had heard about the miracle visited upon this young Jewish fellow, how he had been persecuting the Nazarenes until their Lord Yeshua spoke to him on the road to Damascus and blinded him. Many of the Nazarenes in Damascus had that day witnessed Anania's blessing, restoring his vision.

They overshot their estimations of good will. At best, only some of the Nazarene brethren were neutral to Paulus and those only after being pressed by messengers from Cephas; the majority had something else in mind for him.

The Damascus Nazarenes had always assumed that Anania never came back to Damascus because he stayed with Paulus and Barnabas in Arabia. The Nazarenes in Arabia, like the famous Yohana the Baptizer, were known ascetics living in the wilderness away from the sins of the world. One of these ascetics broke with the desert sect, choosing life in Damascus. Welcomed into the more worldly congregation, they learned the truth about Anania. He told them Anania had left Arabia immediately after delivering Barnabas and Paulus with one attendant who was an outsider to them. A scant amount of speculation revealed but one explanation for Anania's disappearance: Paulus the persecutor must have had a hand in it.

The rage against Paulus surfaced quickly. Jews and Nazarenes alike united against this man of many faces. Instead of the expected friendship in both communities, Paulus had been summarily rejected.

Immediately recognizing the huge risk to their man, the agency's agents in Damascus implemented their contingency plan to smuggle him out of the city and back to his hideout in Tyre. According to plans, the very next evening, under the cover of a moonless night, they lowered Paulus in a basket over the city walls and southwest to Tyre in great haste.

And so, once again, their man with the highest potential, the agency's largest single investment, and the possessor of recommendations from Seneca himself failed to produce. Perhaps it was time to stop investing in him. Was his estimated value based solely on his cleverness admired by his mentors so many years ago? Cornelius was at loss. They were operating in the dark, with Seneca still in exile. Had he been on the scene, the agency would have better primed Damascus for Paulus and avoided this costly failure.

Standing right next to Cornelius when the news was received, Marih knew the Aleph elite had not quite given up on Paulus. Theirs was a culture accustomed to biding their time, waiting for decades or, if necessary, centuries. They had no reason to relinquish their investment in Paulus as long as he was alive. Following this *modus operandi*, Marih and Elisa leveraged the situation with Claudia, managing to convince Cornelius one more time to put a hold on expelling Paulus until further opportunities presented themselves.

Not fully convinced, Cornelius conditioned his acceptance on an attempt at reusing Paulus in Jerusalem. In furthering this angle, they saw to it that the word was spread: this Saul, though still under doubt, was actually being persecuted in Damascus for spreading the word of the Nazarenes. Cephas didn't question this information as it came from his friend and secret protector, Cornelius. So when questioned, Cephas told his congregation he had put all his doubts aside and, in the manner of the Lord, he tended to trust Saul.

Gradually, Paulus, or Saul as the Jews and Nazarenes knew him, met with the members of the Jerusalem congregation. It was difficult to gauge their true feelings let alone their level of approval of this known persecutor of questionable redemption. After all, everybody knew he was a Jew who came from Tarsus and had a Roman citizenship.

That Roman citizenship was what made it very difficult for the Jews to openly endanger him. The life of the Jews in Roman-occupied Jerusalem was tenuous at best, making them suspect everyone and trust no one. A Jew and a convert to the Nazarene ways, maybe. But an ex-Roman... never! The fear never dissipated and made Cornelius' work all the more sensitive.

Saul, in turn, didn't make it any easier for the congregation to accept him. He seemed to have a need to preach the necessity for the sect to be open for the gentiles. Unlike Cephas, Paulus always confronted the congregation with this particular tenet for their new faith. Cephas typically remained quiet.

Just as the centurions began to relax, believing their 'Paulus Project' was taking root, circumstances took a turn unforeseen by any of their contingency plans: Emperor Gaius was assassinated.

Once again, all levels of Roman administration were temporarily paralyzed. The military factions stationed weeks and months away from their lifelines to Rome suffered most. The agency's already tenuous existence became explosive. Informants reported to Cornelius there was now an even higher risk on Paulus' life as Jewish activists asserted their bravery during such times of transition.

As a result, Paulus was ordered to temporarily disappear from the picture. With the dissemination of the Nazarenes among the people of southern Phoenicia, it was no longer safe for him to hide in Tyre. Cornelius suggested Rome. Paulus preferred Marih's suggestion of Tarsus. Paulus had family in Tarsus; perhaps he could work in his family textile business, thereby hiding in plain sight. Also, Tarsus was close enough to Tyre for Elisa to bring Claudia to visit whenever possible. *Let him think it's all his idea*, Marih thought to himself, as he once again guided Paulus and the agency according to the will of the Aleph Lodge.

Twenty One

Making Sense of Human Sense

The ancients among the ancients knew one thing for certain: nothing is more predictable than change. Change is the very definition of life; without change, there is no life. In the paradox of any truly worthy philosophy, in this way change is like death: both are inevitable.

Flowing along with these inescapable changes, Elisa's world view underwent its share of adjustments. Surely, many factors must have played a role, but for her one of them was the most prevalent, the champion of factors, the fork in her destiny, the reason for wakeful nights, and for the inexplicably sweet trances. Love. Magi and scholars could spend forever discussing it; struggle against it as she might, she was just stuck with it.

For years she and Cornelius had been together, yet apart. In some ways it kept their romance fresh. In others it was sweet torture. She managed to hide her urges, asserting her formidable control, while beneath it all her inner woman longed for it. She was done with the trysts by moonlight, the stolen moments when they could divert the attentions of everyone so constantly around them. Wonderful in the beginning, now she wanted more.

She wanted to experience submission to her lover's power, the complete surrender in his arms. She clung to the hope that one day she would be privileged to wake up in the morning next to Cornelius, no longer hiding her feelings from the world. It kept her going. Her memory never lost track of the instant allure she felt for the handsome young man who came to be billeted in her parents' house many years ago. If the gods truly created souls in twos and put them on earth just to watch them cross each other's paths, then surely they also created the hell of the convoluted maze some tortured souls had to endure for the gods' added amusement.

Why, out of all people, did she have to fall in love with this man, a Roman? Or maybe that wasn't the right question. Instead, maybe, why, out of all people, did she have to be a royal subject of the Aleph Lodge? Without that obligation, her life in Caesarea with Cornelius could be just about right.

She told herself she was lucky in so many other ways. For little could offer more reward right now than watching the emergence of her little sister, an intelligent young woman of striking beauty and promise. Elisa frequently saw herself in Claudia Achte and she hugged herself with pride. Eliza had been continuously influenced – to the point that she came to believe her thoughts were her own– taught by her family, the lodge, the priests of Melqart as they created in her a soldier for the cause. In the process they left a damaged woman, ashamed of yielding to normal human emotions and unaware of her deprivation of the most basic, instinctive rights. So well trained was she that she unwittingly played her part in applying the same processes on Claudia. And, as so often happens with each brilliant generation, Elisa added her own flair to the dysfunction.

If life had anything to offer Elisa's personal desires, it had to be now. The winds of time blew this sea in only one direction and no sailor had ever returned. She wasn't getting any younger; every one of Achte's milestones of growth drove the point home. By Elisa's selfish calculations, the Aleph Lodge's singular revenge needn't be sidetracked just because of her bond to one Roman.

Elisa needed validation. Love made her thought processes plausible yet unreliable, and she knew it. The one being who could possibly understand was her brother and best friend. *Marih knows what it's like to love to desperation*, she thought, remembering his impetuous marriage to Ishtar. Elisa left Claudia in Tyre and headed light to Caesarea.

. . .

"I'm here with a thorny matter, dear brother," she said to a pale and cheerless Marih. It wasn't like him to be so glum, and he couldn't have read her thoughts... so what was with this mood?

"What matter brings you here without notice, my dear?"

"A dire one. I need your help."

"Elisa, speak up, sister! What happened? What's the matter?"

"I am in love."

Marih took a couple of steps backwards. With his eyes half shut, he took a deep breath. "Why, that's the best news I've heard today. You almost scared my soul away, sister."

"Not so fast... I am in love with Cornelius."

The way Marih's face froze would have been hilarious under any other circumstances. This face frightened Elisa. "Oh, by all the saints of Melqart, say something!"

He just stood there, stunned. He never expected to hear these words escape Elisa's tongue. Love, yes, but Cornelius? He shouldn't be so surprised, really. Deep inside, he always knew it; he had just let himself deny it for expediency's sake. *No more room for denial; she has laid it out as clearly as the summer sun.*

"Call me a traitor! Call me a failure! Say something!" Her anxiety dissolved into tears.

Betrayed by his brotherly love, Marih opened his arms and held her close as she sobbed out what remained of her self control. This was a side of his sister he had never seen. Surprised by his emotions, he took a swipe at his own tears, hoping she wouldn't notice.

"I didn't mean to... it was never my intention... all my training... I am human, you know." Her words came in a flood between childlike hiccups. "I am no goddess... I deserve... to have a normal life. I can still be loyal, to Melqart and to Tyre and the lodge. I can do that .. and yet be with him, you know."

Marih stroked her hair to calm her down. "Don't fret so. I am here for you, dearest sister."

She pulled back a bit, searching his face. "So, will you support me if I live with him? Will you help me convince the Mother Lodge?"

"I would if I could."

That didn't sound too promising. "So, you... couldn't?"

"It's not what you think, Elisa. We received orders today."

"Orders? What orders? From the lodge?" she wondered why he brought up orders at a time like this.

"Orders from the new emperor, Claudius."

"Ah."

"He wants to leave Judea in the hands of his friend: King Agrippa and his mercenaries. The Roman army is to withdraw."

She stared into her brother's eyes, only now with horror. Even her speedy mind was having trouble keeping up with all the repercussions this news brought to every aspect of her life.

"I am to move to the Tyre camp. Cornelius..." Marih choked at the words, now for Elisa's sake. "Elisa, he has been summoned to Rome."

Her knees buckled and she collapsed to the floor like an autumn leaf.

. . .

The orders hit what was left of the agency and its staff like a lightning bolt. Worse for Cornelius was the jab the news took at his heart. All those years spent conspiring on his own behalf through the guise of the agency would be wasted if he stopped now. The Jews would win again. They took his father's life and now it felt like they were taking a part of his.

As if this was not enough, he was summoned to Rome, away from Elisa. Would she come with him? What if she wouldn't? He couldn't imagine life now without her. She was there whenever he closed his eyes, in his dreams and thoughts. He expected her when any visitor knocked at his doors, whenever a female voice reached his ears, or when Marih was out of town. A stray thought crossed his mind: Is it even possible to meet someone so perfect twice in a lifetime?

Stress just kept piling itself higher and higher all around him. What of the consequences of shutting down the major covert agency projects like Paulus and Barnabas? Surely this was the end of the line for them, abandoned and left to handle their lives midway, as if they had never been parts of some pivotal political intrigue. He couldn't help but wonder, *Does this new Emperor Claudius even begin to realize all the repercussions of his decisions?*

Marih and the Aleph Lodges, however, were seriously scorched by the shutdown of these agency projects. They had achieved profound access and completely permeated the agency. To lose Paulus and Barnabas and similar agents so brilliantly nurtured against their knowledge was more than a mere setback.

In the midst of the emotional chaos, a band of soldiers arrived at Cornelius' compound. One of the soldiers perfunctorily delivered his orders: "Greetings, sir, from Emperor Claudius. We have been commissioned to accompany you to Rome without delay. We must leave immediately."

"Are you at liberty to discuss the reason, soldier?" Cornelius asked professionally, hiding his worries.

"We were given to understand you have gained a favourable position in the eyes of the emperor, sir."

Cornelius immediately assumed an air befitting his impending elevation of status. "Do we have time to stop by Tyre?" Cornelius wanted to see Elisa, talk to her and make plans for the future. He didn't know she was already in Caesarea with Marih.

"Sir, I am afraid our orders are to return by the ship which brought us. We are to take the fastest route back to Rome, through Cyprus."

Cornelius was left no room to maneuver. Even when orders were favourable, the emperor expected them to be executed without question. Cornelius couldn't just leave like this, though. He had years of contacts and responsibilities. He should at least get in touch with Marih, his closest friend, not to mention military peer and agency co-operative. With so little time to gather his necessary belongings, he ordered one of his men to carry a message to Marih: "Tell him I had to leave for Rome on urgent orders. I will be in touch with him as soon as I can. Tell him to pass my regards to his sister, and the family."

Twenty Two

A Friend of a Friend

It had been close to fifteen years since Cornelius left Rome. The city had changed considerably. New buildings and monuments were everywhere. To say he was impressed would be an understatement. It seemed people had been busy making children, too. Either that or a massive influx of people from all over the Empire... most likely, both... for Rome was getting crowded. It did feel good to be back home. And yet, a part of him felt like a visitor, and a temporary visitor at that, one who had left his real life behind, somewhere between Caesarea and Tyre.

Soon after he recovered from the exhausting sea voyage, he was brought to meet the emperor.

"A friend of my friend is my friend," Emperor Claudius stated.

"I am but Caesar's subject," Cornelius respectfully replied with a formal salute and bow.

"I am told that you have been an excellent military man, skilled with diplomacy, and you managed to keep the peace through the most difficult of times in Judea."

He was told? By whom? Seneca? Was Seneca here? Or was it just a general recommendation from the agency? Not missing a beat, he replied, "Most kind of you to say so, Great Caesar. I am but a student of your military. All credit goes to my teachers."

"Your teachers!" Claudius smiled. "Perhaps... However, I trust you because of the advice of this man." Claudius pointed at the door behind Cornelius.

Cornelius couldn't wait to see Seneca again. He had so much to tell him, so much to discuss with him. Their work hadn't been completed and Seneca was the man to make it happen. He turned halfway, never completely turning his back to Caesar. An old man stood there, a shadow in the shadows. Cornelius peered at the shadow stepping forward, a massive smile on his face, arms extended.

He recognized the face he hadn't seen for a long time, a very long time. Simaan Ben Aaron, the man who murdered his father, approached with the dignified stiffness of old age and a chillingly eager grin that reeked of deceit.

He wanted to push him away with both hands. Better yet, punch him in the face, then kick the life out of what remained of this walking corpse. At least that was the scenario quickly unfolding in his vengeful mind.

Should he tell Caesar who this man really was? What better time to make him pay for that horrific deed all those years ago than right here, right now, with Caesar as his ultimate witness! But would Caesar believe him? And even if he did, what would he do to Ben Aaron? Drawing on his innermost discipline, Cornelius denied this one compulsive moment the opportunity to steal away his well-nursed, beautifully meditated, carefully calculated, delectable punishment for the venomous old snake.

Cornelius stuffed all his own venom away and embraced the old man, fingertips carefully curved away into the air as if not wanting to touch the slime on the serpent's back.

"It is about time you returned to us, my son!" Ben Aaron said. "What took you so long?"

Right. Well, that loving fatherly tone wasn't working on Cornelius. "The call of duty, old man," Cornelius forced a smile; any of his close friends would have caught the ruse immediately. Lucky for him, Caesar didn't know what his sincere smile looked like.

"Rome needs loyal people like you. Caesar needs loyal people like you." Ben Aaron held Cornelius at the elbows and pushed him far enough away to study his face without letting go of him. "Caesar wants you here in Rome, among his people."

"An assignment I take with great honour." Cornelius accepted his immediate fate without revealing his guile.

. . .

In the next few weeks, Cornelius heard from Ben Aaron many times how he had influenced Caesar to bring him to his court and have him among the Praetorian Guard – specifically, among his personal protection team. Ben Aaron puffed himself up like a peacock. "I owe no less to your late father... he would have loved to see you here in such a position of honour and trust."

The shrillness of this man's voice mentioning his father grated in Cornelius' ears. To not squeeze Ben Aaron's neck and enjoy his last futile gasp for air nearly took his last bit of self-control, but to listen to this idle banter about his father was simply too much. He dug his nails into the palm of his hand to distract himself. He wondered why he had really been brought back to Rome. Maybe some of the secrets of the agency's covert operations had leaked to the Jews in Jerusalem and then in Rome. Maybe Ben Aaron had been asked to intervene.

That was one option. Too many what-ifs, though. He had time to reason this out; no need to be rash. He would keep on the alert for other parts of the puzzle to fall into place.

So it came around in the due course of events. Cornelius learned that Claudius Caesar was a close friend to King Herod Agrippa of Judea. His friendship with the Jewish king was the reason he granted him control over Judea and ordered the Roman army to withdraw. If Claudius thought the Jews would cease their agitating just because the Roman army departed, he was dead wrong. Cornelius' years in Judea had given him great insight into its politics; he knew very well that the Jewish extremists would now be emboldened to express their greedy aching for autonomy. They didn't really consider Agrippa to be a worthy representative of the Hebrew people, let alone their true king, and they would exhaust themselves in every effort to topple his rule... and Rome's chokehold on Judea.

The question closer at hand was how much Claudius knew. For

example, did he know full well Simaan Ben Aaron was actually a Jewish conspirator, playing both sides against the middle, and even so took his counsel? Or was he listening to him merely in an attempt to pacify the Jews throughout the Empire, especially in Jerusalem?

Everything became more complicated when Cornelius learned Seneca had been exiled from Rome, sent to Corsica following some plot accusing him of engaging in adultery. Cornelius knew Seneca all too well to believe any of it to be true. *The Jews must be behind this*, he thought. In some ways, it was all starting to make sense. Of course they had the army withdrawn, pulling Cornelius and other agency managers back to Rome, thereby abandoning agents in the field. Banishing Seneca sealed the deal. Yes, it was clearly a Jewish plan.

Cornelius sat back, angrily assured by his most recent reasoning. In his books, the Jews were winning.

Like a stranger lost in a foreign land, Cornelius felt he had no trustworthy advisors. Marih was far away, Seneca too, and all his agents had either been let go or had their projects shut down. However, the idea of just surrendering to these circumstances was not an option with this self-reliant militant. He was used to getting things done his way.

While carrying on day after day with his regular duties and acting as if nothing was wrong, in his mind Cornelius considered scenarios and made careful plans for each. With no one to help him test his theories, he eventually ran out of viable options.

One crazy idea kept dominating his thoughts: what if he worked on bringing another Caesar, a Caesar of his choice, to power? One who was not controlled by the insidious Jews? He was getting that desperate. But how could he do it? The idea wasn't completely realistic, mostly because of his proximity to Caesar and Caesar's court. Just because he had the guts to think about such treason didn't mean it was viable. Besides, the risks in it were beyond measure. Still, treason only carries a death sentence if the plot fails.

He was going mad. He had to think of something else...

One evening, drowning himself as usual in nonstop pondering, Cornelius jolted upright in his seat as if cold water had just been thrown on him. That's it! How did he not think of it before? Antonius!

His teacher and patriot soldier from Damascus... he was his father's true friend. Antonius had recently retired to Rome, before the recall of all the legions. He had to find him, immediately.

. . .

Finding Antonius was an easy matter. Cornelius had the resources of Rome's society at his disposal and they were soon reunited. As if resuming a conversation only recently begun, they jumped right into stories and tales that brought each other up to date. Aided by the comfort of Antonius' family and trusted household attendants, Cornelius felt safe to vent all the thoughts that had been boiling up inside. Caesar's palace was no place for this kind of talk. Not unless you had already poisoned Caesar's food.

Antonius was completely aware of Seneca's situation. The surprise to him was the fact that Paulus and the other agents were shut down mid-project. "Cornelius, my son, politics change every day. But agents are the core of continuous projects, all for the glory of Rome. They should never be shut down."

"But we seemed to be thwarted at every turn. Working with Paulus just never led us anywhere. Forgive me, Antonius, for I know your feelings for him, but he's... he's just that young prodigy who dazzles the world with early promise and then never achieves anything as an adult!" Cornelius' frustration was loud and clear.

"No, no. I know Paulus. I know him, Cornelius. If he hasn't achieved his goals it is because the agency has failed him. This man is an asset."

"Antonius, dear father, trust me when I tell you we tried everything with him. Even with Seneca's best-laid strategies, there was nothing more we could do."

"So where is Barnabas now?" Antonius sat forward, sensing he could help and ready to leap into action.

"I left him in Judea. We informed him that all missions were henceforth cancelled, but he decided to stay there as he had nowhere else to go."

"Has Paulus' cover been compromised at any time?"

"No, not really. It hadn't at the time I left him, anyway. He might have decided to strike out on his own now that he doesn't work with the agency anymore." Some doubt had crept into Cornelius' voice.

"Nonsense. Paulus would never do that."

"What makes you so sure? We officially informed him he was no longer employed."

"Cornelius, listen to me carefully: in order to judge a man you have to learn to think like that man. Consider yourself – you have spent years dedicating your life to your causes. What did you do when everything was taken away from you and you were brought back to Rome?"

Cornelius started to see where Antonius was going.

"Did you give up? No, you did not. You planned and plotted and then you sought me out." Despite all his years, Antonius' inner passion for teaching hadn't faded. "If you didn't want to give up your undercover life, what makes you think Paulus... who gave away his life and daughter and good name for his career... would just surrender to these few hurdles that now challenge the agency's projects? Remember this if you remember nothing else: Caesars come and go, but the Roman Empire abides."

"You mean he is still active?" Cornelius wasn't sure he understood what Antonius was saying. "Should I try to seek him out in Tarsus?"

"No. First we must have a complete and comprehensive plan; consider all contingencies. I need to talk to my friend Seneca. You stay here with my family. I leave for Corsica tomorrow."

Twenty Three

A Message of Aid

When the Romans withdrew from Judea, King Herod Agrippa was under tremendous pressure to prove his power of kingship. The grandson and heir in the most recent Jewish dynasty, like any dutiful son in any family business he had learned several tricks of the trade. Of course, these didn't include transparency and honest transactions with the people for whom he worked. No, he had learned defensive maneuvering aimed at retaining power by any means necessary.

Such rulers who find themselves in these positions – as most do, sooner or later – try to identify and eliminate potential risks before they take hold. Unfortunately for Herod Agrippa, by the time he came to power in Judea, the Jewish religious leaders had already solidified so much power centered in the temple at Jerusalem that simply eliminating them was not possible. Expecting no less, he was ready to implement a no-less-devious plan. He befriended them, gave them whatever they wanted, and allied himself with their allies.

They were ready for him. They never forgot his or his family's history as Roman collaborators, so they used and abused the sins of his past to bully him into getting anything they wanted. Once, to appease them, he ordered the execution of James, one of the leaders of the notorious Nazarenes. When he saw what favour this garnered him among the people, he ordered the imprisonment of a number more.

Cephas had a certain notoriety for his interaction with gentiles like Cornelius and his staff, thereby garnering him permission to openly speak about his Nazarene ways. But the news of the Roman withdrawal fell upon him like a death sentence. Looking to save his skin, he immediately started planning his escape from Judea. Lacking courage and initiative, he fled from house to house, hiding among the Nazarene brothers and sisters. When Agrippa gave orders to imprison him, the houses of the suspected Nazarenes were raided and Cephas was captured, along with many more believers, just for good measure.

Agrippa had no intention to commit mass genocide among his people; he eventually freed the Nazarenes, keeping only the known leaders. Perhaps the unluckiest man on earth, Cephas found himself at the top of the list. King Agrippa played his politics like Greek theatre. In a great show of compassion, he made the most of delaying – possibly staying – Cephas' execution. For the time being, it made more sense to keep him in prison and let the Jews agitate for an execution before giving it to them as a gift. It would be a political spectacle he would milk to the last drop.

. . .

At the same time in Rome, Cornelius had been trying to distract his mind from the unavoidable circumstances in which he found himself. Still waiting at Antonius' home in Rome for news of his visit with Seneca, he had no escape from the frequency of finding himself in Ben Aaron's presence. Otherwise, he found Caesar's inner circle of family members to be very pleasant and intellectual company. To an outsider like Cornelius, they were a delight; not too far beneath the surface was the infamous court intrigue perennially fuelling anarchy for the throne.

Among his new friends were the emperor's wife and his niece, sister of the previous Caesar. This niece had a seven-year-old child named Lucius Domitius, to whom she was completely devoted, and adamant about every aspect of his upbringing. Even at that young age, it was clearly evident that he was more advanced than his peers, possessing a natural intellect and artistic tendencies. Great

Uncle Claudius felt the boy needed an appropriate male influence. He found in Cornelius certain gifts all too often lacking among the military ranks; his level of education, political knowledge, analytical skills, and social charm in general made him a very appealing choice for a friend for young Lucius.

Cornelius was starting to accept his new life at court, his longing for Caesarea and for Elisa slowly abating, when a reminder of his previous life emerged. A messenger escorted by a party of Roman soldiers arrived. "I come to you with a message from Centurion Marih of Tyre. His message is of a most urgent nature." The man spoke shyly, having never stood before someone who was so close to Caesar's inner court.

"My friend Marih? How is he? How is his family?" Cornelius' blood surged at the mention of Marih's family. Elisa's image dominated his thoughts.

"They are all well, sir. They send you their regards."

"I am glad to hear it. And so, what urgent message do you have for me?"

"Centurion Marih wishes me to inform you that an acquaintance of yours, Cephas the Nazarene, has been captured by King Agrippa and may well be facing a death sentence."

"Cephas!" Surprised but cautious, Cornelius collected himself. "So who are you? Do I know you?"

"Sir, we have never met, but we know of each other. I am called Simon the Tanner and I live in Joppa."

"Of course I know who you are. You are Cephas' friend. He was in hiding at your place when our men found him," Cornelius remembered.

Relaxing a bit, Simon offered further familiarity, "You may also remember, sir, they didn't really find him so much as they were guided to him."

Taking the hint, Cornelius drew Simon aside, out of earshot of his escorts. "Absolutely. You are one of Marih's agents. Good work."

The man awaited a signal from Cornelius to continue his message about Cephas.

"So what has Cephas done?" Cornelius asked.

"Befriended you, sir."

"I mean, what did he do to deserve the death sentence?"

The man paused a few seconds, letting the heavy silence do the explaining.

Cornelius was quick to answer his own question. "Ah. I see. He befriended a gentile!"

The man nodded. "After the Roman army withdrew, King Agrippa raided many homes of the Nazarenes and, of course, Cephas was the greatest catch among them." Simon made a gesture that perhaps they should remove themselves further for more privacy.

Cornelius casually escorted him onto a small balcony where both could see anyone approach. He continued, "So what does Marih think? Our business is shut down, why should we care?"

"Marih wants to inform you that many of the Roman agents left behind have felt deserted and abandoned and have been asking for a minimum of attention from the agency. Marih fears all these agents, if carelessly left to their own devices, may turn against the Empire. He asks you to remember, even though they are Roman citizens, they are also Judeans."

"Aha." Cornelius squinted in thought. "With all their covert training and knowledge, they most certainly could cause problems for the Empire."

Simon nodded again. "Marih bids me to tell you that these following words are carefully chosen by him: He fears they will turn their support to the festering quest for Jewish freedom and liberation from Rome." Once he detected the effect of his words on Cornelius' carefully practiced face, he continued, "If Cephas is executed, the Nazarenes might turn against the Empire. Their numbers have grown and they have spread all along the shores of the Great Sea from Judea to Rome."

These last words hit their mark. Cornelius had so much invested through the agency's project he could not turn away. They had increased the number of Nazarenes to a point where they could pit them internally against the Jews. The project served many purposes and many points remained in motion. Closing down the agency didn't make these pivotal machinations just stop cold. Their goal of smoothing the way for Rome in Judea surely was as important now as ever before. He had to do something. King Agrippa was Caesar's friend. Maybe he could ask Caesar for a favour.

. . .

Seeking a favour from Caesar proved easier said than done. Once Cornelius had the chance to think about it, he realized how tough a matter it really was. Caesar would no doubt ask him his reasons for such a favour and what could he say? He couldn't tell him that along with some friends back in Judea he was keeping agency projects running despite orders to the contrary. Maybe he could just say that it was a personal favour for a personal friend. Caesar might understand that but in turn be annoyed by having to interfere in such a small matter. And what if Caesar was simply in a bad mood when he approached him? He wouldn't get a second chance to ask.

The urgency of the matter coupled with his sincere desire to keep Marih's entire family satisfied with his actions – not least of all his eternal longing for Elisa – won out over all Cornelius' second guessing, forcing his decision. He made sure Simon the Tanner was given comfortable lodging until he could secure a reply for him to take back to Tyre.

The very next day, he made sure to spend time accompanying Caesar as he went about his business, awaiting the right moment to talk to him privately. He jumped at the first opportunity. He had to make it count.

"Caesar, if I may bother you a moment, there is a small matter of a personal nature on which I would welcome your counsel. I'm a little embarrassed to talk to you about it," Cornelius began as any familiar courtier might.

"Son, you may always speak to me liberally. Is everything alright? I hope you are happy here with us."

"You and your family have been very generous... most kind to me. I have every reason to feel fortunate to be here. This matter actually concerns a friend of mine, someone I befriended in the years I lived in Caesarea." Cornelius stopped in confusion as he saw Caesar's eyes distracted from his for a moment. Following his gaze, his whole plan evaporated as Simaan Ben Aaron walked in on them unannounced. This was the worst timing!

Caesar cordially saluted Ben Aaron, and Cornelius realized he was cornered. He had to quickly find some way to keep from exposing his nemesis to what he was about to ask of Caesar. The vermin was one of Caesar's trusted counsellors; he could not chance any disapproval of his plan for saving Cephas. What should he do? Hiding his panic, his mind went to work. He surprised himself, remembering the feeling he had while in the lower levels of the temple in Jerusalem, both he and Marih scared of being caught in that unfriendly environment. Eerily enough, Simaan Ben Aaron played a part then as he did now.

That's it! His training to act in a tight spot took over. This was just a matter of thinking like an agent again. He relaxed as he felt control of the situation settle in his hands. The key was to divert the story he had planned into something else, regardless of whether it was convincing or not. What really mattered was his *delivery* of the story. If his presentation was convincing, it would give the matter enough weight, and with the proper attitude, he would create an environment for his audience to readily believe his story. This was one of Seneca's premier techniques with his agents, successfully proving its practicality through their field work.

Gathering Ben Aaron into their discussion, Caesar prompted Cornelius in a fatherly fashion, "My son, you were telling me about your friend in Caesarea. What can I do to help?"

"Yes, yes, of course. My friend was not only a comrade at arms, but I billeted with his family when I first arrived in Tyre and we were in training together in Damascus. So, you see, we are more than casual acquaintances. We had graduated together and advanced together as centurions, and have remained friends all these years. He is stationed now in Tyre and has sent a messenger to me carrying his regards and asking if I might come to visit him and his family."

"Is that all? You merely wish to ask to take your leave of my court for a visit to your home away from home?" Caesar smiled his encouragement with Ben Aaron listening all along.

"I would not wish to leave Caesar's court for any other reason. However, my duties at the moment make it inconvenient, so perhaps I might send him a gift of appreciation, perhaps a formal letter of acknowledgement from your court's scribe carrying your seal. He and his family will be awed by your generosity and will carry the honour in their hearts and memories forever."

Claudius chuckled with pride, enjoying his young courtier's polished delivery of hidden praises for Caesar in his simple request. "Consider it done, Cornelius. I admire your sense of duty and value towards the military brotherhood. I will gladly fulfill your wish. The fates are with you, my son, as Simaan is going on a visit to Jerusalem. I am sure he will be able to deliver your message."

Simaan smiled and opened his mouth to declare his readiness for service, but was interrupted before he said a word.

"If you will allow me, Great Caesar," Cornelius courteously replied, "With your permission, sir, I could relieve you of such a trivial matter by speaking to the court scribe on your behalf."

He then turned to Ben Aaron, preparing to offer a gesture of good will. "As for your trip to Jerusalem, I assume you will be departing by ship. I hate to have you go out of your way on such a small errand. Just the same, please allow me to send some of my men to attend you. My messenger and his convoy would be honoured to keep you safe until you are well on your way to Jerusalem."

Cornelius had deftly finessed Ben Aaron at his own game. Caesar's blessings sealed the arrangements and gave Cornelius a most welcomed feeling of control, something greatly lacking in his life these days in Rome. Yes, the results were most rewarding, indeed.

. . .

"And what message would you have me inscribe for Caesar's seal and testament?" The scribe was familiar with Cornelius and his role at the Caesar's court and had no reservations regarding his task at hand.

"Start with 'To my dear' and leave a space. I will write my friend's name by my own hand so he knows it is a gift from me."

"That won't be a problem," the writer confirmed.

"Then please write: 'A friend of Caesar's friend is Caesar's friend.'"

The scribe smiled, as he was familiar with the phrase. Claudius had often used it and it was most appropriate to quote him in this manner as an opening salutation.

"Then leave a space for me to add my friend's name again and write: 'is in Caesar's circle.' Oh, and for those spaces, leave me plenty of room both times as my hand is not nearly as fine as yours!"

"Done. I will prepare it as you wish with all the usual flourishes. Oh, and I will affix the official seal at the bottom so all you have to do is fill in the blanks. It will only take me a few moments for your friend's gift to be ready."

Cornelius didn't bother to hide his smirk as the scribe bent over his vellum and began to write. He figured the court scribe would just interpret it as an awkward smile of appreciation. The scribe blotted the vellum and handed it over. Borrowing the pot of ink and a spare quill, Cornelius took the finished letter to an empty table and filled in the blanks. Having been schooled by the same tutors as the scribe, his hand was a near match.

In a moment alone in the offices of the court scribe, feigning other business, Cornelius had added the word 'confidential' in formal Latin lettering to be visible on the outside of the rolled-up scroll. So marked, Marih would put it in the hands of none other than King Agrippa for his eyes only.

With the scroll tucked safely in the mantle of his robes, he left the palace and headed back to Simon the Tanner, his trusted messenger. This seemingly routine greeting from Caesar read:

'To my dear *King Herod Agrippa*, greetings. A friend of Caesar's friend is Caesar's friend. *Cephas the Nazarene* is in Caesar's circle.'

Cornelius had done all he could.

Twenty Four

And the Gates
Opened for the Man in White

Passover was one of the most celebrated holidays in Judea. Jews of the Roman Empire made every effort to travel to Jerusalem well ahead of Passover to celebrate it with their extended families. Simaan Ben Aaron did not widely announce the reason for his trip. Being a closed society, it was easier for Jews to travel by avoiding explanations to the gentiles regarding their holidays. Unlike the Romans, who invited any and all to their pagan festivals, discreet travel etiquette en route to Jerusalem kept the Jews from having to invent reasons for not inviting gentiles to celebrate this peculiarly Hebrew holy day with them.

The Romans were generally accepting of the widely diverse religions of the peoples they attempted to assimilate into the Empire. They didn't pay much attention to the ceremonial lives of the minorities unless they posed a political threat. Some considered Hebrews haughty and self-serving; they merely took advantage of this freedom of belief as part of their societal approach to Roman occupation.

Marih and his fellow Phoenicians were, in contrast, very aware of their Jewish neighbours' traditions. So when the convoy reached Tyre and Marih received Cornelius' "confidential" scroll from Simon, he quickly formed his plan to deliver the scroll to King Agrippa. He insisted Simaan Ben Aaron accept his hospitality and stay over with the promise that he would escort him the following day to King Agrippa carrying Caesar's Passover greetings.

Marih never passed up a chance to stir up a little trouble. Aware that Ben Aaron was a close confidant of the Jewish religious leaders – so confirmed by seeing him in the temple's back rooms during that graduation mission so long ago – Marih made sure that Ben Aaron knew about the release of Cephas firsthand so that he might relay the story to the Jews. It was probable that King Agrippa was going to smuggle Cephas out of prison and lie to the people, telling them he was executed or had escaped. Marih wanted to make sure the Jews knew that Cephas had not been executed. He wanted them to rage against Herod Agrippa – that Roman puppet!

Before he left for Caesarea with Ben Aaron, Marih slyly plotted with his man, Simon the Tanner. By having Ben Aaron stay an extra day, Simon the Tanner had time to head straight to a Nazarene safe house in Caesarea. While Marih and Ben Aaron made their way to the King's palace, Simon could prepare the unsuspecting Nazarenes for the next step in the scenario.

The Nazarenes had no idea Simon was Marih's man. He told them Marih, the Roman centurion, was a friend of Cephas and was in town briefly visiting the king with a convoy of dignitaries en route to Jerusalem. He then suggested a group of them quietly wait for Marih's convoy outside of town when they departed for Jerusalem. Their purpose was to appear as though they were coming to see Marih and introduce themselves before respectfully asking Marih to pull some strings in order to save Cephas' neck.

While Simon was taking care of his part of the plan, Marih was completing his revised actions. In his original scheme, Marih had hoped Ben Aaron would become alerted at the palace of plans for Cephas' release. Court protocol interfered. Instead of sharing the contents of the scroll in front of Ben Aaron, Marih ended up delivering the scroll to the king without Ben Aaron noticing a thing. Disappointed with these results, Marih hoped that the backup plan that Simon was setting up would work better.

The trip remained uneventful for Ben Aaron until the group of Nazarenes interrupted them on the road. Their intentions were at first unclear, and the company of Roman soldiers did not make Ben Aaron feel safe. If anything, he felt more anxious. After all, the Romans had withdrawn their forces from the area, possibly making some Jews dangerously brave. What if their intention was to slaughter the Roman soldiers?

It was a relief for him to hear their plea.

One of them addressed Marih: "Sir, we have heard that our brother Cephas has been sentenced to die in the next few days. He is to be killed right after Passover."

"Isn't he with King Agrippa?" Marih pretended sincerity.

"Yes, he is. King Agrippa might have mercy on him if you put in a good word for Cephas. He will surely value a centurion's word," the spokesperson pleaded while the others humbly stood by.

"King Agrippa is just..." Marih began.

"We are confident he is, but justice might not be an option for him." The Nazarene brother's anxiety overrode his customary decorum. "His decision will be political to keep the people from raging against him."

Making allowances, Marih dismissed them. "Gentlemen, I can promise you that I will do everything in my power upon my return. I urge you to calm down and offer your prayers for Cephas. Now you must let us be on our way. We have a long trip and time is short. The sooner we go, the sooner I can return to speak with the king." Marih enjoyed the whole act. He made a mental note to commend Simon the Tanner. He was such a valuable Aleph agent, always ready to lend his special hand.

. . .

"If your duties require you to return to Caesarea, please don't feel obliged to accompany me," Simaan Ben Aaron offered politely.

"I really am quite at my leisure, sir!" Marih replied.

A moment of companionable silence passed between the travellers before Ben Aaron casually asked, "Who's this Cephas everybody is talking about?"

"He is one of the heads of the Nazarenes. King Agrippa has been persecuting them." Marih kept his answer brief, as if the topic were of no importance, thereby nourishing Ben Aaron's curiosity.

"So you won't really help the Nazarene?"

Marih looked at Ben Aaron with the arrogant smile of an overconfident Roman military man of a rank. "I was in King Agrippa's presence yesterday when he discussed with his advisors his intention to let that Nazarene man go."

"Oh, so he's not persecuting him after all?"

Yes! Marih thought to himself. He had Ben Aaron's attention. "This is highly confidential information. I trust you understand the magnitude of it. A discussion at the King's palace cannot be divulged to anyone. Diplomacy and privilege are involved. I know you must be accustomed to such behaviour from being at Caesar's court."

"You can trust me, son. I never heard a thing!" And he let the subject drop, cool as could be.

Marih expected quite the opposite. He counted on their conversation being repeated in the backrooms of the temple, with Ben Aaron telling the head priest about Agrippa's plan to betray the Jews by releasing this so-called head of the Nazarenes.

He wished he could be in that hiding place again, overhearing his conversations. Better yet, to have Cornelius there listening with him. Marih caught himself just before a joyous chuckle escaped and quickly saved himself, "We are but servants of our circumstances. We must laugh at our captivity or have it laugh at us."

Ben Aaron nodded his agreement.

. . .

On the night before the assigned court was set to perform their mock hearing for Cephas, King Agrippa's men acted on what they assumed were direct orders from Caesar. They drugged the wine sent to the prison guards with their evening meal. One of the men casually walked into Cephas' cell, unchained him, and walked him out of the jail right into the city streets. When they were in a safe place, he ordered Cephas to disappear for a while or, better still, leave the city altogether.

"If you are ever caught again, the king will execute you. Don't waste this chance," the stranger said to Cephas.

After having to deal with accepting the terrible destiny that awaited him – execution – Cephas thought that the happenings were the product of his imagination. He must have been hallucinating. Was he still a dead man walking? Was this a sort of a game the king played for his amusement? This family was infamous for such actions. Yohana the Baptizer had been beheaded during one of their parties, his head presented on a plate as a gift to his seductive step-daughter.

These thoughts weren't doing him any favours. First things first: he must run and hide at his friend's house. Cephas being himself, fear for his own life overruled any fears he should have for his friends. He didn't give their safety a second thought as he followed the shadows to the safe house.

How did this cowardly man spin such fantastic tales? Before dawn could come, Cephas' story to his Nazarene brothers and sisters was of an angel visiting him and miraculously helping him escape. Well, and why not? They believed all his other stories – like his vision about eating the forbidden flesh of certain animals, which led to the acceptance of Cornelius and other gentiles into the then predominantly Hebrew sect.

. . .

As word of Cephas' escape spread, Simaan Ben Aaron paced the priests' room in the Temple of Jerusalem. The high priest, cleaning the holiest ceremonial items in preparation for Passover, listened carefully to Ben Aaron's unique account. Very few people had his resources; his information came from first-hand encounters within the palaces of kings and Caesars.

"We cannot accept such an act!" the priest bellowed in the safety of his chamber. "If the king shows any leniency with the Nazarenes today, they will be bringing gentiles to the temple tomorrow!"

"Rabbi, King Agrippa has clearly shown his hatred of the Nazarenes. He has persecuted them and executed several of their leaders. His action towards Cephas can only be attributed to a plot of a kind. We have to trust him." Ben Aaron attempted to defend King Agrippa's actions. "Believe me, this is the same man who kicked the Romans out of Judea by way of his peculiar politics. We must trust he knows what he's doing."

The priest freed his hands and stood in front of Ben Aaron, deep in thought. He wanted to believe Ben Aaron; after all, his plea made sense, and the man always gave reliable advice.

"King Agrippa wears his supposed favour with Caesar like a ring on his finger. If we aid in toppling this king of ours," he sneered, "the Romans will be back in no time. We have to protect him. We have to ensure our people don't give any credence at all to this freeing of Cephas; we then must let the matter pass."

Simaan Ben Aaron was very convincing. His argument to keep the peace was wise and well calculated. The priest consented.

Marih had no idea how lucky he was to not get his secret wish to listen to the conversation, for he surely would have choked to death on his surprise. His plan went exactly in the opposite direction! He wanted Ben Aaron to tell the priest that King Agrippa freed Cephas so that trouble would ensue. What Ben Aaron just said to the priest hadn't even crossed Marih's mind. The man's words had secured the peaceful acceptance of Cephas' release.

Where had the Alephs' intelligence failed?

Twenty Five

The Huddle

Several months after Marih's visit, King Agrippa became ill with a terrible sickness of the digestive system. After considerable suffering due to the spurious cures of his sycophantic physicians, he died in agony. Rumours spread quickly: upon his death, intestinal worms came out of his anus and his mouth! Although such a manifestation was not unheard of, the Nazarenes wasted no time ascribing his horrible death to a heavenly punishment and spread the story of the evil king punished by God to be eaten alive by worms.

Some Alephs believed Herod Agrippa was poisoned according to a plot designed by the Jerusalem Lodge. They had no recourse but to kill the king in order to create the necessary Jewish/Roman tension, partially thwarted by Cephas' release. Such elaborate rumours were barely noticed among the ordinary citizens, as they much preferred the wormier details.

. . .

Cornelius had made himself an indispensable expert on Judaism at Caesar's court. Heeding his expert's advice, Claudius Caesar ordered his Roman army again occupy the various outposts of Judea.

Cornelius' sage advice had been prompted by Antonius' return to Rome from Corsica with stunning information. Seneca in exile was no less adept at his machinations for intelligence than he had ever been. On the contrary, his time in Corsica afforded him ample time to focus on the information his minions continued to feed him, biding his time for the return of his agency to active duty.

. . .

One of the main hubs of the Roman Empire, Tarsus was a modern city in every way that mattered. Major investments of Roman engineering and planning had amplified the city's existing infrastructure of harbours, roads, bridges, markets, and teaching centres, creating magnets for students and businessmen alike. Someone like Paulus had no trouble blending into the labour force and melting into the urban culture.

The thriving textile industry beckoned to Paulus. He had grown up in the family tent-making business, and his return was celebrated by them all. He set his mind to mastering the commercial end of the industry. Thanks to his natural charm, he made his own fun where he could find it – especially exercising his talents for trickery. His work with the agency had always been his real passion. He couldn't simply relinquish all his powerful skills, so he turned them about to serve other purposes. His relatives quickly realized Paulus had become an integral part of their business.

One day, at the permanent storefront where his relatives made the large tents, Paulus was negotiating with a customer when he overheard his cousin speaking to a stranger: "I am not sure what that is exactly, but trust me, if any of the tent merchants would have such a thing, it would be me. We have been in this business, at this very location, for generations."

The customer was asking for a tent made of invisible material, a tent that would hide the people inside it. Paulus quickly reacted. He casually interrupted his cousin with an easy question and then tactfully switched places with him; such exchanging of customers was a technique they often used when one's expertise better suited the other's customer. He took the stranger by the elbow and walked him to a quiet corner.

"You're not from Tarsus, are you?" Paulus probed, making sure he wouldn't dupe a local with the invisible tent ploy.

"No, I come from Judea," the stranger said.

"Well, that explains it."

"What do you mean?" The man sounded offended.

"If you were from around here you would have known of the ban on selling these invisible tents. Nobody would admit to having them – not in public, and certainly not to a stranger," Paulus explained.

"So... do you have them?"

"Shhhh! Keep it quiet!" Paulus looked around as if afraid of eavesdroppers. "When are you leaving the city?"

"In two days or so," the stranger said.

"In that case, I will have it ready for you by then." Paulus negotiated the sale for the day the man left the city. But he also had to be extra cautious. "I know where to get them. It is not from this store. The owner of this store should never know about this, do you understand."

"But of course!"

"People pay ten times the price of a regular tent for the invisible ones. I can get you one for just eight times the price."

"What? But that is very expensive! I would pay double, perhaps, but..."

"Shhh," Paulus cut off his protestations. "Sir, I am doing you a favour. Please don't bargain with me, I don't even need to put myself through this kind of trouble. I have a safe job here and I don't need to risk losing it."

"Very well. I will bring you the money in two days."

"Half of it in advance."

"Let me call in my friend, he carries the money." The stranger walked away to a man standing in the crowds a few feet from the store. The other man had his mantle hiding part of his face. Paulus followed his customer to this stranger.

Pushing back his mantle, Paulus found himself face to face with Barnabas, his old friend and agency partner. The whole invisible tent banter had just been a game. A grin of playful revenge by Barnabas saluted his old friend. Their middle man also enjoyed the exchange, bowed his respects, and left them to talk privately.

Barnabas maintained his serious demeanour despite an overpowering urge to hug his friend, celebrating their mutually deft execution of the invisible tent prank. "I will walk by again at sunset.

Follow where I lead."

Paulus nodded once, turned, and went back into the shop. There would be time enough that night for their reunion. For now, not one person in that buzzing marketplace was aware of the two veteran spies scheming in their midst. They still had the touch.

. . .

Barnabas and Paulus had developed an enduring friendship since their early days of enrollment with the agency. They had been teamed up for a number of projects, each necessitating their reliance upon one another in ways that cemented absolute trust. The same thing happened between Cornelius and Marih. These were two friendships built stronger by constant life-or-death interactions, an unspoken bonus for agency loyalties.

Under any other circumstances, the mere sight of Barnabas would have given Paulus great comfort. However, Barnabas' sudden appearance in Tarsus, unannounced and so deviously undercover, swamped Paulus with intrigue. Barnabas was there on a mission of some sort, a sure sign excitement was coming Paulus' way.

As the business day approached its end, Paulus informed his relatives at the store of some errands he had to accomplish before other businesses closed for the day. He bartered the favours necessary for not staying to help close up the shop. He kept his hands busy, finishing his task at hand, but his eyes relentlessly scanned every passerby until he recognized Barnabas casually wandering past the shop, pausing briefly to inspect the goods at the entrance.

Paulus was ready and said his quick goodbyes. He followed Barnabas at a discreet distance. They exited the market area and zigzagged their way through narrow, residential alleys, avoiding the main roads. They had proceeded like this for over half an hour when Barnabas stopped suddenly and bent down as if picking up something he had dropped. He stood up and resumed his walk.

Any agency operative would have understood Barnabas' signal. Paulus didn't flinch. He recognized the target as the door where Barnabas had stooped. He confidently walked straight to the door like a man with a clear purpose. He raised his left hand and knocked with a certain rhythm. After pausing for a few seconds, he knocked with another short rhythm. The door opened.

Taken aback, Paulus raised both arms gesturing a 'what the hell?' He opened his mouth and was about to exclaim, "Teacher!" when a wrinkled yet solid fist grabbed him by the shoulder and yanked him inside.

"Is that how I taught you to act in public?" Antonius joked.

Now Paulus was speechless. His eyes filled with tears and he threw himself into the arms of this father figure, someone who never ceased looking after him. Only two beings on earth could get to him like this: his daughter Claudia and Antonius. This peerless spy of legendary intelligence and unrivaled will stood weak with guilt before his daughter, and became dependent as a child in the presence of Antonius.

At first Paulus did not notice anyone else in the room, his tearful eyes were so fixed on Antonius. Cornelius watched the emotional reunion with new insight. He realized his relationship with Paulus, despite all the years of being his direct case manager, would never amount to the bond he just witnessed. No greater testament could be given to the nurturing character of Antonius.

Paulus was startled when Cornelius stepped forward, but quickly grabbed him in a bear hug as all three giggled like joyous kids at Saturnalia.

"I wanted to bring you a gift," Cornelius said, indicating Antonius. "I hope you like it!"

"This is the best favour you have ever done for me, Cornelius." Paulus wasn't shy now about his tears. He swiped at both eyes with the backs of his hands.

"I am the best favour Cornelius did for you?" Antonius played along.

"Well, maybe the second best favour. The number one favour ever was pulling me out of that Arabian desert Anania had condemned me to!"

The three laughed again. They spent the next few hours drinking wine and recalling various adventures, all they had been through together – their good times and the bad ones, the wins and the losses.

They filled each other in on their lives since the agency folded, forcing their loss of contact. "So, Seneca is stuck in Corsica?" Paulus asked.

"Yes; however, Antonius has established links so I can now be in continuous contact with him. Until we find a way to bring him back from exile, we will work around it," Cornelius explained.

"Work around what?" Paulus wasn't sure... was Cornelius hinting at reviving the agency?

"Paulus, you didn't really think the recall from Rome was the end of it for us, did you?" Antonius teased.

"Not for a minute," Paulus said, faking a confidence he hadn't felt until now. "So what's the plan?"

"We need you in Antioch."

The mere mention of Antioch startled Paulus. Wasn't he to pick up where he left off, his ploy as Saul? Or was this a new project altogether? Antioch was so far from Jerusalem and Judea, what could he possibly do there?

Cornelius picked up on Paulus' puzzlement. "We have made a minor change in our approach. Instead of focusing on the Nazarenes in Judea, we will put our investments where the payoff is more substantial."

Paulus listened vigilantly, like a star pupil sitting in the first row.

"The Phoenicians and the Greeks have shown way more tolerance to these Nazarenes than the Jews in Judea have. Even the Jews living outside of Judea have been more receptive." Cornelius paused to allow Paulus to reflect. "Our goal is to create a wall of defence against the Jews in Judea that will keep them from exporting their troubles to Rome." He paused again. "Our thinking is, if we plant and nourish an anti-Jewish seed among the Nazarenes scattered along the shores of the Mediterranean between Tyre and Antioch, when the time is right we will be able to set them at odds with the Jews. Divide..."

"Then conquer," Paulus finished.

"Exactly!" Cornelius grinned.

"But tell me, how do you envision my entry into Antioch? Are we so sure I will be accepted there?"

"You will be officially commissioned by the new church in Jerusalem to spread the word among the people of Antioch," Cornelius said.

"What?" Taken aback, Paulus was reminded of his last not-very-favourable encounter with the Nazarenes in Jerusalem and Damascus.

"Cephas has vouched for you. He even had the Nazarenes send Barnabas to seek you for this mission. Cephas told them about your charming presentation skills and your convincing defences on behalf of the Nazarene way." Cornelius added, "As very few of them were brave enough to venture outside of their country, they found their proselytizing solution in you."

"You and Barnabas will emphasize certain teachings that will contradict the Hebrew core of their belief system," Antonius interjected. "The original Nazarenes will not be around to watch over you."

"So, what you're telling me is I am ordered to create a new religion?" Paulus spat out sarcastically, "What a blasphemy!"

"I said the very same thing to Seneca when he presented the plot to me," Antonius chuckled. "He said not to worry because it is a divine blasphemy. I remember exactly what he said next: 'He who spares the wicked, injures the good.'"

"A divine blasphemy!" Paulus yelled. "Is it any wonder we love that man!"

Twenty Six

The Sisters

of the Brotherhood

"By dedicating your life to our cause, you earn the respect and protection of our Lord Melqart and you obtain the protection of our lodges over the inhabited surface of the Earth."

Just as Elisa had been compelled to swear it years ago, it was now Claudia's turn; she stood before the Aleph Mother Lodge of Tyre. With every eye focused upon her, she would take advice, prove allegiance, and swear the life-binding oath. Elisa watched Claudia with mixed feelings. Her personal devotion to her people was unquestionable. Elisa knew from firsthand experience that the true consequences of taking such an oath were beyond the comprehension of these young candidates. She had no clue when she proudly and nervously swore herself to the cause that her words were going to deprive her of the joys and blessings of a normal life for the rest of her years.

Elisa knew Claudia was anointed with the fervour of the new convert after the ceremony. She could still remember her own feelings as she set about to change the whole world. Candidates always walked out of the lodge so motivated. The lodge instilled an acute confidence in the candidates; they emerged feeling like puppet masters with the world as their stage. If only these feelings could last, for it would not be long before they discovered they could easily spend a lifetime seeing just one project through to the end.

"Rome will be fun!" Claudia repeated again and again after the ceremony. Elisa recognized the signs: her little sister was trying to hide her nervousness by convincing herself and all those around her that moving to Rome was not truly frightening.

"It will be. Truly! And it is perfectly alright to admit you are a little stressed at the same time. It's a big change, moving away from everything we know." Elisa encouraged her sister to share her feelings. She didn't have that kind of support when she needed it years ago. She had shown such confidence she had even convinced her superiors of maturity beyond her years. Now that she knew better, she wasn't going to let Claudia go through those same nerve-racking experiences alone. "Remember, Achte darling, I will be with you at all times." She hugged her over-confident little sister. "And who knows, maybe you'll get to spend more time with Paulus once we're in Rome!"

Claudia Achte gave an odd little chuckle.

"What was that laugh? I thought you'd like that."

Claudia snickered again. "So it is Paulus we will be seeing more of?"

Elisa thought surely she hadn't been so transparent.

"Are you sure there is no one else in Rome?" These words came in a childish sing-song voice.

Achte was the one person Elisa couldn't fool. Words didn't have to pass between these two, as they understood each other's gestures to the point of some sort of telepathy. Some gossips thought they had the witching way between them.

"You don't have to say it, sister, and I didn't mean to tease you."

"No, you're right, Claudia. I do miss Cornelius. Memories of the time I spent with him in Caesarea are all I have, and they were so wonderful they have kept me going."

"You love him that much." It was a statement more than a question. Claudia knew the answer. She loved getting into one of their sisterly talks of dreamy romance.

Now it was Elisa instead of Achte who was in need of comforting. In a moment their roles reversed and Achte was doing an amazing counselling job. Elisa's little sister was not a child anymore.

Claudia Achte, Phoenician for 'Sister Claudia,' was twenty-one years of age. Though not born a Phoenician, she had become the embodiment of a Phoenician woman in her prime, ready to take on Rome.

. . .

That year, Rome was preparing to celebrate the eight hundredth anniversary of the founding of the city. Elisa and Claudia couldn't have picked a better time to move. The city was hustling and bustling with visitors, merchants, and construction masons. Buildings of all types and sizes were rising, new and renovated, tall and wide. Strangely enough, the man who ordered all the work was not there to enjoy it. Caesar had left on a mission to Britannia to put an end to the turmoil at the periphery of his Empire. Britannia was geographically closer to Rome than Judea was and it posed a more immediate need of his personal presence.

Elisa and Claudia Achte stayed with a Phoenician family in Rome while they became more familiar with the city. The Mother Lodge in Tyre had instructed them to present themselves to the Aleph Lodge in Rome, which in turn would provide them with the support needed to launch Claudia on her mission: to penetrate the society of the Roman senators and other powerful establishments of the Empire. Women had no open presence in Roman society – even their names were diminutives of their male relatives – but they held the power of influence behind the scenes, and they used it effectively. Claudia and Elisa meant to become Roman women of the highest social standing. However, their missions were of a timely nature and they knew they didn't have much of it to waste.

"We should visit Cornelius first," Achte insisted. "Before we get all involved in our work, let's go see him!"

"That's a bit embarrassing, don't you think?" Elisa said.

"Embarrassing?"

"You know, the girl he met in Phoenicia comes all the way to Rome and impulsively visits him among his people. What if he's forgotten about us? What if he already has a woman?" Elisa said.

"Nonsense. Cornelius isn't like that. He's head over heels in love with you."

"Claudia Achte!"

"It's the truth and you know it. Besides, I'm the one who wants to see him. He is a family friend, isn't he? His house in Caesarea was the meeting place for my father and me for years. Even the lodge recommended using him to build my network. You just... come with me!"

Elisa's fragile defences fell away. She had wanted to visit Cornelius more than anything since their arrival in Rome. Now her little sister had brought it up, sparing her pride. But she told herself it was not her pride as a woman, rather as a Phoenician soldier. How could she continue to allow her sentiments to interfere with their missions? However, if their visit should grant Claudia's wish to see an old family friend and they just happened to kill two birds with one stone, all guilt could be assuaged. Besides, the lodge's business could wait; they deserved some personal time.

With the help of their Phoenician hosts the two women arrived at Cornelius' temporary residence in the vicinity of Caesar's palace. Caesar had offered him these prime apartments to keep him close to the palace. Cornelius' inherited palazzo, where a few of his relatives still lived, was by no means anything to be ashamed of, but it was on another side of the city and not practical for his new duties.

Forgetting Roman etiquette, the women didn't send word ahead to expect their arrival. They were disappointed to learn Cornelius wasn't at home and his staff had no further information to give them.

They turned from the door to find in their way a stately Roman woman standing on the portico connecting Cornelius' apartments to others of equal elegance. She appeared to be about Elisa's age, and she held the hand of a pre-pubescent boy. Elisa and Achte apologized for the awkwardness of the situation and split their path, trying to go around the strangers.

The woman confidently smiled. "Were you visiting Cornelius?" It was a curious thing to ask. People here, unlike in rural areas or smaller cities, were not usually given to chatting with strangers or interfering in others' affairs.

"Yes... no, not really," Elisa stuttered. "He's not there, or so we were informed."

"How do you know him?" The woman seemed accustomed to having her questions answered.

"We're old friends," Elisa replied.

"From Caesarea?"

"Yes. Is it that obvious?" Elisa smiled as her inner lioness took over. She didn't like the way this woman was interrogating them and she needed to regain control of the dialogue. "Is it the accent that gave me away?"

"That, a little, but mostly it's your Phoenician charm."

The unexpected compliment caught her off guard. Maybe it was sarcasm. If so, perhaps she was Cornelius' woman. Was this jealousy? If so, Elisa was pretty sure she was jealous as hell.

"My friend here, Claudia, was keen to visit Cornelius. He's a longtime friend of her father's."

"Ah, I see." The woman's smile never wavered. "I am Julia Agrippina," she said and glanced down at the nine-year old boy at her side, "This is Lucius, my son."

"You are the late Emperor Caligula's sister!" Elisa was startled.

"I see my name is known across the Empire."

"With all due respect, my lady, all descendants of your great family command such fame." Elisa felt sick as she said 'my lady.' The blood that ran in the veins of that Roman family was a sordid excuse for royalty. This woman deserved no more recognition than the purple dye for her dress. But, wait, Elisa's own dress had been dyed purple in Tyre, by Tyrian experts no less. She corrected her hasty judgment. This Roman blood wasn't even worth splotching a cloth, so perfectly finished by Phoenician hands.

Elisa was no slouch at holding her truly royal composure. "I apologize for my rudeness; I am Elisa, princess of the Abdmelqart family of Tyre."

"Why don't you come in and wait for Cornelius. He should be returning soon." The woman invited them in as if into her own house.

"We do not want to intrude," Elisa politely hesitated.

"You are not."

She walked them with steady steps to the front door again, then inside to a well-appointed chamber, and sat down. "Lucius has become accustomed to spending time with Cornelius. I couldn't dream of a more suitable man... intellectual, versed in politics, military sciences, and world matters... to be a teacher and friend for my son."

"Actually, there is at least one other person whose knowledge extends leagues beyond mine." Cornelius strode into the chamber, addressing all with the comfort treasured among family members. All his time spent at Caesar's court had eliminated the need for certain etiquettes. He hadn't yet recognized the faces of his two other guests.

"You have visitors, my dear." Julia kept her seat as the other two courteously stood up.

Cornelius' face glowed with sudden delight.

As Julia observed the interactions, her womanly instincts figured it all out. Claudia Achte was surely a family friend; that was true enough. But what had been previously unstated quickly revealed itself to her. Her intrigue for this well-versed teacher of her son expanded yet some more; he was obviously a passionate lover with good taste in women.

In his happiness, Cornelius forgot to salute little Lucius. The boy ran up to him, raising an arm in the air in a practiced military salute.

Julia made to correct her son's play for attention, "Lucius, my dear boy, I know it is sometimes difficult to sort out one's considerable passions, but a true artist should be able to tell when it is time for military formalities and when it is time for other sentiments." Julia spoke as a woman who feared no borders.

Cornelius and Elisa controlled themselves in their greeting. The tremors in their arms and the quivering in their bodies... like two wild horses stamping to be released... fooled no one, except perhaps young Lucius.

"Thank you for playing hostess and greeting my friends, Julia. I apologize I was not here to do so when you arrived. Elisa's brother, Marih, was with me at the military camp in Damascus and I billeted with their family whenever I was in Tyre. From the very beginning we became fast friends. He is a very loyal and skilled centurion."

"You surely know how to choose your friends," Julia teased, hinting at Elisa.

"If you truly trust my choice of friends, you should also trust my choice of teacher," he said.

"Give it a rest, Cornelius. Let's say you are correct; Seneca would be the best teacher for Lucius. But what can I do if he was exiled by order of Caesar?"

Cornelius smirked at Julia's answer. Everybody knew that Caesar had always had quite the attraction to Julia. She could ask for anything. She had everything a Caesar would desire in a woman: the family descent, the personality, the charisma, the proven ability to bear sons, and let us not forget her beauty.

"We'll talk about this another time. Now that you can attend your own guests, I'll give you some privacy. Lucius..."

"Julia, please, my home is yours. It is always a pleasure to have you with us," he said courteously.

"I must see to some singing lessons for Lucius. Alas, there are some things you cannot provide," she teased.

"Claudia is an amazing singer," Elisa suddenly piped up. She wasn't sure she had heard her own voice. Had she just asked Julia and Lucius to stay with them longer? After all, a promising opportunity had just presented itself: cause to create ties, even friendships, within Caesar's court. This was their mission, after all.

"Is that so?" Julia tested, just in case Elisa had offered it merely by way of good manners.

"Absolutely!" There she went again. Elisa's devotion to the cause subconsciously geared her speech. In her ears, the pitch sounded a little too anxious.

"Perhaps Claudia doesn't wish to waste her time instructing a child," Julia said.

"It would be my pleasure, my lady," Claudia confirmed.

"Please, call me Julia. You will find working with Lucius tantalizing. He is an innate artist." She looked to Cornelius for confirmation.

"He is a formidable young man with very promising talents and a passion for learning all things." Cornelius nodded his assurance with his words. "All are desirable features in a promising little Caesar. Right, Lucius?" He placed a hand on his shoulder and squeezed lightly, coaxing an enchanting smile from the boy.

. . .

Claudia Achte began the lessons that very afternoon. The boy's singing was better than they expected: a sweet pre-pubescent soprano with an inspired delivery. A fine artist, indeed. On the sidelines, each with their own agendas, Elisa and Julia ventured into various topics of conversation. Cornelius drifted in and out of the conversations, seeing to tasks that needed his attention. They were a picture of comfortable casualness.

Of course, Elisa had a specific goal; Julia was just enjoying the socializing. No doubt knowing Elisa was of royal descent in her own country made Julia more hospitable towards her. Or maybe her entertainment was watching the chemistry between Elisa and Cornelius. Regardless of her original intent, Elisa successfully leveraged this first meeting and managed to impress Julia with her refinement and intellect. By the time Julia and Lucius took their leave, Elisa and Claudia had secured an invitation for an afternoon in the palace's gardens and another for the celebration planned for Caesar's victorious return from Britannia. Most importantly, Lucius personally asked the beautiful Claudia to sing with him again.

Who would have guessed that Cornelius, the untested young Roman warrior who stopped by her parents' house on his way to Damascus so many years before, would be so instrumental in achieving their Aleph goals? What luck that was... and what a man he had turned out to be! Why must her feelings for him be this eternal paradox, for here before her was the love of her life in the guise of her most productive weapon as an Aleph dead set against Roman tyranny. Melqart gave with one hand and took with the other.

Twenty Seven

A Consensus to

Agree... or Disagree?

Upon the death of King Agrippa, the Roman legions returned to Judea. Marih was once again stationed with his soldiers in Caesarea. On one hand, his office duties kept him busy bringing order back to the region. On the other, the unofficial revival of the agency by Seneca and Antonius fit like a glove. The new directions were to not only support the Nazarenes, but to help widen the rift between the belief systems of the Nazarenes and the observant Hebrews. Had he a third hand, Marih and his Aleph brethren couldn't have been any more thoroughly or gladly busy.

Communications between Roman agents and their leaders, once again including Seneca, had evolved to a higher level. Written letters became a common method of transmitting orders and information. The letters were coded in such a fashion as to be interpreted in a completely different manner should they be read by an outsider. The agency had refined the ciphers Julius Caesar had begun using during his campaigns, almost from the beginning of their inception. Letters intercepted by the legion regulars were utter nonsense by regular decoding methods; these letters were believed to be exactly what they appeared to be – benign messages on mundane topics – and summarily ignored. Only the agency had the codes and the understanding to unlock the actual meanings. Seneca honed the cipher while in exile in Corsica, helping him carry on major operations without interruptions or hurdles. Agents like Paulus could write back to Seneca informing him of updates and requesting advice or help.

Seneca's eventual return to Rome, particularly as a friend to Caesar's court, was a boost to the agency's projects. The agents in the field were heartened by their great leader's return, prompting a new era of espionage to Rome's glory.

In the due course of events, Julia Agrippina became Caesar's wife. Powerful woman that she was, she immediately set in motion the chain of events leading Claudius Caesar to officially proclaim her son Lucius the official heir of the Roman Empire. Lucius' name was changed to Nero in honour of the event.

Claudia Achte had officially become one of Nero's tutors in the arts. Elisa had become Julia's close friend. But Elisa's lusty encounters with Cornelius, the love of her life, were a mixed blessing: mixed because every moment was overshadowed by an intolerable guilt. More and more, she felt that that infernal paradox of her love and her duty would be the death of her yet!

Inspired by his sister's achievements and sacrifices, Marih accomplished his share of glory for the cause. He could take pride in the increasingly frequent troubles in Judea. One incident was a Jewish riot following a transgression by a Roman soldier – or so they thought – taking his clothes off in front of their temple and making lewd insults to their traditions. Another time, a number of gentiles claiming to be newly converted Nazarenes attempted to enter the temple in Jerusalem, rousing the sleeping monster that was the Jewish mob to riot again. Troubles were simmering – the Alephs were stirring the pot – and more Roman troops were called in to keep things from boiling over.

As satisfying as all these machinations were for Marih, none compared to the zenith of his successes: the Jerusalem Council. Guided by the Aleph Mother Lodge, Marih wrote to Seneca suggesting a ploy they knew Seneca could not resist. Seneca practically drooled over the genius of finally bringing the blasphemous teachings of Paulus to Judea, which had already spread among the Nazarenes of Antioch. Now strong and well-established, the organization of Nazarenes – which they were now calling churches – would pose an even greater threat to the Hebrews in Jerusalem. To Seneca and the Romans, this was a major step towards further dividing the Jews before conquering them. But to the Alephs, ah! This was one giant step closer to the very destruction of Rome.

They watched with barely hidden glee as Seneca wasted no time running with Marih's plot. He enlisted the help of all agents in Judea and abroad, including Paulus and Barnabas. A key pawn, however, was Cephas. Cephas was more accepted by the new church in Jerusalem than Paulus was, and more powerful in rank than Barnabas. The three of them met in Caesarea to discuss the need for a consensus to help bring all the Nazarenes together, strengthening the bonds within the organization. They would begin in the homeland of Judea and then move to the provinces where their message was only beginning to arrive. A major challenge for Paulus and Barnabas was convincing Cephas to preach the less orthodox rules they had been employing among the gentiles. Cephas was impressed by the successes of Paulus and came to see himself as a secondary leader to this outspoken Roman citizen, though Hebrew by birth, with his supporters throughout many city-states. Though he lacked the backbone to argue with Paulus' ways, Cephas still clung to the strict conduct of the Nazarenes in Jerusalem, anchored as they were in Hebrew law. He saw conflict here in Jerusalem. Some common ground must be found were the message to survive.

Paulus and Barnabas nearly exhausted their persuasive talents, but Cephas eventually agreed he would do all he could to convince the Jerusalem church and its stubborn leaders of the necessity to loosen some of the rules, at least for those new gentile converts. These new believers made up the richest groups in the Nazarene organization, and their financial support, along with political protection, were essential to the survival of the Jerusalem church and its members. One of the first disagreements to broach concerned the majority of the gentile Nazarenes who were not willing to be circumcised as a sign of conversion. Such a hard and fast rule was a sure deal-breaker. Paulus had already eliminated it from his teachings; now Cephas had to receive the blessing from his brethren in Jerusalem.

Circumcision was not the only challenge. All Jewish adults had grown up accustomed to certain foods and meal restrictions in accordance with Hebrew law. The gentiles had very few dietary restrictions. They would see a high rate of failure to convert if a complex ban remained on what they ate, let alone with whom they were allowed to eat.

Paulus had very high hopes for Cephas as he left to attend this Council of Jerusalem. He should have counted on Cephas' usual tendency to underwhelm, for his accomplishments with the Council came up short and he only partially achieved what they had agreed on when they met at Marih's. Although less than satisfactory for his means, Paulus was oblivious to the fact that these results were quite good enough for Marih and the Aleph elites.

The brethren at the Jerusalem Council hesitantly accepted that the foreign gentiles need not be circumcised, but they still insisted on a mound of old Hebrew dietary restrictions for these new members.

Never short on hubris, Paulus turned his back to the Council and its consensus. He'd make his own dietary laws, and start by taking their demands with a grain of salt. After all, his was the voice listened to by people outside Judea. He was the one spreading the word. There was no reason Paulus should change his ways. Ultimately, it would be his word against the Council's.

Even so, all these triumphs won by Marih and Elisa for the glory of the cause were nearly neutralized. Out of the blue and without a clear explanation for doing so, Emperor Claudius issued a decree expelling all Jews from the city of Rome. Supposedly, a racially cleaner Rome was a much safer Rome; but this would pose a definite impediment to the lodge's goals. The Alephs were just as surprised as the Jews, and the Nazarenes were being ejected because of their Jewish affiliation.

Marih drew a deep breath and went back to the planning table.

Twenty Eight

When Opposite Minds Concur

"I have conquered the Druids in Britannia. The people and the Senate in Rome are happier since I made Julia my wife and announced her son Nero as my heir. As one Empire we all renewed our allegiance and showed our pride via the eight hundredth anniversary celebrations. Yet I still have one problem to see to. I would like to hear what you think of it." Caesar paced anxiously as he spoke. His obvious agitation was somewhat contagious to his friend Simaan Ben Aaron, summoned for a rare private meeting.

"What is it that disturbs the leader of our world to such a degree?" Ben Aaron thought he knew the answer, but his years in politics had taught him great patience in listening.

"Judea!"

Ben Aaron's open expression invited Caesar to continue.

"My friend, despite our various attempts to broker a peace in your homeland, your people are not accepting our efforts." Caesar spoke evenly, gently, avoiding any hint of condemnation. Claudius was a thinker and systematic planner, not given to impulsiveness. Anger was not a dominant trait. "Ever since King Herod Agrippa, once our loyal hand in Judea, died his ignominious death, the situation there has been deteriorating. Our generals tell me they are losing more and more control, living moment to moment with expectations of troubles exploding at any time of any day."

"Caesar, of course you know I am no stranger to these matters." Ben Aaron's voice commanded assurance; he was the right advisor. "It would be a lie if I said I had never given them much thought."

"You have a solution? Whatever are you waiting for?" Caesar's scolding came with a softening smile.

"I don't claim to possess a radical solution, Caesar. However, it has become clear the recently gentle behaviour of the Empire towards the Jewish communities throughout the provinces has only prompted the extremists amongst them to bolder tactics. They no longer fear any retributions of discipline shown from time to time under your predecessors."

Caesar liked what he was hearing. "I was thinking the same thing. The more we give, the more they ask for!"

"It seems to me that some military action of unmistakable intent might become inevitable," Ben Aaron said.

"You're suggesting we launch a war? But we just returned from Britannia; our treasury is weakened."

"Perhaps not a war, not just yet. The Jewish diaspora, as the Greeks would say, within the Empire is more widespread than that of the Celts and their Druids from Gaul into Britannia, before Caesar forced their seclusion to the tribes scattered across those islands today. No, I am suggesting postponing any military actions Caesar might be thinking of until the timing is optimum."

"And just when is this damned right time supposed to be?" Caesar's voice rose with frustration. "When they start rioting and rampaging inside the city of Rome at our very doorstep?"

"To the contrary, it seems once again our thoughts are coinciding."

"Simaan, my friend, I am asking you to speak your mind openly. Do not pose your thoughts in courtly flattery. I am nearly out of patience, so I promise you my lenience in advance. There are no bad ideas at this time; I want to hear them all."

"I suggest expelling the Jews from Rome."

Caesar froze. Was his hearing failing him? How could this possibly help matters? Upon first thought, the idea seemed stupid.

Yet this man's reputation for brilliance was beyond reproach, so there must be more to it. Without saying a word, Caesar planted his feet, body facing Ben Aaron, while partially turning his head as if giving an ear to the speaker.

"By expelling the Jews from Rome you can slowly concentrate their numbers in some cities or provinces, areas far from Rome. Once concentrated – and thus controllable – they will pose less of a risk on the body of the Empire when any military attacks become necessary. Most importantly, Rome itself will be far removed from any acts of retaliation."

Caesar slowly resumed his pacing. Such a ploy had never crossed his mind. He had done similar cleansings before, but on a much smaller scale, fewer people, smaller groups – never an entire ethnic race.

"Has such a thing ever been attempted before in the history of the Empire?"

"More than thirty years ago, Tiberius attempted to expel them."

"Ah, yes, I remember. That didn't work then; why would it now?"

"Because Tiberius Caesar drafted four thousand soldiers from among the Jews in the newly assimilated provinces and expected the allegiance of a Roman citizen. When these legions eventually returned to Rome, their families came back with them. How can you say no to the families of four thousand well-trained soldiers? That was his big mistake."

"Indeed, the people wouldn't accept expelling loyal soldiers... and, well, four thousand of them can cause a lot of damage should they become angered, not to mention the rioting by all their kin," Caesar thought out loud, reasoning to himself.

"We will place the blame on them for instigating the expulsion order. The announcement will originate by Rome's decree of intolerance for religious conflicts, especially the different sects of Jews with their inner clashing over their sects and cults and various beliefs, their segregated synagogues, and the harbouring of hatred towards any who oppose their orthodoxy. Therefore, they all must leave Rome, no exceptions, and be settled elsewhere," Ben Aaron explained.

"Has this really been happening?"

"Not to a great extent; the divisions exist, but in Rome they're still being civil about it. In Judea, however, they've gone far past the stage of civility, so as a people they will believe the announcement to be true."

"You're a good friend and a loyal advisor, Simaan. I wish the rest of the Jews thought like you. You know, Rome can be their best friend or their worst enemy. It has been so all along. As to their best interests, they unfortunately keep making the wrong choices," Caesar said politely to his Jewish friend.

"If I may look after my self-interests, Caesar, I realize this plan could mean that I, too, must relinquish my position in Rome."

"Not necessarily, Simaan. We will speak of it again soon."

"If I may impose upon your generosity once more... I don't need to emphasize to Caesar the risks I am taking by even discussing such a matter. If my people discovered the slightest hint of my involvement, I and my entire family would be first on their target list."

"This discussion never happened. I look after those who look after Rome."

. . .

That same evening, Caesar was in the process of concluding his consultations when he summoned the one remaining advisor.

"This is a matter for your expertise, Cornelius. I need to know what you think about it."

"Caesar, I am at your service." Cornelius had no idea what the matter could be.

"I am expelling all the Jews from Rome."

Cornelius stopped cold, blinking. He must have missed a word somewhere. Caesar couldn't have just said what he heard. It was impolite to ask Caesar to repeat himself, so what to do? Perhaps just pretend to be thinking and maybe Claudius would say something more to clarify?

Silence.

Perhaps not. "Caesar, forgive my ill manners, but may I ask for your indulgence and... may I hear the matter stated again?"

Claudius chuckled, taking a certain delight in his little game. It had been such a very long day. "What would you say, my trusted centurion, were I to expel all Jews from the city of Rome?"

There was no doubt this time; Cornelius heard very well. "That would be the most perspicacious decision by any emperor... ever!"

Claudius laughed aloud this time. "I'm not used to you being compulsive, Cornelius. Could there be any emotions behind your suspiciously quick response?"

Cornelius suddenly felt like an inattentive child being scolded by his teacher for a wrong answer.

Seeing him hold his breath, Caesar patted Cornelius' shoulder. "Just joking with you, my son. Knowing you as I do, I have no doubt you must have given this matter plenty of thought before now. Yes, even before it ever came to my mind."

Cornelius relaxed and answered with conviction, "Indeed, I have. Their presence in Rome gives them the impunity to challenge Caesar's rule in Judea."

"It seems all my advisors are in harmony about this matter. I cannot believe it took me so long to think of it."

"All your advisors... your non-Jewish advisors, if I may ask?" Cornelius had a certain person in mind.

Claudius paused a few seconds, but quickly came back, "Of course, non-Jewish advisors. This is a sensitive matter, you know." He honoured Ben Aaron's request for secrecy.

"What do you plan to do to those Jews close to the court?" Cornelius hoped to hear the right answer.

"Well, I don't have many of them, do I?" Claudius tried to make light of the question.

"Like Simaan Ben Aaron," Cornelius put in before Caesar was able to change the topic.

"Oh yes, he's an old family friend of yours, isn't he? Well, don't be concerned, Cornelius, he will be safe. I will give him the choice to stay or leave, and will protect his assets and business either way."

Cornelius indeed wanted Ben Aaron to stay in Rome. He wanted him nearby to keep a grip on him until the right time came.

"Remember, Cornelius, I look after my friends."

"One of your divine traits, Great Caesar."

Twenty Nine

He Who Taught Me a Letter

Although the Aleph brethren saw the expulsion of the Jews as a setback, they were still in a good position to guide their plan towards the destruction of Rome. They were surely ahead of their position ten years ago. If ever anyone understood the cycle of life and the game of destiny, it was the Phoenicians and their Aleph leaders. They believed that few things were destined to last, and a fall must follow every rise. Simply put, they were willing to bide their time.

Keeping this philosophy in mind, the Alephs knew Claudius' decision to expel the Jews could just as easily be reversed based on his – or the next emperor's – slightest whim. In the calm before the inevitable storm, Elisa gathered her rewards as she found them, mostly in her desires for Cornelius. A propitious turn of destiny for the Alephs saw Claudia become Seneca's newest prime project.

Upon his return from Corsica, Seneca was asked by Julia Agrippina to guide her son's education as would befit a Caesar. The talented Nero was to receive the best education from the most intelligent minds in Rome. Seneca never disappointed in the arena of purposeful planning. Ever resourceful, he knew how to use every tool in his box. Claudia's growing friendship with Nero became the golden medal in his collection.

If Paulus' daughter followed his instructions – which, in his arrogance, he took for granted – they could tighten their clasp on Nero and the future of the Empire, and thereby rule the known world. Seneca's altruistic philosophies would never overtly rank ruling the world as an objective. It was his loyalty to Rome which sought a permanent ending to all sources of trouble as the means to achieve the ultimate Roman triumph. The high morals of his stoic calm raised his intentions above those of a selfish, narrow-sighted, power-hungry, common man.

. . .

"My dear boy, when we are faced by powers we cannot resist, the intelligent thing to do is to adopt it as our own choice, for destiny guides those who embrace it and drags down those who resist," Seneca explained to the young Nero, who had just reached the age of majority at the age of fourteen.

"But how do I know I can't resist a power unless I try?"

Nero's questions always spoke to his intelligence. Not many people in Seneca's life had stumped him as often as Nero had. This last question made Seneca very proud and, in a very real way, validated his teaching abilities. One needs to understand a philosophy and its reasoning before being able to ask such a question.

"If the matter brings you agitation, do not fight it. Running with the wind gives you speed. Befriending destiny is a source of serenity. So if your fight begins with agitation, you'll have your answer: it is a force you shouldn't resist."

"But sometimes I feel... I feel when I am angry I can be stronger. Agitation and anger prompt me to make better decisions." Nero argued with his teacher as if arguing with a peer.

"It might seem so on the face of it, but this way leads to unrealistic rationalizations."

Seneca took a deep breath, inflating his no longer vigorous fifty-five-year-old chest. "Anger can be useful if tamed, like in battle." Seneca slowed his pace to allow Nero time to arrange his thoughts. This master teacher chose the right speed and the right tone to suit his pupil's needs. "But when making decisions, remember this: Reason wishes the decisions it provides be just. Anger wishes its decisions to seem just. It cares not whether it is just or even if the outcome is successful."

Nero thought about it. "So one only claims his angry decisions were the right ones, in retrospect, but given the opportunity to do it all again without anger, he might make another decision?"

"That's my young Caesar!" Seneca clapped his student on the shoulder.

The sound of light steps approaching distracted Nero. While distractions were strongly discouraged by Seneca, Claudia Achte was always an exception.

"My dear Seneca, isn't it time you stopped being surprised by Nero's abilities?" Achte's flattery was honey to the young man, twelve years her junior. At twenty-six years of age, Achte had all the magic of the classic Mediterranean beauty, the charisma of her father Paulus, and the intellectual vigour of her adopted sister Elisa. She complemented her words with the slightest touch of her scented fingers to Nero's neck, a touch that would seem innocent to bystanders, but not to Seneca. Their young student had developed quite the infatuation for his singing teacher. Achte deftly maneuvered the aristocratic boy's weaknesses and social gaffes.

Julia Agrippina had managed to simultaneously raise a son of incomparable genius and deprive him of a normal social life. In her opinion, there was no time to waste on matters that diverted her son's path from the throne of the Roman emperor. And despite his young age, she was especially cautious about his relationships with females. Seneca had noticed this and wasn't sure if she did it just because she assumed it was the correct way to raise her son, forgetting that a young man's needs are different from her needs as a grown woman. Seneca never ruled out other options, chief among them being Julia's ambition to rule Rome as the mother of Caesar. His eyes recognized a woman who had been a sister to an emperor, became the wife of the next emperor, and now had positioned herself to be the mother of one who would eventually be the new emperor. Not many women in history had played such a variety of roles with such finesse.

Seneca appreciated Julia's influence with Caesar allowing his return from Corsica, but something deep down in his gut always raised invisible flags of warning with this woman. Could it be that this philosopher of colossal capabilities and commanding personality was, somewhat, intimidated by Julia? He would never admit it, of course, yet her innate confidence shook his. He aimed to keep on her good side, especially as he came to fear the impossibility.

In light of Julia's dominant role in Nero's life, Seneca secretly encouraged Claudia to cast her nets about Nero. The plotters made full use of their favourable positions at court and with Nero. It was crucial that Julia be kept in the dark – not too difficult a task as Nero himself was too afraid to admit to his mother any feelings or desires he might have. And so Claudia Achte remained, in Julia's eyes, merely the talented singing teacher from Tyre, with an age sufficiently greater than her son's to safeguard against feminine distractions.

"Isn't it almost time?" Seneca asked.

"The play is a week from now. And as the masters insist, practice makes perfect," Claudia replied.

"And art refines the heart. I'll leave you two alone."

"Don't forget, you promised to start taking me to the Senate court to watch the trials." Nero's reminder sounded more like a command.

"I won't forget. I will talk to Cornelius about it, as he provides court security and knows the schedules. I will choose something interesting. Until then, happy acting!"

Thirty

A Friend of Caesar!

And a Friend of Rome?

Cornelius returned to the city after a two-day trip to the peripheries of Rome with the emperor. Heart-wrenching news awaited him; Antonius had become acutely sick and suddenly died. Cornelius' great sadness reminded him of learning of his father's death. Antonius had filled the void his own father's passing had left in his life, almost to the degree of supplanting his father's early influences.

Other news helped break the sharpness of Antonius' death. He was about to become a father. Elisa had been keeping to home, in apartments next to his, shared with Claudia Achte. The two were elated despite their unofficial status as a couple. Elisa knew the Mother Lodge would not object, as she would designate the pregnancy as an element of her project. Cornelius had the social and military rank to easily create a diversion. The natural thing was to wed, and so they would.

Marih traveled to Rome to attend the wedding celebrations. The Mother Lodge made use of him while there to attain a major milestone. He was their best asset to close the deal. Marih was on a mission.

. . .

The news that brought Cornelius sadness was nothing short of devastation to Paulus. Antonius was half of all the family he had. The other half was his daughter Claudia.

. . .

"We need your help!" Marih told Cornelius and Seneca in a closed meeting after the wedding. "We have managed to prompt the governor of Syria to accuse Ananias, the high priest of the Jews, of acts of violence."

This was welcome news indeed. Ananias was well known for his avarice and brutality. He was one of their worst enemies and he got in their way sometimes, yet nobody fought the Nazarenes as effectively as Ananias. He once brought Paulus to trial on trumped-up charges, creating extra work for everyone in the agency by making them pull every string they could to keep him from harm. Yes, Ananias was trouble.

"Will he be sent to Rome?" Seneca asked.

"Yes, but in Rome, as you know, our agents are restricted. Seneca, you are our only hope," Marih pleaded.

"I do not have my former influence here, you know. Caesar's clear orders forbid I discuss these matters with him. My sole official function is to educate his heir, Nero." It was generally known Claudius Caesar had allowed Seneca back from Corsica merely to placate Julia's demands. But he refused Seneca's participation in any facets of political or military life. He had clearly banned him from communicating with the agency. These restrictions forced Seneca to work covertly with Cornelius, Marih, and their old cronies in the agency. They were forced to fund their activities through money gathered by the centurions from bribes – a common source of wealth for many – or from donations by richer Nazarenes to Paulus and Barnabas and other agents, or even directly to the centurions who offered them protection. They were creative, if nothing else, struggling to keep their pet projects afloat.

"Maybe I can influence Caesar. He tends to consult with me on these matters based on my service in Judea," Cornelius ambitiously offered.

"We can make sure Nero attends this trial. It is time to coach him on the many dangers of the Jews." Seneca never passed up an opportunity to exercise long-term planning.

"Consider it done," Cornelius affirmed.

. . .

In a few months Ananias arrived in Rome for the trial. Everything seemed to go according to plan. Cornelius couldn't wait to see Simaan Ben Aaron witness his infamous friend Ananias when he was hung or, better yet, crucified. These enemies of the Empire were to witness a day from their own Gehenna, a true hell on earth.

Seneca brought Nero to court after several detailed lessons regarding the enemies of the Empire, coupled with indirect messaging from Claudia about the dangers of the Jews – from her personal experiences as a neighbour in Tyre. Contrary to Seneca's interests, Claudia and the Alephs had no interest in hurting the Jews either for who they were or what they believed in or did. Their sole interest was in creating trouble for Rome and bringing the Empire closer to its destruction. In a twisted way, they had common goals with many of the Jews who sought freedom from Rome, yet the Alephs would expediently sacrifice them for their cause. Such is politics.

On the day of the trial the evidence supporting Ananias' participation in acts of violence was overwhelming. It was difficult for Cornelius to hide his glee. In anticipation of the verdict, Cornelius celebrated heavily. Upon stumbling home that night, he found quite a different reality.

"That Ben Aaron swine had a lengthy meeting with Caesar today!" Elisa told her husband.

"How do you know?"

"Nero told Claudia. Caesar had Nero attend their top-secret meeting."

"Not very top secret, was it?"

"You know, Nero doesn't keep anything from Achte."

"So? What happened at the meeting?"

"They're acquitting Ananias!"

"No!" he bellowed. Almost immediately he plunged into a mental stupor, his hopes and confidence shattered. He was so close to his revenge, so close, and now helpless… again.

She let him alone with his sobering thoughts. After some time, his voice cracked as he grasped at anything in his disbelief, "Is Claudia sure? She didn't misunderstand … she heard those words exactly?" He wanted to yell, lash out, punch somebody. Another part of him wanted to curl into a ball in the corner and pitch a fit like an infant until he got what he wanted. He fought back against displaying such embarrassing weakness in a Roman centurion, thankful only Elisa could see him now.

"Ben Aaron told Claudius that Ananias had always been one of the pillars keeping peace in the area. He said Ananias was a politician of the first degree and a friend of Rome. He knows how to manage the Jews and diplomatically kept them subdued, as evidenced since he took over after Agrippa died. And Claudius trusts Ben Aaron, as always."

Cornelius found no rest that night. He thought of sneaking into Ben Aaron's apartments and murdering him. Why did he hesitate? Would he ever find his revenge, or would he just take whatever came, like a coward? Only Elisa's presence kept him from doing something he would surely regret by the light of day.

But the morning only confirmed Claudia's disturbing intelligence. Ananias had indeed been acquitted despite piles of evidence to the contrary. He was allowed to return to Judea, stronger than ever before.

Cornelius wasn't the only one burning from this defeat. The relentless Aleph lodges were shaken to their core by this unforeseen result. They did not figure Simaan Ben Aaron into their equations. They had underestimated the influence of this solitary man in their analysis and projections. Really, who was he? How could he have such an effect and how much of a role had he played in their previous setbacks? Had he been an element in events such as suppressing the Jewish riots against the Romans and the late King Agrippa? Had he a hand in suppressing them again after the release of Cephas? Was Ben Aaron the proverbial stone the masons of the Aleph Lodge ignored to their detriment?

Aleph lodges were put on high alert across the inhabited world. Their singular mission: Identify Simaan Ben Aaron.

It wasn't long before their fears were confirmed. A breach in common practices at the Jerusalem Lodge had led to ignoring incoming intelligence where Simaan Ben Aaron was concerned. A minor error led to their major underestimation of the value of set protocol, allowing local judgment to override what would have otherwise identified Ben Aaron as a significant player. Such behaviour caused his name to slip through the cracks and fail to come to the attention of the top decision-makers. The Mother Lodge had no tolerance for such errors. Corrective action was immediately taken; several found their ranks greatly diminished, some their reputations marred forever.

Reliable information about Simaan Ben Aaron was disseminated to the new operatives in all the lodges, and a plan of action was quickly developed. It was imperative for Marih to go back to Rome carrying the new intelligence to his sister Elisa and to Claudia Achte: Simaan Ben Aaron was categorized by the Senate as 'a friend of the Empire.' This category contained a number of strongly trusted diplomats, usually high-status businessmen who provided foreign support to a subcommittee of the senators involved in top-secret operations of the Empire. Such a designation protected said diplomats from the frequent changes in military directions or even in Caesars. The Senate was more stable, riding out these political tempests, and so were these diplomats. Of course, in return, people like Ben Aaron gained immeasurable security allowing them to maintain their businesses and wealth. As such, they would automatically enjoy the friendships of successive Caesars and avoid unwanted animosity from any pandering Senate subcommittees.

In other words, Ben Aaron was considered a special kind of Roman agent who reported directly to the Senate and could exercise diplomatic privileges in any of his missions, unlike the agency, which reported to the military and was led by Caesar, a far less stable arrangement. The two entities, the agency and these 'friends of the Empire,' supposedly worked for the same ultimate purpose, but had no direct accountability or visibility with one another. A clever few could play this quirky little communications problem to considerable advantage.

Returning to Rome, Marih was crystal clear regarding his

directions from the Mother Lodge: until a viable plan was put in place, Cornelius was to remain in the dark about this information on Simaan Ben Aaron. The Alephs had yet to thoroughly comprehend one strategic contradiction: if Simaan Ben Aaron was a friend of Rome, why had he murdered Cornelius' father?

Thirty One

Unholy Priest

Those who failed to recognize High Priest Ananias as a single-minded power-monger did so at their peril. His despotic dictatorship through his position at the temple became intolerable, causing the Jewish people to continuously bring complaints before the Roman courts. Despite the regard the Hebrews held for Ananias' office of high priest, he was one of the few in their history who had manipulated his position to such a degree the people rose up against him as one voice of frustration. He ignored them and continued to shrewdly maintain his position by greasing the wheels of politics, paying bribes and offering political favours to the Romans or any other entity that could benefit from his conniving.

However, upon his acquittal and return from Rome, Ananias sensed true danger about him. The dissatisfaction with the judgment was palpable. Many had hoped he would die in Rome. In his perverse way, he planned to strengthen his political position with the various minorities agitating against him by way of secret deals with their leaders, all while showing a public face of conciliation for the demands of the majority: the observant, conservative Jews.

. . .

He would begin with the Nazarenes. Ananias summoned Cephas

for an undisclosed meeting.

Cephas cringed at the summons. How could he go alone to meet with the infamously violent and untrustworthy fraud? But what choice did he have? Driven by his primary motivator, fear, Cephas sought refuge at Marih's.

"Just like Herod Agrippa, I think he's planning on capturing me to gain favour with the anti-Nazarenes," Cephas whined in panic.

"An intriguing theory, indeed, but I think you're overreacting. Ananias has just survived all those accusations of excessive violence, unforgiveable in a supposed holy man. He's probably going to lay low for a while, if anything." Marih's opinion was more than trivial analysis. By now he had become one of the top analytical minds of his age, not only among his Aleph brethren in matters of politics, but also in the Roman Empire. No less among the latter was his position within the agency. His years of experience and the nature of his work gave him the advantage when working with any manner of ambiguity.

"Maybe so, but I'm not taking that risk. No, I will not go to see him. Perhaps I should leave for Antioch and hide there for a while until all this settles."

"Cephas, my friend, calm down. Have I ever let you down?"

"Marih, don't get me wrong, I trust you, I do. But Ananias I cannot trust. You know what he thinks..."

Marih cut Cephas short with a voice soaked in reason. "Cephas, Cephas, just listen to me." He knew this man's levels of fear well enough to use them against him. "How about this? I will see him with you!"

"You will? But he summoned me alone for a closed meeting. What do I tell him?"

"Don't worry about that. Let me guarantee your safety like I always have."

"Marih! Would you? Would you really? Oh, how can I ever thank you for tolerating me? I know I can trust you blindly. I know that. Just tell me what you want me to do."

"Nothing right now. Stay here with me for a few days and gather your strength. I will ask Ishtar to see to your comforts personally. And I will contact Ananias to set things up. I will invite him here, an added advantage for us. Even so, I am sure he will not refuse my arrangements on your behalf."

Cephas' face relaxed. An invitation here? So much safer than walking into that demon's den.

The Alephs' intelligence brains had more in mind than merely helping Cephas. Their top priority still awaited a resolution: ironing out the folds in Simaan Ben Aaron's role.

. . .

Just as anticipated, Ananias rushed to accept Marih's invitation, especially when presented as a matter of routine alignment between Jewish and Roman authorities.

To protect himself against his enemies, Ananias arrived *incognito*. Graciously receiving Marih's warm welcome, he accompanied him to an isolated underground chamber where a surprise awaited him. Cephas sat there alone, pale as wax, eyes bulging and jaw tight.

"Ah! A pleasure to see you, Cephas. I had been awaiting your reply. This is good timing." Ananias' political mind jumped into action. This much was evident: Cephas was scared of him and had sought out Marih's protection.

Cephas smiled and stood up in respect to the high priest's office. "The pleasure is mine, Rabbi."

Marih directed his speech to Ananias, "I would have preferred the comfort of our meeting around a dinner table, but please, forgive me, the nature of our meeting dictates different circumstances."

"In truth, I appreciate your understanding of my situation and keeping this meeting private. Perhaps we can discuss business more efficiently this way," Ananias said.

"Indeed. Rabbi, it would give us pleasure if you were to guide this meeting." Marih offered the courtesy to his guest to set the agenda, when in reality he was asking him to expose his strategy first.

"Thank you, centurion." Ananias nodded, taking the bait. "As you know, many people are unhappy with the Nazarenes' deviation from Jewish law by allowing gentiles to mix with them. Forgive my bluntness, but I feel it is best to set agreements based on plain speaking and clear understanding."

Cephas had so many things to say in response to these

accusations, but he sat mute. He wanted to defend the reasoning behind the Nazarenes' way and explain their teachings, maybe tell about the miracles and visions that had happened to him, but for once he retained these thoughts in his mind. Besides, he was not the one who had been the most deviant in this regard. Paulus was the one carrying the banners of change and travelling the world teaching against the laws of Moses. He felt his ire rise in his throat, but his tongue remained still, allowing for the occasional dry swallow.

"The Empire, as you well know, has strict rules regarding freedom of belief. I am sure you have a suggestion taking this concept into consideration," Marih diplomatically argued.

"Am I to understand the Empire chooses to defend these Nazarenes despite the potential unrest which may ensue?"

"The Empire chooses to keep the peace by respecting its own laws, a practice that we know from experience benefits all involved. One would hope you, Rabbi, with your renowned wisdom and judgment, would manage to provide the needed balance between the Nazarenes and the temple... and any of the other sects, for that matter."

"When you speak of the Empire, to whom do you refer?" Ananias cut to the chase. He knew Marih's position in Caesarea, but he surely didn't speak for the Empire in this matter.

Marih openly smirked. "Why, the Roman forces from Jerusalem to Tyre, of course. This is for whom I speak and this is who will support and protect our deal, should we have one."

Ananias became edgy. He took a studied pause, arranging the folds of his robe, to regain his composure. "Here's what I can do: I will try to limit the persecution of the Nazarenes, but Cephas and his friends must follow Hebrew law."

An expert at negotiation, Marih's tone changed to assert authority. He would prove beyond any doubt intimidation was his weapon and not Ananias'. "Here's what will happen: you will stop the persecution of the Nazarenes in Judea." He stared Ananias directly in the eye.

Ananias took a deep breath, breaking the tension. "That sounds doable. There's no reason to persecute any who follow the law."

"In Judea!" Marih said.

"In Judea," Ananias repeated, at first not sure why Marih said so. "Follow the law in Judea, of course."

"The Nazarenes may do whatever they want outside of Judea," Marih asserted plainly.

Ananias didn't like that part one bit. He didn't see it coming. In certain ways this meant the Nazarenes were still free to antagonize the Hebrew law, but from a distance. Pretending to be obedient only inside the boundaries of Judea was a joke, a bad one. Nobody would buy into that. Ananias' gut told him Marih had just presented his best and final offer. For some reason unclear to him, the Nazarenes were under Roman protection. He puzzled on this turn of events for a moment. The Romans had always cared for the contentment of the majorities in order to keep the peace. Regardless, he wasn't there to bargain on behalf of Judaism, he was there to secure his own position. If that's what the Romans wanted in return for their cooperation with him as the leader in Judea, they could have it.

"It seems we have an agreement." Ananias forced a conciliatory smile.

"On our part, I will have the Nazarene brethren in Judea announce their respect for Hebrew law and recommend reprimands to those outside Judea for teachings deviating from it." Cephas, overly joyous with Ananias' agreement, half-wittedly volunteered to Ananias what Marih had just won by his negotiations on his behalf.

Ananias jumped at the opportunity, agreeing to Cephas' unexpected gift with a cynical laugh.

Marih almost had a heart attack watching Cephas hand his opponent exactly what he had fought to protect. The worst of it was, Cephas didn't seem to realize the consequences of his offer. He was just happy to have his head safe from Ananias' persecution. What a fool! Marih couldn't help but wonder how Cephas had managed to achieve a leading position among the Nazarenes with such naivety. Then he remembered, but of course, it was he, Marih, and the agency that made Cephas who he was. The same attributes that made Cephas a pliable pawn for the agency – chiefly fear and half-wittedness – had proven to be a double-edged sword. Ah well, it wasn't the end of the world. After all, Paulus and Barnabas would surely manage to rectify the matter.

"Dear Cephas, I would hate to keep you any longer and bore you with the technical matters the rabbi and I have yet to discuss." Marih thus politely dismissed Cephas. His original plan was to continue the discussion in Cephas' presence, but not after this last self-destructive contribution.

"I will leave you alone. I know my way out." Cephas bolted like an obedient student anxious to satisfy his teacher.

Ananias maintained his cynical smile, watching Cephas beat his hasty retreat, then asked in a relaxed tone, "Was there something else on your mind?"

"Do you know what saved you at your trial in Rome?" Marih pounced.

Ananias squinted in surprise. "I was found not guilty by the Senate's high court. I thought you knew that."

"I thought we agreed to be clear and straightforward, no games," Marih said.

"In that case, I am sure you know very well the emperor himself pleaded for my case. It seems to me you are the one playing games here."

"Do you know we almost lost you?"

"Lost me... what do you mean?" Ananias wasn't sure he was following.

"The emperor's advisor on Judea and its matters is my friend and the previous centurion here in Caesarea. Cornelius, son of Silvius. I am sure you remember him very well."

"Indeed, a generous and understanding officer. I enjoyed working with him when he was here."

"Cornelius, at my advice, argued on your behalf. He convinced Caesar your presence was necessary for the peace."

Ananias' smile stretched wide. "Why! How can I thank you? I appreciate your trust."

"But we almost lost you," Marih emphasized.

"Aha?" Ananias was ready to hear.

"There was some unexpected advice from a friend of the Empire. Said advice recommended replacing you with someone else."

Ananias' expressions turned grave.

Marih studied his reaction. His approach was working. "We

almost lost you... to that advice," Marih spaced his words as if trying to explain something complicated.

"Who was it?" Ananias asked angrily, avoiding direct eye contact with Marih.

"That is not the question you should be asking. The question is, why?" Marih pretended his interest was on behalf of Roman welfare.

"Why what? Why people stab each other in the back? Isn't it human nature? I don't know why... who was it? Who was the cheap bastard?" Ananias' limited scope made him sound like a madman. He was clearly angry about something as yet unknown to Marih.

Marih maintained his silent scrutiny. His eyes penetrated Ananias' lack of patience, and he let him reveal the chaos in his mind.

"Who else could it be? That spawn of Herod Agrippa, of course. He wants to assign a high priest of his own choice. He never liked me and guess what? I never liked him! And he dares call himself Herod Agrippa, as well. He is *nothing* like his father!" Ananias spat out his disgust.

Marih watched with deep interest as Ananias revealed the hatred he was capable of and thought of all the attractive scenarios possible should it be properly channeled against Rome. He kept a straight face. "Why, Ananias, I am surprised... you are truly unaware, aren't you?"

Ananias fumed. He did not take that comment kindly.

"I really thought you might have some idea, but maybe you don't know your friends... or enemies... as well as you think."

Ananias was clearly agitated. The idea of having an enemy he didn't know about scared him to his core. People in his position couldn't survive such weaknesses. He had to be aware of all his surroundings and be ready to defend or attack whenever needed. One small lapse of attention could be his last act on earth.

"Simaan Ben Aaron," Marih stated with a friendly tone, as if to reassure Ananias that he had his back and was there for his protection.

"Simaan? Why? What's in it for him? The rascal! What's he up to now?"

"Relax, Rabbi, relax. Remember, you are safe now and we'll work on this together."

Ananias took a deep breath. Realizing he must regain his

composure and think straight, he ventured, "So why did he do it?"

"I do not know. I was hoping you would tell me. We are just as surprised as you are. He must be working for a third party."

"I have known him forever. He never cared for anything more than his wealth and the Roman blessings of his wealth. Though I will attest to his many good works for the poor throughout his life."

"But he has done things contrary to this image, things a simple and peaceful businessman wouldn't do."

Ananias seemed puzzled by Marih's last comment. Was he referring to this last act of betrayal when Simaan spoke against Ananias to Caesar? Or was there something else he didn't know?

"For example, years ago he murdered an aristocratic Roman, a partner and supposed friend of his, cold bloodedly." Marih carefully searched for clues in Ananias' gestures and reactions.

"He did?"

Ananias seemed sincerely puzzled. Did he not know Ben Aaron had poisoned Cornelius' father? Perhaps these Jewish priests didn't really gather as much information as one would expect. True, the high priest at that time was someone else, Caiaphas, wasn't it? But one would expect the rest of the priests, including Ananias, to pass along such information.

"The man he murdered was the father of Cornelius, the same man who defended your case in front of Claudius Caesar. Ben Aaron betrayed the trust of this close friend, killing him with poison in his wine." Marih had just finished his sentence when Ananias unexpectedly burst into laughter.

"You heard of that?" Ananias chuckled. "I have to congratulate you on your amazing intelligence. This story was only told inside very tight circles of priests. Obviously there is more betrayal in our ranks than we ever imagined."

"So you did hear of it? Why does it make you laugh?"

"Because you have amazing intelligence, just not enough of it." Ananias resumed his chuckling.

Marih was starting to be annoyed, but he had to continue to play the friend. He forced a laugh himself. "What's so funny, then? Do share, my friend."

"That was a lie. Simaan never killed Cornelius' father."

"How do you know? Do you really trust the man after knowing what he did to you?" Marih probed.

"I don't trust Simaan, but I trust myself."

Marih's face showed a clear need for more information.

"I made the story up. I made it up and convinced Simaan to tell it to Caiaphas." Ananias paused to give Marih the time to grasp his tale. "After the death of Cornelius' father, Simaan was scared. Thinking he had lost his biggest ally in Rome, his position there would be weakened because he was a Jew and his wealth might be affected. He needed to be recommended as a friend of the Empire by the pro-Roman Jewish royalty. The royal court here wanted any such person to possess favour with the high priest – at that time, Caiaphas. Simaan sought a way to help him come closer to Caiaphas. I brought the solution. He paid me well and I made up the lie for him. I knew what resonated well with Caiaphas. So, Caiaphas thought he had a Jewish spy in Rome, the royal court liked Simaan's seeming acceptance by the high priest, Simaan secured his rank, and I got my money."

Marih sat for a moment, speechless, yet trying not to look as stunned as he was. This was more than enough for Marih to make his conclusion. Simaan Ben Aaron was truly a friend of the Empire and a peace-seeker. In other words, he was a serious obstacle to the Aleph Lodge's efforts to instigate trouble with Rome. Yet another fault in the Alephs' intelligence became evident where Ben Aaron was concerned.

"Most interesting. It doesn't really change the matters at hand. I just wanted you to be aware of Simaan's position towards you. I will keep my eyes open and will let you know if I learn something. You too, keep me informed if you figure out his motives." Marih tapped Ananias' shoulder. "Needless to say, only a closed circle around Caesar knows what I told you. If you shared it with anybody, it could well anger Caesar himself."

"We don't want to anger Caesar, do we?" Ananias joked. "But seriously, I appreciate your trust and confidence in me. You watch my back and I watch yours."

"I want you to watch Cephas' back," Marih reminded.

"Say no more."

Thirty Two

The First Time
is the Most Difficult

Now that Simaan Ben Aaron had been identified as a major pillar in maintaining the Roman-Judaic peace, the Aleph Lodge proposed to cut their losses by eliminating him from the equation altogether. But simply murdering Ben Aaron would be a waste. The Aleph brethren had a more elegant plan: they would employ his death to support their other projects.

In their usual manner of carefully timed, patient maneuvering, this new mission would make use of Cornelius' existing hatred of Ben Aaron by portraying their potential victim as an enemy of Rome. No purpose could be served now by revealing the truth of Cornelius' father's death: that he really had died from spoilt wine and not by Ben Aaron's hand. Marih felt a pang of regret at not relieving his old friend's mind, but a vendetta so long nurtured would surely be hard to let go. Let Cornelius serve his purpose for their cause instead.

Once Ben Aaron was disposed of, Claudius would be convinced peace would be better served by allowing the Jews to return to Rome. They would cast aspersions on Ben Aaron's earlier counsel. Rather than fostering good will, they would produce evidence the move had emboldened the extreme Jewish sects' plotting by concentrating the Jews in Judea for a major uprising.

One more flourish to their plan would be the support of Ananias. Marih had finessed the high priest to give false witness against Ben Aaron, asserting he had indeed worked with extremists.

Such was the first version of their scheming. However, in the middle of their preparation, Julia Agrippina – that iron force behind the throne of Rome – had Claudius Caesar announce the wedding of his legal heir and her son to Caesar's daughter. Nero would marry his stepsister Octavia.

Julia's plan cemented her son's succession to Caesar's throne versus the son of Caesar's own body. In little more than a year, Claudius Caesar would be dead, in a manner many ascribed to Julia. All hail Nero Claudius Caesar Augustus Germanicus, Emperor of the Roman Empire!

The time had come at last for the Aleph Lodge to carry on with their plan to eliminate Simaan Ben Aaron. This change of scenario better suited their purposes. Nero was oblivious to their control, either directly through Claudia or indirectly through their manipulations of Cornelius and Seneca. If anything were to go awry with one avenue, they still had another. Besides, it would be much easier to convince Nero to allow the Jews back to Rome than it would have been to have Claudius reverse his own decree.

. . .

"Since the death of Claudius, Ben Aaron has been visiting Octavia, the previous empress, regularly. Rumour has it that he was Julia's consultant on the murder of Claudius Caesar," Claudia Achte offered as casual dinner conversation with Elisa and Cornelius.

"Where did you hear this news?" Cornelius was immediately intrigued.

"Julia's slaves," Claudia Achte said, pretending indifference.

The next morning Cornelius flew to Seneca carrying the tale. They now risked losing control over Nero. If Julia had listened to Ben Aaron's counsel, the Jews might somehow exercise influence over the new Caesar. Something had to be done. After much deliberation – and taking into consideration the sensitivity of their positions and the complexity of Ben Aaron's network within the Empire –

they decided to bring his case to the public court and let the law do their work for them. Seneca in turn counselled Cornelius: by law he could not only take his revenge but he would be able to legally put his hands on Ben Aaron's wealth as compensation. This turn of the screw would further punish Ben Aaron in his final moments, seeing all his life's work handed to Cornelius.

Elisa's husband shared the plans with his wife at lunch. That very same afternoon, Elisa rushed the intelligence to the Roman Aleph Lodge. For them, taking Ben Aaron to court was a bad idea. The possibility of the court acquitting him would expose all the lies the Aleph brethren had built up around him.

With no time to waste, Claudia was instructed by the lodge to enlist Nero's help. She told him that Ben Aaron was working with extremist Jewish groups who were, among other things, organizing riots against the Empire. She said she overheard him in conversation about the matter with a stranger while awaiting audiences with the Palace Court.

"I also think you should know this about him..." she caught her tongue, as if hesitating.

"Know what, Claudia?" Nero's curiosity was piqued.

"I hesitate because it feels wrong to share a secret not my own, but you know I don't keep secrets from you. You are my best friend." Her deceit was honey on her tongue.

"You are my best friend too, Claudia. You know you can trust me. Anything in the Empire you want, anything! You can have it. I hope you know that." Nero had more than just friendship in mind. His new marriage posed no barriers for Nero Caesar. His lustful heart belonged to Claudia Achte. His unfortunate wife didn't have a chance next to this adventurous, artistic yet classic example of female pulchritude. The fact that Achte was twelve years older than Nero made her all the more attractive to the emotionally deprived adolescent.

"Well... would you promise to keep my secret?"

"I promise you."

"I believe the source, Nero, I do believe Simaan Ben Aaron murdered Cornelius' father by poisoning his wine, many years ago." She studied Nero's reaction for a brief pause. "Cornelius always knew, but he could never find a way to do anything about it."

"What are you saying? How did Cornelius know?"

"I admit now... Cornelius is my source. He confided to Elisa and me a tale of his military graduation mission in Jerusalem, how he was hiding in secret rooms beneath the Jewish Temple when he overheard Ben Aaron telling the High Priest how he murdered his father so he could manipulate Cornelius' influence in Rome."

"The poor man! He heard it with his own ears? I would have jumped the traitor and strangled him with my bare hands!"

"Cornelius is the consummate patriot. Like his father before him, he has always held the interest of the Empire above all else. He didn't want his rash actions risking the peace of the Empire or tainting his family name." Claudia skillfully defended her sister's husband. "Anyway, I just wanted to tell you this because now... well, now Simaan Ben Aaron is trying to advise your wife and your mother."

"I have to stop him... I have to..."

"My Caesar... my dearest friend... you promised me you would keep it a secret," she begged.

"But... do you want me to leave such a pest in my palace and let him harm me and the Empire? Claudia, my dear, we have to do something."

Claudia quietly wept. For once her skillful manipulation of Nero was also part of her real life. Her tears were genuine, but not for the reasons he thought. With lust and what remained of his youthful guilt simultaneously eating away at his heart, he took her head into his arms and wiped her tears against his chest. "Don't cry, Claudia. I'd rather take a dagger in my heart than see you cry."

She shrieked at the mention of a dagger in his heart. "Whoever would hurt my Nero shall cease to walk upon this earth! Do whatever you want with Ben Aaron... kill the bastard, if you want." She hoped he would literally fulfill those last words.

Nero gently raised her off his chest, composing her to sit comfortably, and crossed the room to the door. He whispered something close to the ear of the guard waiting outside and returned to Achte, continuing his caressing and consoling.

Within an hour the guard returned. Claudia Achte's own heart jumped in her chest when she saw the guard had Simaan Ben Aaron in tow. This was too good to be true, and her tears were triggered anew. Best of all, the old man had no clue why he had been summoned.

Nero took him by the hand and brought him to the middle of the room. "Do you know who I am?" Nero asked.

Nero's tone sent shivers up the old man's spine. "Caesar of the great Empire of Rome," came the reply of a true courtier.

"Do you know what happens to any who conspire against Caesar?"

"He shall not live!" Ben Aaron prayed to his one true God that Nero was only amusing himself with some of his playacting and was not being serious. He looked to Claudia for explanation, but the tears in her eyes weren't what he wanted to see. In a moment of denial, he assumed Claudia was the one at risk; perhaps Nero caught Claudia betraying him and she was the object of his questioning. "Has Claudia wronged Great Caesar? Has she angered you somehow?'

"Oh, you are a master of manipulation, aren't you? Working with the terrorists and betraying the trust of Claudius Caesar… wheedling your way into my court by influencing my mother and my wife… and now you try to twist your way out of my trap!"

"Caesar, these are untrue accusations! I beg you, allow me to defend myself." The old man's knees threatened to fail him.

"Defend yourself? What could you possibly say that I would believe? You didn't kill Cornelius' father? You didn't poison his wine?"

Hearing this ancient reference to Cornelius' father, Ben Aaron realized the conspiracy had its roots in Jerusalem. Only the priests knew that story… that lie!

"Caesar, I can prove it's not true… let me…" Simaan's words caught in his throat.

At that moment the tip of a slender dagger, a lady's dagger, slid through his left side, its handle held tightly in Claudia Achte's fists, one on top of the other. A practiced murderer could have done no better, slicing through his vital organs. Simaan wanted to turn around to see the one who had done this. He wanted to tell her he forgave her. He wanted to use his last moments of life to pray to his

God for peace. He wanted to tell the emperor he needn't feel guilty when he learned the truth in the future. He wanted to say he had lived for a good cause and was willing to die for the very same cause. His last thoughts reflected an innocent man's pure nature... the good deeds he hoped would survive him. But no words came. All that was left for him were those flashes in his mind before his aged heart gave way.

Nero stood in fear as he watched the falling body slam against the floor. The man just died, right there before his eyes, in his very own chamber. He, Nero Caesar, would be accused of this murder. His breathing was heavy. What would Caesar do?

"Caesar!" Claudia called in despair.

Nero heard Claudia as if hearing the word for the first time in his life. That's right. I am Caesar! "Guaaards!!" Even his own voice was a sound he had never heard before. It sounded like... Caesar.

He was Caesar.

Nero ran before the rushing guards, catching up Claudia and carrying her outside of the chamber. He ordered his guards to dispose of the body of the traitor.

Coincidentally, standing just at the entrance to the throne hall, Julia caught a glimpse of her son. Unsure of the situation, and why he had Claudia in his arms, she rushed after them.

"Claudia, dear, what happened? Are you hurt?"

"I apologize, my lady, forgive my appearance. I must look a fright." Claudia's face was still stained with tears and she used it in her pretence.

"This is all your doing, Mother! You and your traitor friends you have brought into my court!" Nero scolded.

Julia was taken aback. "Nero! I am your mother."

"And I am Caesar... Mother!"

She shrieked at this new behaviour from her son. What shock could cause him to speak to her in such a manner? Her instincts drew her in a panic back to his chamber. Before she got to the door, two guards were carrying away a body.

"Stop!" she commanded. A dead man would surely explain her son's conduct. Carefully looking at the face, she couldn't believe her eyes. This wasn't a burglar or assassin or errant servant of some kind. It was one of the most important Jewish diplomats in the city of Rome, an honoured friend of the Empire.

As she darted back to her son, many scenarios played in Julia's mind. Perhaps an intruder had killed Simaan and scared her son into thinking he was next. Or possibly it was an accident of some kind.

"Nero, what happened to Simaan?"

His face was contorted in a horrible sneer. "He got what he deserved, the murderer!"

"What are you talking about, what has he done?"

"Where would you like me to start, Mother? How about the poisoning of Cornelius' father? Or his plotting with the terrorist Jews, thereby convincing Claudius to expel them from Rome so they could regroup in Judea. You want to hear more? Do you? Or do you already know the rest?"

Julia stood stunned. Nero could not possibly be talking about the Simaan Ben Aaron she knew. He and a very few like him were all the reason behind the diplomacy still managing any control in that hotbed of Judea. He was no terrorist. She learned this firsthand from Claudius Caesar just before his death.

"Do you know what people are saying, Mother? They say he helped you kill Claudius!" Nero leaned forward in confrontation, face to face with Julia, challenging her very position in his court.

Julia Agrippina summoned every ounce of her formidable will and delivered a firm backhand to Nero's right cheek. No hesitation, no faltering. Under usual circumstances, she would have prevailed and regained control. However, there was nothing usual about this moment. In her automatic display of control, she had failed to read the situation before her: her son Nero had just moments earlier fully come to the realization of his total power as Caesar. It was most unwise for the mother of Caesar to slap him at all, let alone before his heart's desire.

With a roar of fury he called Caesar's guards. However, in removing Ben Aaron's body, the guards had wasted no time informing Cornelius of what had just happened. He answered the call for guards himself along with several of his soldiers.

"Take her to her chamber and keep her under locked guard until I say otherwise!" Caesar held his trembling arm in the air, pointing accusingly at his mother.

"These are lies, Nero! All of them, lies! Simaan Ben Aaron was loyal to the Empire, loyal to you!" she screamed in defence as the guards respectfully restrained her and bore her away.

"Claudia does not lie, Mother!"

Claudia? Claudia was Nero's source? The name fell on Julia's ears like the beating drums of war. She snapped one arm out of the grasp of the soldiers and turned sharply, throwing daggers with her eyes at the venomous Phoenician viper.

Claudia's body shook in a moment of doubt. But only a moment.

Thirty Three

The Envied
Should Trust None

The same name that drummed into Julia's ears soon became legend in every Aleph lodge. Tales of heroism and chronicles of bravery were attributed to the deeds of Claudia Achte. Many had heard of the near-magical feats of this triumphant young Phoenician and others even spoke of the return of the spirit of Hannibal to avenge the Phoenician glory. Very few knew her actual roots: Claudia, daughter of Paulus the Roman spy from Tarsus, who was himself of Jewish birth. Only the inner circle of brethren knew her true secret being: sworn Aleph warrior, baptized by the Mother Lodge of Tyre.

Cornelius was now in eternal debt to Claudia Achte for punishing Ben Aaron for him. He devoted himself to her protection and dedicated his military men and informants to keep any enemies away from her, especially Julia Agrippina or those who would do her bidding.

Seneca was no less proud of the daughter of Paulus, whom he considered to be his best man. In his mind, she was but a cub of that lion. They were both products of his making. He would put aside his stoic philosophies and sometimes revel in his view from on top of the world. Even Caesar was a puppet in his hands.

Nero fulfilled his pledge to Claudia by allowing the Jews and the Nazarenes back into the city of Rome; she found a most devious way to return the favour. In his lust for her, she had become his bronze goddess from Tyre, thereby providing her with the means to lure him into a world beyond his imagination, a world his aristocratic wife Octavia could never comprehend.

The Aleph missions immediately benefited from the new freedoms with Julia Agrippina's removal from the palace. Nero Caesar pursued another of his cravings, the beautiful Poppaea Sabina, and Claudia helped him realize his untapped desires. She led him to believe her only desire was to provide brilliant venues for his happiness, knowing her openness would subliminally enhance her influence over him and bind him to her. Unlike his jealous wife Octavia, she encouraged him to indulge himself.

Despite all her newfound power at court, one matter ironically escaped her reach: helping her father. The Nazarenes were experiencing a uniquely prosperous period across the Empire, even in the city of Rome. But in Jerusalem, Paulus was not having as much luck with his mission. He had been captured in Jerusalem by the men of Ananias. The high priest had no intention of breaking the deal he had with Marih. Indeed, he captured Paulus to save his life. His open preaching against the Jewish laws put him at risk of being killed by the people, not the temple. Ananias sent him to Caesarea to be protected by Roman Governor Felix. Having no clue of Paulus' work on behalf of Seneca, the governor kept Paulus in prison in order to satisfy the Jewish population and maintain the peace.

It was a hospitable imprisonment. Lost in the bureaucratic quagmire of the Empire since Nero's full realization of his divineness, Paulus took advantage of what amounted to little more than a house arrest. By this time, Paulus found himself supervising a widespread network of agents from a position of influence he had never thought possible. In fact, he didn't really need to be out in the field working on his projects day in and day out. His agents were doing all the work; he could coordinate their moves much more efficiently from one safe place. Writing letters to his flock spread across the Empire became his *modus operandi* and Felix's prison his headquarters; the governor had no idea what was going on right under his nose.

All the fluctuations of the turbulent reigns of a succession of capricious Caesars had driven the core of the agency underground. For some time Seneca had been running the whole project independently, thanks to Marih and Cornelius, his pillars in Judea and Rome. As far as the agency operating above ground was concerned, Project Paulus and Project Barnabas had been shut down long ago.

Claudia's helplessness persisted for the same reason Felix didn't know about the project and Nero had remained blinded to it. Informing Nero of the various delicate operations of his Empire postulated too many unpredictable outcomes, so Seneca's decision was to not take any additional risks at this time. Thus Nero remained uninvolved in the matter of Paulus of Tarsus, now Felix's indefinite guest. Even though Marih had managed to ensure no harm would come to Paulus beyond his gentle imprisonment, the imprisonment stretched out longer than originally planned.

In the course of events outside the agency's influence, Ananias was removed from his position as high priest at the Hebrew Temple. This troublesome development was immediately compounded by the assignment of a new governor, replacing Felix. These changes jeopardized Marih's ability to ensure Paulus' safety. Seneca cooked up a plan in short order. He sent word to Paulus advising him to raise his case before Caesar in Rome. This was a right of every Roman citizen across the Empire, although it was rarely practiced. Very few defendants ever had enough nerve to stand before any of the Caesars. For most, opting to serve time in prison seemed the safer choice.

At first the new governor thought he had no choice but to grant Paulus his wish, especially when another prominent Roman citizen and centurion – Marih – pleaded his case. Nevertheless, a pressing priority for this new governor was to be on good terms with the Jews. To serve both ends, he looked to find a way to return Paulus to Jerusalem, putting the onus on the Jews to try him there. But first, he needed to shore up his case by proving Paulus had committed an offense justifying the governor's refusal to send the case directly to Caesar. Using his influence, Marih advised the new governor to take advantage of the pro-Roman counsel of the ruling Hebrews, Herod

Agrippa the Second and his sister Berenice.

Marih had long ago established himself as an ally and trusted counsellor to Agrippa and Berenice, so he pressed them to speak in favour of Paulus. Theirs was a relationship steeped in political maneuvering, each deftly securing their positions with the assistance of the other. Hidden agendas were understood; each performed their favours from time to time without questioning motives on either side. As long as benefits flowed freely in both directions, who cared? The system worked.

Their highnesses insisted upon speaking with Paulus first. They clearly disagreed with his preaching and laughed at his attempt to convert them. But to the governor's disappointment, they claimed to find no reason why the man should be considered dangerous or worthy of a complex Jewish trial.

And so, with their testimony, Paulus was put in the company of Marih's soldiers and brought to a ship sailing for Rome. The ship was a Phoenician commerce vessel with many ports of call on its lengthy tour. Paulus would not see his trial before Caesar for least three years.

. . .

Seneca made certain Marih understood he must delay Paulus' return to Rome as long as possible. Nero was unbalanced and therefore unpredictable. Nero Caesar had recently murdered the intractable Julia Agrippina through an unbelievable series of highly implausible attempts. Some were very complex, set up like toy blocks to tumble in a particular manner.

One time he ordered the devising of a ceiling over his mother's bed that was to collapse at a certain trigger, crushing her. She survived it. His engineers then built a boat designed to founder and sink, drowning her. When it failed to sink, another of his boats was immediately dispatched to collide with hers. She swam to safety.

Rumours finally surfaced of several assassins sent to stab her so expertly that it would appear to be suicide. Those who saw the corpse said she looked just as beautiful and stern in death as they had ever seen her in life. Still others refused to believe that she had really died, insisting the assassins were so scared of her that they agreed to give her a sleeping potion of the blowfish making her appear dead, just to fool her conniving son. That rumour was pure silliness, of course, for Nero would have insisted on seeing the wounds himself in order to verify her death.

All in all, Julia's grip wasn't so easily shed. Not even death would free Nero Caesar from her iron grasp. Nightmares stole into his sleep, pushing him to the edge of insanity. Waking visions of her scolding him confounded his mind. In trembling fear he lost hold of reality and called upon Persian conjurers to send her ghost to hell where she belonged.

Seneca preferred Paulus stay away for a while. Claudia needed time to regain and secure her control over poor, demented Nero Caesar. Only twenty-three years old, he was never more susceptible to her wiles than in his current condition.

. . .

After several brief stops, the Phoenician vessel dropped Paulus and Marih's men on the island of Malta while it ferried various trading goods back and forth among the immediate islands. Malta was a major Phoenician settlement and a haven for Aleph elites, creating a friendly environment for the lodges to conspire and plot. Paulus never questioned all the doors opened to him in every Phoenician port and the surrounding cities, and so enjoyed spreading his version of the Nazarene way, preaching against the Jewish laws.

The signal came from Seneca at last: it was safe for Paulus to sail to Rome. Paulus and Marih's men concocted a story explaining how their ship had been wrecked among the smaller islands in a terrible storm. They had to wait until the weather permitted another ship to arrive in order to carry on with their voyage to Rome. Of course, anyone familiar with the sea lanes and seasons would have found all these excuses hard to believe. First, the distance from Malta to Rome was nothing compared to the distance already covered from Caesarea to Malta. Second, the length of time they had waited in Malta was totally unnecessary for a seasoned traveller. For such a brilliant man, Paulus was surprising malleable. To placate Paulus' people on the mainland, they couldn't resist spicing up the tales whenever possible. They told of Paulus being struck by a poisonous snake while in Malta. His resulting sickness required care and caution in handling their valuable captive, hence the delay.

. . .

Nero's priorities remained scattered. Now busy with plotting to rid himself of his wife Octavia, he deferred peripheral responsibilities – such as court hearings – to his staff and his Praetorian guards. Taking full advantage of his position, Cornelius was able to guide the Paulus case to appear before his own court. Without much fanfare, he acquitted him and Nero trustingly signed off on the judgment. At last, Seneca's favoured spy was able to sit by his side, in Rome, and resume their plotting for their perennial war against the Jews.

The Alephs gladly sat and watched their schemes unfold, unknowingly executed on their behalf by Seneca and his gang. Their bliss was short-lived.

Poppaea owed her position as Nero's lover to Seneca and Claudia. Claudia had encouraged Nero to pursue her against his mother's wishes. Poppaea's continuous encounters with Nero by way of Claudia's machinations had gone beyond expectations. She was older than Nero but younger than Claudia; even so, she became possessive and spiteful whenever Nero spent time with Claudia, and a dicey fire of jealousy consumed her belly.

Poppaea's first jealous wielding of her power over Nero resulted in the exile and eventual murder of Octavia, creating an uproar of public disapproval. Undeterred, Poppaea turned her spite toward Claudia. Unlike Poppaea, Claudia never underestimated Nero and did not take his actions lightly. Nero had learned one lesson from Claudia Achte that would stick with him for the rest of his life: as Caesar he could solve any of his problems by simply eliminating them, be they problems of things or people. Achte had created this monster herself the day she murdered Simaan Ben Aaron in his very presence. She knew now to watch Nero carefully, for Poppaea was proving dangerous... as much to herself as to anyone else. Seeking to pour oil on the troubled waters, Claudia and Seneca blessed Nero's marriage to Poppaea.

Whenever Claudia left her scent on Nero – for he could never give up his passions for her – the territorial Poppaea was driven to act, but soon realized her weakened position. She felt the squeeze of the tight and powerful gang of operatives, choked by Seneca, Cornelius,

Claudia, and their supporters at the palace. She was forced to devise a plan of her own. She would build her own network of supporters, encouraged by a thread she discovered among the Praetorian Guard. No court is without its intrigues, and there were those among the elite military who envied Cornelius and Seneca their everlasting positions of influence with Caesar. They were ready and willing to give Poppaea a hand.

. . .

"My lady, your suspicions were wise," said her contact among the Praetorian dissenters. "Caesar's advisor and trusted consultant, Lucius Seneca, is involved in matters beyond my ability to contemplate, let alone judge."

"Speak up!" Poppaea encouraged. "The Praetorian Guard need not fear any truth discovered on behalf of Caesar's safety. But, if you fear judging such actions, leave it to your empress. Leave it to me."

"I fear no consequences, my lady. I merely fear an error in judgment when it comes to Caesar's choice of friends and counsellors."

"You are an honest man and I know your loyalty to Caesar is beyond reproach. Tell me what concerns you."

"During Seneca's recent absence, my men searched his office, just as you ordered. They found many suspicious letters. They took a sampling and brought them to my attention." As the officer spoke, Poppaea's hopes of finding the key to eliminate Claudia from her life were lifted. "My lady, my first thoughts were perhaps Seneca was involved in some sort of undercover operation. Then one of the letters stood out among the others. I believe you will find it of utmost significance." He politely waited until Poppaea inquired as to the contents of the letter.

The officer produced the scroll, unrolled it, and read:
"PAUL TO ANNAEUS SENECA, greetings:
Whenever your letters are read, I think of you as present, and imagine nothing else but that you are always with us. Soon, we shall see each other in close quarters.
I desire your good health."

Poppaea listened carefully but was puzzled, obviously unable to connect the dots.

The officer volunteered an explanation: "My lady, this letter comes to Seneca from a man who was imprisoned by our governor in Judea for two whole years before being sent to Rome to stand trial before Caesar."

"So, was he tried?"

"Yes, but not by Caesar. He came before a court convened on behalf of Caesar. The judge was none other than Cornelius with Seneca in attendance. They heard his case and acquitted him." He hoped this pretty little trophy wife of Nero's would grasp the implications of his report.

"So, they helped a friend? Is that a bad thing?"

"Not just any friend, my lady. This man is a leader among a Jewish sect called the Nazarenes. They have been and continue to be a source of recurring troubles for the Empire in Judea. Why, their original leader was executed for that very reason, years ago. Continued conspiring with such vermin is a matter of treason against Rome, if I may be so bold as to offer my opinion, dear lady."

Poppaea's pretty smile spread across her face. It did little to hide the fire behind her eyes. Finally! she had heard what she needed to know in plain and simple clarity. She had her evidence: Claudia and her cohorts were traitors against Rome, against Nero Caesar himself! If this didn't keep her tempestuous Nero away from Claudia, what could?

Thirty Four

A Walk on the Beach

"And with the permission and blessings of Melqart, the Great Architect of Life, I now declare this lodge duly open and ready for business. We are gathering this night as brethren of the highest degree of the Lodge of Tyre, the degree of our Master Hiram, to discuss the pending business of our late brother Hannibal."

That meeting of the Aleph Mother Lodge in Tyre would have been one long-remembered by historians – had it only been known to them. It was springtime and Melqart showered his blessings everywhere: the sea was friendly, the moon lit the stony paths of the city by night, the sky was uninterrupted by even a hint of clouds, and the morning sun brightened the blooming orange trees, boosting the moods of locals and visitors alike. The overpowering sense of well-being encouraged the Aleph brethren to proceed with their patient discussions of the perfect timing to launch their greatest campaign.

If there ever was a time and a place for their enemies to decimate the powers behind the Aleph lodges, it was then and there. Everyone who was anyone was in attendance. Masters of lodges from all through the Mediterranean and stretching far into the hinterlands came to put their mark upon this auspicious gathering. Every word of the discussions would be evaluated and every vote counted. These powerbrokers squeezed in side by side, packing the hall to overflowing. Peering eyes surveyed every face, trying to identify their heroes and heroines.

"That must be Claudia Achte," one man whispered.

"Claudia is younger and tougher. I think Claudia is over there, the tall girl with the tattoo," another man replied.

The visiting lodge masters took turns speaking. Those for and those against gave their justifications and reasoning. Those against were amply outnumbered. Then, they voted. At last it was time to launch an offensive against their archenemy and ancient foe. Their revenge had been simmering for generations; their ceaseless planning had stoked the fires. Now they would take their places at the table and serve up destruction, beginning with the city of Rome itself, feasting on the mayhem.

If the Alephs believed in such silliness as augurs and portents, they would have claimed the most propitious omens were favouring their efforts. Nero was under Claudia Achte's control. The Nazarenes of Paulus had sufficiently invaded the Empire, even unto Rome. Among them were hundreds and hundreds of Alephs planted as gentile converts to the new religion. The Jews in Jerusalem had reached their threshold for tolerance with the latest Roman governor who made one blundering mistake after another thanks to Marih's masterful misdirection. Last, but by no means least, the most powerful of Caesar's Praetorian Guard, Cornelius, was like a precious ring on Elisa's finger.

"...As our Aleph brethren burn the core of the city, Elisa will hinder Cornelius and the Praetorian Guard until the job is done. She will persuade them the city is being burned by order of Nero Caesar. Meanwhile, Claudia will distract Nero by employing his obsession for art, thereby saving him from the fire. He must remain alive for the people to blame... he must be the focus of their hatred, once the fire is contained and the inevitable chaos ensues. Marih will expose Barnabas, Cephas, and Paulus to the Jews as Roman agents, which will further fuel the smoldering war between the Jews and the Nazarenes, scorching the Romans with their flaming religions. Brothers and sisters: in their chaos we will flourish! In the ashes of their destructions, we will grow like a forest of cedars on Mount

Lebanon!"

The master of the Mother Lodge delivered the blistering outline of the carnage to come with all the fire and brimstone that burned legendary Sodom into the Dead Sea. The Phoenician people were only marginally aware of the revenge being kept alive on their behalf. It was their priests of Aleph who had carried this burning ember of revenge deep in their breasts for generations upon generations, nursing it so slowly only those in the lodges could lay claim to true fervour. Yet because of the brethren, all the while everyone had prospered and grown. The commoners had no idea there was an elaborate hidden agenda behind their leaders' otherwise tolerable governance. Now these powerful orders flowing from the Mother Lodge would cut across the classes, break up families, separate spouses, slaughter the children, destroy property and promises, and lay waste the innocent. Collateral damage is a very ancient concept.

For in the hive mind of the Aleph brethren, all was allowed in the name of revenge. Just as their temples had been desecrated by the Roman filth of occupation so many years ago, now the children of this accursed enemy must be sacrificed for the honour of Melqart, the vengeance-craving god who thirsted for blood.

These were a people who didn't forget, a people who rose from the ashes time after time... after time. The design of the long-fallen Melqart temple shaped all their lodges; the pillars of His temple were still mimicked in every ceremony they held all across their world. They lived for a purpose and died for that purpose: the revenge of the God Melqart, the Aleph and the El.

. . .

After the vote, all commands became non-negotiable. Swaying of minds, lobbying for one's argument, and all other forms of debate had been relegated to history. A truly democratic body, for or against, once a majority was decided, all Alephs put aside the losing arguments and were expected to steadfastly and literally perform any and all duties assigned to them.

That night, back at Marih's house in Tyre, the women couldn't sleep. In their minds, it was all too easy for the lodge master; he so matter-of-factly read out the orders one would have thought he was handing out awards, even though he tried to dress it up in rally cries. Now that the hour had come, it didn't rest easy with Elisa and Claudia. More than twenty years ago, Elisa's heart would at times resist being thrown into a life with no other purpose but to serve the cause. She manipulated her world until she was offered a path combining her two passions: Tyre and Cornelius. Her trials were at times severe, but her rewards had been many.

Up until tonight, that is. Swimming in her thoughts, she now stared her orders directly in the face. She had just been ordered to deceive the man she loved and had built a family with. Putting love aside, Elisa could not comprehend how the lodge she had served so selflessly could now cast aside basic considerations of human nature and the simple but fundamental moralities modern civilizations agreed made life worth living. Something as basic as caring. After all these years she realized lust and love and passion were not what bound her to Cornelius. It was caring. How could she harm the person for whom she cared so much, the father of her children, who trustingly relied on her care?

In her restlessness she debated with herself. On the other hand, she thought, Cornelius would have not been in her life at all had it not been for the lodge and her assigned missions. Her royal blood bound her to the Alephs, and in return for her life of privilege she was obligated to carry out her sacred mission, keeping her promises to her royal house, her nation, and her god. Tyre depended upon her. Her personal feelings and emotions, her very life, were but transient trivialities written down in the Book of Life. From infancy her parents had taught her, 'Victories are born from the wombs of sorrow.' That was how her ancestors found courage to jump on tiny boats and risk their lives in the open sea, seeking glory and prosperity for many generations yet to come. These ancestors resisted the most brutal Mesopotamian warriors. They chose death over surrender to that Macedonian conqueror. Neither Nebuchadnezzar nor Alexander had been able to force this people to bow before them. From the ashes of their burnt cities the glorious phoenix kept rising. Such pride deserved any and all sacrifices for vengeance.

Elisa felt her head was going to explode.

Claudia tossed and turned in her own bed. She was thirty-nine years old. Like Elisa in her youth, her own stomach had twisted into knots of rebellion more than once. She frequently balked at the realization of her life as a pawn in the hands of old men who sat on their phony thrones in their lodges of self-acclaimed greatness. She pushed her defiance deep within her psyche, her indoctrination beyond question or reproach, but this time their scheming went beyond her tolerance. Paulus was her father! She was too little to remember much of anything before being brought to the royal household in Tyre. Their gentle programming always taught her to love her father and not blame his Jewish ancestry or Roman allegiance, as it was not his fault to be born a Roman Jew. Had she thought to question the Phoenician ancestry, they had already firmly supplanted their racial superiority in her very soul. It never occurred to her before, and she marvelled at it now; but she was so well-trained it got fleeting attention. It was truly amazing how her mind skipped right back to implanted memories of her father, how she had been taught that his actions were also not to be despised for he was being misled by the Roman agency. And now, her adopted people plotted to hurt him, a man in his sixties! Her mind had swung back again. She thought of other ways he might die. He could just as easily be killed by extremist Jews or conservative Jews or any number of Roman organizations should any of them ever learn he had spent his life working for an unofficial intelligence agency run by Lucius Seneca. Treason, just like beauty, must be in the mind of the beholder.

. . .

"I cannot sleep either," Claudia said. She stood with her face against the cool plaster, as if likening her current circumstances to hitting a wall. Elisa had already been sitting up in the dark, silently, for quite a while.

"You want to take a walk on the beach?" Elisa asked.

Claudia threw a cloak about her shoulders as her reply. Elisa followed in the dark. No torches lit, they went silently along the coast, shivering just a bit from the spring breezes coming off the sea. Aside from their dark cloaks, only a dagger strapped to Elisa's waist protected the sisters. They felt more secure under cover of darkness.

"Thinking about Paulus?" Elisa started.

"Is it wrong to?"

Elisa turned her head to Claudia, her little sister's eyes peering ahead with little more than starlight to show their way. The darkness provided a luxury of privacy as they shared their thoughts. "I think it is healthy to be thinking about your father."

"Then why do I feel so guilty?" Claudia's tone was flat, incompatible with her words.

Elisa's eyes watered in the sea air, though she knew it was more than that. What could she to say to Claudia? Nothing made sense to her anymore. What devotion to any cause could ever make hurting one's own beloved parent acceptable?

"You know, by manipulating the Praetorian Guard, Cornelius may be accused of treason or negligence. Either way he may be severely punished." Claudia stopped and turned to the sea, the gentle waves of the ebb tide playing peek-a-boo with her toes. The darkness of the horizon over those unknown depths offered a greater sympathy than anything these now devious assignments by the lodge ever could.

"How would I live with myself if I harmed him?" Anguish slipped past the knot in the willful Elisa's throat.

Claudia tried not to flinch; she was scared of breaking down herself if she were to see her sister weeping. "Then maybe you shouldn't."

Elisa wept quietly.

"Really. Just how binding are these orders... how binding are our vows to obey?" Claudia said defiantly. For the first time in her life, she found the courage to question the lodge, the very core of the elite Phoenician religion and their sacred way of life. "You realize... it was you and I and Marih and Ishtar, and others like us – our generation – who brought the lodge to this point in time. Real-life flesh-and-blood people like us who went out and made these things happen, gave those old men in their aprons and regalia all their successes and glories. It's been our everyday decisions and tactics out there in the world that they take credit for today... putting our lives on the line every hour of every day, not for a month, not for a year, but for decades... lifetimes. We put the power of our decisions in the hands of the lodge masters, not the other way around. We are Phoenicia,

Elisa... we should be the ones making the rules, not them."

Achte's rebellion was music to Elisa's ears, the forbidden melody of disobedience. But accepting such upheaval at her age was not just a matter of making a decision. She had grown up and spent the majority of her life following a certain belief system, how the world functioned, and she accepted her part in it. Dropping this understanding now meant admitting all her life had been misdirected, a waste. Such a daunting admission could prove fatally depressing.

Elisa repeated a trite old phrase as if divinely inspired, "You cannot teach an old dog new tricks." She wiped her tears as she spoke.

For the first time that night, Claudia turned to her sister. She heard Elisa's words, but she was not convinced she meant them. She let her entire being speak her support, whatever it needed to be.

"I know that sounded silly. In the moment I couldn't think of anything more enlightening. But you know what I mean. I will do what I do best, what I was born to do," Elisa confirmed.

The two women walked back to the house, with no further need for words. Claudia heard Elisa's cryptic decision. She didn't quite understand it and maybe didn't want to understand it, let alone agree with it. What she really didn't understand was why Elisa did not ask her if she was going to comply? Did Elisa expect her to follow her lead? Or perhaps not. Perhaps Elisa just didn't want to influence her decision. It might have been her way of saying, 'I won't judge you whatever you do.' Perhaps there was one more explanation: one that disturbed Claudia even though she thought her level of disturbance had already peaked. What if Elisa in fact wanted her to go ahead with her defiance? What if her sister believed defiance was the right action, but she couldn't follow through? Elisa might want Claudia to do what she couldn't get herself to do – such actions they both knew could only lead Elisa to deeper regrets.

Back in their beds, they were more awake than before, their minds racing through the remainder of the night.

Thirty Five

Beware the Jealous Woman

"The empress has the letter, sir," the Praetorian Guard informed his commander Tribune Flavius.

"Does she understand its value and what it means?"

"I explained it to her, sir. She understands that it implicates Lucius Seneca in an act of treason," the guard confirmed.

Flavius stifled his snicker; he summoned some sincerity and graciously praised his loyal guard for a job well done.

Flavius Scaevinus was a Praetorian tribune commanding a cohort of a thousand soldiers. As the Praetorian Guard were entrusted with the life and safety of Caesar, they were the closest to his person, his palace, and his inner circle. Any breach in loyalty of the Praetorian Guard could have grave consequences on Rome itself.

Nero's Praetorians were positively infected.

The very rich Roman senator, Gaius Piso, counted among his many possessions the loyalty of Tribune Flavius. Aristocratic Gaius had his eyes on the emperor's throne, for everyone knew Nero's days were numbered. He had helped set that clock himself by insidiously exaggerating Nero's faults and campaigning against him in the Senate. His long-term plan was aimed at his promotion via his generous distribution of wealth and support to the people.

Nero's public relations were sorely lacking and easily manipulated by people like Gaius. Occasionally Nero helped them along without any prodding at all, like when he killed Julia and Octavia.

Political tricks of all sorts were tolerated within the republican measures of the era, with the exception of attempts to replace Caesar. Any such subversion quickly caused heads to roll. The operative word here is 'attempt.' Gaius' plan was to remain undercover until the right time and make sure not to fail. On the day the secret came out, it had to be definite, final, and mortal to Caesar.

. . .

Returning to Rome from her trip to Tyre with Claudia under the ruse of visiting her parents, Elisa found Cornelius fuming and flustered. This was not at all like him.

"Somebody has meddled with Seneca's documents!"

"Somebody? Somebody who?"

"That's what makes me crazy. We cannot be sure, but if I didn't know better, I'd say Poppaea is behind this. Her jealousy of Claudia is out of control, making her very dangerous."

"Can she really be that harmful?"

"I don't know, but in our position, any small mistake can have disastrous repercussions. It would all fall upon one man's word. If Caesar suspects the slightest thing, he can end it... end us, with just one word."

Elisa shared her husband's distress, though for a slightly different reason. These unforeseen circumstances could radically affect the Aleph plans. If Cornelius lost ground to Poppaea or her men, he could be removed from his place of honour in Caesar's court. Without him in place, the Aleph plan would have a gaping hole.

She wasted no time relating the seriousness of these developments to the master of the Aleph Lodge in Rome. They had to move quickly to identify the source of danger, then clarify the risk to the operation, ultimately deciding whether they should abandon it, revise it, or just carry on. Word was spread to all the operatives, but they would not jeopardize the momentum of the plan unless absolutely necessary. The burning of Rome must be this very summer, as the heat dried to brittle tinder not only the city but the tempers of the citizens, all equally primed for the flames of vengeance.

. . .

Jealousy is a foolish emotion, and Poppaea gave the word new meaning. She blindly followed her basest instincts, uncalculated and destructive. It wasn't long before she brought her evidence – the found letter – to Nero's attention.

Nero justified the letter to his wife. "My love, Seneca is a peerless philosopher and the wisest man I know. I am not his only admirer. He must receive many letters of this kind."

"Not a letter from a man like that, a man actively working against my Caesar's Empire."

"What man? What do you know about him?"

"The author of the letter goes by the name Paul of Tarsus, sometimes Paulus, but his real name is Saul. He is a Jew and preaches for the glory of a new god higher than Caesar and for a law higher than the Empire's!" She spoke in such detail that Nero had to be suspicious of such knowledge beyond her usual comprehension.

"Where did you get all this information? And since when do you care so much about politics?"

"Oh, stop insulting me, please! Politics aren't the sole realm of your little Claudia! You are blinded by her slyness. Open your eyes and look around. You will see a reality quite different from the one she sings into your divine ear. Others plainly see it. Why, all your Praetorians know it."

"So that's what's at the bottom of this. How many more times than the thousands I've already told you: you don't need to be jealous of her. Take care, Poppaea, for you know this topic angers me!" Nero turned away with hasty steps towards the door. His sudden fury took control and he stopped in his tracks. He turned on Poppaea, taking her thin neck in his tight clasp. He hissed between clenched teeth, "You speak of this once more, woman, and I swear it will be the last time I hear your voice!" With that, he pushed the frail beauty off her balance and stormed out, leaving her gasping in a pile of costly silks upon the floor.

Nero's anger toward Poppaea cooled in a few days, as it always did, but this time it was replaced by unsettling doubts. *If she is right and all the guards know this Paul or Saul or whoever and his influence over Seneca, why hasn't anyone told me about it?* he thought, wavering on the edge of paranoia. Of course, no one would admit to giving the letter to Poppaea, for that would mean they had conspired to hide state secrets from Caesar.

"Wait a moment! I am Caesar! These silly courtly intrigues are no barrier for me! With this letter in hand, I will confront Seneca myself and dig out this treason by its very roots!" This time his thoughts were very out loud. He grabbed the letter in one hand, felt his sword's hilt in the other, and dashed out, full of purpose.

Before he reached the door of his chamber, Claudia Achte silently appeared from the shadows, startling Nero out of his resolve. She made sure they were alone, Nero's hot eyes following her around the room. With the assurance of accustomed privilege compounded by lustful depravity, she climbed Nero's rounded trunk and wrapped her legs around him; the move was a specialty of the Devadasis, the temple courtesans of India, and Claudia's mastery of it made Nero her puppet. His former fury and wrath settled in his spine and exploded, transformed into the artful expression of two connoisseurs of celestial lust – two bodies fastened together by the authority of the stars – or perhaps by Melqart.

Thirty Six

On the Hour

King Herod Agrippa the Second had been playing games with the ancient religion of Judea with great dexterity. He presented himself as the protector of Judaism by way of reviving the temple and the holy city of Jerusalem. Despite his astute finessing of the One God and His chosen people, he suddenly found himself in pressing need for a political victory to fortify his position against the zealot Jews, for they had never stopped accusing him of being a Roman sympathizer. With the reconstruction of the temple now completed, a new distraction needed to replace it in order to keep the people busy and marginally accepting of their king.

The king's desperate situation came to Marih's attention. His informant was none other than the former high priest Ananias. After losing his title and position to another priest, Ananias found a safe haven at King Agrippa's palace and financial comfort by working for Marih.

"I have something sure to gain you favour with King Agrippa," Marih said, baiting his hook. He had never felt uncomfortable in his dealings with this paragon of greed and selfishness. People like Ananias could be bought for the right price at any time and for any reason.

"I like the sound of that," Ananias responded, his salacious voice dripping with avarice. His grin stretched over stained, uneven remnants of teeth. "But why don't you start by telling me what you want in return."

Marih smirked. "This one is on me, in the name of friendship."

"People actually do that? Well, I'll not stand in the way of brotherhood. I am all ears."

"You are going to provide your king with the political distractions he's been searching for."

"Aha..." Ananias bent forward, the better to hear.

"Three Nazarene names, three Roman spies." Marih paused to watch Ananias' face as he tried to make the connections.

"Three Nazarenes who have been spying for Rome?" Ananias repeated, rephrasing for clarity.

"That's right."

Ananias looked directly at Marih. "Big names?" His tone reflected immense interest.

"The biggest." Marih pointed to the sky.

"The biggest! Cephas?"

"Uh huh," Marih nodded.

"Is this some joke? Don't you want him safe and sound?"

Marih smirked again. He let out a little more fishing line, knowing Ananias would eventually take the bait.

"Aha! His time has come, I guess."

Marih nodded.

"Don't toy with an old man. Who are the other two?"

"Paulus and Barnabas."

Ananias, stunned, took a step backwards to regain his balance. "You really meant it? These are the biggest. But the king will not want to try Roman agents. The governor would never even attempt it!"

"The king needs the support of the high priest, so he will expose their whereabouts to said high priest and then let him work with the governor." Marih explained, "King Agrippa gets his political score, the high priest gets his evidence to capture the Nazarenes, and you get the king's appreciation and more."

"You never cease to impress me. Of course, you have omitted

your part of the deal," he said, his ugly teeth emerging again.

Bending his knees to bring his face down to the grizzled old man's level, Marih loudly whispered, "This conversation never happened. You don't know me."

"But how can I prove this? The king will require proof."

"This is your proof." Marih picked up a scroll from among several others in a pile in the middle of planning table.

Ananias snatched it from him impatiently, unrolled it, and buried his face in it for few minutes. "Is this *the* Seneca?"

The letter was written by Seneca and directed to Paulus and Barnabas with instructions related to their projects. Marih had once intercepted one of several letters, saving it for a day like this.

"Yes, one and the same. The king knows him well." Marih didn't want to give too much information to Ananias. If something went wrong and Seneca suspected his agents were uncovered, Marih had to protect himself as the source. He would let Ananias take the story to King Agrippa, rather than tell him directly.

"This implicates Paulus and Barnabas. But what about Cephas?" Ananias was still unclear on several points.

"It's implied. He is their leader and guide, isn't he?"

"Well... I suppose so. It could be implied. But is it the truth? Is Cephas really a Roman spy?" Ananias, despite his natural bent for foul treachery, shivered at the thought of the Nazarenes being led by a Roman spy.

"Does it really matter?"

"No." Ananias had his answer: Cephas was just a pawn; he was being set up. He rolled up the scroll and tossed it back onto the pile. "No. Why would it?"

. . .

Marih's Aleph operatives, the ones who were their eyes everywhere and sometimes planted ideas where they would best grow, informed the Nazarenes that the High Priest had placed his hands on some evidence, putting him in the position to persecute them despite local Roman protection. He did not intend to have the Nazarene leaders captured right out of the blue; rather he wanted to stir the pot, build up anger and tension, and keep the level of chaos just below the boiling point in Judea until it was the perfect time to let it boil over.

Despite his age, Cephas could be surprisingly quick when resorting to his best defence: hiding. He didn't even bother to confirm the news. The rumours made out that local Romans like Marih were helpless, so he turned his back on the new church and took off for Rome, to his Roman friend Paulus. The High Priest couldn't reach him there.

Barnabas, on the other hand, took the trouble to verify the accuracy of the information by going directly to Marih. Beneath his Roman centurion guise, the Aleph spy delighted in having no good news for him. Barnabas decided to head to Cyprus, his homeland and birthplace. Friends and family would give him refuge until things calmed down. But the time he wasted to verify the information proved to be a dreadful misstep. The orders of the High Priest arrived in Cyprus before him, bearing undeniable proof of treachery in Seneca's own handwriting.

Friends and family were speechless with shock, but only for a moment. The disclosed particulars were enough to move them to action. With the might of the Law of Moses behind them, Barnabas received a special homecoming: stoned to death on his native soil.

Perhaps there is something to be said for the ways of the coward. For the time being, Cephas' survival technique proved to be the most effective.

. . .

On the eighteenth night of the month of July, certain Aleph brethren who were planted among the Nazarenes saw to a gathering of their church in Rome. The announced purpose was to discuss how they could best support their brothers and sisters in Judea, now under persecution by the High Priest. They met in the dead quiet of night, among the warehouses in the merchants' quarter, far away from the residential districts. Under the light of a nearly full moon, devoted Nazarenes silently picked their way between the sparse shadows to the meeting place.

As the two leaders of the church made ready to make their way to the meeting, Paulus and his guest Cephas were stopped at Paulus' doorstep by a man bent over, hands on his knees, gasping for breath. "Rabbis, stay here! Do not go to the meeting!"

"Who are you, son?" Cephas asked the man, bending to hear the words through his panting.

"Milichus... I am... a believer in Yeshua... a student of your teachings... masters, please hear me." The man finally caught his breath, deeply in and then out. *I have their attention now,* thought the Aleph operative as he stood to face them. "I work for the Praetorian tribune, Flavius Scaevinus, my lords. He just gave orders to his guards to attack the Nazarenes gathering in the warehouse district."

"What? But why? They are gathering in peace!" Cephas nearly shrieked. "We have to warn them!" Cephas immediately regretted what he just said. But he had to pretend. Such a response would be expected from him.

"No, Rabbi! It is too late. You cannot help them now, you will only endanger yourselves."

Paulus was in no hurry to set himself up for any more trouble. Summoning what passed for fearful concern, he pled, "So what can we do? There must be something... some way to aid them?"

"My brothers in Christ, I recommend you stay here until things settle. This is all I can say. I have to return to my post. Be safe in the name of Yeshua." And with a deep bow, the man dashed away into the night.

. . .

At Cornelius' house, Elisa had finished writing an official order in her practiced hand: on behalf of her husband, the Praetorian Guard are urgently commanded to send a hundred soldiers to the merchants' district, there to surround a group of Nazarenes planning to riot. They are to force them into an empty warehouse loaded with dry timbers and mercilessly set it to blaze. She stamped and sealed the letter using her husband's official Praetorian seal.

Elisa had put their children to bed several hours earlier. At the door to her house two soldiers were seated, as usual, guarding the family of this Praetorian tribune.

"Soldier!" she called with authority but with a face full of urgency. "Go find the tribune and be swift! Tell him the children are sick and I need him to come without delay." Elisa knew Cornelius was doing his late night tour on the palace, a routine he kept from his earliest days at Caesar's court.

As the soldier ran to fulfill her command, she hurried next to one of her husband's Praetorian centurions. This centurion's post was not part of Cornelius' nightly routine, so to this man she handed the written order.

"My lady, forgive me, but this kind of action within the city of Rome requires either the Senate's approval or Caesar's."

"I am but a messenger, centurion." She lowered her eyes and continued, "I was told that this is a matter of utmost urgency. Caesar's life is in danger! If we do not carry out this command and harm comes to him, we will all be held for acts of treason." She stepped close to the young patriot and clasped his left shoulder, drawing his face closer to her sweet breath. "These are the difficult times when the gods test the trueness of men. Your Caesar is in need. His very life calls out for his Praetorian defenders. You are the pride of Rome and the elite of the Empire. Of course, it is your choice to overlook protocol, but I hope you choose wisely." She shook his shoulder encouragingly, turned with the confidence of one accustomed to obedience, and steadily retraced her steps back to her apartments. Beneath her actions was a heart pounding into the pit of her stomach. If the soldier didn't comply, the whole plan would fall apart. There would be no time to try something else.

From behind her a familiar military cry reached her ears. Elisa closed her eyes for a couple of seconds, took a breath of relief, and kept walking. The centurion was readying his men.

Eyes open, Elisa still couldn't see. Hot tears blinded her.

. . .

Cornelius returned to his house in a panic. His wife had never sent after him in such a fashion before. The matter would have to be very serious indeed. Upon arriving, he was alarmed to find the children in bed and Elisa nowhere in sight. The guard who had remained at the door explained she had gone out in a hurry, leaving no messages.

Checking on the children again, it was obvious they were very ill. Their little bodies were cold with a clammy sweat; they were lethargic, eyes closed, breathing heavily. Perhaps his wife had gone herself to fetch the court healer, but perhaps not. He couldn't take any chances.

"Guard!" he cried out. The guard appeared, awaiting directions.

"Fetch the healer! If he can't be found, seek one outside the compound who can come right away." Cornelius felt helpless. His children had come to him at an age much older than most of his peers. He was very attached to them.

He sat by the fitfully sleeping children, mopping their brows and stroking their soft cheeks... and waited.

Thirty Seven

Story Has It,

He Watched and Fiddled

After that wild, unplanned sexual encounter, Claudia enticed Nero to leave the city with her and go to his villa in Antium. Her pretence was that Nero Caesar must rehearse for his appearance in the play he had planned to perform for his adoring public, something never done before by any Caesar. Antium, Nero's birthplace, was a seaside destination southwest of Rome where many aristocrats built lavish villas for their hedonistic escapades away from the eyes of Rome.

Nero didn't need much persuading. He didn't feel like confronting Seneca about the letter right now. He would deal with it all later. And so the two lovers headed out of the city chasing the sweet, sea air and whatever other surprises his lusty Claudia had planned for them.

They had barely begun his rehearsal in the small amphitheatre at the villa when a messenger barged in upon them. This sudden breach of courtly etiquette would normally draw an unreasonable penalty, but before Nero could unleash his rebuke the man burst out:

"Mighty Caesar, Rome is burning!"

"What do you mean?"

"A huge fire began in warehouses of the merchants' district and is rampaging through the city. The cisterns are not full enough to supply the fire brigades with water and the winds are whipping the flames and spreading them quickly to all quarters."

"Aren't my guards working on the matter?"

"Caesar, forgive me for bearing this suspicion, but some say the Praetorian Guard started it." The messenger paused a few seconds, obviously afraid to continue.

"Speak up, soldier!"

"It was the Guard who attacked the Nazarenes, supposedly upon your orders. They packed them into an old warehouse and set the dry wood to blaze, burning them alive."

Claudia kept her face aloof, as if nothing she heard passing between Nero and the soldier was of her concern. Behind her distant eyes, the carefully executed plan unfolding in Rome was indeed a command performance, and she sat with the audience, enjoying the spectacle as it played out in her mind. And now the climax:

"I gave no such orders! That's absurd! Why would Caesar burn his beautiful city? This is treason! Treason, I tell you! I will find out what is going on! Those responsible will pay with their lives!" Nero dropped the instrument in his hand and bolted from the theatre, back to Rome. Claudia followed silently, and amenably.

. . .

When Elisa left the centurion preparing for his attack on the Nazarenes, she didn't immediately return to her children. Instead, she went to Milichus, the Aleph operative serving under Tribune Flavius Scaevinus. She asked him to warn Paulus and Cephas not to go to the meeting.

"What do I say to Cephas about how I came to know about this?" Milichus asked.

"Say that you heard Flavius give the orders," Elisa instructed. "Assuming you are one of the Nazarenes, Paulus and Cephas will never tell on you."

After dispatching Milichus to Paulus and the simpering Cephas, Elisa climbed atop one of the seven hills of Rome where she could clearly see the warehouses below. From a small grove of cedar trees, she waited silently, watching the scattered torches along the dark road. She watched as the torches converged and the blaze of a much bigger fire gained prominence. Beneath these cedars transplanted long ago from her native land, she fell face down on the ground, her head to the southeast, in the direction of Tyre and the still sacred ruins of Melqart's temple, and prayed.

A few minutes later, she stood and dusted from her clothes the foreign soil along with the dry needles that carried the scent of her place of birth. She took a final look at the fire and whispered to herself, for she wanted to hear her own voice speak these words at last:

> "In memory of two hundred and ten years since the burning of Carthage by Rome and seven generations of Phoenicians restless with devotion to you, Lord Melqart, this night the Romans will watch their city fall to ashes, a mighty sacrifice at your feet and a fitting testimony to your magnificence."

Like an automaton magically set to motion in the Temples of Alexandria, Elisa set her feet towards home, her emotions blunted.

. . .

Cornelius was going crazy waiting for the healer. Where was Elisa? Nothing made any sense. He was helpless and afraid without her. The healer who came back with his soldier was not the court healer but came with recommendations. Still, he was worse than useless as he had no idea what ailed the children. Fearing for his life should he fail a family so close to Caesar, the healer promised to return with certain preparations he claimed could at least counteract the mysterious symptoms.

Head down, listening for any sound of Elisa, Cornelius finally heard a commotion at the entrance. His guards were quarreling with someone. In a moment, Praetorian Tribune Flavius Scaevinus was at the door with a number of soldiers at his heels. The guards were outnumbered and Flavius entered the house in an authoritative and vulgarly intrusive manner. The Empress Poppaea was at his side.

"You gave an order for your soldiers to attack the Nazarenes in the absence of the emperor and without approval of the Senate." Flavius expected no rebuttal to his accusation.

"My lady," Cornelius began, maintaining a calm he did not feel. He saluted the empress then turned to Flavius: "What orders are these? I gave no orders this night!"

Flavius handed Cornelius the scroll Elisa had written in his name. As Cornelius read, a million thoughts raced through his mind. The most convincing had Flavius and Poppaea attempting to frame him with trumped-up charges of treason. He knew very well of their desire to push him and Seneca out of the way so they could assume power and influence over Nero. Cornelius wasn't going to give up so easily.

"This letter is forged! Flavius, this is a treacherous act of disloyalty towards Rome. Caesar will not be swayed by this feeble attempt by power-hungry traitors! I suggest–" Cornelius was interrupted by Flavius' abrupt orders to his soldiers.

"Strip him of all weapons and hold him captive!"

Cornelius' mind was overwhelmed from all directions: fearful thoughts for his children's lives, the absence of his wife, and now this setup with the forged orders compounded by the absence of Caesar or even Seneca to defend him in his time of need. Never crossing his mind was the possibility of Elisa's involvement in these matters.

Cornelius stepped back from the soldiers, pleading for time. As a citizen of Rome, and one of position, he must be allowed time to explain, especially to tell about his sick children in the other chamber and the imminent return of the healer. Flavius ignored him and pushed his men to act fast, leaving Cornelius no choice but to fight back – but bare-armed, and not wanting to harm an innocent Roman soldier for merely following orders. His impotent defence gave Flavius the opportunity he hoped for. Cornelius was resisting arrest: a traitor obviously attempting to escape justice.

In his conspiracy with the aristocratic senator Gaius Piso, Flavius had long believed one of the best and most permanent solutions to their plan for taking over the Empire was Cornelius' death. With a strong arm Flavius pushed the soldiers aside and placed a dagger's point above Cornelius' heart. He drove the point deep and Cornelius fell immediately at his feet.

Stepping out of the way of the expected oozing life force, Flavius ordered Cornelius' guards, "You two! take care of this, a corpse of a traitor, but a Roman soldier nevertheless." He turned to Poppaea, "My lady, I apologize for you having to witness such a scene. But it is necessary in order for you to personally explain to Caesar exactly what happened." Poppaea nodded in wide-eyed abhorrence.

Now but a short distance from her home, Elisa arrived in time to see a crowd of people coming out of her house. Her steps were steady, but her heart sunk to the pit of her stomach. Not knowing exactly what to expect, she kept telling herself that nothing mattered anymore. She had fulfilled her life's objective. Rome was burning.

She certainly wasn't prepared for the gory scene just inside her door. Her own two house guards stood over the body of her beloved, motionless in a slowly spreading pool of blood, a dagger buried hilt-deep in his chest. Despite – or perhaps because of – all her training, she froze for an undetectable moment before ordering the confused and scared soldiers to fetch surgeon just in case he still lived. Her only goal was to be left alone with her husband, and she immediately went to work.

She dragged him away from the pool of blood, unavoidably leaving a trail. Straightening his still-living limbs, arms at his sides, she left the dagger as it was. Elisa went to her children and gathered up their warm but now lifeless bodies, carrying them to the main chamber. She began muttering a continuous prayer, chanting in her ancient language. With one of the tiny heads next to his father's, she aligned the tiny forms, head to foot, in a straight line and at an angle to form a 'V' shape with the bodies.

She brought out the cup she had prepared earlier, the same one she had made the children drink from before putting them to bed. Oddly curious at such a time, she took a small sip. *So this is what poison tastes like.* She had given her babies an amount sufficient to kill them slowly after first putting them painlessly to sleep. But Elisa had a different plan for herself. She would drink the full cup. She had been told the poison in this amount would act quickly, but she would remain painfully awake. Pain wasn't a deterrent; in fact, she welcomed it.

She lifted the cup to her lips, sealed them upon the rim, and gulped the cruel draught, leaving one swallow's worth in her mouth. Lips still wet, she leaned her face over Cornelius' and placed a final kiss on his mouth, letting the last mouthful of poison in her mouth flow into his – their final kiss a kiss of death, a kiss of mercy.

Elisa lay across the bodies of her family, making the shape of an Aleph, ". The first letter in the Phoenician alphabet, the symbol of the great Tyrian God Melqart, ensured the blessing of this ultimate sacrifice of her family in His honour.

. . .

Three hours later, Cornelius opened his eyes. His own loyal guards had dragged the healer back through the screaming panic engulfing the burning streets of Rome. It was too late for the children or for Elisa, but Cornelius still had a breath in him. The dagger had not actually found his heart. Because Elisa left the dagger where it was, it had kept him from bleeding out. The healer found Elisa's cup of poison with traces still in it. He recognized it and knew its other properties. While the poison had killed the others, it might have saved Cornelius' life. The nicked vessels close to his heart bled enough to convince anyone he was dead or soon would be, but the poison hadn't been enough to finish him off; instead the vessels clotted thanks to the toxin, preventing further loss of blood.

Understanding his family was gone from him forever, and at the hand of his adored Elisa, Cornelius fell unconscious again. It was days before he woke up, speechless and paralyzed in the lower limbs. The dagger had missed his heart but not his spine.

And Rome continued to burn.

Thirty Eight

A Scapegoat by Design

Upon arriving in Rome, Nero was informed of the alleged treason and subsequent death of Cornelius. His head was swimming. Too much of everything, everywhere, going on all about him. Cornelius, a traitor? Disappointment tangled with doubt. He had the presence of mind to order Seneca under immediate house arrest and protection by his guards until he had time to investigate the charges and discover the truth. He also sent his soldiers to Cornelius' house to provide aid and protection to his wife and children, assuming they were still alive.

His first priority was to aid the people of Rome and save the city from the damning fire spreading out of control, feeding on houses and livelihoods of the poor and the rich alike. He personally went into the streets of the city, helping those in need, fighting new outcrops of fire, blending with his troubled people. It was almost a week before the fire was controlled. Maybe it was not so much controlled as it had run out of any more Rome to burn. Even Nero's own palace fell before the flaming carnage. Thousands upon thousands of people were homeless. To aid the citizens, Nero ordered temporary relief tents be erected wherever possible, including in his own pleasure gardens.

But no matter what he did, the rumours had lives of their own and refused to die. Chief among them was that Nero had ordered his Praetorian Guard to burn the city. Eyewitnesses had seen Nero's own Guard start the fire in the merchants' warehouse. No other explanation would placate the people. Once a lie is planted, the truth must struggle for light.

. . .

"And I asked the centurion where he got such orders, and he handed me a written order under Cornelius' own stamp." Flavius repeated the story to Nero for the fifth time. The four previous times he hadn't had Nero's complete attention as the emperor was too focused on all the emergencies at hand. Now that the fires were out, he honed in on the facts behind that night.

"Why would Cornelius do such a thing? What's his motive? He had everything he needed and more: position, money, power, a beautiful family, friends, respect, our love and trust. No. No, this just doesn't make sense," Nero thought out loud.

"You saw the letter with your own eyes. He sent his guards to burn the city."

"Flavius, this cannot be true!" Nero shook his head, appalled at the idea of Rome burning by the act of his Praetorian Guard, no matter who ordered it. "Assuming Cornelius did write that letter, he never ordered the burning of Rome! The letter ordered the burning of the gathering Nazarenes!"

Flavius remained silent against Nero's sharp response.

"All that aside, how do you explain finding Cornelius' family all dead by him?" Nero scorned the Praetorian tribune, but he was mostly annoyed with the mystery confronting him.

"Caesar, the people are demanding an answer. They want to know who burned Rome. If we don't tell them the truth about Cornelius' treason, they will continue to lay the blame on the emperor's head. Rumours are merciless, sir."

"No! I will not accuse Cornelius as long as I remain unsure of his guilt. This is not how Caesar treats his loyal subjects."

"But, sir, I..."

Nero abruptly stood. "Flavius, come with me."

"Where are we going?"

"I owe Seneca a visit," he said with serious direction.

"Seneca?"

"Just before the fire, Poppaea had her hands on a letter sent from a Nazarene leader to Seneca. I need to resolve that."

Flavius turned to gather up his arms and made to follow Caesar, who was already out the door. He knew the letter well. "So now the cock comes home to roost," he murmured to no one there.

. . .

Seneca had trained himself all his life to accept his destiny and live as if he were a servant to life, embracing its highs and lows with an open heart. Even so, he found no reason behind this house arrest. Was he being punished or protected? The arrival of Nero and Flavius together relieved his boredom, and lit a spark of fear.

"Caesar, you bring honour to my house," Seneca welcomed.

"Ironies of ironies. I see the fire did not find its way to your door," Nero smirked.

Seneca noted the sarcasm but didn't get the hint. Taking a moment to gather his thoughts and make the appropriate reply, he shook his head, "No... no, I do not know if this is luck or if it is a curse. Knowing there is such devastation beyond my door makes me want to give them my house and go sit with the rest in the tents."

"I have always called you teacher, Seneca. You have taught me better. So cut the nonsense!"

Seneca's jaw audibly snapped shut. He looked to Flavius for explanation. Flavius didn't have the guts to attempt to explain Caesar's bluntness.

Nero turned on him, and in his infamous tone which too often edged on insanity, he quietly asked, "Who is Paulus?"

"Paulus? I beg your pardon, Caesar, many people bear the name."

"You know perfectly well who I mean! Paulus the Nazarene leader, and do not attempt to deny you know him. I have a letter from him sent to you. It indicates a very friendly relationship."

Seneca stepped back and perhaps would have fallen were it not for Flavius standing just a little too close behind.

"It appears Caesar has hit a nerve, eh, teacher?" Flavius hissed in his ear.

"Caesar, whatever you may think you know of this man, he is

first and foremost a loyal Roman soldier and a secret agent with the Imperial Intelligence Agency – for decades. He has spent his life as a spy for the sake and glory of the Empire since the reign of Julius." Flavius grabbed him, ready to strike him for his insolence, but Seneca shook him off his arm.

"Stop!" Nero yelled at Flavius. Turning to Seneca, he now threatened, "I swear on my own head if you speak anything besides the truth from this moment forward, I will have you fed to the beasts while you dangle from a rope."

Seneca looked Nero unflinchingly in the eye, thereby giving his pledge. "Paulus is a Roman citizen from Tarsus. A student of the famous General Antonius of Damascus, he was tapped for our intelligence agency more than thirty-five years ago. From Damascus, his cover was carefully nourished as we first planted him in Judea as a Jew. However, with time, the agency found a better approach to weaken the Jews. There was a small group of them who took issue with the Hebrew law and seemed to be continuously agitating the people while angering the temple priests. We call them the Nazarenes, you have heard of them. Sometimes they call themselves Christians, by way of claiming their dead leader had been anointed. Many Caesars before you, my lord, have attempted to crush these peoples of Judea. The Hebrews have a legend of a Messiah, they call him, a deliverer. They pop up like a yearly crop of... well, let us just say they have a most peculiar knack for surviving our various assaults. So we decided to use them to our advantage, giving them support as we proceeded to divide and conquer. Paulus received new instructions to join the Nazarenes. We made sure he steadily attained a position of leadership. He brought a new twist to the formerly all-Hebrew sect by permitting gentiles, or non-Jews, to join. Paulus is very good at creating itches hard to scratch."

He had Nero's complete attention. Even Flavius had backed off a bit.

Seneca took a seat and rested, trying to catch his breath. At his age, merely talking could be an effort. Before he resumed, he remembered his duties as host and called for the comfort and refreshments for his guests.

"So you are saying these Nazarenes are the product of our

agency?" Nero asked.

"Well... in certain ways, yes."

"Why have I never heard of this? Have you heard of it, Flavius?" Nero watched Flavius shake his head, but in a way that indicated a certain admiration for the subterfuge. Nero and Flavius were intently listening to the deepest secret of the agency, aware that Seneca was rolling out a summary of one of the most brilliantly conceived projects and a massive undertaking the likes of which neither had ever known.

"Allow me to give you context, my lord. When Emperor Gaius came to rule, his trust in the military was very shaky and he feared many of the people in positions of power. In his ignorance, he eliminated several projects and shut down the agency for a while. You may recall I was under house arrest for some time. Some of my men – including Cornelius, who would come to be your loyal tutor – went underground, so to speak. That is, they kept these projects going because of their loyalty to always serve the Empire regardless of the emperor of the moment. Such patriotism put them continuously at risk of death, as any Caesar upon a whim could call it treason."

Seneca stood up and approached Nero, who had been gazing at him the way he had for so many years, the good student giving total attention to his devoted teacher. "Great Caesar, I guarantee Paulus' patriotism as I guarantee my own. Here, look."

Seneca led them to the corner table where he had been writing. "I was composing a letter to Paulus, just before you arrived. My letters to the field are carefully written. I employ a method making my orders to my agents intelligible only to them. Should anyone other than my men intercept them, the letters will seem to be of only benign matters. So it is when I write to Paulus. If any of the Nazarenes see it, they will only see a letter of support to them. However, in my code, I tell Paulus we must identify the villain who used the burning of the Nazarenes as a diversion to burn all of Rome, thereby smearing Caesar and his Praetorian Guard for good measure. The Nazarenes were always intended as a weapon against the Jews of Judea, not against ourselves, our Caesar, or the Roman people."

Nero and Flavius read the letter.

>*Hail, my dearest Paul. Do you think I am not in sadness and grief for your innocent people who are so often condemned to suffer? Worse, should the whole people of Rome think you so callous and prone to crime you are supposedly the authors of every misfortune in the city? Yet let us bear it patiently and content ourselves with what fortune brings, until supreme happiness puts an end to our troubles. Former ages had to bear the Macedonian, Philip's son, and after Darius, Dionysius, and our own times endured Gaius Caesar. To all of these, their will was law. The source of the fire, which all Rome suffers, is plain. But if humble men could speak out what the reason is, and if it were possible to speak without risk in this dark time, all would be plain to all. Nazarenes and Jews are accused as contrivers of the fire. Whoever the criminal is whose pleasure is but that of a butcher, and who veils himself with a lie, he is reserved for his due season. And as the best of men is sacrificed, the one for the many, so he, vowed to death for all, will be burned with fire.*

Nero paced back and forth across the room. Flavius and Seneca grew more nervous with each turn, dreading the unknown depths of Nero's capricious mind, knowing only full well what he was capable of bringing down upon them all.

"Soldiers!" Nero's cry sent shivers down his companions' spines. "Seneca, tell them where they can find Paulus. I want him brought here immediately."

His orders were obeyed without debate. Only an idiot would battle Nero when his genius, evil or otherwise, was in action. Within the hour, Paulus was among them. The fox he had always been and his advancing years had not dulled his ample talents. Trying to read the circumstances in which he now found himself, he watched every move, every gesture: a twitch of a cheek or a jolt of a finger – no matter, he saw it all. Next to Paulus, Nero was a precocious upstart.

Nero, thinking himself in command of the interrogation, had made sure Paulus knew nothing of why he was summoned. He handed him the letter Seneca had been writing, which Paulus could not have seen, and asked him to explain it to them. Paulus read the situation like an open book, as if he had been sitting with them an hour earlier, listening to all Seneca had said. He realized the futility of a crafty lie. Only the truth would suffice. He decoded the letter, explaining what he understood from it, all of which was compatible with Seneca's explanation.

A palpable silence followed. Pragmatic Flavius was the first to break it. "Our dilemma remains. What are we going to tell the people of Rome? The people are waiting for the results of our investigations. They still accuse Caesar and his Praetorian Guard for the fire."

"You mean you don't know who caused the fire?" Paulus asked, truly incredulous.

The men froze in mid-action. As one they thought, *Did Paulus just imply he knows the cause?*

"Caesar, I apologize for my boldness. How could I assume you don't know... surely you know." Paulus bowed slightly in apology.

Nero came forward and grasped both of Paulus' shoulders. "Do you know who caused the fire?" Nero seemed friendly and encouraging, precisely as Paulus intended.

"The Nazarenes!" Paulus looked around as if surprised nobody knew.

Seneca couldn't believe his ears.

"Yes, I was about to write to you, Seneca, to see if you knew and, if not, to inform you. I just learned about it myself." The master manipulator succeeded once more in driving all accusations away from him. "The leader of the Nazarenes in Judea, Cephas, had plotted to forge Cornelius' order and asked Cornelius' wife, who was ignorant of the matter, to deliver it."

"But why would this Cephas plot to send the guards to... to burn his own people?" Nero asked.

"Precisely for the very purpose which has come to pass! He martyred his people while managing to burn all of Rome."

"The bastards!" The walls shook with Nero's cry.

. . .

Two days before the revealing meeting at Seneca's house, Claudia Achte visited her father. The ensuing heart-to-heart talk tore down ages-old walls of secrecy and deceit that had been built up between the father and daughter. Claudia had just lost her sister

Elisa. She had paid her dues to Melqart and burned Rome. Now a free soul, with a real princess' certainty and a warrior's determination, Claudia sought to protect her father with the only weapon she had: knowledge.

The shock of learning about the Aleph Lodge, a covert organization who had instigated relentless plots spanning hundreds of years with the sole purpose of undermining Rome, would have been sufficient to throw an entire Empire into a crippling stupor. But lucky Claudia, her father was no ordinary Roman. Her father was Paulus. Even with the bitter realizations this news brought, Paulus was ultimately not so different from his daughter. All that mattered to him at this moment was one thing and one thing only: his daughter Claudia.

As she chose him, he chose her.

They put their heads together and agreed to blame the Nazarenes, thereby setting themselves free of fault. Even in her newfound openness with her father, Claudia didn't reveal the ultimate irony. For by accusing the Nazarenes she was fulfilling the lodge's last demand of her. The Alephs needed to create chaos in the city and Paulus needed to keep the accusations far from him, especially after Seneca's house arrest and what happened to Cornelius.

Paulus, now in his sixties, was resigned. If he had to give up Cephas, even Seneca and the agency, he would do it for his Claudia.

Thirty Nine

Death by Truth

In the proceeding months, Nero gave no rest to the Nazarenes in Rome. He captured them in groups, fed them to the beasts, tore their bodies apart, even burned them to light the night. All was done in public. Before long, the people of Rome – who had cried out for their punishment – came to pity the Nazarenes.

One difficulty in the beginning was sorting out the Nazarenes from the rest of the Jews. The military received unexpected help on that front: the Aleph operatives planted among the Nazarenes turned against their "brethren," giving testimonies and thus saving the lives of the Phoenicians among them.

Nero continued to keep Seneca under house arrest, directly due to Flavius' influence on Caesar and by his strategic use of Poppaea. Flavius had to keep Seneca out of the picture. Impressed as Nero was by the corroborated testimony and evidence of Seneca and Paulus, Flavius was still able to convince Nero of Seneca's irresponsible actions outside the official Imperial Intelligence Agency. Without the counterbalance of the other departments of the Empire, the Nazarene problem got completely out of hand. Seneca could protest with his loyalty to Caesar and the Empire until he ran out of breath. The ashes of Rome were an immeasurable asset for her enemies throughout the known world.

Nero's sentiments for his old teacher wouldn't allow him to order Seneca's execution. But Poppaea's persistent nagging and Flavius' fabricated accounts did the sage philosopher no good. Luckily for Seneca, Nero kept himself preoccupied with persecuting the Nazarenes and rebuilding the city. So Seneca languished, his talents useless to anyone. Such luck as this was debatable.

. . .

Special directions from Nero ordered Cephas be kept alive. As the alleged leader of the Nazarenes, his case warranted unique punishment. As the rumour among the Nazarenes would have it, the missing Paulus had in fact been beheaded. They expected a similar fate for Cephas, the disciple of Yeshua.

Cephas was brought before Nero, to be interrogated by Flavius. "Are you the leader of the Nazarene terrorists?"

"Their leader died many years ago. I am but a poor man, servant to the people."

"Do you deny that you gave the orders to burn Rome?"

"I deny every word of that accusation, sir. My message is one of peace, not as a means of bringing more trouble into the world." Cephas tried to explain, but pessimism seeped into his soul as Flavius mocked his speech.

"I was warned you might say so." Flavius clasped both of his hands behind his back, stretching his shoulders for what might prove to be a long and enjoyable interrogation. "A real leader should proudly and honourably take responsibility for his actions and on behalf of his subjects. You are the worst of the worst, an insult to your people as well as a terrorist." Flavius chuckled and spat on Cephas' feet, as Nero watched silently from the half-shadows.

"Flavius, let's finish this," Nero said, snatching the theatre of torture away from his tribune.

Not quite ready to relinquish his own terrorism, Flavius continued, "How do you wish to die, enemy of Rome?" he asked, thus informing Cephas of his pre-determined fate.

"Sir, I am innocent, I wish you believed me, I did not do anything to warrant my death..."

"Alright, alright," Flavius toyed with him some more, giving him an inkling of hope that his resolve could be swayed. But only a few seconds of hope. "You will be crucified like your teacher. No, wait! I say your teacher was most certainly braver than you and no doubt died like a man. Therefore, you will be crucified upside down! How about that, you poor excuse for a man?"

Cephas fell to his knees.

. . .

Claudia and her father set about making the wisest of counsel for themselves. They reasoned that with Claudia's major contribution to the burning of Rome being behind her, staying in Rome was too high a risk. Poppaea's jealousy was unmanageable and undermined Claudia's influence at court, not to mention limited any direct contact with Nero Caesar. Nothing that remained here was worth the trouble it brought, so they decided she should leave.

But she wouldn't sneak out through the toppled gates in the dark of night. She would leave with as much dignity as she could muster, so she chanced one last audience with Nero. She laid her reasoning regarding Poppaea before him and he admired her decisions, ascribing them as she did to her love for Caesar and her wish to eliminate all sources of strife between him and Poppaea so that she could bear him an heir. By way of assuaging his guilt - an emotion he had from time to time despite popular opinion – Nero offered her a choice of palaces in several cities including land and house staff. His skewed understanding of society and the world in general may have nurtured a dangerous genius with criminal tendencies, but he never lacked generosity towards those who showed him kindness.

Claudia chose Sardinia to live out the rest of her life. She didn't reveal her intention to take Paulus with her. Nero didn't know he was her father and she surely didn't explain why she chose Sardinia. The island had long been a hub for Phoenician colonies and trading lanes across the Mediterranean. The Aleph Lodge there was powerful and welcomed the legendary Claudia Achte among them.

. . .

"Caesar, I have one last wish, should you see fit to grant it." Claudia felt sure in her request. "Please, may I pay my respects and say a final goodbye to Cornelius. He was like a brother to me and I may never see him again."

"I could refuse you nothing, even now. I will always remember your noble sensibilities, Claudia. A true artist you are." Nero held her at the waist. "You could do me a favour in return. Take Seneca with you. He has been begging for permission to see Cornelius. Even Caesar can admit to gratitude to these former tutors of mine; they are not bad people, they just made a mistake. Too bad for all of us it was such a very big mistake." Claudia nodded her assent, and Nero took it to mean just a little bit more. He bent to savour her lips and... well, old habits die hard. It was just his way of saying goodbye.

The next day Claudia and Seneca were at Cornelius' bedside. The house, once bustling with life, was little more than a mausoleum now. The children playing, their father's important guests, and mother gracing all with her bottomless wealth of knowledge and experience, all were ghosts in the shadows. Such a price to pay for such grace and gentility, for like many gods before and after him, Melqart gave and Melqart took. Cornelius now lay under an absurd house arrest, an insult to the speechless, paralyzed man, unconscious much of the time, a prisoner in his own body.

Seneca and Claudia sat on either side of Cornelius, watching his chest rise and fall, the rattling of his lungs as he breathed the only sound in the room. The guards and caretakers had given them the courtesy of privacy.

"I am leaving Rome," Claudia said quietly.

"A wise decision. Too late for me." Seneca, now sixty-nine years old, bore his destiny as the stoic he was.

"Yes, it is... too late for you."

Her words had a calm ruthlessness. Seneca wasn't sure she realized just how cruel her comments would seem to a man sentenced to death by the empty passage of time. Always the gentleman, he granted her the benefit of the doubt.

"Nothing personal, Seneca. You were always good to me. Mind you, you always assumed I was little more than the poor, sweet daughter of your premier spy, to be kept in comfort in order to ensure his loyalty."

By now, Seneca had no doubt Claudia Achte understood perfectly the weight of every word she spoke. But what in the world was she talking about?

"Sooner or later," she softly mused, "reality comes around to bite us, doesn't it? Funny, how the sweet girl turns out to be a special agent against Rome, the one who manages to use you and your projects against you to achieve her own people's goals."

Seneca leaned forward and placed both hands on the side of Cornelius' bed. The world was turning upside down; his breathing was now louder and faster than Cornelius'.

"Oh! I'm sorry, do you need help? Should I call a guard? No. Better not. They don't like you, you know; they think you are some sort of traitor." Claudia's dripping sarcasm soaked into Seneca's chest and he gasped for air.

"You didn't expect this turn of events, did you? Had no idea what you were doing, taking a little child from her father and placing her with a royal Phoenician family – respectable strangers, weren't they? – all so you and your little agency of secrets could be freer to manipulate the world about you! Looking back on it all, that's rather nastier than anything I did, don't you think?"

"How much are you involved?" Seneca nearly choked on his words, his wheezes more audible than the invalid's between them.

"Hm? Really? You want to know? Trouble talking? Nod once if you want me to continue." She smirked in a way he had never thought her capable, as if a demon had taken possession of Paulus' innocent daughter. But no, perhaps he was hallucinating. Then her next words affirmed she was all too real.

"Down to my bones, Seneca. I became as my adopted family, a Phoenician true to the God Melqart and of the Aleph Lodge that supports his realm throughout the known world. Everywhere Rome is today, we were there first, and we will remain long after your legions are gone. I have dedicated my life to the destruction of Rome and all the little people like you along the way. And do you want to know something? There is no taste quite so savoury as vengeance."

"Elisa... Marih... all involved?" Still struggling for his breath, he managed only a few words.

"How else do you think the Nazarene religion spread so widely, so quickly, so bloodlessly? Well, until my darling Nero lent his special talents, anyway. But I digress. Did you really think your plans were so effective? Or maybe it was just luck!" She was truly enjoying this. "The Aleph lodges across the Empire ordered their members to help, especially by joining the Nazarene movement as they spread their message among the gentiles."

She leaned closer to Seneca's perspiring face, creating an arch over Cornelius' near-lifeless form. "I wonder if you've given any thought to how the Roman and Greek Nazarenes – Christians, I think they call themselves now – came up with the idea of a holy trinity? Cephas?" She gave a tiny, quiet laugh. "We Phoenicians wove our own belief systems into the Nazarene sect. We taught them that Yeshua was a god become human and not a human become god. We gave them the idea of a virgin mother and a holy family, dietary customs, how they should dress. Paulus just went with the flow, dressing it up here and there with all those letters he wrote in exile. Dear father, he spent a little too much time alone and got off track now and then. But without knowing it, he complied with your orders by welcoming gentiles into the new church... gentiles who were Phoenicians, first and foremost. You wanted a religion that contradicted Judaism. We made sure he found it."

"Stop." Seneca closed his eyes.

"A little too heavy on your ears?"

"No. Not mine." He put his hand on Cornelius' hand. "They say unconscious people can hear. Will you have mercy on this innocent man? Cornelius doesn't deserve to hear this," Seneca begged.

"Your compassion is touching, truly. But he's not so innocent, old man. Cornelius had a consuming revenge which made his manipulation a bittersweet bonus for some of us. He gave in to his desires for revenge in his own way, not realizing he was such easy prey."

Seneca knew she would not resist further elaboration. He was her captive audience, and she would have him... them... hear her out. Though what she was about to say would have satiated his curiosity any other time, right now he wished her to remain silent. He didn't want to know. He didn't want Cornelius to know. He saw all his life's work shattering in front of him.

"When Cornelius was a young man, just out of military training, he thought the Jewish merchant Simaan Ben Aaron had killed his father. He was consumed with hatred of not only him but all Jews everywhere. An unreasonable extension of his hatred, but there you have it. He built all his life around something he had no idea was nothing more than a misunderstanding. So quick was he to hate, he never took the time to investigate. Some strategic technician he was! Not sounding so innocent... or brilliant... anymore, is he?"

Like a crow picking out the eyes of its fallen prey, she insisted on pronouncing every word clearly and hurtfully, "Simaan Ben Aaron thought he was just playing a little political game, never realizing we had directed his fabricated scenario to the High Priest in order to gain favour in the eyes of his temple. That Cornelius should be there at the precise moment to hear him was the happiest of accidents. You see, he never harmed Cornelius' father and never intended to harm the Empire. Quite the contrary, he cared more about keeping the peace than for his own personal gain or even his own kind."

"Why are you telling me all this? Aren't you afraid?"

"You will die soon. You are a singular man, Seneca, an analyst and a philosopher and, in many ways, an artist, like me. I appeal to the artist in you, to your need to understand what went wrong before you die. And please, go tell Caesar. Everything you say now will only serve the opposite purpose. Any desperate man in your place would try to find an excuse to save himself, his reputation, his good name. Not knowing or appreciating the true Seneca as I do, I'm quite positive that's what they'll think." She looked up at the shadows lengthening on the ceiling with a cold smile.

As if Seneca needed one more reason to tax his weak heart, Cornelius' right arm jolted, jumping up in the air for a split second before falling back on the bed, beside his otherwise non-responsive body. Seneca's jaw dropped, his lungs desperately gasped for air, and his eyes widened, though full of tears. With what remained of his strength, he howled, "Guards!"

They carried him back to his house to be tended by the healers. Claudia departed with the evening tide for Sardinia.

. . .

In the morning, the guards found Cornelius' still body. He had heard every word Claudia spat out, leaving him no reason to linger in this world. Sometime in the night he joined his beloved Elisa and their babies, waiting for him in the shadows.

Papal Chair;

in the Wrong City?

After the ignominious death of Cephas, very few of the Nazarenes were still brave enough to live in Rome. Even fewer were prepared to publicly associate with the new religion.

With Paulus' advancing years and no one left of the agency to expose him, he saw no harm in building upon his relationship with the Nazarenes as one of their leaders. No one knew he was the hand behind Cephas' capture and demise. Once an agent, always an agent, he supposed; besides, these old habits died hard. So why not maintain his role with the church just in case he ended up needing them in the future?

He arranged for Cephas' body to be washed, scented, and carried to a Phoenician commercial vessel sailing for Tyre. Two Phoenician wine merchants were given directions to preserve the body in a watertight wooden cask, filled with wine vinegar. Upon arrival, they made sure the body was delivered to Cephas' friends in Tyre who gave it a respectful burial, discreetly so as not to irritate the Jews who still held him in contempt. The burial was in a small town south of Tyre, next to his father's tomb. To the west of the small town was the main road into Judea. Hidden in plain sight from the Jewish and Roman population, it became the best-kept secret of the local Nazarenes and took hold in the religiously friendly land of the Tyrian Phoenicians. Many called the little town by the name of the sacred body that lay in it, Simon Cephas, as his late teacher Yeshua had called him. They further concealed its purpose by shortening the name by ways of code: Sime.

. . .

Known as Paul to his Christian friends, Paulus stayed in touch by writing letters on various matters from his home with Claudia to the churches springing up all around the Mediterranean.

Claudia maintained a more active role in Roman politics. The Phoenicians in Sardinia were excited to have the accomplished Claudia Achte among them. Her skills remained undiminished and she quickly rose to a leading position, proving time and time again her allegiance to the cause. With the aid of the local Aleph Lodge, she built a memorial for her sister Elisa in the Temple of Eshmon, another name of their God Melqart.

Under the very noses of the Romans, the Aleph elites met at the temple to celebrate what the Sardinians believed was nothing more than an annual feast day for the Phoenician locals. They had just received news of more trouble for their enemies in Rome. Nero Caesar had just captured a group of his closest advisors and accused them of treason.

. . .

The Aleph man Milichus, who served under Flavius Scaevinus, consistently provided reliable intelligence on the Praetorians. He became privy to a scheme being prepared against Nero. Following the advice of the Sardinian lodge and Claudia's invaluable knowledge of the inner workings of Nero's court, Milichus planted the news with Nero's secretary: Gaius Piso and Flavius the Praetorian tribune were planning to overthrow Caesar.

Claudia may well have had some bias by advising the Alephs to inform Nero of the plot. By avoiding his death at this time, she reasoned, the fracturing of the Empire would only worsen. What they didn't realize was that their Aleph heroine had reached a stage in her long life of intrigue where personal feelings swayed her judgment. Perhaps she truly was convinced that the wisest course to follow was the saving of her art student's life.

Nero captured scores of soldiers and senators and, in a state of panic fuelled by his madness, gave into his craze to cleanse his Empire. He had just rid the city of most of the Nazarenes, pushing the rest of them towards Asia Minor. He had no problem initiating a new spree of executions. He ordered all court cases be expedited, including those he had postponed indefinitely – like Seneca's.

The conspiracies of Gaius Piso and his followers ended in disaster for everyone involved. Just as Claudia had predicted, the political split actually did widen between the people, the politicians, and Caesar. The trials were brutal.

In the middle of hearing a long day of cases, Seneca was brought in. Offering his own defence, he began, "Caesar, I plead to your divine humanity. You are the brilliant embodiment of all arts and magnificent architect of our culture, feeding the glory of Rome and increasing its power. Caesar, I humbly ask you remember my nurturing guidance in your youth and allow me to speak with you in private," the frail Seneca spoke in a peaceful voice unheard by most of those intently listening.

How could a man being sent to his death speak with such calm? This stoic before them was not a fake. Seneca was true to his beliefs and he had made peace with his destiny. However, not all were moved by the graceful dignity of the man before them.

"Caesar! I object! This man's audacity is unforgivable!" one of the judges yelled, causing a murmur to rise in the crowd.

Nero lifted a hand, shushing all speakers. To everyone's astonishment he stood and walked to an unoccupied side chamber "Bring him."

"Great Caesar, I thank you for indulging an old man." When they had withdrawn to just the two of them, still visible to the body of senators but private in their speech, Seneca quietly continued, "I must offer confessions of my follies. I attempted to influence the powers of nature. It is my fault I ignored the signs of what surely would have come to pass, ignoring a natural force more powerful than I could predict. The Nazarene movement that I attempted to manipulate in order to aid Rome instead became its curse, causing it to be burned to ashes." Seneca could see Nero's inner struggle with sending his teacher to his death. "Allow me to make this easy, and right. Allow me to commit suicide without continuing the trial. Before the judges I will admit to conspiring with Gaius Piso – though totally untrue, my lord – and let that stand as my accusation."

Seneca searched the face of his former student as he tried to hide the trembling of his eyelids. Despite all his recent cruelties, he sensed his delicate young prodigy was still there with him. "For the sake of Rome, for the sake of the Imperial Intelligence Agency and the soldiers who have dedicated – are still dedicating – their lives to their Empire and emperor, let us not uncover the agency's work and place many more lives at risk as recompense for my mistakes. Let us not discourage your dedicated soldiers and any other agents who might yet come into your service by giving them cause to doubt or otherwise be afraid of performing all the good that comes from working with the agency."

Nero turned sharply from his teacher, keeping his back to all who were watching intently from the outer chamber, wiped his eyes, and cleared his throat. Then, pulling himself up to his full magnificence, Caesar walked steadily and quickly back to the court. Seneca followed.

Calling for silence, he announced, "Hear me! Lucius Seneca has just admitted to me his role in conspiring with Gaius Piso to overthrow the throne of Caesar and take control of the city of Rome. I see fit that he receive the same sentence as Gaius himself."

The rest of the judges agreed with Caesar, but the audience watched dumbfounded and in complete disbelief. No one thought Seneca's case had anything to do with Gaius Piso; they were under the impression Seneca had been imprisoned a long time before the conspiracies. Though many could not accept what had just happened, who among them would object at such a time as this?

But what people couldn't say in open court they said in private, and rumours spread like the fires that had already consumed Rome: Seneca was not guilty. For all the good their grumblings did, a logical explanation was never found. If Seneca accepted his fate, what could they do?

. . .

Seneca did not protest because the outcome came about exactly as he had asked. He allowed Caesar to save face, and in return was given solitary confinement before his sentence was commuted. He died by way of opening his own veins.

The news gave a boost to the Aleph lodges all across the Mediterranean. They daringly roused the conservative Jews who now saw the Nazarenes as Greek and Roman – gentile – intruders to their religion. The fire of Rome the year before, followed by the Gaius conspiracies and the decimation of Nero's inner circle, distracted the people while the confusion continued to poison the very core of the Empire. With the core rotting, the peripheries felt the loosening of the reins. Chaos ensued, just as the Alephs had expected.

For their part, Judea wasted no time. The Jewish rioters attacked the Nazarenes, singled out Roman soldiers whenever they had the opportunity, and invaded the palaces of Jewish Roman puppets, including King Herod Agrippa the Second. Within the palace grounds built by Herod the Great, the Jewish nationalists sought their prey, Ananias, the previous High Priest. The lucky hunt found him hiding in an aqueduct. With no mercy in their hearts, they killed him on the spot.

Milichus, the Aleph operative who had exposed Gaius Piso's conspiracies, leveraged the trust he earned with Nero for a final act of glory before disappearing, some said to Claudia's palace on Sardinia. Destitute of trusted friends or family, Milichus found Nero easy prey indeed. A combination of factors neatly converged, making his job easier, though who's to say they happened all on their own?

Perhaps Nero was bored with Poppaea, or his madness and paranoia had destroyed any trust he may have ever had in her. For when Milichus informed Nero of his wife's secret Jewish heritage, and reminded him of the Hebrew precepts commanding any son she carried to honour his mother's religion, Nero never questioned the report, and acted upon it. He kicked the pregnant empress to death.

No one, neither Aleph nor Roman agents, were present when he killed Poppaea; but those who witnessed the scene afterwards told of the horrifying distortion of Poppaea's body. They concluded that Nero Caesar must have not only kicked her, but jumped on her belly, instantly killing her and the child within.

Whether as a brilliant act of damage control or one of true remorse, Nero gave his beautiful Poppaea a royal funeral, worthy of any empress of Rome.

. . .

Soon after, Nero sent one of his generals to Judea to settle the score with the Jews, once and for all. Vespasian was given strict orders not to seek or otherwise broker peace with the Jews - the old-fashioned methods of gaining their alliance by fulfilling some of their demands would henceforth cease. The Roman military knew no restrictions. Vespasian's sole purpose was to eliminate the potential of future revolts or troubles in Judea by any means necessary. Caesar would have no more of these blights upon his reign, these Jews or the Nazarenes or anything coming from either one of them ever again.

All the vengeful retributions in the world could not sustain Nero. Before long his loneliness pitched him into a deep depression. At age thirty-one, he realized he was no longer young and beautiful; he had burned all his bridges, and in moments of clarity he knew it. Even Caesar couldn't just go out and create a new life full of a loving family and trustworthy friends. His mounting paranoia kept his retainers at a distance.

With no inner circle to inspire reasons for living, the idea of cutting to the chase became more and more appealing. In the end, even a mad genius was no genius at all. His rationalizations were very convincing to his audience of one.

In the last month of the spring of the fourteenth year of his reign, the gentle artist forced by his conniving mother into the sandals of a Caesar, the tormented victim of a cruel life in an even crueler age, by his own hand finally found his gateway to freedom.

Forty One

As You Sow,

So Shall You Reap

With the death of Nero, the already crumbling Empire fell into complete chaos. Civil war erupted in Rome as four Roman emperors gained and lost the throne that one year.

All the while, Vespasian had been consistently building military power and accumulating political respect due to his neutral position within the politics of Rome. Being away in the battlefield enhanced his status. Eventually the people of the Empire made him emperor; in turn, he assigned the task of suppressing the Jewish revolt to his son Titus.

Titus had a unique style compared to his predecessors in Judea. His manner inflicted a wound on the Middle East that would fester for two thousand years.

The Phoenicians could not predict Titus' fist of steel incessantly hammering Judea, besieging Jerusalem and the other surrounding strongholds, and destroying every last stand of resistance. The ultimate coup was the destruction of the Temple of the Jews, the centre of their religion and very existence. Destroyed six hundred and fifty-six years earlier by the Babylonians, Rome's assault led to the looting of its contents and tens of thousands of Jews being taken as slaves or dispersed throughout the provinces as refugees. Judea became a true Roman Province. For hundreds of years to come, the Hebrew people lived *persona non grata*, banned from returning to their homeland.

In due time, Titus inherited his father's role as emperor and oversaw the solidifying of the *Pax Romana*, crowning the Empire with peaceful glory once again.

But in the ruins of the temple, the hidden meeting place for the Aleph Lodge of Jerusalem became exposed. The Imperial Intelligence Agency acquired a succession of delectable findings about the lodge, but never connected any of it to the Phoenicians. They found documents implicating certain conspirators in a plot to destroy Rome; they also found artifacts – things like compasses, squares, hammers, and other tools used at the time by engineers and builders – but failed to make the crucial connections. It was obvious to the agency that the relics held symbolic meanings as evidenced by their treatment: polished and cleaned and stored neatly in preparation for future ceremonial activities. Special notice was given to the signs of the Aleph, many of which were bundled in groups of three. But time and time again, their analysts made no connection with the Phoenicians. They suspected that a secret, most likely Jewish, group had attempted a large-scale revolt across the Empire. Unable to make the concrete connections for any further actions, the documents and relics were packed away, eventually becoming the property of the new Roman Christian Church. In eras to come, the captured relics would be interpreted as symbols of evil.

. . .

Some five hundred and forty years after the destruction of the temple, a secret Jewish tribe in Arabia met behind closed doors. The occasion was to commemorate the destruction of the temple in Jerusalem. The hated Roman Empire had been supplanted by the Roman Christian Church. As Jews in exile in Arabia, they had never ceased their longing to return to Jerusalem.

This Jewish tribe was secretly conspiring to empower an Arabic military leader who, with his own band of soldiers, had become a force to be reckoned with. These soldiers had come to live by the laws of Moses and commemorated the destruction of the temple by facing west to Jerusalem when they offered their prayers, but they had no inkling of what their Jewish supporters had in mind for them.

In his blessing concluding that fateful meeting, the Jewish tribe's rabbi casually prophesied concerning these soldiers they intended to manipulate, "One day may the unbridled might of these men fulfill our revenge against the Romans. Then we shall return to our fathers' land and the Lord's city of Orashalim."

. . .

What had once been a project by the Imperial Intelligence Agency to divide the Jews against themselves evolved way beyond its original scope of intent. In the following centuries, the teachings of Paulus – ironically drenched and enriched with Phoenician myth and practices – became the basis for the new Roman religion. The Judaic flavour had been almost completely excised.

The agency's traditional labelling of the relics from the Aleph Lodge beneath the temple as evil had been assumed by the church. However, the legendarily infamous symbols would one day come in handy. The Knights Templar, a rich and powerful cadre of crusader monks, attracted the attention and the jealousy of King Philip of France. Bent on claiming their fortune, the king and the Pope framed the Templars, accusing them of heresy and implementing evil symbolism in their rituals. Ever since, the Roman Catholic church has banned practitioners who appreciate the ancient Phoenician symbolism and still finds that "the faithful who enroll in Masonic associations are in a state of grave sin and may not receive Holy Communion," and "membership in them [Masonic organizations] remains forbidden."

Front cover image is adapted from:

"The Death of Seneca"

By Jacque-Louis David

1773

www.ingramcontent.com/pod-product-compliance
Lightning Source LLC
Chambersburg PA
CBHW030025180626
46810CB00001B/211